Three Gold Coins

Also by Josephine Moon

The Tea Chest
The Chocolate Apothecary
The Beekeeper's Secret

Three Gold Coins

JOSEPHINE MOON

First published in Great Britain in 2018 by Allen & Unwin

First published in Australia in 2018 by Allen & Unwin

Allen & Unwin
c/o Atlantic Books
Ormond House
26–27 Boswell Street
London WC1N 3JZ
Phone: 020 7269 1610
Fax: 020 7430 0916
Email: UK@allenandunwin.com
Website: www.allenandunwin.com/uk

A CIP catalogue record for this book is available from the British Library.

Set in 12/16.5 Minion Pro by Midland Typesetters, Australia
Printed and bound in Great Britain by CPI Group (UK) Ltd,
Croydon CR0 4YY

Paperback ISBN: 978 1 76029 197 6
E-book ISBN: 978 1 92557 517 0

10 9 8 7 6 5 4 3 2 1

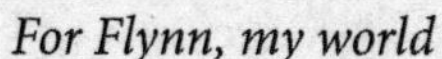

For Flynn, my world

He mustn't know.
He mustn't know.
He mustn't know.

1

Lara

Lara Foxleigh felt the slight tremor in her legs with every step through the narrow cobblestoned street and knew it wasn't just from the jet-lag; every moment since she'd arrived here yesterday had tested her confidence. Of the many times in her life she had imagined herself in Italy, it had never been for the reasons she was here now. She could only hope this had been the right thing to do.

She stumbled on the uneven ground and nearly fell. Cars with tinted windows beeped in frustration and a swell of people diverted around her and continued on their way, a human river gushing towards the mighty Trevi Fountain, whose splashing water she could already hear in the distance. She righted herself and hurried forward. As she did she caught sight of an old man ahead of her who also stumbled at that moment. She felt an instant wave of empathy for him.

His snow-white hair was brushed neatly to one side and he was stooped, a noticeable hunch between his shoulders. With his right hand he worked the end of his walking stick between the cobblestones.

A young woman in flashy gym gear held on to his other arm, steadying him as he lurched through the push of tourists and the swift Vespas that wove impatiently through the cramped space. The man seemed so out of place here.

But then so was she.

He tripped again and his companion righted him. It wasn't done unkindly, but it wasn't loving either. Lara couldn't explain why, but there was something about him that made her want to stay close; perhaps it was just her affinity with someone who needed help to navigate this world.

The old man and his companion turned the corner around a tall building, a large family bustled their way in front of Lara, and the narrow street gave way to a wide space with the fountain commanding the arena. Blue sky stretched above her, and bright sunshine beat down on the Fontana di Trevi and the hundreds of people packed into the square.

All she could do was stare. She'd seen photos of it, but its sheer size was staggering. Corinthian pillars—three storeys high—with a towering sculpture of the god Oceanus in the centre stood over imposing waves of sculpted water. Muscular, bearded tritons thrashed from the sea, taming winged horses. Clear water roared over shelves of white stone and plummeted into the pool below.

For a few moments she stood there, allowing herself to forget the reason she was here, on the other side of the world.

People squeezed past each other to get closer, the lucky ones sitting on the edge of the pool, smiling for pictures and tossing coins backwards over their shoulders. Lara felt a small, unexpected smile flutter to her lips. The fountain was mesmerising. The cacophony of pummelling water muffled the hum of her anxiety.

A flash of red caught her attention. It was the old man's shirt. He was leaning hard on his young attendant, lowering himself to the edge of the pool, wedged between a man sporting a Union Jack tee and a young Japanese girl with a Hello Kitty bag. His assistant said something to him and he waved her away. She melted into the crowd. He gazed around to the fountain's pool behind, its light blue floor littered with silver and brass coins, and Lara did the same.

The water was beautifully clear, calling to her, a relief from the tenacious summer heat that was holding strong into September. Maybe it would wake her up, two espressos having had little impact on her jet-lag. She inched closer. At the very least, she could cup some water in her hand and wash her face or wet her hair as so many others were doing.

'*Mi scusi*,' she said, needling her way through and down the steps. Simply by chance, she found herself a few steps from the old man, who sat quietly, his head bent. She kept her eyes averted, conscious she'd been staring at him.

At the edge of the pool, the water reflected the clouds in the sky above. She cupped her hands under the water then threw it over her hair. It trickled down the back of her neck. She breathed deeply.

I am in Rome.

It was ludicrous.

Lara splashed herself some more, then straightened and reached into her bag for three gold euro coins. She turned and threw them, one at a time, over her shoulder. The first to ensure her return. The second to bring new romance into her life. The third to guarantee marriage. She imagined that each landed in the water with a tiny *plink*. Undoubtedly the ritual she'd read about online was all rubbish, but it did seem to be the thing to do.

Nearby, the old man rested his cane against his thin leg. He moved his veiny right hand over to join his left. With great gentleness, he touched the gold ring on his finger.

Lara watched, sadness welling, her emotions always just under the surface. He pulled the ring easily off his bony finger and lifted it to his eyes, studying it as though reading an inscription. Then he kissed the ring and flung it back over his shoulder. It made barely a splash before sinking to the bottom of the pool, just one more shiny object among hundreds of others.

Lara lurched forward, leaning over the edge, splashing into the water, trying to catch sight of the ring. But it was hopeless.

'Your ring!' She turned to him, bending to his level. He faced her, his eyes blue and bright, though he seemed to look right through her.

'Why did you do that?' She searched the water again, her eyes darting. Tourists with backpacks and bulky cameras jostled her and tried to wedge between them to pose for photos.

'Leave it,' the old man muttered.

She opened her mouth to argue but stopped; he had clearly done it deliberately and she had no right to tell him what to do. But, still. It seemed wrong.

'Leave it,' he repeated, with a British accent.

'You're English!' She squatted down beside his knees, looking up into his face. 'We've still got time to find someone who can help us get your ring back, if you want to.'

'No.'

'They collect the money every day. Someone will be able to get it. There's a policeman over there. He's busy right now but there'll be another. We need to report it if you're going to get it back.'

'Are you deaf? I said no. I wouldn't have thrown it if I wanted to keep it.'

Lara was taken aback. 'I heard you.'

The lines on the man's face were deep and there was a shake in the hand that held the cane at his knee. She didn't know if these things were normal, or if it was because he was angry, or maybe even because of the heat. She straightened to scan the crowd for his assistant, but couldn't see her anywhere. She lowered herself to the man's level again, this time resting on the edge of the pool, angling her body towards his.

'Where is your . . . person, the woman who was with you when you arrived?'

He looked at her sharply. She assumed he was wondering how long she'd been watching him, and discomfort prickled under her cotton shirt along with beads of sweat. She forged on regardless. 'Is she a relative? A carer? Can I call someone for you?'

The man looked away from her; she'd been dismissed.

'Okay,' she said, 'I'll leave you alone.'

She stood and walked away, feeling the air hit the backs of her legs where they'd been sweating on her uncomfortable perch. Sidestepping and ducking through the crowd, she reached the very edge of the throng, over near the gelateria, and turned for one last look.

He was still alone, a small, solitary, vulnerable figure; she couldn't leave him there until she was sure he'd be alright.

She kept her eyes on him, letting them roam occasionally to look for the young woman who'd disappeared, or to wave away yet another street vendor trying to sell her bottles of water or a selfie stick. Hordes of people hustled her from her spot as they ordered their gelato. But still she hovered.

It was only after the heat had risen into mid-morning and the crowds thickened more, when the old man had wiped the sweat from his brow and temples, once he'd started to look up and stiffly position himself to peer first to the left and then to the right, when he'd checked his phone several times, and when he'd made two attempts to get to his feet, his hand shaking terribly on his cane, that Lara pushed her way back through the crowds, down the steps and to his side.

He looked up at her and closed his eyes for a moment as if trying to control his frustration.

'Let me help you,' she said, in a tone that made clear there would be no arguing.

'If you must,' he said softly.

2

Far out, he's not a lost dog.

Lara smiled at Hilary's text message. It would be late in the evening at home in Brisbane, but her friend was still trying to wrangle her three children into bed and had texted Lara for some moral support. It had been either that or vodka, she'd said. So Lara had told her about Samuel.

You can't just take an old man home to your apartment in Rome. Now there's a sentence I never thought I'd say.

But he needed help.

Lara turned on the air conditioning in the living room. She'd already put it on for Samuel in the bedroom. The old man had grudgingly lain down on the queen-sized bed.

It was crazy hot in the city, his carer had disappeared—and had taken all the

money from his wallet—and
I couldn't think straight in the crowd.
He looked in danger of collapsing.
I had to do something.

So you just bundled him into a taxi and
took him home?

Pretty much. It felt like an emergency
or something.

Something like finding a dehydrated, weak kitten abandoned on the side of the road. A kitten with a fierce tongue, as it turned out. Her new house guest was none too pleased that his paid carer had filched all his cash. But after an initial burst of outrage over the theft, Samuel had deflated, apologised for his obscenities and allowed Lara to take him by the elbow and help him into a taxi, where he sat in silence till they got to the flat.

Lara could have tried to call a doctor, but she didn't know anything about the medical, welfare or aged-care systems in Italy and she certainly didn't have enough Italian to work it out quickly.

You're such a kind person.

Lara took a moment to consider Hilary's summation of her personality. It was generous, really, given she'd handed Hilary her resignation notice out of the blue, without enough time for her friend—pretty much her only friend these days—to find a replacement for Lara's role as property manager in her boutique real estate agency. But there'd been no time; she'd had to get as far away from Brisbane as she could.

In reality, it was no great loss for Lara. She'd only taken the job last year because she needed the money, it was local and part-time, and she hadn't wanted anything too taxing. Unfortunately, chasing rent, filling in forms and delivering eviction notices had been slowly killing her. The job was filled with conflict, which made her queasy and sleepless (well, *more* sleepless) and made her scratch at the inside of her left wrist until it was red and raw. The only good thing about the job was that she'd made a new friend in Hilary, her first friend in a long time. Plus the money she'd earned had largely gone into her bank account and stayed there, meaning she could now be here in Italy with no pressing financial worries. She had a bit of time up her sleeve to work out a proper plan.

Despite Lara's abrupt and unexplained departure, Hilary, bless her, still seemed to love her. Although Hilary didn't know everything about Lara, she knew enough. Her eyes had quickly spotted the red claw marks on Lara's wrist when she came to say goodbye, and she had asked no questions.

I've got to go. The kids are destroying the house. Text me updates.

Lara looked around. What was she doing? She'd only arrived at this flat around ten last night. It was a great Airbnb apartment, on the top floor of a copper-coloured five-storey building. It had an expansive balcony running down one side, and her host had taken her out there to show her the sea of lights, with the dome of St Peter's immediately recognisable nearby.

He'd shown her where everything was and how to use the numerous keys to the lift door, which opened right into the apartment, and the ones to the metal grate doors that opened onto the balcony, and the gates at the front of the building. As soon as he left, she'd collapsed into a deep, exhausted sleep.

But right now there was no sign of jet-lagged weariness, because adrenaline had spiked her blood. What had she done? What was she going to do with the elderly man resting in the bedroom?

She pulled shut the large wooden-framed windows against the heat outside. She was just considering phoning Sunny, waking her up and asking for advice when a sound startled her.

'I, er . . .'

Lara turned to see Samuel in the hall, stooping, one hand on the wall to prop him up.

'Oh, hi, I thought you were having a rest.' She stepped towards him till she was within reaching distance in case he fell.

'I need help,' he said. His gaze was directed at the floor, whether from embarrassment or because it was just physically easier she wasn't sure. She winced, looking at him. It must be so uncomfortable, painful even, to have that sort of curvature in your spine.

'What can I do?' she asked, uneasy. She had no idea about aged care. Was he hungry? Did he need help to go to the toilet? Had he wet the bed?

Until two days ago when she left Brisbane, she'd been living with her mother and sister, helping to raise Sunny's children, Daisy and Hudson. With those two kids around, there wasn't a bodily fluid she hadn't wiped up at one point or another. But could she do the same for an elderly stranger?

'I need to get home,' he said.

'Oh, of course.' *Relief.* 'I can get us a taxi, or an Uber. I'll come with you,' she said. She would make sure he got home safely and then leave him be.

'My home is in Chianti,' he said, lifting his chin to make eye contact. It was a strong chin; his face had good bones beneath that papery skin. The colour of his eyes, even at his age, was stunning.

'Okay, great,' she said, reaching for her phone so she could book the Uber car.

'Chianti is south of Florence,' Samuel said.

'Florence?'

'I came down to Rome on the train this morning. Reeba came with me. I hired her through an agency in Florence. She's from Algeria, a student on a gap year, travelling her way over to the US, or so I was told.' He paused. 'I didn't realise she'd use my trip to Rome as her passage to get one step closer.'

'I'm so sorry that happened to you,' Lara said. 'It's very unfair and not your fault—'

He cut her off. 'The theft is an insult, but not my biggest problem. I need to get home by this evening. I'm needed there.'

'Are you sure? You've had a shock and an already stressful day by the sounds of it.' She inched a chair closer to him while she talked.

He huffed at that but leaned further into the wall.

'I . . .' He started to speak, then closed his eyes as if the idea of asking for help was excruciating. 'I need help to get to Termini and then find an ATM so I can pay you for a cab. But I also need help to walk,' he said, the words bitter.

'Do you think it's wise to get on the train again today? It takes a couple of hours or so to get from Rome to Florence, doesn't it? Train stations are crowded and tiring, in my experience. Is there anyone who could pick you up from the station at the other end? Do you have some family, a neighbour, a friend . . . ?'

'No one,' he said, haltingly, as though only just realising the true difficulty that lay ahead of him, having to manage on his own. His words hung in the air.

No one.

Sadness washed over her. She had no knowledge of his life, of course, of how or why he'd ended up so alone, and certainly no idea why he would come to Rome for nothing more than to throw away his wedding ring. But here he was, a vulnerable man who needed help, certainly, but also one with fierce determination to get on with his life, no matter how challenging it might be. She respected that. She wanted to help him get home again. It was just that right now, she was a stranger in a strange land. She had no idea how to catch a train here, let alone drive on Italian roads. She had no connections here. No home of her own. No food in the house. No plan.

But she looked at Samuel, at the tremor in his legs as they fought to hold him up. She remembered him throwing his ring into the

Trevi Fountain and wondered what awful thing had happened to make him do that.

'I'll drive you,' she said, allowing the words to tumble out of her mouth before she could think too much about them.

He looked at her again, decades of pride still fighting with the greater need to accept help. Even he must have known he was reaching his limits for the day.

'I could hire a car, um, I suppose. I've got nothing else to do, really, no plans or anything. I haven't even unpacked yet. Not that I need to, as I organised myself into a carry-on bag only. I'd hoped to see more of Italy and head up to Tuscany anyway,' she went on, nervous but determined to help. 'I could start my sightseeing today.' She smiled, encouraging him to accept her motives.

Samuel looked back down and nodded once. 'I'll pay you, of course, for your time, the petrol—'

'No. Definitely not. Consider it my good deed for the day.' She wiggled her shoulders in some sort of attempt at jolliness, whether for his benefit or hers she wasn't sure.

Samuel gave a small shrug.

Lara manoeuvred the chair closer to him still. 'It will take me a bit of time to organise a car and finish up here, so rest your legs while you're waiting, if you like.'

She was relieved when Samuel lowered himself heavily into the chair. She pulled her phone from her pocket to google rental cars in Rome. Samuel would know the way, she assumed, but she'd better get a satellite navigation system to help. And she'd need more coffee before getting behind the wheel to tackle Italian roads. As well as the challenge of driving on the opposite side of the road, during her few short hours in the city she'd witnessed the loose observation of traffic rules.

Oh dear. Lara tried to conjure up Sunny's capable, practical nature and fearless attitude to life. Or even her mother's organisational skills and steady calm under pressure. Any of those qualities would be welcome right now.

She took a deep breath, closed her eyes, counted to five on the inhale, six on the exhale. Then she gave herself a rousing internal speech. She could do it. She *had* to. This man was depending on her. She was his lifeline! She was practically a *hero*, for goodness' sake, the one thing standing between him and . . .

'Wait, what is at home that you need to get back to, if you don't mind my asking?'

'Goats.' He smiled for the first time since she'd met him. 'I need to get home to milk my goats.'

ꕥ

Goats!

She was driving the scariest roads she'd been on in her life, Fiats whizzing past her at sickening speed, buses and trucks overtaking her with rude hand gestures, all for goats with huge udders waiting to be milked. Sitting beside her, Samuel had refused to put on his seatbelt, claiming it wasn't the done thing in Italy.

She was on her own in a foreign country, making it up as she went along, Samuel sitting tensely and mostly silently beside her in the passenger seat, occasionally arguing with the prissy navigation system, which called itself Liesel. According to Samuel, Liesel was intent on taking them through industrial estates and traffic congestion on roads that any local with half a brain knew you should avoid.

They made it out of Rome proper and onto the motorway, where hopefully they could stay all the way to Chianti. They settled into an easier rhythm and Lara even managed to peek occasionally at the scenery sweeping by, blue-grey mountain ranges and endless fields of crops broken up by rows of cypress trees. They climbed the winding mountain roads towards Chianti as the day stretched into late afternoon. At last they arrived at a steel automatic gate and Samuel gave her the numbers for the keypad so they could turn into the driveway.

Lara's heart rate slowed and she loosened her white-knuckled grip on the wheel as they crunched slowly over the gravel and pulled up next to his seventeenth-century stone villa and parked under the trees.

'Oh, wow,' she murmured, admiring the tall peach-washed walls and the red geraniums spilling out of terracotta urns.

Samuel struggled with the car door.

'Here, let me help you,' she said, unclipping her seatbelt and jumping out, rushing around to his side.

'I can do it,' he snapped, stabbing at the ground with his cane.

'I'm sure you can, but let me help anyway,' she said, reaching under his armpit and helping him to his feet. 'You must be tired.'

Once he was steady, she stepped back, but not too far, smiling at him. In truth, she felt like a freaking champion right now, a tiny girl who'd conquered a mountain.

He looked at her. She looked at him, waiting for something, anything from him to acknowledge her tremendous achievement. But nothing came.

'Well,' she said, squirming inside. She wanted to make sure he got into the house okay; also she very much wanted an invitation to take a look inside the two-storey villa and at the grounds, and maybe even to meet his goats. She also needed to visit the bathroom after all those coffees.

Hell, an invitation to stay for dinner wouldn't be too much to ask, would it? After all, she'd just dropped everything to bring him here. Her adrenaline was falling fast, and suddenly she was exhausted.

She reprimanded herself silently for thinking he owed her anything. She'd come here willingly—in fact, she'd practically bullied him into letting her help him. She'd given her help with no strings attached.

It was just that the view from this villa—the strict rows of grapevines, the lines of cypress trees spearing into the sky, the grove of olive trees nearby, the blue mountains and the hazy sky—was exactly like every movie about Tuscany Lara had ever seen. She was dying to stay a bit longer.

'Are you going to stand there all day?' Samuel asked.

'Oh, right, of course.' She stepped to the side and automatically reached for him as he began to walk.

'I'm fine,' he said, shrugging off her hand.

She shut the car door behind him with a click. Just then, she heard some cranky bleating.

'I'm coming,' Samuel called, shuffling across the grass and heading around the back of the villa towards the noisy goats. Some irritated banging on the stable gate came in reply. They sounded stroppy, rather like their owner.

'Can I come and meet your goats?' Lara asked, excited now to see them. After all, they were the reason she was here.

Samuel didn't answer her. Lara trotted behind him, her travelling boots steady on the ground. She could see the animals, two brown bodies with straight horns, standing up on their hind legs with their front hooves all the way over the top of the wonky wooden gate. Their barn was a homemade job for sure, with odd angles and gaps between boards, and a rusty metal roof.

As Samuel arrived at the barn, the goats' insulted bleating reduced to mellow grumbling. Lara was instantly seduced by their sweet faces.

'Oh, look at them!' They stretched out their soft noses and lips to inspect her hands. Their yellow eyes with horizontal pupils were inquisitive. Their coats were the colour of maple syrup, with black legs and faces. She looked down and could see their full udders waiting to be milked; that didn't look comfortable at all.

Samuel struggled with the wooden slide bolt. 'Blast!'

'Here,' Lara said, jumping in to help. This time, Samuel didn't argue. She was pleased to see he had a lot more colour in his face now that he was back home.

The wooden slide snagged, then released, and the gate swung open. The goats cheered and made a dash for freedom, shouldering Lara out of the way.

She squealed. 'No, no, no, come back,' she pleaded helplessly as they skipped away, tails in the air. One of them lifted her head, sniffed, then let out a loud snort.

'I'm so sorry,' she began, but Samuel entered the barn, leaving his cane at the gate, and lurched around collecting buckets and a three-legged milking stool.

'They'll come back,' he said. 'Leave them.'

The goats were happily stationed under an olive tree, plucking at its green-grey leaves, wagging their tails with glee.

It was evening now and the light was falling, but not quickly. It was a beautiful soft light, making everything appear muted and romantic.

'Here.' Samuel thrust a metal bucket at her. 'Rattle that. They'll come running.'

She took the bucket and watched as he set himself up on the stool near a squarish wooden structure set out from the wall with an odd shape cut from the middle. It was some sort of vice, she realised, something to clamp around the goat's neck and keep her still while she was milked.

'What are their names?' she asked, reaching into the bucket and scooping up cylindrical pellets of food.

'Meg and Willow,' he said.

She turned around and shook the bucket, the pellets rattling against the metal sides. 'Meg! Willow! Come for dinner!'

She didn't need to ask twice. Both goats galloped back, their pendulous ears flapping as their hooves drummed across the earth. The one with the pink collar got through the gate first and shoved her head into the bucket, nearly knocking it out of Lara's hands. The other goat, this one with a blue collar, wasn't far behind and rammed her body against the first goat so she could get to the pellets too.

'Over here,' Samuel said, pointing to a small trough on the other side of the wooden vice.

Lara wrestled the bucket away from the goats—with more difficulty than she would have liked to admit—and poured some pellets into the trough. Both goats followed and tried to get their heads through the vice.

Samuel tutted at them. 'Only one goat in the crush,' he said, drawing the blue-collared one away. The first goat calmed and ate from the trough in peace. Samuel pulled a metal lever and the crush closed loosely around the animal's neck. The other settled into eating from the bucket beside Lara's legs. She ran her fingers through the animal's hair.

'Gosh, they love their food,' she mused.

'They're Italian.'

Lara laughed out loud at Samuel's dry humour. 'Which Italian mamma is this?' she asked.

'Willow,' Samuel said.

'Hi, Willow,' Lara said, scratching her neck. To her delight, the goat murmured back as if saying hello.

Lara looked up, beaming, to see Samuel watching her.

'She likes you,' he said, a note of surprise in his voice.

'I like her,' she said, running the flat of her hand down Willow's spine. Willow wagged her tail and let out a noise that was almost a purr—a big, creaky goat purr.

'Did you hear that?' Lara said, amazed.

Samuel sniffed and turned back to Meg, placing a bucket under her udder. 'The chickens need feeding too,' he said.

Lara shook her head at the audacity of this old man. He had his back to her now, his hands working rhythmically and expertly under the goat to send needles of milk spitting into the bucket at his feet. He rested his head heavily against Meg's side, using her for support and working by feel, not sight.

Lara opened her mouth to say something, to get him to acknowledge she'd just made a huge effort to save his backside, but stopped. Instead, she inhaled the smell of the grassy hay at the back of the stable, wood smoke somewhere in the air, and the distinctive but not unpleasant aroma of goat.

'Fine,' she said, with a touch of petulance, and left the stable in search of the chickens. She couldn't imagine they'd be hard to find. And sure enough, as she walked down the hill, passing the house, there was a large chicken coop, partially built into the hillside, with its roof the same height as the top of the hill. She could hear them as she got closer, murmuring and clucking, settling themselves for the night. The coop door was in the same rustic, handmade style as the goat barn, and stood wide open.

She assumed the door needed to be shut to protect them from foxes and roaming dogs, and dragged it closed behind her. It dragged over the ground. She could fix that, she realised; she'd just need a shovel to dig out some earth to give it room to swing.

A few chickens of varying colours strutted out from their roost, clucking with interest to meet the new person, their feet making swishy noises through the straw.

'Dinner's coming.'

She looked around for where the feed might be and saw a toolshed nearby, also built into the slope of the hill. She wandered down to it, simultaneously aware of her need for a bathroom and in complete awe of the view, and stepped inside. She paused in the dimness, waiting for her eyes to adjust. She could make out various shapes of tools and hardware, a shovel and two metal drums. Bingo.

Inside the first drum she found a bag of mixed grain. It was heavy, but she pulled it up as high as she could to check the packaging. She noted the Italian word for chicken, *pollo*, and a picture of a rooster. She worked a metal scoop into the grain, then straightened and turned.

There, standing in the doorway, was a man.

Lara jumped, one hand flying to her chest, and spilled some chicken feed on the concrete floor.

The man held up a silhouetted hand in apology.

Lara recovered herself, embarrassed. 'It's okay, you just startled me—too much coffee.' Regaining her wits, she quickly assessed the man as best she could in the low light. He was a bit taller than her, with curly hair pulled up loosely in a man bun at the back and soft facial hair. He was possibly mid-thirties, a few years older than her, though the beard made it tricky to tell. He was dressed in a holey old green t-shirt and shorts, with blue socks and rubber shoes.

'You sp-sp-sp—' he paused, his eyes blinking and his head bobbing, lost in a moment of rigid stuttering, '—speak English?'

'*Sì*,' she said. She'd dropped her eyes while he struggled with his words, but now raised her gaze to meet his dark eyes.

'Matteo,' he said.

'Lara,' she said, and held out her free hand. '*Ciao*.'

'*Ciao*.' He took her hand in his. It was warm and strong but not too strong, and roughened, but not too rough.

'I am looking f-f-for Samuel,' he said.

'He's with the goats.' Lara gestured up the hill.

'Are you the n-n-n-new *badante*?' Matteo asked.

'*Badante*?' She had no idea what that was. 'No, I just . . .' God, how could she explain the day? 'I gave him a lift home.'

Matteo tilted his head as though not sure what she was saying.

'I drove him home. In the car.'

'Ah, *sì*.' He didn't seem in any hurry to finish this conversation and she was trapped here, by virtue of the fact that he was blocking the doorway. She glanced down at the scoop of chicken feed she was holding, wishing he would move out of the way. She was wrung out and stiff from driving and still had to feed the chickens before she could find a loo.

But since he wasn't moving, she asked, 'How do you know Samuel?'

'He is my great-uncle.'

'Uncle? But he told me he had no family,' she said, suspicious now, on edge.

Matteo lifted his shoulders defensively.

She returned the motion, feeling spontaneously proprietorial towards Samuel. She'd only known him for half a day but she felt like she'd rescued him—from a thief, dehydration, falls in the street, perhaps further robbery or even assault, hunger—when no one else was there to do it. He'd been defenceless. What sort of family left their elderly relatives to travel across the country with unscrupulous carers?

'Do you know he was in Rome today, all alone?'

Matteo frowned.

'He was robbed. I had to drive him back.'

Matteo lifted his chin, considering her. Then, as her unexpected surge of self-righteousness fell away and she realised he was likely in no way at fault, she felt starkly vulnerable.

No one knows where I am.

A cold sweat beaded on her neck.

'I'm sorry,' she said, wanting to take back her words, unoffend this man—this man who had her trapped in a dim shed halfway around the world from anyone she knew.

Stupid, stupid Lara. You should know better.

Matteo opened his mouth as if to respond, but just then there was a crash from up the hill, bleating from the goats, and a yell of pain from Samuel.

Matteo turned and ran up the hill. Lara dropped the chicken feed and followed suit.

Inside the barn, Samuel lay on the ground, the buckets of milk spilt over the straw bedding. He was on his back, holding his wrist, his face screwed up in anguish.

3

Sunny

Sunny Foxleigh—or 'Foxy', as more than one boyfriend had tagged her, thinking he was the first genius to come up with it—lay awake in her bed, her two young children asleep in the room next door. She could hear Hudson's snoring through the wall. It clearly didn't bother Daisy. Her daughter could sleep through an earthquake, her earnest, busy mind probably just as busy during sleep, with no time for distractions.

Sunny covered her face with her hands, trying to will sleep to come. The rough edges of paint on her fingers brushed against her nose.

The handle of Eliza's door *scritched* and the hinges creaked. Soft footsteps padded along the passage. Her mother obviously couldn't sleep either.

Sunny flung off the bedcover—a light blanket, all that was needed in September in Brisbane—and followed Eliza to the kitchen, blinking as her eyes adjusted to the light. Her mother was reaching up on tiptoe, into the top cupboard where the tea and coffee were kept, along with the Milo which had to be stored out of reach to stop Hudson eating it with a spoon.

Eliza jumped as Sunny approached, and clutched the tea canister to her chest.

'Couldn't sleep?' Sunny asked, grateful to have someone else awake in the middle of the night. It made her own anxiety about *him* easier to bear.

Eliza squinted, lacking her glasses. 'I was worrying about Lara, alone on the other side of the world.'

Sunny's shoulders slumped. 'Me too, among other things. That, and Hudson's snoring.'

'It's rattling the walls,' Eliza said, moving to the kettle and flicking the switch. She held up the tea canister, questioning.

'No, thanks.' Sunny leaned against the bench, catching sight of the red paint stains across her navy cotton pants. She didn't care much for clothes and had never been one for pyjamas, happy to simply fall into bed in whatever she was wearing. She'd slept quite soundly on many couches in many people's homes wearing her jeans. Sleep had never been an issue for her. Until the past week, anyway.

Sunny did love the winter pyjama sets on her children, though. Somehow, her estimation of her mothering efforts inched up a notch when she got the end part of the day down pat—dinner, bath, pyjamas, teeth, stories, bed. Regardless of the chaos two active five-year-olds could create throughout the day, the world was restored to some sort of order in the blissful, relieving silence that fell once they slipped into dreamland.

And then Hudson started to snore.

She studied Eliza's hair as her mother moved about the kitchen. It was flattened on one side and Sunny wondered if she could suggest a newer, trendier haircut—something shorter, a close crop that showed all the different colours of ageing with pride—rather than the slightly too long misty-grey bob Eliza had been wearing for so many years.

She blinked, rousing herself, and voiced her greatest fear.

'Do you think he knows?'

The kettle clicked off and steam floated gently across Sunny's neck. Eliza looked away, jiggling her chamomile teabag.

'God, I hope not.'

4

Lara

Lara woke at dawn, opening her eyes to see the thick wooden beams that held up the terracotta roof tiles above. A welcome cool breeze blew through the open double doors of the villa's balcony, shifting aside the curtain to give her a glimpse of a sky not long emerged from darkness. The unfamiliar house was quiet. She eased herself up off the achingly hard mattress and stood to stretch and massage out the kinks and knots. Her feet were silent as she crossed the floor and stepped out onto the balcony to drink in the sight of dawn over the Tuscan valley.

Yesterday evening, before a goat had darted under Samuel's feet and sent him to the ground, she'd only been able to capture the view in broad brushstrokes—mountains, trees, vineyards. Now, with the sky turning a gentle rose colour, she could pick out the details of the many properties that made up the bowl of the valley in front of her. From her vantage point up on the ridge, she could see a mustard-coloured villa to her right that loomed over its yellow fields, next to a white church with a belltower. To her left, four white villas nestled close together, overlooking a slope planted with rows of green vines. On the other side of the valley, a road wound through clutches of ancient cypress trees, cars zooming between the trunks. And then there was the imposing villa up on the highest hill, a dull grey colour, neglected perhaps, but at least double the size of Samuel's.

She stood there for a moment, remembering all that had happened last night. Samuel's accident. The short trip to the hospital in the nearby village of Fiotti-in-Chianti, the three of them in her hire car because Matteo's truck was only a two-seater and someone (Matteo) had to sit beside Samuel to hold ice on his arm. The doctor telling Samuel he had a broken wrist and would have to stay in hospital overnight. In rapid Italian, with Matteo translating for Lara, the doctor had lectured Samuel about needing help at home, telling him that he couldn't go home without someone to care for him. The word *badante* had come up several times.

Carer. The young woman Samuel had been with in Rome had been his *badante*. But she hadn't done a lot of caring as far as Lara could tell. Lara had stared at Matteo, waiting for him to say that he or someone else in the family could care for Samuel. But Matteo had turned away from her, murmuring something to Samuel. Samuel shook his head and patted Matteo's arm in reassurance.

'I can do it,' she'd heard herself say from the corner of the hospital room. Matteo's shoulders had dropped with relief; his eyes had softened.

Samuel had accepted. But only because he said it wasn't enough notice for the usual agency to help him and, besides, he would never trust them again after Reeba. Then he worried about his goats; they would need milking in the morning. So Matteo had said he would stay overnight at the villa and teach Lara how to milk.

As cute as they were, Lara was robustly horrified at the idea of having to milk the goats, but hoped she'd managed to hide that from Samuel.

Through these conversations, she'd started to gather tiny pieces of information about Samuel's life. For the past fifteen years, since his wife had passed away, he'd slept in the downstairs bedroom, unable to ascend and descend the stairs safely anymore. Samuel had told them to find themselves rooms upstairs but not to go into the first bedroom on the right because that had been his and his wife's.

His wife's name was Assunta.

Now, with dawn's misty optimism moving gently across the balcony and into her bedroom, Lara was still coming to terms with the fact that she'd landed in Rome only a little over twenty-four hours before and had spontaneously offered to care for an elderly man in a four-hundred-year-old villa in Tuscany. The world sure moved fast when you weren't busy chasing late rental payments for Hilary, or watching *Dora the Explorer* and building skyscrapers with Daisy and Hudson. She missed them already.

When they'd left the hospital, around midnight, she had asked Matteo to drive. Too bad about the insurance risk for an unlisted driver; she could barely keep her eyes open. At the villa they'd climbed the stairs together, Matteo carrying Lara's bag for her. She was too tired to take in much, feeling as though she'd covered a week's worth of experiences in one day. They'd stopped at the top of the stairs, Matteo so close that she could smell the antibacterial soap he'd used to wash his hands at the hospital. The door of what must have been Samuel and his wife's bedroom was closed. She'd looked up from the round brass handle to Matteo's face. His dark eyes reflected the moonlight streaming through the window on the landing.

He broke eye contact first and stepped away. Her gaze followed his back as he moved to the other two bedrooms, switching on the lights inside.

'Your choice,' he said. She could see how weary he was too, his face pale.

'It doesn't matter, truly. I'm a stranger here. You pick one, please.'

Matteo shrugged and pointed at random. 'Thank you,' he said, holding her gaze for a moment. 'My u-un-cle was lucky you were there for him today.'

'You're welcome,' she said.

He passed her the bag. 'Well, goo-d-d-d night.'

''Night.'

Their bedrooms were on either side of the bathroom, which had a deep iron bathtub, some missing tiles and a dripping tap.

She should go there now, actually, and try to freshen up. She wheeled her whole carry-on bag to the bathroom, as it seemed easier than fishing around in it for what she needed.

Her mother had urged her to pack lightly. 'Sarah from work had her luggage go missing once on an overseas trip and it took three weeks for them to find it and forward it on,' Eliza had warned, sitting on the back steps of the house and watching Daisy and Hudson play in the sandpit under the leopard tree. 'She was home again before they found the suitcase. She'd spent her whole holiday without her clothes or medicines or shoes.'

Lara had been hanging out her washing, running through mental lists of things to organise before she left—copies of her passport and travel insurance, tiny bottles to take on the plane until she could find proper supplies in Italy, prescriptions filled and medicines packed, a doctor's letter, a good pair of travelling boots. Sunny had helped, booking her the apartment in Rome, printing out her flight itinerary and labelling her luggage. Lara's nerves had been bad that day, she remembered. A late season westerly had aggravated the raw skin on her wrist.

Later that night, Sunny had come to Lara's granny flat in the backyard while Lara had been laying out shirts, dresses and pants on her bed. Sunny's long blonde hair was piled on top of her head. She was wearing one of the many handmade aprons that she collected from op shops to wear while painting, preferring the softness of well-worn cotton to some hot, plastic material. Each piece became a work of art in its own right as layer after layer of paint splashes was added to it. That night, Sunny reached into the front pocket of the yellow gingham apron and presented her little sister with a tube of paw paw ointment for her wrist. That simple, caring touch had almost undone Lara. Her eyes had filled, but Sunny had taken her by the chin and spoken sternly to her.

'You can do this, Sprout.'

Lara *had* done it. She'd got on the plane, and now here she was in a villa in the Tuscan hills.

She found a towel in the rickety wooden chest of drawers in her room, which stood below an oversized framed print of Raphael's angels, and took it to the bathroom, where she showered, standing in the deep old tub, and cleaned her teeth. She dressed in a pair of ultra-light white cotton pants and her favourite flowing three-quarter-sleeved shirt. V-necks always served her well, making the most of her bounty—a bounty every woman on her mother's side of the family shared, except for Sunny. Her older sister was slim and toned, with small breasts that were annoyingly perfect for every style of clothing.

In the mottled bathroom mirror, Lara looked weary and washed out, obvious shadows under her dark brown eyes. Her chestnut hair was wet from the shower, but she didn't have a hairdryer, so all she could do was comb it out to air dry. She fished around in her toiletries bag for her tablets, which she took first thing every morning, and swallowed them with a handful of water.

Matteo's bedroom door was still shut.

The concrete steps with the wrought-iron railing allowed her to go quietly downstairs—that was the beauty of a stone house as opposed to the Foxleighs' wooden home back in Brisbane, which creaked and popped with movement day and night.

The staircase snaked fully back on itself so that when she reached the ground floor she was confused as to where they'd come in last night. As she wandered, she got lost several times, with the house seeming to twist her around and send her out into yet another courtyard or entranceway. One door that seemed to lead to a bedroom actually opened onto what must have once been the receiving room, with huge double-wood doors to the outside and a marble fireplace.

A short hallway led to a large L-shaped living room, with several couches and a shiny black Steinway & Sons piano. The room's alcove held another deep fireplace, with green velvet upright chairs, footstools, walls lined with shelves of books, both Italian and English, on music, food and art, piles of sheet music, an old record player, a large tobacco pipe collection, metal servants' bells and red woven rugs. More doorways, more windows and more confusion for Lara. There seemed to be double wooden doors everywhere she turned, leading to yet another room or opening to the beautiful outdoors.

Beneath the house was a dusty, cluttered one-bedroom flat, with a spiral staircase leading up to the kitchen. And it was the kitchen that fired her imagination.

It was easy to visualise generations of women bathing babies in that wide stone sink, filling it up with just enough water for the baby to splash. They'd chop onions, garlic and tomatoes on a wide board on the wooden kitchen table. Maybe a dog lay on the terracotta tiles at their feet. A young girl, learning to cook alongside her mamma and nonna, would carry in potatoes and carrots, stored produce from the vegetable garden; perhaps she caught the baby's hands as he reached a little too far over the edge of the sink.

Another girl would be on the other side of the kitchen's half wall, bent over the fireplace where centuries of meals had been cooked. Maybe she'd be hanging a cast-iron pot over the flames and boiling water for those potatoes. From outside would come the sound of an axe falling rhythmically into logs, the sharp crack as the wood split; the son carried it inside, complaining that he was hungry.

This was a home built for big families, life spilling out of every corner.

'*Buongiorno*.'

Lara spun on the tiles, startled by Matteo's sudden appearance—the silence of this house worked for others too. He stood tall and offered no smile.

'*Buongiorno*,' she managed to reply.

'Is there c-c-coffee?' he asked, coming closer to her. He was still in yesterday's clothes, though his socks and shoes were missing. He peered around the kitchen.

They rummaged around in silence, looking for the coffee. Matteo found ground beans in a terracotta pot near the salt and pepper.

'Thank God,' he muttered.

Lara laughed. 'You need a coffee?'

'I cannot th-think straight without one. I make no sense until the caffeine has reached my b-b-brain.'

'I think you're doing okay,' she said, with just the tiniest edge of flirtatiousness, she was appalled to note. She felt heat rush to her ears.

He looked at her sideways, just quickly, while spooning coffee into the pot. 'Did you sleep well?' he asked.

'I did, thank you. I was so tired. I don't think anything would have woken me.'

Matteo added water to the pot and set it on the stove. 'I am very grateful that you are able to st . . . ay and h-h-help Samuel. I feel . . . not good enough that I am not able to do more.'

'Do you work?' she asked, then felt ridiculous. Of course he would have responsibilities, a job and maybe a family of his own.

'Yes,' he said, 'and there is no one else in the family who will help him.'

Lara wondered at his use of the word *will*. Was that intentional or a slip of translation? His English did seem exceptionally good. But families were complicated; she knew that better than most.

'I'm sorry if my uncle was less than gracious to you yesterday. He can be . . .' Matteo rocked his head from side to side, a cheeky glint in his eye. '. . . I think the word is *contrary*?'

'That's probably the right word,' she said, grinning in agreement. 'Your English is excellent.'

'I s-s-studied at university,' he said, rubbing one eye with the palm of his hand, still struggling to fully wake up. Suddenly, he looked down at his clothes from yesterday. 'I need to get changed. The coffee will be ready soon. Perhaps we should talk over breakfast.'

'That sounds like a good idea,' she said, and firmly told herself to ignore the fluttering of attraction she felt watching the back of his neck as he walked away. As if her life wasn't complicated enough right now! Fantasies of romance were the last thing she needed.

5

Lara and Dave

Lara was nineteen when she met Dave at the Peaceful Valley Animal Shelter, about forty-five minutes from her home. She was wearing men's working overalls, trying to be like her sister, because Sunny was so much cooler than her. Not that she would admit that to Sunny. But Sunny was the sort of person who could pick up some ugly old jumper from an op shop and add a scarf and on-trend bracelet and look dazzling and edgy and oh so bored with the world. Her sister was living in a share house in West End, hanging out with other struggling artist types, painting by day and working in a bar at night. Lara wore the overalls hoping to catch just a bit of Sunny's self-assurance. In drama classes, they made her feel like she belonged alongside her gregarious classmates, and they also did nicely here at the shelter.

Lara and Dave had both been assigned to clean the cat cages. She'd seen him here a few Saturdays back. When she'd seen his name on the duty roster she'd hoped she might have a chance to be partnered with him. Then, one day, she was.

'Hi, I'm Dave,' he said, holding out his hand. He had almond-shaped green eyes and thick curly brown hair and an easy confidence.

'I'm Lara.' Now she felt slightly underdressed in her overalls, next to Dave with his tucked-in collared shirt, belted jeans and clean shoes. She took his hand and he held hers for a touch longer than necessary, and her hopes soared. She just knew that he was different to all the boys at uni. The silly boys who kicked cans at lunchtime or skived off in lectures as if they were still in the back row of maths class in high school. The boys who compared their weekend drinking binges to see who got the most slammed. The boys who stank of either body odour or cheap deodorant. No, Dave was nothing like them. He looked quite a bit older, for a start, and took pride in his appearance. And the fact that he was here, on a Saturday, volunteering his time at the shelter just like her, said it all.

They cleaned thirty cat cages together and Lara cuddled every inmate, letting them push their heads up under her chin and purr and purr. Her heart broke a little with every one she had to return to the cage, locking the door behind it. She'd always wanted a cat or a dog, but Eliza had firmly said no, vet bills would cost too much and pets made it hard to go on holiday. Not that that argument mattered at all, because they almost never went anywhere. Eliza had finally given in and allowed her a pair of guinea pigs in the backyard when she was in primary school. But Lara was determined that the moment she moved out of home she was getting a cat or a dog, maybe both. She would let them sleep on her bed at night and curl on her lap while she worked on her laptop.

She shared this with Dave when their tasks were finished and they were having coffee in the shelter's kitchenette—which was really just a nook with a boiling water unit on the wall.

'What would you call it?' he asked, stirring his instant coffee and grimacing at the rainbow-coloured oil slick that floated on the surface.

She shrugged. 'I don't know. It would depend on the cat. They're all so unique.'

'Like you,' he said, staring at her in a way that made her feel he could see right inside her. 'You're different. I can tell.'

How did he know that? She half smiled, nervous under his attention. She *was* different. Could he see into her mind?

'I meant that in a good way,' he clarified. He leaned back in his chair and she felt his withdrawal from her like a small puff of cold air.

'No, it's fine,' she laughed, hoping she looked natural and carefree, wanting his attention back on her.

'It's clear that you care about something other than yourself. You've got a big heart. I like that.'

She smiled and stirred her tea with her plastic spoon, too flattered to look at him.

'When I was younger, I . . .' He hesitated. 'I had some difficult stuff going on with my father. Someone with a big heart helped me out. Probably saved me, really.' He smiled, though it seemed empty, as if raw pain was just below the surface.

Lara nodded her understanding. Maybe that was what he saw in her—shared childhood experiences. 'I get that. My dad wasn't easy to live with either.'

Dave adjusted his shirt collar, as though embarrassed, and cleared his throat. 'Anyway, forget that. It doesn't matter.' He sat up straighter and changed the topic. 'I'm renting, which is probably a great thing—otherwise I'd be bringing home half the shelter every week.' He swept a rogue curl to the side, a gesture she found endearing, then blew cooling air over his terrible coffee in three short puffs.

Lara listened to the ever-present barking of dogs in the concrete and chain-wire kennels at the back. It was a cold day, grey and windy. She wanted to take them all hot-water bottles and blankets.

'It's devastating, isn't it?' she said, feeling a sense of hopelessness at the overwhelming flood of animals that just kept coming. 'I don't know why we do it to ourselves. Coming here is torture, really. It always takes me a couple of days to recover.'

Dave's eyes grew serious. 'I could help you with that. Both of us here together, you wouldn't have to feel so alone with your pain.'

Lara gulped. 'Wow.' No one had ever said anything like that to her before. Normally, people would just tell her not to worry so much. She was intrigued. 'What do you do?'

'I'm a psychologist.'

That dampened her excitement.

'I have a placement in a general practice on the south side and I'm studying again, to become a medical doctor.'

'How old are you?' she asked, surprised. He didn't look *that* much older than her.

'Twenty-eight,' he said. 'And you?' He was flirting back now, she was sure.

'Nineteen.'

He whistled gently between his teeth. 'I thought you were older, only because you seem so mature and you're here volunteering. Shouldn't you be out somewhere cutting up the dance floor or protesting in a rally?'

'I'm a bit clumsy for dance floors,' she said, and he laughed. 'And I prefer the company of quiet people and animals.'

'I do too.'

Lara shifted in her seat. Her interest was ignited by how similar they were, though his age and profession did make her feel a bit weird. She felt older than her peers, but not nearly as adult as a twenty-eight-year-old psychologist. A *psychologist*, of all things. What were the chances?

'When are you next here at the shelter?'

'Next Saturday,' she said hopefully.

He nodded. 'Good. Then I'll see you again.'

6

Lara

Lara and Matteo pulled together scrambled eggs and caprino cheese on toast for breakfast. Samuel had goat milk stored in glass bottles in the fridge and what looked like homemade caprino. Just outside the kitchen door grew basil and cherry tomatoes, and down in the chicken yard Lara found four golden-brown speckled eggs.

Matteo had scrubbed up nicely, with a fresh white collared shirt and faded jeans highlighting his golden skin and his strong—but not too muscly—body. Too many muscles made her flinch.

They sat at the kitchen table, both enthusiastically tucking into their food. Matteo picked up a chunk of caprino and chewed, murmuring his appreciation. 'That is good cheese,' he said, his face more relaxed and alive now that the coffee had kicked in.

'I couldn't agree more,' she said, licking several crumbs off her finger.

'Have you w-w-w-worked as a *badante* before?' he suddenly asked. It was a reasonable question. Everything had happened so quickly, there had been no time for reference checking.

'No,' she said. 'But I've been helping my sister to raise her twins since they were born. They're five now. I know it's not the same, but I think there would be some crossover of skills—cooking, washing, housework, medicines, bathing.'

'Of course,' he agreed.

'I've also had a job with a real estate agent. I'm happy for you to call my employer if you like.'

He waved the offer away. 'I've al-already seen you act honourably.'

'Well, thanks.' His words made her feel unexpectedly proud.

Then he told her that he lived and worked at a goat farm and dairy, not far away, which produced goat cheeses; that he'd studied animal science at university; that he had three older brothers, all married, all living up north; that his mother lived alone in Fiotti, the nearest town, as his father had died several years ago; and that he came over whenever he could to help Samuel.

She told him that she lived in a granny flat outside her mother's house, and that Sunny and the kids lived inside the house with Eliza, and that they'd been living together to support each other since the twins were born.

'But I needed to get away for a while,' she admitted, her mind flying to the other side of the world. She would text Sunny straight after breakfast.

'I understand that,' he said, his dark gaze holding hers long enough to make her look away. 'I would like to do this too sometimes,' he chuckled. 'My mamma?' He gave her a look that might have conveyed several things.

'She is hard work?' Lara asked, trying to clarify.

'*Sì, sì*. But I am stuck with Mamma,' Matteo said, giving a smile that suggested he was actually happy about that, despite the hard work. Just then his phone pinged in his pocket and he pulled it out to study the screen, his jaws working through a mouthful of tomato and basil. 'You see—here she is. My mamma.' He held up the phone and gave a *what can you do?* shrug.

'How long are y-y-you here in Italia?'

Lara used her knife to cut open a cherry tomato. 'I don't know. I don't have a flight home booked yet.'

Matteo nodded approvingly. 'Living in the moment,' he said, and drained the last of his coffee.

Living in the moment. Mindfulness. It was the catchcry of the millennium and the backbone of her therapy.

Suddenly, Matteo gave her a huge smile and placed his knife and fork together on the plate. 'The ladies are waiting. We go milk now.'

'Right,' she said, slightly alarmed.

'I'll t-t-teach you,' he said, standing, beckoning to her to follow.

Naturally, if Samuel had a broken wrist and she was going to be his *badante*, she would have to milk as part of her job—for however long she would be here. But out in the barn, her nerves sizzled as she settled herself onto the milking stool at the warm flank of Willow, who was tugging at hay and raising her back legs impatiently. Matteo knelt beside Lara, his shoulder and arm pressing against her as he reached for the goat's udder to demonstrate. A stray curl brushed her cheek as he moved to settle Willow, murmuring to her in Italian. Lara couldn't understand his words but his tone was soothing.

'First we must wash the teats,' he said, producing a small plastic bowl with some soapy water. 'I do one to show you.'

She watched him wring out a green washcloth and clean around one teat and up into the udder a little.

'You have to really clean the tip,' he said, paying excruciating attention to one of Willow's *nipples*—because let's face it, that's what they were. Lara shifted on the stool, feeling long-forgotten sensations in her own.

Matteo handed the second washcloth to her and she took it, wrung out the water, and reached under the goat to wash her other teat gently. 'Sorry, Willow,' she muttered. The goat kept eating, unperturbed. Lara put the washcloth down, relieved.

'Now we milk,' Matteo said. He put a small container under Willow's teats. 'Each teat is separate. You have to milk both sides.'

'Okay,' she said, wishing she'd brought a notebook and pen.

'You don't pull down like this,' he said, pulling Willow's teats until they stretched in a manner that made Lara wince. 'You push up, like a baby goat.'

He wrapped his thumb and first finger around the top of the teat, just below the bag, and pressed upwards gently. 'Then you use the next fingers to squeeze the teat.' He did it slowly, moving his middle finger and ring finger downwards in turn, to direct the milk. It squirted out. He did it again, this time a little faster with more rhythm.

'It's like playing a recorder,' she said, observing his fingers working together but independently, as if playing different notes.

Matteo gave a little smile, though she wasn't sure if he'd understood what she'd said. After he'd released a few squirts from each teat he stopped and picked up the small container.

'This?' he said, indicating the milk. 'This we throw away. D-d-dirt, bacteria.' He tossed the milk onto the straw, then picked up a stainless-steel bucket to begin again.

'Squeeze and roll,' he said, reinforcing the movement. 'Now your turn.'

'Oh God,' she said, taking a deep breath.

Matteo chuckled. 'It's easy.'

It was *not* easy. Lara couldn't get anything out of a teat for ages, and Willow got stroppy with her and shuffled her legs about, twice almost landing a foot in the bucket. Lara was afraid to squeeze too hard. She tried squeezing one teat at a time, and squeezing both together. But she couldn't coordinate her fingers.

Beside her, she could feel Matteo's body vibrating as he tried to suppress his amusement.

'Stop laughing,' she said, 'you're distracting me.'

'Look.' He demonstrated again how to do it—and milk flowed out easily, of course—and then how she was doing it, like a drunken sailor trying to pull down rigging on a sailing ship, until they both fell into fits of laughter.

'Stop,' she said, breathing deeply. 'I need to focus.'

He moved out of her way and she tried again, but she was trembling with embarrassment and giggles. She couldn't help thinking that this really was a bizarre thing to be doing less than two days after arriving in a strange country and with this kind-of-lovely man disturbingly close to her.

Matteo reached over, laid his strong arms along hers and covered her hands with his. 'Like this,' he said, slowly and gently directing her fingers. It was terribly difficult to concentrate on learning the movement with the warmth of his skin awakening her own.

But then it happened.

'Look!' Lara squealed. Satisfying streaks of milk were zinging into the metal pail.

'You are doing it,' Matteo said, lifting his hands away to allow her to take over. 'Very good, Lara, keep going. You are a natural,' he enthused.

'*Cosa sta succedendo qui?!*'

Lara and Matteo both started and turned towards the barn gate. Standing on the other side was a long-legged woman with shiny dark hair, expensive-looking sunglasses and a crisp white shirt opened lower than Lara would ever dare. Essentially, she was a living image from a fashion magazine.

Matteo jumped up and went across to speak to her, and the woman shouted back. Italian words and hand gestures flew between them, Matteo's tone placating and the woman's accusing. Lara made out the word *badante*, and a sharp finger was pointed in her direction. And Lara almost felt the slap as she was put firmly in her place: she was the servant girl perched on a stool at a goat's udder, and she'd been caught flirting with the elegant lady's man.

After Matteo and the goddess had departed—she in a shiny red automobile spraying up stones and Matteo following in his truck—Lara finished the milking and took the buckets to the kitchen where she located bottles and poured in the milk, feeling so proud that she'd achieved her first task as a *badante*. She made herself a second coffee and sat out the back of the house, admiring the amazing view over the valley. She needed to check in at home. It would be late afternoon there. She pulled out her phone.

Hi Mum and Sunny, is everything okay? Xx

Everything's fine, Sprout. Just enjoy yourself. You're in ITALY! Don't waste your time worrying about anything back here. The kids are fine. All is good. I'll tell you if you need to know anything. X

Darling, where are you? Are you still in Rome? Mum x

So much has happened so quickly. I'm in Tuscany and have taken a job as a carer for an old man. Staying in a villa. Have just learned to milk goats!!! Trust me, it's not easy!!!

Well that sounds wonderful. I wish I was there with you. I've always wanted to go to Tuscany. I'm just back from my mahjong group—such a great bunch of ladies. I must have them over for tea. It's good to be making new friends at my age. Keep me posted. Mum x

Next, Hilary's name popped up. Since Lara's sudden departure from the agency she was managing rentals. She'd sent a series of photos, each one worse than the last.

No wonder you left. Look at what the tenants at 42 Dura Street left behind.

Lara scrolled through photos of burns in the carpet, a year's worth of rubbish festering under the house, broken blinds, graffiti on walls, and . . . oh . . . the bathroom.

The bond money won't even scratch the surface of how much it will cost to fix this. The owners will be devastated. I should have been paying you danger money. It's too late for me, Lara. Save yourself. Stay in Italy. It's the only sensible thing to do.

Poor Hilly Billy. What a nightmare ☹

Lara scrolled through the photos again, simultaneously glad she wasn't there and dreading the day when she'd have to go back. Hilary had said she could have her job back whenever she returned, and as stressful as it was Lara knew she might have to take it, at least till she got back on her financial feet. But that was something she could worry about later. For now, she looked up from her screen, taking in the tall purple and grey-green blooms of the lavender surrounded by buzzing, industrious bees, and took a deep breath. Despite the circumstances that had led to her swift departure from her family and job, she could almost feel Italy starting to work its charm on her, convincing her that everything in the world was beautiful and good. She wanted to believe it, so badly.

7

A clerk from the hospital phoned Lara later that day to tell her in broken English that Mr Samuel Baker was ready to go home. Lara found Samuel in a patient transfer room. He was sitting in a reclining chair, his left arm in its cast propped up on a pillow, his right hand holding his phone to his ear. He was speaking in Italian, his voice rising and falling, his jaw jutting. Short sentences. Exasperated sighs. Then it was done.

'Hi,' Lara said, smiling, trying not to be intrusive.

Samuel's eyelids were heavy over those blue eyes, his pale skin so translucent under the fluorescent lights that his veins showed. The bright green paint on the walls didn't help his pallor.

'Is everything okay?' Lara ventured, nodding to his phone.

Samuel let out a puff of frustrated air. 'My daughter, Giovanna.'

'Is she coming to see you?'

'No. She lives in London. Wants me to go and live with her. Thinks this is *a sign*.' His eyes softened a little then, almost as if a small smile was brewing at this mystical notion.

'What do you think?'

He shook his head almost imperceptibly, but said no more.

'How are you feeling?' she asked, leaving the family argument behind them. She perched on the arm of the recliner next to his. There was only one other person in the room, his eyes cast down at a newspaper.

Samuel grunted. 'In need of a decent meal,' he muttered.

'Well,' she said, buoyed to think that this was something she could help with, 'let's get you home and get that sorted. I'm okay in the kitchen. I could whip you up something really nice if you tell me what you'd like.' She hoped he wasn't too much of a carnivore; she ate a little meat but didn't relish handling it.

He raised the knobbly pointer finger of his right hand. 'Before we go, let's get a few things straight.'

'Okay,' she said, bracing herself.

'How long will you be here, in Italy?'

'I don't know yet.'

'How long will you be staying with me? If you plan on going soon then I'd rather find an assistant from somewhere else.'

Lara sensed his nerves beneath the bravado. It was an awful feeling, she knew, to be vulnerable. 'To be honest, I can't say for sure.' His eyes pinched in the corners. 'But I would like to help you out for a while. If you're happy to have me, of course. I can get you references and so on, if you like.'

He nodded curtly, but seemed relieved that she wasn't rushing away for the time being. 'We need to agree on the terms of your employment,' he said, trying to recover some control.

'Good idea,' she said. 'In fact, I have a notebook and pen here in my bag—let's write it down, shall we?' If real estate had taught her anything it was to take scrupulous notes.

Samuel eyed her bag as she pulled out the notebook.

Lara clicked her pen and smiled at him. 'Ready.'

He held out his hand for the notebook. She passed it to him, along with the pen. He scribbled down a figure with his right hand; the writing was shaky and the penmanship from a different era. He passed it back to her. 'I'll pay cash as you obviously don't have a permit to work here. It will include your board in the villa and use of the car.'

'The car?'

'I have an Alfa Romeo. Bought it in 1995 and it's still going.' He said this proudly, with a lift of his chin. Everyone liked to feel they'd made a good purchase, especially when it was an expensive one.

'Oh yes, I saw that,' she said, remembering seeing the square-jawed bonnet of a black car under a terracotta-tiled carport with vines proliferating over it. Never having been interested in cars, her eyes had just ticked over it.

'Hours are six to six a day, with a two-hour break in the middle.'

Six a.m.

'Hm. What about duties?' she said, narrowing her eyes at Samuel. He was old, frail and in need of help, but she suspected he was far more cunning than one might think.

'You'll be my personal assistant,' he said, narrowing his eyes back at her.

'Give me some examples,' she said, tapping her pen on the page.

'Shopping, cooking, cleaning, taking me to appointments. I have to come back here in a couple of weeks to have this changed,' he said with disgust, raising his left arm with the heavy cast.

'What about helping you with showers and getting dressed, things like that?'

Samuel huffed and looked to the ceiling. 'Maybe.'

'And what about looking after the goats . . . the milking?'

'Have the goats been milked this morning?' he asked, his eyes widening, and she could see it clear as day: the goats were the thing he loved most now. She felt for him.

'Matteo gave me a lesson in milking and we sorted it out.'

Samuel nodded, obviously relieved. 'Yes, I suppose I'll need you to help with the goats too. And the garden.'

The garden? She was hopeless at gardening. She loved planting seedlings with Daisy and Hudson, watering them, watching them grow and bloom, then picking the flowers or the beans or snow peas or strawberries. But that was it. Once that first flush of blooming life had passed her interest faltered.

Lara considered the figure on the notepad in her hand and the extensive list of duties, uncertain if this was something she should commit to. She certainly wouldn't abandon Samuel right now—he needed her. He'd been through a lot since yesterday morning and it was showing.

Besides, where would she go? She had no plans, and a job like this would buy her more time as she wouldn't have to dip into her savings. She felt somehow bonded to him now, as though she was *meant* to be here, ever since she had been in the right place at the right time at the Trevi Fountain. Speaking of which, why had he thrown his wedding ring away? She was dying to know. And as for herself, maybe keeping busy was just what she needed to stop having nightmares about . . . *him*. A spiralling sense of helplessness was to be avoided right now.

'Okay, look. I can do all this, and I'm happy to help you. But I want Saturdays and Sundays off,' she said firmly. If she was going to stay in Tuscany, she'd at least like to explore a little.

Samuel raised his chin. 'Saturday afternoons after one o'clock, and Sundays,' he countered.

'Alright, I agree. Deal?' she said, holding out her hand to him.

'Deal,' he said, and shook it.

8

Samuel

Samuel sat uncomfortably in the *badante*'s hire car, his wrist aching and his shoulder even more so, having been wrenched dreadfully in the fall. The sling was pinching a nerve in his neck. And this girl drove so slowly, barely reaching the speed limit. What a joke. No one obeyed speed limits here. Italy was a country of *Life*, capital L. And if he could turn back time he'd be enjoying that life, flying along the road on a Vespa, preferably with no helmet (yes, even despite what had happened to Lily) and no shoes. And above all, with his dear Assunta at his back, her strong arms wrapped around his waist and her cheek resting on his shoulder, her long hair flying out behind her, shouting with joy, shouting at him to go faster.

That was the Italy he'd fallen in love with.

He'd been born in London just months before the outbreak of the Second World War. His father served his duty overseas, coming home to London just once through the duration of the war, to their small flat in the East End. Long enough to heal a sprained knee and father a second son. But not long enough to fall back in love with Samuel's mother. Henry went off to war again and never returned. Not because of death, as Samuel and his brother were told, but because of love. *Marisa.* He went to live in Italy, to start a whole new life, and they never saw him in the flesh again.

It was only when Samuel was a teenager that his mother had shared the truth. Henry had left them. All of them. His father wasn't a hero at all, dying in battle. He was a coward, a deserter of their family.

So at twenty years of age, Samuel kissed his mother goodbye and set off to find this deserter, to push him up against a wall and make him explain what was so great about this country and that woman that he'd left his wife and children to live in poverty. Samuel's childhood memories were of shivering under thin blankets and eating boiled tripe, of wearing the neighbours' older boy's shoes to school, and ducking threats of eviction from their home.

But then Samuel had arrived in Italy. It was sunny and warm. It was colourful. It was full of music and art and affection and amazing food. It was in every way *alive.*

And there was Assunta, with red ribbons in her long hair and a laugh so loud it made everyone turn to look. She threw her whole body into laughing—she arched her back and slapped her sides or someone else's arm, her frame shimmering with the sound.

Words flew out of her mouth with passion and urgency, whether in affection or admonishment, or both.

Samuel, my darling heart, when will you fix the leak in the roof, eh?

Tomorrow, my love, tomorrow.

Both the country and a woman had stolen his heart and he never returned to England. It turned out Samuel was no different from his father. He didn't even bother to find his old man. They'd both walked away from their lives and Samuel could understand why.

Now, the *badante* pulled into his driveway and parked the car next to the old olive tree, and his memories drifted away like the shifting fogs of his childhood.

'Home, sweet home,' she said, smiling as she unbuckled herself.

Sweet. That was definitely a word he would use to describe this girl. She was unlike any *badante* he'd had before, motivated by genuine concern for his welfare, he could tell. But he also knew enough about people to suspect she had secrets of her own.

He let his eyes roam over the villa. It was still in great shape. That was the beauty of these buildings: they were so solid. They'd been standing for hundreds of years and would be for hundreds more.

He looked down at the plaster cast around his wrist.

If only he could say the same for his body.

9

Sunny

It must have been some sort of universal law that children only ever got sick and had to stay home from kindy when their mother had planned a huge workday. Hudson and Daisy flopped lethargically on the lounge watching children's morning television, their cheeks flushed. Small 'milk bottles', containing watered-down juice and crazy straws, sat untouched on the coffee table in front of them.

Sunny said goodbye to the kindy director, who'd informed her that hand, foot and mouth disease was going around, and disconnected the call.

'Great. Now we'll all get some cow disease and have the authorities coming around to shoot us.'

She turned to see Daisy watching her, eyes wide.

'Did I say that out loud?' Sunny asked, grimacing.

Daisy nodded.

'Sorry, poppet. I was joking. It was a bad joke. You don't have a cow disease. Just a regular human one.'

Daisy knew a little too much about anatomy and physiology. She pored over pictures of germs and antibodies and white blood cells. Whenever she bumped into something, she would hold up the offended limb and say, 'I've hurt my bones. Now I'll have to go to hospital for an X-ray to see the jagged pieces.'

Sunny felt Hudson's forehead again—warm, but nothing that would ring alarm bells—then brought one of the drinks to him. 'Come on, buddy, you need to drink something.'

'My voice hurts,' he said. At least he was talking today. Some days they could barely get a word out of him.

'Me too,' Daisy said, her lips moving but nothing else.

'Mm. Open up and show me,' Sunny told Daisy. She shone her mobile's torch light into her daughter's mouth. 'Ulcers,' she said. 'Ouchy.'

'Very ouchy,' Daisy agreed.

Paracetamol was what they needed. That should at least get them drinking and eating again.

Sunny tapped her teeth together, frustrated, and went to the fridge to find the bottle, trying to let go of the great hopes she had for the old wooden door downstairs. It had a wonderful grid window divided into fifteen panes of glass. She had been planning to clean it up, sand it back, paint it, and then sand it again to make it 'distressed'. It was part of a big project for a local bed and breakfast. The owners were renovating and redecorating throughout the house and relandscaping the grounds. The door was to be hung horizontally behind the desk in the reception area, each square filled with a heritage photo of the building. The owners had chosen her to do the job based on her Instagram photos of the items she'd completed over the past five years. This was the biggest job she'd taken on yet.

She administered strawberry-flavoured paracetamol first to Hudson and then to Daisy, and both of them sucked it down willingly.

Usually, Lara had Thursdays off from the agency, so if she hadn't been in Italy she might have been able to help. And Eliza would normally step in whenever needed, but she had left early for some sort of women's meet-up breakfast and said she wouldn't be back till the afternoon. She *might* have said what she was doing after breakfast, but Sunny might not have been paying attention. Thoughts of *him* had been playing on her mind.

Sometimes she thought of moving out, just her and the kids. This life of being planted in one spot—and at her mother's house—wasn't what she'd ever imagined for herself before the children came along. But her insufficient income was the barrier, and until she grew her business, or the kids were at school and she could take a second part-time job, she would have to be patient. It was just that every now and then the wind would blow a certain way, as if it was trying to lift her up and tumble her away like a fallen leaf, destination unknown. But then there was Lara, and Sunny had made that promise a long time ago to look after her.

'Mama, what's the difference between a giraffe and a penguin?' Hudson asked, his usually serious dark eyes wide with mirth.

'I don't know, what?'

'Flippers!' He proceeded to fake laugh.

'Funny,' Sunny said, smiling, though obviously it wasn't funny at all.

'And now for my magic show,' Hudson said in a ringmaster's voice, pulling himself up to sitting. That paracetamol must have worked in seconds.

'First, I'll make you disappear.' He pointed at Sunny and narrowed his eyes. 'Abracadabra!' He made a whooshing noise.

Daisy sat up quickly, adjusting her glasses as if waiting for Sunny to actually disappear.

Sunny joined in and began to pat her body. 'Wait a minute, where am I? Where'd I go? I can't see me.'

Daisy's eyes were wide. 'You're indivisible.'

'Help!' Sunny cried.

'I'll save you, Mama.' Daisy launched off the couch and threw her arms around Sunny. 'I've got you.'

Hudson followed. 'I've got you too.'

They all fell onto the floor in a tangled mess.

'No, I've got *you*,' Sunny said, wrapping them up in a big bear hug. And she was never letting go.

10

Lara

The first couple of days with Samuel went by in a daze. Surprising herself, Lara slipped into the new time zone and slept fairly well at night, only waking a few times to roll over and adjust her hips on the hard mattress. But she didn't lie awake for hours on end, worrying about the day to come. Neither did she ruminate over the day that had just been, re-examining it from all angles to see if she had said or done the wrong thing. A lot of stress had simply fallen away. There was something about the Tuscan hills that was luring her into a place of hope that maybe the problem back home would just go away. With every hour that passed with no word of bad news from Sunny, Lara relaxed further into her surroundings as one might ease into a hot tub to relieve stiff and aching muscles, feeling each knot loosen and soften.

There'd been some awkwardness between her and Samuel, like a cello and an electric guitar trying to find a melody, but that was to be expected. At least they both spoke the same language; that helped.

She tried to be sensitive to Samuel's needs and feelings. It must be dreadful to be alone at this stage of life and needing help from strangers. And it wasn't even as if it was 'the kindness of strangers' anymore, because he was paying her to help him. She intuited that he would never be able to trust that she actually *wanted* to help him.

Overall, he was coping well with his injury. He was clearly made of tough stuff. From time to time she had to help him get around the ground floor of the villa. He could still use his walking stick in his right hand, but with his left arm in the sling he was even more unsteady than he'd been before the accident. She also needed to help him get in and out of the shower. For the moment, he had a plaster cast on, which couldn't get wet. Next week she would take him to the hospital and he would get a mouldable splint that she'd be able to take off for him. But for now he had to wear a plastic bag over the cast in the shower. He kept his underwear on too. He clearly hated the process, ordering her around and snapping at her.

She drew on her experience of looking after the twins, brushing their teeth and hair, putting on their shoes and so on; this really didn't seem so different. Except that back at home she wasn't the primary carer; there was usually someone else around to help. For the first time, she was caring for a dependant on her own.

The bathroom on the ground floor had already been modified for disability access. Lara noticed that Samuel was able to undress himself with one hand as long as there were no buttons involved, and she suddenly realised why older people often seemed to dress so shabbily. It wasn't just that they were on limited budgets and bought cheap clothes, it was because it was easier to deal with trousers that you could simply pull down with one hand, rather than having to undo zips or buttons. And the same went for shirts. She practised it herself so she could understand what Samuel had to do, and found she could undo buttons with one hand but she certainly couldn't do them up. She could only take off a shirt by leaning forward and pulling it from the back over her head and arms. Shoes were tricky—slip-ons were the key.

Right now, it was lunchtime. Samuel was sitting in one of the green velvet wingback chairs facing the sleek piano. It was another hot day outside, but the villa's thick stone walls provided significant insulation. Samuel had asked her to put on a record from his vintage collection: a Mozart concerto, number eight. It was uplifting, with lots of happy violins and a chatty piano. She wasn't into classical music herself—she was more of a pop person. But it was surprisingly enjoyable there in the background and she found herself chopping tomatoes and fresh oregano from the garden with a lightness of touch. She was making pasta for lunch.

Samuel had told her that he ate pasta every day, and there was a stash of packets in the pantry. She hadn't had to go shopping yet, which was a relief; she wasn't keen to tackle the roads again. Today she was making a rich red sauce using the tomatoes in his garden, making it up as she went, with onions, garlic, oregano and basil. She was going to present the pasta with grilled zucchini on top, curls of grated cheese and yeasty bread on the side.

Her phone buzzed on the kitchen bench, its screen splattered by tomato juice. It was a message from Sunny. Lara's heart leaped to her throat. But she quickly saw she needn't have worried.

Whatcha up to?

Making pasta and sauce for lunch. Listening to Mozart.

How bloody sophisticated. We just had fish and chips for dinner. It was puppet day at kindy but the kids have been sick so couldn't go. The teachers decided since the kids missed out that I could pick up the ghastly marionettes to take home for the weekend. Now Chucky 1 and Chucky 2 are sitting at the table and staring at us.

Don't turn your back on them whatever you do!

Pretty sure you've got the better deal. Love you.

Love you too x

Lara put her phone back on the bench, relieved that one more day had passed with no news of *him*.

11

Sunny

On Saturday morning, Sunny took the kids with her on a garage sale run. Early spring was a classic time of year for a good clear-out, and there were a lot of sales in the area today. Hand-drawn signs had lined the streets all week, with balloons and streamers at traffic lights to garner attention. Anyone who was practised at finding gems and bargains knew they had to be up at dawn, and so she was. She'd put the kids in long-sleeved tops before they went to bed, so they'd get up already dressed. They wouldn't be in them for long, not once the sun had climbed a few degrees into the sky.

Hudson had no shoes on, which was normal for him—she'd long let go of any idea of trying to keep him shod. Shoes, clothing tags, new clothes, heat, cold, roughness, prickliness, hair-brushing, teeth-cleaning, nail-cutting, hair-washing, bandaid-applying—for Hudson, everything was a challenge. Strangers had told her, 'Get a jumper on that kid,' or stared at him and asked her, 'Why isn't your son wearing shoes?' She'd been the recipient of disapproving looks at kindy when he turned up wearing the same paint-spattered t-shirt as the day before because when she'd tried to wrestle him out of it he'd screamed so much that she was terrified someone would call the cops. The most obvious diagnosis, she assumed, would be the same as for Lara and their father, Leonard.

Bipolar affective disorder, though Leonard was type I and Lara type II.

Leonard had tried different medications but none of them seemed to work. Often, he simply refused to take them. In Sunny's memories he was either non-verbal, not answering when spoken to, or insisting they lock all the doors and close the curtains because The People were following him. Sometimes he was lavishly generous, coming home with flowers and jewellery for Eliza and toys and lollies for the girls, picking them up, whirling them around and talking of holidays on tropical islands. This part of the manic episode was exciting, and Sunny would think that maybe he was better now. But then the crash would come and the three of them tiptoed around him, waiting for him to explode at the smallest thing.

He would disappear for weeks at a time. After years of this, Eliza stopped calling the police to notify them that he was missing. They'd stopped caring long before that anyway. There was nothing they could do, they'd said, to prevent a man from walking out of his house. For many years, Eliza had pretended to her friends that her husband was busy with work, rather than admitting that he would prefer to live a life on the streets. At least, that was where he told her he was. She could never know for sure. She became quite masterful at lying to her co-workers and friends, though the latter diminished in number as she attempted to conceal the chaos in her home.

The two sisters had responded very differently. Lara was the earnest, hardworking, sensitive one, always trying to help, convinced that if she was just good enough, quiet enough and helpful enough then Leonard would be happy. Sunny was the wild one, with no tolerance for Leonard's behaviour. She used to take off too, from her early teenage years. Maybe her restlessness was something she'd inherited from Leonard. Or maybe it was the only way she could cope. Instead of striving for peace like Lara she embraced instability. Sunny often thought how ironic it was that of the two of them, it was she who was now living the life of responsibility.

Sunny plucked a rubber ball from the garage sale table and clenched it in her fist. She needed to channel her anger at the memories of having to explain her father's strange behaviour at birthday parties, or walking home from a school dance alone in the cold and dark because he'd forgotten to pick her up, or the time his fist landed on the wall right beside Sunny's head. She could still remember the puff of air on her cheek as his knuckles broke the plaster. The dent in the wall remained for several years until Eliza got sick of it one day, mad as hell with Leonard, who'd been gone three weeks with no word. Eliza plastered over that dent the way she covered over so many emotions in order to keep their lives going.

Sunny watched her children running wild on a stranger's lawn. Daisy had put on a pair of fairy wings and was pretending to fly by running in circles, her purple gumboots leaving a trail through the dew on the grass. Sunny watched her daughter, her chest thick with emotion. How she adored that little girl. It was such a privilege, this mothering thing. It wasn't something she'd ever given much consideration before it happened. It had never been part of her vision. But then it did happen, and the course of her life changed in a moment.

A fellow fossicker reached across Sunny to pick up a battery charger, and accidentally elbowed her in the arm. 'Oh, sorry,' the woman said, putting her hand on the spot she'd bumped. 'Are you okay?'

'All good,' Sunny said, with a smile and a wave of her hand. The woman grimaced another apology and wandered away, carrying the charger with her.

Sunny picked over battered board games and one-eyed dolls, frying pans missing handles and rocking chairs that didn't rock. Next to all the crappy bric-a-brac lay a pile of dusty items that looked as though they must have been stored under the house for decades. Metal tubs and rusted gardening tools. A milking pail. An ancient baby's cot that wouldn't pass today's safety standards. Interesting stuff, but nothing of use to Sunny's current upcycling venture, and she didn't have room at home—that was to say, at her mother's—to store much more stuff.

Hudson tackled the residents' corgi to the ground, and the small dog growled at him and nipped at his wrist.

'Baxter! No!' the girl at the stall yelled. 'I'm so sorry,' she said to Sunny. 'He's never done that before.'

'It's fine, really,' Sunny said.

Her son let the dog go and it ran away. He howled, holding his wrist. Sunny crossed the grass to Hudson, who was half crying and half raging with indignation that the dog had bitten him.

'It's okay,' Sunny said, bending to rub his back and inspecting his wrist. Nothing but red skin and saliva.

'It bit me!' he bawled.

'I know. But I think you squashed him and hurt him. Dogs can't talk, so he couldn't say so. He only had his teeth to tell you.'

Just like that, Hudson stopped crying and got up, his attention caught by a balloon that Daisy had taken from somewhere and was bringing to him. 'Here you go, Hudson,' Daisy said, handing it over. He ran away with it. Hudson was always moving, unless he was asleep or in front of a screen of some sort. Maybe it wasn't bipolar. Maybe it was ADHD. Or maybe he was simply five.

Sunny smiled and pulled Daisy in for a hug. At least her daughter liked to be hugged. She knew it wasn't her fault as a mother that Hudson didn't much like to be touched, but she craved his body, wanting him to lean into her and cuddle her back, rather than stiffening up, or wriggling away, or becoming completely disengaged and floppy.

Maybe it was autism.

Or maybe he was just five.

'Thanks, Daisy,' she said, kissing her daughter's cheek. It was warm from all her running around. Sunny helped her pull up her long sleeves.

'Can we call Aunty Lạ La in It-a-ly?' Daisy said, over-pronouncing the unfamiliar word.

Sunny lifted one of Daisy's long plaits over her shoulder. Her daughter had incredibly thick hair for one so young—a lot like Lara's. 'Well, it's night-time in Italy. She might be asleep. We don't want to wake her.'

'When she's awake, then? Can we call her then?'

'Of course,' Sunny said.

'I'm going to tell her about my puppet show,' Daisy said, grinning and jigging up and down. Daisy had already forced Sunny and Eliza to sit through one puppet show with the nightmarish marionettes. It looked like they might be treated to another yet.

Sunny levered herself off the ground. She was somewhat stiff from taking apart a wooden bed frame yesterday, sawing it and sanding it to turn it into a bench seat, then painting it turquoise.

'Come on, let's get your brother and go find something fun to do. There's nothing here for us. I'm in the mood for an adventure.'

12

Lara

Lara was still in bed, enjoying the view through the open double doors onto the balcony, watching the light over the mountain range slowly changing from pale rose to a misty lavender, when her phone buzzed beside her.

Sunny.

'Hello?'

There was a slight delay at the other end and then, 'Aunty La La! I'm Daisy!'

'Hello, sweetheart.' Lovely Daisy was exactly as her name suggested: cheerful, bright, dependable, resilient. Sunny had asked Lara's opinion on the name, holding her baby in the hospital, the smell of antibacterial gel strong in the air.

'Do you think it fits?' Sunny had asked, the tip of her nose twitching slightly, desperate to get just the right name. 'I've been thinking she should have a really strong name, like Valencia or Audrey or Kendra. But I just keep thinking she's a Daisy.'

Lara had reached out her fingers and wound them around the tiny fist and Daisy had opened her eyes, deep pools of wisdom, and looked right at Lara, spearing her with love. 'Yes,' Lara had said, a tear rolling down her face. 'Daisy's perfect.'

'How are you?' she asked now, thrilled to hear Daisy's voice.

'Good. Guess what?'

'What?' Lara winced, bracing herself.

'We got a puppy!'

Surprised and relieved, Lara swung her legs over the side of the bed. 'Where from? What sort of puppy?'

'A black one. We got her from a woman who had a sign on her fence at her house.'

'Ah, I see. And what's her name?'

'Midnight,' Daisy said. 'I got to name her.'

'Well, that's a beautiful name,' Lara said. 'What does Grandma think about this?' She remembered all the times she'd begged her mother for a puppy and been refused.

'Grandma loves her. She got a baby sling to carry Midnight around when she's asleep.'

Lara smiled. Although Eliza had resisted pleas for a cat or dog over the years, she had always helped Lara to nurse orphaned or injured birds in the garden. Perhaps that was what Lara should have done when she was young—just accidentally 'found' a puppy.

'She's going to sleep in my bed,' Daisy went on. 'Here she is—can you hear her?'

Lara could hear faint grunts and pants that suggested poor Midnight was being dragged up to the phone.

'Say hi-iiiii,' Daisy sang from the background.

'Hi, Midnight,' Lara obediently crooned to the pup. 'Daisy. Daisy! Daisy? Can you hear me?'

'I was just handing Midnight to Hudson so he can give her some milk.'

'Oh, okay.' Lara was disappointed that Hudson wasn't clamouring to speak to her, but not surprised; his phone anxiety wasn't specific to the person on the other end. 'Can you text me a picture of Midnight? Ask Mum to help you.'

'Oh no!'

'What?'

'She's just wet my bed. Ohhh . . . popsidoodles!'

Lara giggled despite herself. She could never hear Daisy's trademark exclamation without laughing. Her niece had heard the word on television one day and adopted it as her swear word of choice. She was a particularly attentive mimic, so it was a good thing that was the word she'd chosen; both Sunny and Lara could be a bit careless with their language, much to Eliza's disapproval. Their mother was far too refined to swear.

'I've got to go and deal with this,' Daisy said wearily, sounding just like Sunny. 'Bye.' And she was gone.

Lara sat on the bed, holding her phone. The kids had a puppy. She remembered conversations with Dave about getting a puppy, and how disappointed she'd been when they didn't get one. And how glad she was now that they hadn't.

The memories of Dave unsteadied her.

A warm shower lulled her back into herself, and she popped her pill and dressed, ready now to help Samuel get up and about and to make his breakfast.

Downstairs in the lovely stone kitchen, Lara brewed coffee and arranged a plate of sweet pastries she'd found in the freezer and heated gently in the oven. It was the tradition in Italy, she'd been delighted to discover. Now she had a licence to indulge in a chocolate-filled croissant (a *cornetto*) for breakfast. She couldn't wait to take Samuel's car into the market to buy fresh ones.

It was going to be an exciting day. Her first official half-day off would begin as soon as she'd done some washing and cleaning and prepared lunch and dinner for Samuel. She planned to drive her rental car to the Florence depot and then, with some divine intervention, catch a bus back. From tomorrow, she'd start driving Samuel's Alfa Romeo around. And since tomorrow was also a day off, that meant she could explore the area. Her feet moved more lightly around the kitchen as she imagined where she might go.

First, though, she had to milk the goats, and each milking had been taking ages to accomplish. Matteo's instructions had helped, but she was still a novice. Her nervousness about the task was made worse by the fact that Samuel insisted on coming out to the barn to supervise her.

'You've got to do it right or they'll get mastitis,' he kept telling her.

He was sitting beside her on a stool, offering suggestions. 'Slower. Go gently, now. She isn't finished; there's plenty more in that teat. Make sure you wash the end of that teat so no germs go up there—we don't want mastitis. Come on, pick up the pace or we'll be here all day.'

She felt bruised by his irritation, but she reminded herself how important the goats were to him and how frustrating it must be to watch her fumble around. Occasionally he demonstrated a bit with his good hand and she saw how the simple act of milking his goat relaxed him. So she bit her lip and endured his impatience.

Back in the house, Samuel eating his pastries in the living room and Lara in the kitchen bottling the warm milk—which would settle today, leaving a thick layer of delicious cream on top—their new-found peace was interrupted by the sound of tyres on gravel. A throaty engine gave a final cough as the ignition cut.

'I wonder who that is,' Lara said, half to herself and half to Samuel in the other room. If he heard her he didn't respond.

She shut the fridge, wiped her hands on a tea towel, and went to the front of the house, stepping out through the huge Roman doors and crossing the small open courtyard to the covered patio area, with that immaculate view of the Tuscan hills.

Matteo came towards her, dressed in sloppy work clothes and with his hair pulled back, just as he'd been when she'd first met him. Her gaze locked with his and her breath hitched a little. She remembered his hands on hers, teaching her to milk. The heat of his skin. It confused her. After Dave, she didn't think she would ever respond to a man's touch again.

'M-m-morning,' he said.

'*Buongiorno*,' she replied.

Just then, another visitor appeared behind Matteo. He was a young man—younger than her, anyway—and he was the complete opposite of Matteo. Where Matteo's hair was dark and curly, the new man had straight, shiny hair, white blond. While Matteo wore old, holey clothes, this new man wore brand-new linen. He looked like a department store mannequin.

'Hi,' Lara said to the newcomer.

'Good morning,' he said, his white teeth flashing in his angular face. And gosh, if he didn't have the most groomed eyebrows she'd ever seen. She had to admit that, so far, Italy was living up to its reputation for beautiful people. Except she could tell from his accent he wasn't Italian. But still, he was *in* Italy.

'This is Henrik,' Matteo said. 'He is W-woofer.'

'Sorry?'

'Willing Workers on Organic Farms,' Henrik explained. 'I'm doing a science degree.' He slid his hands into the pockets of his taupe linen pants, accidentally tearing the edge of a pocket as he did.

She felt for him. That was something she would do.

He studied the loose threads for a moment, muttering to himself, then moved on. 'I'm here for six months doing research.' His accent sounded Scandinavian, but his English was perfect, just like Matteo's.

'He is working at our dairy farm,' Matteo said.

'With the goats?'

'Microbiology is my specialty,' Henrik said, by way of explanation.

'Henrik thinks maybe he w-wants t-to get more experience growing vegetables,' Matteo explained.

'Matteo told me about his uncle's inability to work his land anymore. It's a shame to waste land when it could be used for good,' Henrik said. 'I thought maybe I could work it for him and he can get some vegetables in return. The dairy is not far from here. Domenica—the manager—she says maybe she doesn't need as much help with the goats right now, so it makes practical sense. Crop production is more difficult going into autumn, but I like a challenge.' Henrik worked at the edge of a loose brick with his toe.

'Right, well, I'm sure Samuel would love to hear that,' Lara said, though she wasn't at all confident. 'Come in. I'm making coffee.'

They followed her inside, the cool of the villa noticeable right away as they passed through the doors. Samuel was still seated in his favourite wingback chair and all the pastries were gone, she noted.

Lara motioned for them to go over to him while she scurried into the kitchen to make more coffee. She'd learned that Samuel, though still an Englishman, didn't drink tea anymore but instead liked his *caffè* short and black, something that could be thrown down like a shot of vodka. She took a punt that the others liked it that way too. In Rome, she'd seen men standing at cafe bars, drinking their macchiatos and chatting to the barista the way men in Australia would stand at the bar in a pub, drinking beer. Samuel drank upwards of six coffees a day.

She heard Matteo introduce Henrik to Samuel, and then a lively conversation began in Italian, which was disappointing as Lara couldn't follow it. Apparently Henrik was fluent in at least three languages. Lara had learned only a handful of Italian words in primary school, but they'd stuck with her. And those few Italian lessons in a hot classroom on Friday afternoons had planted the seed of a dream to one day see Italy.

She approached the men with the tray of coffees, as well as a glass of water for Samuel and his daily vitamin D supplement for his osteoporosis. She'd picked a few small white flowers that she'd spotted growing in the lawn and put them in a glass. She guessed that they were probably the equivalent of the yellow dandelions that grew voraciously back at home, which she loved but most people considered weeds. She hoped Samuel would think they were sweet; she'd been trying to think of small ways to lift his spirits.

Matteo and Henrik had pulled up chairs and sat facing Samuel. Henrik sat with his legs crossed, a loose tendril of blond hair shifting in the slight breeze that circulated the room, his gaze intense as it held Samuel's. The conversation must have been going well, because Matteo looked pleased (or was that *relieved*, she wondered), Henrik was smiling, and Samuel looked more optimistic than she'd seen him since they'd met. She guessed that he'd be happy to have another goat attendant around and not to have to rely solely on the inexperienced Australian *badante*.

Lara placed the tray carefully on the small table between the men. Samuel gave no thanks and made no obvious indication that he'd seen or appreciated her flowers. She retreated, but not too far, perching on the piano stool and feigning interest in the sheet music that sat nearby.

The happy chatter continued and Samuel's face softened into something approaching a smile. Lara was truly pleased. She could help with Samuel's physical needs, but it was clear as day that he needed more. He needed family. Maybe his daughter was right that he should move to England to be with her.

'*Grazie*,' Matteo said, lifting his tiny coffee. Henrik took his and wrinkled his nose as he brought it to his lips, but sipped it anyway. Perhaps he was more of a milky latte man.

Then they all raised their cups to each other in salutation and threw them back, Henrik perhaps a little too quickly. He tried to cover up his splutter but his watering eyes gave him away. Poor Henrik; she could recognise a fellow klutz a mile away.

A deal seemed to have been reached.

'Mm,' Matteo murmured. 'Lara, you make good coffee.'

'Thank you,' she said, feeling a blush inching its way up her neck.

'Samuel s-s-s-said you need to go into Florence to . . . d-d-drop off your car?'

'Yes, this afternoon after I've finished here. I'll need to find a bus back. Do you know of any that might come this way?'

'I c-c-can follow you and bring you back. I'm heading that way to visit my mamma,' Matteo said, casting an eye at Samuel.

Lara did a quick family tree in her head. Matteo's mother must be Samuel's niece. That meant that either her mother or father would be Samuel's wife's sibling.

'Really? That would be so great,' she said, both relieved that she wouldn't have to work out the bus routes and excited at the idea of spending time alone in the car with Matteo.

But then she remembered the supermodel who had interrupted their milking session.

Still, she'd like to get to know Matteo better and she'd certainly like to find out more about Samuel's family and why he was so isolated now.

'That would be fantastic, thank you,' she said. 'I finish here at one o'clock.'

'I'll be here,' Matteo said.

13

Lara and Dave

Five months after they met, Lara and Dave moved in together into a two-bedroom townhouse that allowed one small pet, and wasted no time in discussing whether it should be a cat or a dog. Lara put forth her case.

'I've never had a dog,' she said. 'It's my life's dream.'

They were sitting on Dave's two-seater leather lounge. As he was older than her and had been living on his own for a number of years, he had managed to acquire everything needed to set up a place. So he'd moved it all into the new place and she hadn't had to do anything more than bring her clothes and books, a few knick-knacks and some pictures to hang on the wall. It didn't matter that it felt like his home, not hers. They would collect new things together over time, and then it would be *theirs*.

'I know, honey,' he said, taking her hand. 'But you and I are gone throughout the day, so no one would be here to look after it. It would end up barking all day and then the neighbours would complain and then we might have to move out or rehome the dog.'

'That's true,' she said, defeated, laying her head back against the bright red and blue Peruvian rug she'd brought with her, which was lying over the back of the lounge.

'Cats are quiet and don't need so much company.'

'Okay, we'll get a cat.'

Together, they chose a two-year-old moggy from the shelter where they'd volunteered. The adoption coordinator was so happy when she handed Pepper over.

'What a great love story,' she said, watching Lara snuggle Pepper against her chest, kissing him on the head. 'You met here and now you're in a relationship and taking home your first baby.'

'Okay, let's not get ahead of ourselves,' Dave said, scratching Pepper under the chin, a look of adoration on his face. He'd told Lara he wanted kids, sure, but not yet. She was still young and he was working hard in the clinic and studying to become a doctor. So he'd asked her to go on the pill early in their relationship, and handed it to her every day at seven in the morning, along with the other medications that kept her brain straight.

The coordinator laughed. 'Look at you two—you'll be back for more.'

Pepper was a black and white 'tuxedo' cat, with a white chin, chest and paw tips. His whiskers were so long they reminded Lara of a seal's. From the moment they brought him home, he made himself comfortable. He walked around the whole ground floor, then climbed the stairs carefully, the tip of his tail twitching, to assess each room upstairs before finally settling into the middle of their bed.

Lara lay down with him, the sound of his purring like music to her ears. She rubbed his fine ears carefully. 'I love him so much already,' she said. Dave was watching her. 'I can't believe I ever thought we should have a dog.'

'He's perfect,' Dave said, and joined them on the bed. The three of them lay there, soaking up the moment of being a little family for the first time.

Lara and Dave spent two days showering Pepper with love and toys. Dave popped out to get a lasagne for dinner and came back with little balls with bells, catnip-spiced cloth mice, and a ball of string. Pepper immediately jumped down off the bed and began to play.

'You are so great,' Lara said, hugging Dave tightly, laying her head along his collarbone. 'I love you so much.'

'I love you too,' he said. Then he kissed her. Then he pushed her gently to the bed and claimed her mouth and her breasts and her body, his passion all-consuming, till she lost all sense of herself and just became his.

They skipped dinner and stayed in bed, while Pepper explored the shoes in the wardrobe, making himself a little nest. Every time Lara tried to get up, Dave pulled her back till she gave in to him. She'd never felt so needed and desired. She lay in his arms all night thinking what a wonderful turn her life had taken, after so many hard years with her father when she was young, and then many more hard years trying to keep up with her schoolwork and maintain friendships, hiding the shame of being *not right*.

In the early days of their relationship, Lara had mustered up the courage to tell Dave about her mental illness and about the things it did to her—the long depressions, the irrational behaviours, the all-night study fests, her obsessions, the wrist-scratching and insomnia.

He'd listened carefully, then kissed her on each temple. 'I love your brain,' he said. She'd scoffed, but he'd taken her firmly by the shoulders, forcing her to look at him. 'No, I'm serious. You are different, yes, but this is what I do for a living. Clearly I love people like you.'

She finally fell asleep in the early hours of the morning, which always left her dopey and incoherent the next day. And it was from this state of deep unconsciousness that Dave woke her.

'Lara, wake up.' He was shaking her gently.

'Huh? What's up?'

His eyebrows were pinched with worry. Alarmingly, his eyes filled with tears. 'It's Pepper. He's gone.'

'What?' She bolted up from the bed. 'What do you mean? He was just here, last night, playing.'

'Oh honey, I'm so sorry.' He wiped his hand across his mouth. 'You must not have quite closed the back door last night when you went out to fetch your shoes.'

'No, I did, I always shut it properly. I double-checked and triple-checked.'

'When I went down this morning to make you a coffee, it was open. I can't find Pepper anywhere. You mustn't have caught the latch properly and he must have opened it somehow and run off. They say to make sure you lock cats inside for weeks before you let them out—'

'But I didn't—' She was up now, naked, scrambling for clothes.

'—because they always try to go home.'

'Shit. Shit! We have to find him. He could get hit by a car or something.'

'I'm onto it,' he said, holding out his hands in a *steady on* fashion. 'I've already called the shelter and told them to look out for him because he might be heading back there.'

'Oh God, I can't believe this.' Lara started to cry, panic, guilt, horror and disbelief all fighting to take charge. *Why was she so fucking hopeless?!* 'I closed the door, I'm sure of it.'

Dave moved to her and pulled her to his chest, wrapping his arms around her. 'It's okay. We'll find him. You mustn't blame yourself. It was an accident. I know you didn't mean to do it.'

Lara was sobbing now, hysterical. Pepper was her cat. She already loved him to the moon and back. She was so stupid. She felt her mind unstitching, preparing for a huge fall, already sensing what she would one day know for sure. Pepper was gone, and he wasn't coming back.

14

Lara

When Matteo returned to escort her to Florence, he'd changed his clothes. Suddenly, the kind-of-sloppy-but-adorable farm boy had shapeshifted into a smooth estate manager. His smartly cut white shirt was made of some natural fibre—bamboo, perhaps—and fitted him perfectly, while his khaki pants had clearly been professionally tailored to sit at just the right length above his shoes.

'H-hi,' Lara said, suddenly developing a stutter of her own.

'*Ciao*,' he said, smiling beatifically at her, removing his sunglasses to reveal a cheeky glint in his eye. She suspected he knew exactly what effect he was having on her.

She was glad now that she had made the effort to clean up too. She wore a bright blue v-necked cotton dress with a gentle fifties inspiration, giving shape to her breasts, the skirt flowing out around her. Not that her breasts needed any more emphasis, but she'd found that it was simply easier to dress for them than to try to hide them.

Henrik, accompanying Matteo, had also changed. He'd adopted

dark denim overalls over a checked shirt and even had a straw hat. With his fair hair and heavy boots, he closely resembled an attractive scarecrow.

'*Ciao*,' she greeted him.

'*Ciao*,' he replied, then headed off in the direction of the goats, who were tethered under the olive trees.

She'd left Samuel with plenty of prepared food and made sure he had everything he might need, reminding him to call her if he got into trouble. He said he would milk the goats with Henrik this afternoon, and seemed somewhat relieved that she was leaving the house for a bit and giving him back his space.

Lara followed Matteo into Florence, rolled into the car park of the rental office and cut the ignition, thrilled she'd managed to get the car back without any mishaps. She dropped the keys in the return box then climbed into the passenger seat of Matteo's two-seater truck, the door emitting a loud squeak as she closed it.

'So,' he said, pulling out onto the road to head back towards Fiotti-in-Chianti, 'where would you like to go n-n-now?'

'I was thinking of exploring the village. Everything's happened so quickly since I arrived. I haven't had a chance to go yet, and I don't even know what's there. I'll need to do some grocery shopping for me and for Samuel soon, but I'll take his car back on Monday to do that.'

She checked off lists in her head to work out if there was anything urgent to do. There *was* one thing.

'I really need some chocolate,' she said, laughing, a touch embarrassed to say it out loud.

Matteo smiled and nodded. 'Chocolate is important. I c-c-can drop you at a shop in Fiotti,' he said. 'It will make you happy, I'm sure.'

'*Grazie*.'

There was a short silence, then, 'Or I could sh-sh-show you around town? Give you a guided tour?' He looked at her sideways, just quickly, then changed gears as they headed up a hill past rows of vines.

Her heart actually fluttered. Was he suggesting a *date*? It couldn't be. Surely he was just being kind, Samuel's great-nephew who was taking an international visitor under his wing.

'I would love that,' she finally said.

Matteo smiled again and wound down the window, which she gathered was his truck's version of air conditioning.

'I would like to pick up some chicken to make Samuel something nice. I saw a recipe online for a creamy Tuscan chicken dish.' She paused. 'It's probably not really and truly Tuscan at all, but it looked good. I'm hoping it might cheer him up a bit.'

'It sounds good to me,' Matteo said, shifting the truck's gears with a clunk. 'I am almost never organised enough to c-c-cook for myself. I have mostly lived alone since moving f-f-from my university flat. I pretty much live on antipasti, something I can eat fast.'

She noted two things. One, that he lived alone, and two, that she had to stop herself from inviting him to join her and Samuel for dinner.

'I think it's always easier to cook for and take care of others rather than yourself,' she said, 'and I'm glad I've got this opportunity to help Samuel. It makes me feel good.'

'He is very strong,' Matteo said. 'I wish the rest of the family could see that.'

'Where *is* his family? Why is he alone? Aside from you, of course.'

'He has a daughter, Giovanna, but she lives in London with her husband, Marco. They moved because their daughter, Lily, got a music scholarship over there. But they stayed there after she finished and now she travels the world playing piano.'

'Talented woman.'

Matteo nodded. 'She is amazing. Her brother, Antonio, lives in America.'

'Does Samuel have any other children?'

'*Sì*—Gaetano. But he and his wife followed Giovanna and Marco to England because their daughter, Aimee, is very close to Lily. And I think also because there were some problems in the family. So they all built their life there.'

'That's sad,' she said.

'I think some families are just travellers. Living on the goat farm, I see so many travellers come through. It is easier these days with internet and phone.'

A strong, hot wind blew into the vehicle and lifted her curls. Lara pulled an elastic tie from her wrist and wrestled her hair into a loopy bun at the nape of her neck. The roar of the wind took the pressure off having to attempt any witty conversation and, content for now with the information from Matteo, she leaned back to enjoy the views from the winding, uphill road. They passed red-roofed villas; and rectangular stone apartment blocks with dark green shutters, tiny strings of washing lines between the window edges—maybe a metre wide—with tea towels or socks blowing in the wind, window boxes with brightly coloured flowers, and teeny balconies with potted olive trees; in every direction she saw blue, grey and green rolling hills.

In Fiotti, they wandered the narrow streets lined with three-storey apartment blocks with the yellow rendered walls typical of the area, many with shops on the ground floor. Lara knew the region was famous for its terracotta, and the rusty red bricks paved the foot-paths. Large plant pots stood with flashy green pines at doorways to flats and cafes.

The shop Lara wanted, the one with the chocolate, was called a *bottega*, which essentially meant a shop but with the connotation of the shopkeeper being a master at what they did, according to Matteo. It had wicker baskets overflowing with chocolate. Its domed concrete ceiling had been painted with a night skyscape, a moon and stars, and paint had flaked away, leaving patches of grey showing through. It should have been messy, but was somehow romantically artistic.

Shiny tins of tea sat in rows, bottles of wine lay in pyramids near wooden barrels, hessian bags of coffee adorned the walls and huge jars of lollies glinted under the ceiling lights. Lara felt sure this store could satisfy any wicked craving she might have. She left with enough chocolate for two weeks, she hoped.

Next they stood at a *caffè* bar, where Matteo ordered them both a coffee and exchanged a few pleasantries in Italian with the cashier. The silver-haired barista was quick, and before Lara could take in the red chairs at the empty tables and pastries in the cabinet, coffees appeared in front of them.

'*Grazie*,' she said.

She was struck by the way Matteo tenderly held his coffee cup, bringing it to his cheek. 'Why do you do that?' she asked.

'To test the temperature, to see if it is ready,' he said casually, appearing not at all offended by her query.

Lara stared at him, completely speechless. The way he handled his coffee . . . it was so sensual and so different to the way Dave had handled his.

She finished her drink quickly, wanting to move on from this place and the memories it was triggering.

A gelateria caught her attention with its rainbow of seductive-looking flavours. Matteo must have seen the look on her face.

'Would you like a gelato?' he asked, one hand reaching for his wallet.

'I really would. But I'll get it,' she said, waving his hand away. He'd already bought her the coffee.

'I'll have one . . .' he paused while a series of tics took over his neck and face, 'too,' he finished, pulling out a ten-euro note.

'*Grazie*,' she said, trying to calm her heart. This *felt* like a date. And okay, she was thirty-one and not a teenager, but she also hadn't dated or slept with anyone since . . .

A long time.

And this was a crazy thing to even think about, because the man was only buying her an ice cream. No one had mentioned anything about sex. Not everything had to lead to sex. The 'rules', if there were any, might be totally different here from back at home. Ice cream was just ice cream, wasn't it?

'What flavour?' Matteo asked. The white-aproned attendant behind the freezer case had his metal scoop at the ready.

'Tiramisu, *per favore*,' she said.

'*Vaniglia, per favore*,' Matteo said.

They took their cones into the street, the gelato already melting. Lara sat on a stone wall, peering down into the piazza below. The market-day stalls filled the space, with pop-up tents and a classical guitarist in the centre serenading the people. One stallholder was selling *zucche*—pumpkins. But his pumpkins were like nothing she'd ever seen before. Each basket on his trestle table held a different type. The one closest to her had palm-sized dark orange ones, like miniature jack-o'-lanterns. There were pure white ones, also palm-sized, and yellow-and-green-striped ones. Yellow ones in the shape of pears, with white pinstripes. There were even bright red ones, like capsicums.

'I never knew pumpkins could look like that,' she said between licks and slurps of her completely wonderful gelato. 'This is so great,' she said, indicating her ice cream.

Matteo swung his legs so that his heels kicked the stone wall, reinforcing her feeling of being a teenager and 'going around' with a boy after school.

Maybe this was what love did? Made you feel young.

Listen to yourself. What she was feeling was not love, just the sweeping, romantic magic of Tuscany that had seduced her with a beautiful and charming life that was spontaneous and full of possibility. Either that or she was on the edge of a new upswing of a mania episode.

'I know vanilla is boring,' Matteo said, licking his lips, 'but it makes me think of being a boy on holiday with the family down by the sea, all of us hot and exhausted after swimming all day, our skin burnt and our feet blistered from the hot sand.'

See! She wasn't the only one feeling too young for her body right now.

After their ice creams, they found a small shop with cured meats, olives and cheeses, which also happened to sell some everyday grocery items. She managed to buy fresh chicken breasts for her recipe, along with cream, sun-dried tomatoes, garlic and spinach leaves. Matteo translated to help her get bottled chicken stock and a wedge of *parmigiana* cheese.

When they were back out on the street, the large belltower above the basilica began to peal a call to Mass. Lara pulled out her phone to snap photos of the church to send to the kids. Matteo was relaxed beside her, seeming to enjoy the sights and sounds as much as she did, rather than fidgeting and wanting to move on.

'W-w-would you l-l-like to come to my mamma's place with me?' he asked quietly. 'I am going there for dinner.'

Lara put her phone away to look at him. His eyes searched hers, a soft vulnerability in them that made her heart melt. She held up her bag of groceries. 'What about my chicken?'

Matteo smiled. 'I love a girl who loves her chickens. We have a saying here—*I know my chickens*.'

'What does that mean?'

'It means when you know someone so well that you finish their sentences, or know what they're thinking. Like an old married couple.'

'That's cute.'

'Come,' he said, and held out his hand for her bag. 'We'll put your chicken in Mamma's fridge.'

Matteo's mamma lived in a *casa* just outside the hubbub of the village centre, overgrown gardens and bushes surrounding it and a bit of land at the back, from what Lara could see. Fields of crops lay in the distance. At two storeys tall, with peaked roofs and terracotta tiles, the *casa* was the same shape as Samuel's villa, just a lot smaller. Its outside walls revealed its origins, Matteo explained.

'This would have been a poor person's house,' he said, touching the yellowish wall fondly. The rows of bricks were interspersed with mud, branches and sticks. Lara surmised that the people who'd built it had simply needed a house and had pulled together whatever they could find. It was a testament to tenacity, bringing together scraps to build something solid, which was how she felt sometimes, having to knit back together the torn pieces of her mind and heart. She found it inspiring, and touched the wall, running her fingertips over the bumps and lumps, feeling the lingering warmth of the day.

Matteo moved to a short add-on adjoining the house at a right angle. He pulled on the handle of a large metal plate that sat on a ledge of about waist height. The metal scraped over the bricks as he removed it. Behind it was a deep opening. Lara bent down to peer inside.

'This was the oven they used to bake their b-b-bricks,' he said.

'Oh, wow.' She couldn't begin to imagine having to build her own house from scratch, let alone baking the actual bricks to do it.

'Good for pizza now.' Matteo smiled, putting the metal plate back in place.

'You cook in there? Wood-fired pizzas?'

'All the time,' he said, dusting his hands off against each other.

'Matteo?' a woman's voice called from the other side of the wall.

'*Sì*, Mamma,' Matteo replied, and raised his eyebrows at Lara. 'Come,' he said, indicating over his shoulder with his head. 'This way.'

Lara followed him, the plastic bag of chicken rustling as she walked. As they went up the two small steps and through the open door of the house, Lara could hear multiple voices inside.

Matteo began to call out in Italian and she followed him down a hallway lined with bunches of flowers and herbs hanging upside down from hooks on the walls. She couldn't see past him until they entered the kitchen, which fanned out in a circular fashion.

Several people sat around a large wooden table, and every one of them stopped talking when Matteo and Lara entered. Lara frantically tried to take them all in and piece together who they might be.

There were two white-haired men over near the gas stovetop, both nursing glasses of red wine. To their right was a woman of around Eliza's age, with bright red hair in a bun, bright red lipstick to match, and a piece of cheese in her hand. There was another woman around the same age, black hair with a streak of white through the front, one arm leaning on the table, the other hand in midair as though she was partway through a story. A small girl of maybe six in a pretty pink dress sat playing on an iPad.

Beside Lara, Matteo stopped short. Sitting in front of him was the long-legged supermodel that had appeared at the goat barn the other morning. She turned to face him and flashed a wide smile, which gave way to a steely stare when she caught sight of his guest.

Lara waved a hand feebly, her plastic bag of chicken rustling.

No one said a word.

15

Matteo, although clearly surprised to find the supermodel at the table, recovered himself quickly.

'*Buonasera a tutti. Vi presento* Lara,' Matteo said, putting his hand lightly on her back. 'She's f-f-from Australia. She helps Samuel. She is his new *badante*.'

At the sound of Samuel's name, the woman with the white streak in her hair lifted her chin, set her jaw and crossed her arms.

Matteo addressed Lara. 'This is my mamma, Lucia.'

'Hi,' Lara said, a little too brightly. Lucia was Samuel's niece and she eyed Lara sternly.

'Th-th-this is Mamma's friend Gilberta, and her husband, Mario.' This was the woman with the bright red hair who, thankfully, gave Lara a huge warm smile, and the man closest to her, who raised his glass of wine in greeting. Okay, not too bad there.

'This is Costantino, a family friend, and his g-g-graaanddaughter, Teresa.' A nod from Costantino and a shy smile from the young girl on the iPad.

'And this is Alessandra.' The supermodel's chest was rising and falling in angry breaths beneath her sunflower-yellow strappy dress. She flicked her long, glossy hair off her shoulder, completely ignored Lara and spoke-shouted in Italian at Matteo.

The others at the table shifted in discomfort, while Lucia pursed her lips and nodded along in agreement with Alessandra's words. Clearly, Lara was unexpected and unwanted, at least by the mother and the girlfriend. At least, that's what Lara assumed Alessandra must be. She was certainly acting that way. Whatever was going on, Lara was stuck here for now; Matteo was her ride home.

Matteo held up his hand to Alessandra, who had risen from her chair to better enunciate with her hands. He turned to Lara. '*Scusa*, for a moment.'

'Sure,' she said, trying not to make eye contact with the elegant, fire-breathing beast in front of her.

Matteo reached out and took Alessandra by the wrist and drew her from the kitchen.

As Lucia appeared to have forgotten her manners, her friend Gilberta stepped in. 'Please, Lara, come have a seat. Tell us about you.' She'd half risen from her chair, leaning across the table and indicating the free seat next to the little girl.

Lara sat down gingerly. 'Thanks, er, I mean, *grazie, grazie*,' she said.

What the hell was going on here? Why did Matteo bring her here if it was going to cause such unpleasantness? She couldn't see how this could possibly end well.

And also, she still had chicken in her hand.

Gilberta looked down at the plastic bag Lara was clutching.

'Oh,' Lara said. 'I'm very sorry, but I am wondering if I might borrow your fridge?' She pointed helpfully to the fridge in the corner. 'Chicken,' she said, indicating the bag. Then, remembering the right word, '*Pollo*.'

'Ah!' Gilberta translated for Lucia as she reached over the table for the bag, which Lara gladly handed over.

The two men in the corner resumed their conversation, perhaps bored with all this carry-on. Lucia went to the stove, lifted the lid from a pot and began to stir with a wooden spoon. It smelled like vegetables of some sort; Lara hazarded a guess that it might be lentils. That would be good if she was to stay for dinner. This awkward situation would have been much worse if there had been something like a baby pig in that pot.

'Are you here long time?' Gilberta asked kindly, sitting herself back at the table.

'I'm not sure,' Lara said, distracted for a moment, wondering what Sunny was doing right now, wondering if she needed help. She forced herself to focus, and smiled; at least Gilberta was trying. 'No return ticket to Australia yet,' she clarified.

'You will fall in love with Italy,' Gilberta said dreamily. 'You will not want to go home. These Tuscan hills are alive with dreams.'

Lucia crashed the lid back onto the pot, making Lara jump.

'Italy is beautiful,' Lara agreed. 'I haven't seen much yet, but I've loved all of it.'

'Ah . . .' Gilberta sighed, her eyes going bright. 'You must forgive me; I am easy tears,' she said, wiping at them.

'I am too,' Lara said, recognising a kindred spirit in Gilberta.

Gilberta put her hand on her husband's shoulder and Mario reached up and patted it, while continuing his conversation with Costantino. 'These days I just take photos of the hills but once I used to dance across them. I used to be on the stage, singing, dancing, acting,' she whispered, a nostalgic smile on her red lips.

'Really?' Lara was instantly charmed and felt even more kinship with the woman.

'Oh yes,' Gilberta said. 'They were the wonder years of my life.'

Lucia came and sat back down, pushing a glass of water across the table at Lara.

'Oh, *grazie*,' Lara said, eager to connect with Matteo's mother too. But Lucia was already leaning over to Teresa, talking to the girl about the puzzle she was doing on her iPad.

'And what about you?' Gilberta said. 'What you do for work?'

'Many years ago, I did a bit of acting too,' Lara said.

'No!' Gilberta said, smiling at the coincidence and placing her hand on her heart. 'But that is fanatical!'

Lara assumed she meant *fantastic*.

'Some days it was,' she agreed, thinking back to the days of tight schedules, unruly children, quick-fire costume changes and cheesy but catchy song lyrics. The thing about being on the stage was that it forced her to be in the moment. There was a welcome sense of escape—total freedom to inhabit the role of someone other than herself. It was a relief not to be her. 'But those jobs finished.' *Because of Dave.* 'And then I did a few different things, and lately I've been managing rental houses. Real estate work.'

'Ah,' Gilberta said, frowning a little. Lara wasn't sure if she totally understood, but it would do for now. 'And are you married?' Gilberta asked, nodding towards Lara's left hand, which was tucked under her right.

Lara pulled it out and held it up to show Gilberta. 'Not married.' Lucia glanced up to check for a wedding ring too, she noted. 'And no children,' Lara said, to forestall the next question. Without warning, her eyes grew misty.

'Oh, *tesoro*,' Gilberta said, her hand flying to her heart again. She reached across the table. '*Bambini* will come when they come.'

Lara nodded, embarrassed, swiping at her eyes with the back of her hand.

Lucia had paused to watch Lara and shifted in her seat. Lara supposed she was unsettled by her guest's brief but startling emotion.

Then Gilberta tapped her husband's arm with the back of her hand, instructing by the sound of it and gesturing to Lara, and he nodded. She patted Lara's hand, then withdrew her bosom and arms from where they'd lain on the table while she'd dispensed comfort, sitting up straight once more. She winked at Lara. 'It is time for aperitifs,' she said. 'The men will get.' Then she reclined in her chair with her hands knitted on top of her belly.

The men got up and began to pull glasses from a cupboard with a stained-glass door. Lara took her moment to excuse herself and look for a bathroom, not so much because she needed to go but because she needed a break from the intensity of the room. She was hoping to run into Matteo somewhere along the way, but there was no sight or sound of either him or Alessandra.

In the bathroom, which had a small bathtub with rusting edges and many shelves of lotions, potions and perfumes, she splashed her face with water and checked her reflection. She pulled off the hairtie and ran wet hands through her curls to give them some bounce. She put on fresh lipstick and wiped away a few smudges of mascara. Then she pulled out her phone to send a text to Samuel, just to check if he was okay—she wanted him to be okay, of course, but if for some reason he wasn't, it would be a great excuse to go home early. She needed to get out of here.

His answer: *I'm fine*. So that ended that chance to escape.

She tried Hilary. It would be midnight in Australia, but the chances of Hilary being up were still good. She was an avid reader, and the only time she got to read uninterrupted was the middle of the night.

> The goat man took me home to meet his mamma and have dinner. Now has disappeared with gazelle-like model creature and I'm stuck hiding in the toilet in hostile territory. Help!

Hilary wasted no time in replying.

> Grab the wine and the cheese (because I just KNOW there will be wine and

cheese—it's ITALY, right??) and run as fast as you can! The goat man doesn't deserve you xx

Lara was startled by the sound of a feisty argument going on outside in the garden. Listening, she thought she recognised Matteo's voice in the fray. She put down the wooden toilet seat and climbed on top to peek out of the small window high above, knowing it was totally inappropriate but also desperate to see what was happening. Standing on tiptoe, gripping the stone windowsill with her fingertips, she could just see Matteo and Alessandra seated on a stone bench under a large tree, surrounded by purple and white flowers waving in the breeze. Unable to follow the rapid Italian, or even intuit by tone of voice—she'd realised that even a normal conversation in Italy could sound like an argument—she had nothing to go on but body language.

Matteo was half facing Alessandra, one arm resting on the back of the bench seat, his knees pointing in her direction and the other hand gesticulating as he spoke. Alessandra was more upright, her tanned knees together, her legs crossed at the ankles. She had her hands clasped together at her chest as if praying, or pleading.

Lara's fingers slipped on the edge of the sill and a fingernail bent backwards. She lowered herself, swearing viciously till the pain subsided, turned the nail back the way it was supposed to go, then gripped it tightly to ease the pain. It probably served her right for spying.

A warm breeze puffed in through the window, lifting the white cotton curtains across the top of her head. She climbed up again to give it one more go.

Out on the bench, Alessandra was crying now. Lara could hear her sobs and saw her wiping her face. She felt a pang of pity for the woman but a small moment of victory too, something she wasn't proud of.

This was crazy! She barely knew Matteo. He owed her nothing. In fact, they *were* nothing. Nothing at all. This was just some whirlwind crush, and whatever was happening between those two had been going on for a lot longer than she'd even been in the country.

And Lara didn't even want to entertain the idea of romance. Okay, she actually might *want* to but she shouldn't, especially not in a foreign country and especially when it was only a temporary stay.

But just as she was about to step down again and start behaving like an adult, Matteo reached out his hand and cupped Alessandra's face. She nuzzled her cheek into it like a cat. And then she pulled him to her and kissed him.

Lara whimpered and dropped down onto her heels so she was facing the stone wall. She took a breath, then carefully climbed off the toilet seat. She smoothed her dress, and held her head high as she returned to the kitchen, where a huge platter of olives, sun-dried tomatoes, capers, crackers, cheeses and dried fruit had been placed in the middle of the table.

Gilberta was laughing with Lucia and they each held a wine glass with something peachy orange in it. Gilberta looked up and gestured to Lara. '*Cara*, come, sit, eat.'

But Lara stayed standing. 'Um, Gilberta, Lucia, I'm so sorry, but I have to go. Samuel needs me,' she said. 'I need to get home and I need, well, I'm wondering . . .' *Too many words, Lara. Make it simple.* 'Could you please drive me home?' she asked, making car-driving charades. 'I'm not far away, or so I'm told, I'm not exactly sure . . .' She trailed off uncertainly.

There was a pause, then several people spoke at once, translations and discussion going on. She heard Matteo's name, as well as Alessandra's and Samuel's.

'Matteo is busy,' she said, raising her voice to cut through the chatter. 'I just need to get home to Samuel.'

Lucia spoke, finally, her expression unreadable. 'Mario will drive you.'

❧

Mario didn't speak much English but that was fine with Lara. As he drove, he sang in a voice she guessed was classically trained. He occasionally pointed out something he thought might be of interest to her, and she tried to murmur in the right places. But it really was a short drive home, only six or seven minutes. Mario let the car idle in the driveway as she got out, and she noticed him peering through the windscreen, taking in the villa, maybe wondering where Samuel was, wondering if he should come in. She couldn't know.

She waved goodbye as Mario reversed away.

It was still only early evening, and the sun had a while to go before it sank behind the hills. Lara wandered to an open stone deck at the back of the house and lay down on a reclining sun bed perfectly situated to take in the views. From inside the house she could faintly hear more classical music.

She was spent emotionally. The lovely bubble of happiness that had carried her away had shattered like a snow globe around her. It was all so ridiculous; she was ashamed of her runaway emotions. She was angry with herself for letting the pendulum of her mind swing so far out from the reasonable centre. She could not and would not allow herself to fall. Not here. Not now.

16

Samuel

From his chair next to the fireplace in the living room, Samuel heard a car pull up, the door open and the *badante* offer her thanks. If he wasn't mistaken, that was Mario's voice in response. Fleetingly, he thought of clambering out of his chair and going to meet his long-missed friend, but the car drove away before he could even pull himself to his feet. His unexpected disappointment was tempered by his relief. He took a deeper breath and realised, with a rush of shame, that he'd been worried the *badante* might not return. It shocked him down to his slippered feet. It was not that she was particularly wonderful. He'd had *badanti* better at making coffee, and certainly better at gardening. She wasn't indispensable, though he did enjoy her cooking. He wasn't anxious about *her* leaving, specifically. But between the notes of Vivaldi, sneaking in around the memories of holding Assunta close to his chest and dancing at their fortieth wedding anniversary, a window opened somewhere in his awareness of himself and he knew the awful truth.

He was afraid.

When he'd broken his wrist, he'd crossed a line. It was the first fracture of his life. And with a kick to his guts, the next thought—it probably wouldn't be his last.

He'd thought he'd handled ageing well. He'd sensibly made the decision to close up his and Assunta's bedroom and move downstairs while he could still choose how to do it, though granted, Assunta's death had prompted the decision. The room held too many memories, too many regrets. Over many years, he'd made modifications to the house. Renovating the downstairs bathroom had been the biggest, but it was something he knew many older people left far too late. Not him. He planned to stay in this house till his dying breath, no matter what arguments his children might present as to why he should move over to England to live with them. *This* was where he was closest to Assunta, and this was where he would stay.

But how much longer would that be—a month, a year, ten years more?

Until now, he'd got by with *badanti* for housework, shopping and cooking. Travelling to Rome with a *badante* was a new experience. He'd known he'd need help to get through the manic streets of the city and to the Trevi Fountain. He couldn't ask Matteo to help. Not because Matteo would have refused, but because Samuel didn't want him to see what he was going to do there at the fountain, throwing away the ring Assunta had chosen for him. Matteo was his only link left to Assunta's family, and while at times Samuel had tried to refuse his great-nephew's help and push him away, on the inside he was crying with relief that someone still cared.

There, he'd admitted it. His stubborn pride and ruthless convictions could carry him only so far. He'd once thought he could shoulder the burden of Assunta's passing alone, and had deliberately distanced himself from her family, letting them hate him.

Even Carlo.

But Samuel had to be strong for his wife, no matter how much he missed the closest person he'd ever had to a brother over here.

It wasn't just Carlo, though; he missed them all. He missed having people near him who knew his past, who wanted to share plates of food cooked in his kitchen, to open *vino* and let it loosen tongues and shoes until everyone was dancing under the lantern-lit trees at night. To laugh and joke in that easy way one could with family.

How would things change if he told them all the truth? What would it do to Assunta, who he knew with all his heart was watching over him?

He heard the *badante* pull up one of the sun lounges outside to watch the sun set. How long would she stay here? He didn't know anything about her.

He felt his lips twitch into a smile. It was obvious to him that there were sparks between her and Matteo. An image flew unbidden into his mind, a coupling of Matteo and the *badante* and a whole new family to fill this villa. Where had that idea come from? He tried to extinguish it from his mind, but instead he could see Assunta smiling at the image, her round cheeks and long black hair, her dark chestnut eyes sparkling with glee. She loved a bit of matchmaking.

He shook his head lightly at her, but gave in to her will as he usually had.

Lara. The *badante*'s name was Lara. Maybe she was the answer.

17

Sunny

Sunny shoved water bottles and muesli bars into her denim handbag, checked her phone was in there, and fetched some more tissues as the kids still had runny noses from their mad cow disease. At least the blisters in their mouths and on their hands and feet had dried up. She paused mid packing to watch her mother.

Eliza laid out the lace tablecloth with care, then placed on it the blue vase containing the cascade of fragrant jasmine she'd just clipped from the front porch, where it wound its way along the balustrade. The mahjong women would start arriving any moment. She was nervous, Sunny could tell. Right on cue, Eliza wiped her hands down her dress, smoothing out imaginary wrinkles.

Her mother had only retired at the end of last year from her role as an executive assistant in the state parliamentary chambers. She'd been there for thirty years. They'd sent her off with a huge bouquet of flowers and a gold watch, as well as throwing her a lavish morning tea. The Minister for Agriculture, for whom she'd worked most recently, reportedly gave a flattering speech about how they simply didn't make public servants like her anymore. Eliza had said she'd seen a few eye rolls between the younger staff members at that. Sunny bet it was true, though. She'd been sorry she hadn't been there at that morning tea. Her mother had worked so hard to hold the family together.

Eliza laid out the teacups and saucers, while Sunny hunted for matching shoes for the kids. She was sure they had at least eight pairs of shoes between them, but she could never seem to find a complete pair.

Her mother's scones were in the oven and the mouth-watering scent wafted through to the lounge room where Sunny was on her knees peering under the couch. She'd told Eliza she would take the kids out to give her some uninterrupted time with her mahjong group, but the aroma of those scones was enticing and the missing shoes almost weakened her into changing her plans. There was a cold wind blowing, and she'd much rather be drinking tea and eating scones than out with the wild mini-people.

At last she found Hudson's missing shoe and hauled herself upright again.

'The place looks beautiful,' she said, gesturing to the peach-coloured napkins on the table.

'Not too much?' Eliza asked.

'No, it's perfect.'

Eliza touched her hair. 'I know it's silly to be nervous about something like this at my age, but I hadn't realised how much I'd miss work and the chats with others in the tearoom. Jenny and I always dissected *Madam Secretary* the next day, and Helen and I always ran the Melbourne Cup sweep. The younger girls even asked my advice on relationships.' She scoffed. 'If only they knew!'

Sunny grimaced, thinking of how much Leonard had put her mother through.

'But it was like incidental exercise, except it was incidental socialising. It all disappeared overnight.' Eliza's face fell. 'I didn't realise

I'd given so much of myself to the chambers that I'd failed to cultivate a social life outside of it.'

Sunny went to her and hugged her tightly. 'You had good reason to want to escape into something else.'

Eliza patted her back and pulled away. She looked Sunny up and down. 'You look lovely. A bit harassed . . .' she touched Sunny's forehead, 'but still beautiful. You have such a knack for layering clothes.' She adjusted the teal silk scarf around Sunny's neck. 'I spent so much time worrying about you when you were a teenager, and now look at you! A strong, loving and capable mother.'

'Some days,' Sunny said, going back to her handbag. 'Daisy! Hudson! It's time to go!' she called.

'Really, you don't have to go,' Eliza said. 'The kids will check everyone out and then leave us alone. We'll be terribly uninteresting to them.'

'No, Hudson's in a mood,' Sunny said. 'I don't want to ruin your morning tea with a screaming meltdown.'

Just then, Hudson rolled across the floorboards on his skateboard, lying on its deck. 'I'm hungry,' he grumbled.

'You just ate,' Sunny said.

'But I'm hungry,' he whined, jumping up from the skateboard and launching it so it ran into the wall.

'Hudson!'

'It's okay,' Eliza said, picking up the board and handing it to Sunny.

'Sorry,' Hudson muttered.

'We're going. Where's Daisy?' Sunny said.

'Here I am,' Daisy answered, wearing yellow and black tights, a pink tutu, a Snoopy t-shirt and blue gumboots. Eliza smiled at Sunny in an *isn't she adorable?* way and Sunny felt her forehead relax.

'Okay, let's go. Hudson, you need shoes,' Sunny said, getting her keys.

'I hate shoes.'

'I know. But it's the rule. If you want to go to the fete, you need shoes.'

Hudson groaned and flopped down on the ground.

'Bye,' Sunny said, waving to Eliza. 'Say bye to Grandma,' she said to the kids.

'Bye,' Hudson mumbled, his face still planted into the floor.

'Bye, darling,' Eliza said, kissing Daisy, and then Daisy and Sunny walked out the door.

'Wait for me,' Hudson called, jumping up and running after them.

'Bye, Hudson,' Eliza called.

Sunny bustled the kids towards the car. She slung her handbag into the front and opened Hudson's door, then headed around to the other side to open Daisy's.

Out on the street, she could hear the gentle whir of a slow-moving car. She glanced up briefly, but kept instructing the kids. 'Sit up straight, Daisy, or your seatbelt won't reach. Hudson, leave the bee alone and get into your seat, please.' Daisy opened a kids magazine on her lap.

The car in the street slowed right down and hovered just before their driveway. Sunny looked up. It was a blue sedan she didn't recognise. It wasn't a neighbour, she was sure. It was probably one of the mahjong women. The car's windows were tinted, but she smiled congenially, welcoming her mother's visitor.

But the engine didn't cut. It continued to hiss quietly, and suddenly the roots of Sunny's hair tingled. She straightened, staring at the car, trying to see through the window. The moment seemed to stretch out forever.

Sunny deliberately closed the door on Hudson, then walked around the front of the car and closed the door on Daisy. She placed her hands on her hips and glared at the car, mad now, despite the nerves that flickered beneath her skin.

The car's wheels began to roll again, and it drifted past them and out of sight.

18

Lara

Matteo arrived in his beaten-up truck just as Lara was shutting the gate to the goat barn, her pail of warm milk on the ground, the smell of wet sawdust and fresh lucerne in the air. The sound of the goats chewing with greedy glee had lifted her spirits. It was lucky she'd had to be answerable to someone today, that 'someone' being the goats, even though it was Sunday, her day off; she'd barely slept a wink all night, riddled with angst over her misplaced feelings for Matteo and the memories of Dave that came with them. Her limbs were heavy; her spark had dimmed. Depression tugged at her like sticky black mud. It was only the insistent bleating drifting through the windows that had forced her to move. Thank goodness for the goats. Thank God for medication.

'*Buongiorno*,' Matteo said, approaching, sunglasses perched on top of his curls and a brown man bag over his shoulder. The top few buttons of his shirt were undone to show a sprinkling of chest hair. He greeted her with a huge smile. 'I was going to h-h-help you to milk,' he continued. 'Mamma told me you had to leave early yesterday because Samuel needed you.'

'Yes, that's right.' She squirmed.

'But then he sent me a message this morning asking me to come.'

'Did he?' Lara looked over at the villa, towards the open doors that led into the kitchen. Samuel had been preparing himself a breakfast of prosciutto and cheese on croissants when she'd left him. She'd tried to assist, but he'd kept swatting her away. He was more capable with his wrist in a cast than she'd thought he might be, actually. He certainly hadn't needed her help last night or this morning. She had to take him back to the hospital tomorrow to have his cast changed to a mouldable splint, and that would mean he'd be even more independent. She thought he was looking forward to it; his mood seemed to have improved and he didn't even grumble at her for taking so long to get to the goats. She wondered what he was playing at, messaging Matteo.

'But I see you've done a go-ooo-d job without me,' Matteo said, grinning encouragement at her, admiring her pail of milk.

Behind her, Meg bleated and Willow banged on the door. They were eager to get out to forage around the grounds. She would let them out once she knew the pail of milk was out of the way. They had a habit of shoulder-charging through the gate before it was fully open and galloping down the hills, their tiptoed feet making a small thunder rumble as they went. They would kick up their heels and wag their tails, talking the whole time with excitement as if they'd been locked up for a month, not just overnight.

'Thank you.' Lara felt a flicker of pride, but really any skill she may have gained was largely due to how tolerant the goats were. Lara liked to think they approved of her. Willow, perhaps sensing how fragile Lara was this morning, had been especially affectionate, breathing in her ear and nibbling at the collar of her shirt. 'I'm happy to do it.'

She reached a hand over the gate and rubbed Willow behind her ear. The goat leaned into her and murmured with pleasure, then spun around and presented her butt for scratching, wagging her tail and snuffling in delight. It was a Willow trademark. Meg was less physically affectionate, preferring to show her approval by grumbling at Lara like a stern but kindly schoolma'am.

Matteo bit his lip and watched her, perhaps wondering about her quietness this morning. 'I'm s-s-sorry for leaving you alone yesterday. I had to sort things out with Alessandra. Mamma, she . . .' he wobbled his head from side to side, 'she thinks she knows best. You know?'

'Not really.'

'Mamma thinks that Alessandra and I . . .' He folded his arms across his body, then released them. 'Well, she has ideas. She wants me married, you know?'

Lara nodded, noncommittal. She assumed that what Matteo was saying here was that Alessandra was his mother's ideal daughter-in-law, and to that she had nothing to add.

'But sh-sh-she is n-n-not,' he said.

'Not what?'

'My woman of choice.' He eyed her steadily. 'And I have told Mamma this many times. But she thinks I need help to find a wife.'

'Why?'

He gave her a look that said, *Are you for real?*

Lara felt for him. He wasn't the perfect package; neither was she. She got it. Still, she took a deep breath and let it out slowly. 'I saw you kissing her,' she said.

Matteo narrowed his eyes. 'You were watching?'

'No. Well, I went looking for you. I didn't know my way around, and I saw you. You and her. Her and you.'

He looked at the ground and scratched at the back of his neck before looking back at her, irritated. '*Sì*, she tried to kiss me. But I pushed her away.'

'Oh.' Lara hadn't watched long enough to see that part.

'There is nothing between Alessandra and me anymore.'

'Okay.' Lara thought she might be pleased about that, but her dark mood was making it difficult to think straight. An uncomfortable silence ensued.

Matteo looked up at the sky. 'We're lucky this great weather has continued,' he said, obviously keen to move on. 'The heat will be g-g-gone soon before we know it.'

She waited, not knowing what to say, wondering why he was bothering to spend time talking to her when he clearly had come to see Samuel. She'd been deluded to think that there was any chance that he was interested in her. She'd let her feelings run swiftly in the wrong direction, something she'd certainly been guilty of doing before—it was par for the course for someone with her diagnosis—but which she thought she'd learned to control.

Matteo reached for the shoulder strap of his bag and pulled it to the front, opening the zip. He pulled out a plastic bag. 'I have your chicken and parmigiana.'

She'd completely forgotten about that.

'I remember that you want to make Samuel a special Tuscan dinner.'

'*Grazie*.' Lara stepped forward and took the bag, her fingers touching his, and an unmistakable pulse zinged up her arm. 'Um, did you want to come inside?' she asked, gesturing down the slope to the villa.

'*Sì*,' he said, and reached down to take the pail of milk before she could lift it.

'Just a second,' she said.

She returned to the barn and pulled the slide bolt to let out the goats, who sprinted away, then turned to face each other, rising up on their back legs and slamming their horns together, play fighting, their tails wagging with glee. Lara laughed. And it felt good. Maybe she could shake this dark mood after all. She was still smiling when she turned back to Matteo.

'*Andiamo*,' she said.

He smiled at her. '*Andiamo*.'

Let's go.

They walked silently down the grassy hill and past the herb garden near the kitchen doors and into the cool inside. Matteo lifted the milk up onto the wooden bench while Lara put the chicken and cheese in the fridge.

Samuel came in, bent over, his broken arm held across his body, his other hand on the walking stick. He was now much steadier than he had been in the days immediately after his fall. It was good to see.

'*Buongiorno*,' Samuel said, smiling at Matteo. Matteo greeted him and put his hand affectionately on Samuel's shoulder. It was easy to see that he truly cared for his great-uncle. They conversed in Italian for a few minutes, Samuel even chuckling at something Matteo said, while Lara cleared the kitchen benches and sink, packing the small dishwasher in the corner of the room and turning it on.

She heard her name and the word *formaggio*, which she recognised to mean cheese, and wondered if they were talking about her plans for dinner. She turned around, smiling—the only thing she could do when she couldn't understand what they were saying. They were both looking at her and talking rapidly. Then they seemed to agree on something, and Samuel nodded and left the room.

'What was all that about?' Lara asked.

'Samuel asked me to teach you how to make ch-cheese,' Matteo said, standing tall again after having bent down to chat to Samuel.

'Cheese?'

'*Sì*. He usually makes it himself, but can't now with his wrist. He is hoping you might enjoy learning? He says he knows it is your day off, so the choice is yours.'

'I would love that,' she said, welcoming the distraction. 'Will we go to your goat farm, or will we stay here?'

Matteo rocked his head from side to side, considering. 'I think we will stay here today. We will keep it simple.'

'Okay, sure.'

'We will save the goat farm for another day,' he said, giving her a smile that in any culture she was sure was flirtatious.

ꕥ ꕥ

They started by passing the fresh goat milk through a fine steel mesh to collect any dust or hairs that might have settled in it.

'We'll begin with ricotta,' Matteo said, pulling aside the curtain under the sink to fish through the saucepans for a large one to suit his needs. 'It is very easy.'

'Good,' Lara said. 'I'm going to find a pen and paper to write notes as we go. Back in a moment.'

She skipped up the stairs and went into her room to fetch her notebook and a pen. She also took a moment to visit the bathroom, putting on some tinted moisturiser and a little lip gloss, and finishing with a swipe of mascara. She adjusted the ties around her floral crossover shirt. Looking in the mirror, she was, if not pleased, *content* with what she saw. She'd learned that making the outside of herself look good could help the inside feel better too. And she needed to lift her mood today.

Back in the kitchen, Matteo had taken off his sandals and was standing barefoot on the terracotta tiles. Behind him were garlic cloves and iron pots hanging on the walls, as well as a crucifix and an original painting of a little girl with an English collie. Lara had been waiting for the right moment to ask Samuel about it, to ask him if the girl was his daughter.

'Right,' she said, opening her notebook. 'Where do we start? Do we need to pasteurise the milk?'

'No, no,' Matteo said, 'we never p-p-pasteurise milk at the d-d-dairy. The m-milk has living bacteria that keep it in balance and give it taste. When you pasteurise, you change the way the milk behaves, you change the taste, the texture. It tastes all wrong. But we are going to heat it,' he said, putting the large pot onto the gas burner and igniting it. 'All we need for ricotta is milk, salt and lemon juice.'

'Lemon juice?' she quizzed, making sure she'd heard correctly.

'*Sì*.' He began pouring the goat milk into the pot. 'We heat the milk and just before it boils we add lemon. The milk will split into the curd and whey.'

'And that's it?'

Matteo grinned, passing her a large wooden spoon. '*Sì*. You need to stir while it heats.'

'I had no idea it was so easy.' She stirred the milk silently while Matteo cut open a lemon and squeezed some juice, the sound of the gas humming between them.

Matteo came to stand beside her to better view the pot. She could feel the warmth from his body and it made her feel connected to him, somehow.

'Do we need a thermometer to know when to add the lemon?' she asked.

He grunted in response. 'If you are a beginner, yes, a thermometer helps. You cook the milk to ninety-three degrees.' He turned to look at her proudly. 'But I know what I'm doing,' he said, and winked.

The smell of the lemon was sharp and refreshing and she inhaled deeply, revelling in its clean, uplifting notes.

After a time, the milk began to change in almost imperceptible ways.

'Getting closer,' Matteo said.

The colour deepened and the volume seemed to take on an energy, not thickening, but somehow inflating. Not simmering, but swaying.

Matteo nodded and lifted the cup. 'When the lemon goes in, very soon, you'll see the milk split. Keep stirring, but only for a little bit, only until you see the curds begin to form. Stir for another one or two seconds, then stop. If you keep going, you will break up the curds.'

'Okay,' Lara said, far more confidently than she felt. It all sounded very precise and she didn't want to mess it up. Her whole morning's milking effort was in this pot. But she didn't get too long to fret about it, because all too soon Matteo tipped in the lemon juice.

'Keep stirring,' he encouraged.

Then she saw it. Like magic, the milk split before her eyes.

'Keep going,' he said.

She held her breath, stirring, poised to stop on command.

'Yes, now,' Matteo said.

She whipped out the spoon and he turned off the gas, then turned to her and grinned.

'You did it,' he said.

She gave a small whoop, her whole mood changed with this achievement. 'What now?'

'Now we will strain off the whey.' He pulled another pot and a strainer from under the sink. 'You hold this and I'll pour.'

Lara did as she was told, feeling far more important in her role of strainer-holder than was probably warranted, but excited by the success of their cheesemaking. Matteo used cloth holders to grab either side of the large pot and bring it to the kitchen bench, lifting it to pour.

'Careful you don't get splashed,' he said.

He poured the pot's contents slowly, the pale, cloudy whey rushing through the strainer into the second pot while the chunky off-white curds huddled together, and then nodded in satisfaction. Whey was still slowly trickling from the curds in the strainer.

'Now we strain this through cheesecloth,' he said, pulling open a drawer to reveal piles of folded soft, crinkly white cloths. Yet another container was produced, this one much smaller, and he laid a cloth over the top, holding it taut. 'Into here,' he said, indicating with a nod that she should tip the curds into the cloth. Afterwards Matteo gathered up the edges of the fabric and twisted it, forcing the curds into a smaller and smaller ball as they released even more whey.

Lara watched, fascinated, then picked up her notebook to write a few things down.

Matteo gave the ball a few more squeezes. 'We won't take all the whey out,' he said. 'It will dry out the ricotta. But we want most. Can you please find me a container for it?'

'Yes, of course,' she said, dropping her pen and ferreting around in the cupboards for a plastic container with a lid. 'How about this?'

'*Perfetto*,' he said.

He tipped the ricotta into the container. It tumbled in in lovely soft piles.

'Now we just add *sale*,' he said, looking up at the spice rack.

'*Sale*?'

'Salt,' he clarified. He pulled down a teapot with a spoon jutting out from under the lid. 'Here we are.' He took the teaspoon and sprinkled some over the top of the ricotta. 'Now stir,' he said.

Lara found another teaspoon and stirred the ricotta till she thought it was mixed.

'And it's done,' Matteo said.

'I can't believe how easy that is,' she said. 'I'll never buy ricotta again.'

'You can add lemon rind too,' he said. 'You just g-grate the skin and sprinkle it on the t-top.'

'But there is a lot of whey compared to the curds,' she said.

Matteo nodded, peering into the pot. It seemed like there was litres of it. 'The cheese is the fat,' he said. 'The whey is the water and protein. But you can use it. You can feed it to goats, or chickens or pigs. You can drink it, too.'

'Like bodybuilders,' she joked, holding up her arms and pretending to flex her muscles. He eyed her arms approvingly and she felt herself flush.

She sneaked a peek at Matteo's biceps, which were evident under his shirtsleeves. She supposed all that work on the farm and in the cheese factory would naturally give him the types of muscles most people had to lift weights for in gyms.

'What should I do with it now?' she asked. Left on her own, she'd probably throw it away, but she sensed that would be frowned on by people like Matteo and Samuel, who spent a lot of time making their own food.

'You can boil your pasta in it,' Matteo said. 'Or just drink it for n-nutrition.'

'Okay.'

Matteo looked at his phone and muttered to himself. Lara's heart sank.

'I am sorry, but I need to go now,' he said, his brows knitted.

'Of course.' She itched to ask him where he was going, but it was no business of hers.

'It is my mamma,' he explained. 'She needs me to help move some furniture so she can vacuum underneath it.' He gave Lara an apologetic look.

'Right. That's important, of course,' she said. 'All those dust mites are bad for your health.'

He scratched at his collarbone and bit his bottom lip, sheepish. 'But w-w-w-would you like to know more about cheese? You could come and visit the f-f-farm.'

'*Sì*. That would be great,' she said, weaving her fingers together to stop herself from reaching out to touch him.

Matteo suddenly smiled, as if relieved she'd agreed. 'You have my number, yes?'

'Yes.' They had exchanged numbers after they had left the hospital, so Matteo could check in with her about Samuel, or she could call Matteo if needed.

'So, I will send you a message,' he said.

'That would be great. I'd love to learn to make more cheese—and I would really love to meet your goats,' she said. 'Meg and Willow have really grown on me. I think I might be becoming a goat person.'

'There are worse things,' he said. 'I must go now. Say goodbye to Samuel for me.' Before she could answer, he stepped forward and took her by the shoulders and kissed her on each cheek.

'Bye,' she said, taking a deep breath as he strode from the kitchen. She let it out very slowly, wrestling to dampen her excitement, which was once again fighting to get to the surface. How quickly her feelings today had swung from gloom to gladness.

19

Lara and Dave

Lara didn't have any friends to speak of. After uni, most of her school friends had gone overseas to travel and work in pubs or use their degrees, meet love interests and share cramped flats in dodgy parts of London. She'd finished her arts degree last year, but had never made any real friends there either. She hadn't joined any sporting teams or theatre groups, and alcohol was not a great mix with her medications, so the uni bar was never in her sphere.

Unlike most of her peers, she wasn't hooking up with guys; she'd been so lucky to find her love early on and to have skipped all that messy dating business. Not to mention the STDs and pregnancy scares. No, she was blissfully happy with her reliable, steady guy, thanks very much. He was exactly what someone like her needed. He sheltered her from the many ups and downs that could have come along to destabilise her, and for that she was deeply grateful. He was her anchor, always knowing what to do.

She'd looked for jobs, but there wasn't a lot on offer for an arts graduate. She'd picked up acting gigs in local shopping centres during school holidays, and she waitressed a little, but the hours were mostly in the evenings and Dave missed her.

'I work all day at the clinic or at the hospital and then you work at night,' he'd said one evening, placing in front of her a bowl of macaroni cheese that he'd made himself. He sat down to join her. 'Maybe this would work better if you saw your job as being my personal assistant or something. Then you could work from home, so to speak, and we'd be able to be together at night like normal couples.'

She put a forkful of macaroni in her mouth. 'Mm. That is good.' She chewed and then swallowed, while Dave sipped his wine and gazed at her. It was an intense gaze that took in everything about her so he could be one step ahead, and she knew meant he would get his own way. Still, she went through the motions.

'But what about money?' she said. 'How would I help to pay the rent, or have money of my own?'

'Why do you need money of your own?' he asked.

She scoffed. 'Everyone needs money to, I don't know, buy clothes and a coffee here and there, pay for car repairs or go to the movies.'

'But that's the beauty of this arrangement,' he said, placing a hand on her wrist. 'You look after me and I'll look after you. I have more paperwork and admin than I know what to do with most of the time.'

That was true. Being a psychologist seemed to require almost as much time on paperwork outside of the consult room as it did actually counselling; Dave was forever writing in his leather-bound book. Add to that studying for a medical degree and it took a lot out of him. He needed her to help him. Then maybe he would rely less on Vicki.

Many times he'd mentioned Vicki, a doctor in the same surgery where he practised psychology. She seemed to have become something of a mentor. He spoke to her on the phone frequently, quick conversations that always made him laugh, and for which he never offered an explanation, which made Lara feel spiky with jealousy, something she was ashamed to admit. Dave was so wonderful; she owed him so much. Besides, he talked to Vicki in front of her, so it wasn't like he was hiding anything.

Still, Vicki's name made Lara's body go hot with misplaced suspicion. Dave was faithful to her, of that she was sure. He whispered to her in the dark, telling her how much he loved her and how he didn't know what he'd do without her, that she was a beautiful, unexpected gift that had landed in his life. He wanted more of her, not less. That was why he wanted her to be at home at night.

He had high needs. He had to lose himself in her to cope with the stress of his career and study. He craved her skin. He wanted her. It was the least she could do to be there for him.

'I spend way too much money at the corner shop near the surgery, buying third-rate sausage rolls and toasted sandwiches,' he said. 'You could earn money, right there, by making my lunch each day.'

'That wouldn't take me much time. I should be doing it for you anyway,' she said, feeling guilty she hadn't thought of it already.

'Well, what about that screenplay you've been saying you want to write?' he said, picking up his own fork and loading it with pasta. 'You'd have the time and freedom to work on that.'

Okay, that was appealing. She'd enjoyed the acting jobs she'd done, but really knew that her talent, if she had any, would be more suited to an off-stage role. She'd been wanting to write a screenplay for years, a historical piece set in Melbourne after the Second World War, with the influx of European migration and the booming businesses that followed.

Still, she wasn't entirely convinced. Would she really find cleaning, cooking and being a little homemaker at Dave's service satisfying? But then, did she find waitressing, washing dishes and mopping floors in cafes and restaurants satisfying? Not really. And it would make Dave happy, and that was what you did in relationships, wasn't it?

And what if this was Dave's way of moving them closer to something more official, like marriage, or maybe children? Not that she was even sure if she could or should have children. There were a lot of medication and genetic questions around that. But if anyone could help her through it, surely it was Dave.

'Look, no pressure,' he said, getting up, withdrawing from her, the slight tilt of his chin alerting her to his swiftly changed mood. He was miffed.

Shit. She owed him so much. She reached for his hand as he passed her chair, and pulled him to her. 'Don't leave, please.' She needed him. 'Thank you. I accept.'

20

Lara

With his mouldable splint in place, Samuel was noticeably cheerier. Lara had even heard him singing softly to himself as he pottered about in the garden. She was surprised to find that she had to watch him even more closely, stopping him from doing too much. Like now.

'Here, let me help you,' she said, moving swiftly to his side as he tried to use his left arm to pull up a large, out-of-control tomato plant that needed staking.

He grunted at her and reluctantly let go of the tendrils that swayed like a many-tentacled sea monster intent on not being caught. 'I shouldn't have let it get so big,' he said.

'Never mind, we've got it now,' she replied, happy to be of service and somewhat appreciated. She looked up from where she was crouched, tethering the creature to the wooden stake, to see her employer looking wistfully over at Henrik. The Swede was stripped to the waist, raising a hoe above his head and letting it fall with a thud into the soft earth. His tanned abs glistened with sweat.

The chickens scratched and fluttered around him, waiting to snatch the worms unearthed by his hoeing.

'Do you miss gardening, Samuel?' she ventured.

'I miss most things.' He looked at her directly. 'It's true what they say—youth is wasted on the young. You have no idea what you've got, you take everything for granted, even something as simple as being able to go upstairs in your own home, or stake your bloody tomatoes.'

Lara winced as she accidentally tied her index finger to the stake, momentarily cutting off the circulation to the tip. She pulled it free and shook it. 'I can understand that. I'm only thirty-one but already I've got a rap sheet of regrets.' She shook her hands free of dirt.

Samuel raised a veiny arm to shield his eyes from the sun. 'Everyone has regrets from their twenties,' he said, his white eyebrows rising. 'You're still quite dense at that age.' He managed a rueful smile.

Lara returned his smile, equally rueful, and picked up the second stake to bang in with a small rubber mallet. 'So you think there's still hope for me then?'

'Almost certainly.'

'I hope you're right,' she said, puffing a little as she tossed the mallet to the ground and wrestled another portion of the wily bush into line. It was surprisingly heavy and unwilling to bend to her direction. 'I don't think this tomato bush knows what's good for it either. Look—if it stays all bent over like this, it won't produce fruit and it'll suffocate and die. It doesn't want to be pulled into line, but if it will just let me—' she growled with frustration as a piece snapped off in her hand, '—it will be so much stronger and more productive.'

With a final grunt, she finished ensnaring the bush and stood up, stretching her back. 'There, all done.'

Samuel nodded at her. They passed a moment in silence, each watching Henrik but for entirely different reasons, she presumed.

Then she remembered something. 'I've been meaning to ask you about the painting of the young girl with the collie dog in the kitchen . . . is that one of your children?'

Samuel shifted his weight and leaned more heavily on his stick. He took so long to answer her that she began to wonder if he was going to reply at all.

'That's Liliana, or Lily, our youngest, and her dog, Beth. Lily was seven when that was painted.'

Lara remembered Matteo mentioning a granddaughter Lily, but not a daughter. But she smiled, picturing the mass of blonde curls and the pink dress with the frilled white collar. 'She looks sweet—or were looks deceiving?'

Samuel wiped the back of his splint across his mouth. 'She was a devil,' he said, but his tone was soft.

There was something in the way he said *was* that made Lara flinch. She moved closer to him and he followed her lead and turned to go down the two steps to the back door of the house. She went with him, her hand placed on the inside of his upper arm so she could steady him if necessary. They made it down the steps safely and she released his arm. He resisted her less now than when she'd first arrived, trusting her more, she hoped. She followed him into the kitchen, where he stopped in front of the portrait. Lily had amazing blue eyes to go with her blonde locks.

'She got her colouring from your side of the family, then.'

Samuel nodded, then moved into the living room and slumped heavily into the three-seater green velvet lounge that matched the wingback chairs. 'The first two—Giovanna and Gaetano—are both dark like their mother. Lily was different from the start.'

Lara searched for a way to learn if Lily had passed away without asking outright. 'Do you see much of your children now?' She perched on a single chair opposite Samuel. This was the most he'd spoken to her since they'd met.

Samuel eased himself back against the cushions. Lara sprang to her feet to adjust them for him and he nodded his thanks before she returned to her chair.

'They're in England,' he said, by way of answer.

Lara eyed the sleek piano in the room. She'd dusted it yesterday. 'Musical family?' she asked, nodding towards the instrument.

'My granddaughter Lily—named after Giovanna's sister, of course—is a concert pianist. That's why they went to England. The fact they have English heritage made things easier.'

She wondered about the difficulties in the family that Matteo had alluded to, but didn't want to push him. 'Do you play?'

'No,' he scoffed. 'That was all Assunta.' He smiled warmly. 'She'd play for hours, totally immersed in the music, losing track of time. She was constantly late for appointments.'

'I have a sister who is very similar. Painting is her thing, that and woodwork and recycling old things for new purposes. She's got real talent, too. But if you try to get her to a parent–teacher interview on time . . .' She shook her head. 'No chance.'

'She has children?'

Lara scratched at the inside of her wrist before she could stop herself. 'Twins. A boy and a girl. Five years old.'

'That's a great age,' Samuel said, lifting his feet off the ground and swinging them up so that he was supine on the lounge.

A warm breeze shifted through the room. A sudden squawking fury exploded from the garden—some poor worm was being drawn and quartered by the chickens, she imagined.

'Daisy and Hudson both have very definite personalities. They're such little people, ready to go out and attack the world with everything they've got. Daisy wants to be a doctor. She's ghoulishly fascinated with anatomy books. Hudson's totally different—if we ask him what he wants to be when he's older, he says, "I'm still working on that."'

'Smart lad.'

'What about your grandchildren?' she asked, still trying to piece together his family tree.

'Lily's brother, my grandson Antonio, is on Wall Street. He has a green card and has no children, no wife and no plans to come back to Italy as far as I know. Our son Gaetano married Sarah and they emigrated to England. They live in London along with their daughter, Aimee. She'd be about your age, I think. I should know.' He rubbed his forehead then, as if trying to remember exactly, before giving up. 'Anyway, she's completing a science doctorate of some sort.'

There was a long silence, during which Lara tried to fill in the names on the branches of Samuel's family tree in her head. Then, because she was terribly inquisitive, she asked outright, 'And what happened to your Lily?'

'Car accident,' he said bluntly, with almost no emotion, rather as if he'd practised saying it over the years in a way that caused him the least grief. 'She was twenty. Her boyfriend was driving. They both died.'

'I'm so sorry. It must be the most awful thing in the world to lose a child.' Lara shouldered grief too, but nothing comparable to his. She had a new understanding of his stoop, his spine buckled over by that load.

Samuel didn't respond.

'And what about Matteo?' she ventured, wanting to keep him talking while he was in the mood. 'He's your niece's son, is that right?'

Samuel gave a small nod.

'And . . .' Lara searched for the right words, but in lieu of anything tactful, she just blundered on. 'Is he the only one who comes here to help you?'

The old man folded his hands neatly on his chest and stared at the dark wooden beams in the high ceiling above them. 'He's the only one who doesn't believe it.'

'Believe what?'

He waited a moment, his eyes fixed and glassy as they stared up. When his voice came out it was soft and scratchy, and Lara had to lean forward to hear his words.

'That I killed my wife.'

21

Sunny

Sunny swirled her hot chocolate with chilli, sitting cross-legged on her sister's bed out in the granny flat, her phone in her hand with the message from Ari open on the screen. She'd come out here to think, but the email had caught her by surprise.

A job for Sunny on the Sunny Coast?

She lifted her eyes from the screen. A full-time job? That was unexpected.

Lara had left her little place clean and tidy, but it still smelled of her rose perfume. Mind you, if Midnight kept coming in here with her at night after the children were in bed, the place would smell like dog soon enough. The lamp beside her—a paper lantern imprinted with woodfolk—cast a soft light over the bookcase. Neat rows of novels dominated the shelfscape, but wedged in here and there were nonfiction titles.

Thrive!

Bipolar and You.

Think Yourself Happy.

Recover, Rejoice.

After Lara's Big Breakdown, Sunny had questioned herself. Was she bipolar too? Sometimes she'd wondered if it was an invisible time bomb just waiting for the right trigger to set it off. With both their father and Lara diagnosed with bipolar affective disorder, Sunny was, apparently, seven times more likely to develop it too.

When she was younger, Sunny had been cranky a lot of the time; even she recognised that. But she was a steady, oxen cranky. No flare-ups. No falls. Despite the genetic risk, she was certain she'd missed it. She'd been lucky; she must have inherited their mother's sturdy psychological profile instead.

But when it came to the twins, there would be no way to know for sure for a long time yet. Daisy was pretty straight and even-tempered, while Hudson was a rollercoaster of emotions from one minute to the next. Then again, when Sunny and Lara were younger, everyone thought Lara was the straight one, the good one, the one who would go far in life. And there was Sunny, the wild one, the one with no plans for her future. Look what had happened to Lara, the high achiever, the teacher's pet. Looks could be deceiving, as they all knew only too well.

Midnight squirmed against Sunny's leg, chewing a rope toy, her puppy breath still sweet. Sunny ran her hand down the pup's body and Midnight gurgled appreciatively and turned to chew Sunny's hand with her razor-sharp teeth. Sunny had barely thought twice about adopting Midnight. That was the sort of person she'd once been all the time—impulsive, spontaneous, living in the moment. But everything had changed when the twins came along.

Before she became a mother, she'd take a job one minute and quit it the next. Move in with musicians, then pack up and go home to live at her mother's. Sleep with this man over here, but love that one over there. She'd lived like a gypsy. Enjoyed her freedom. This job offer from Ari tugged at those old feelings, tempting her to take to the road and start over.

Sunny rubbed Midnight's delicate velvet ear between her fingers.

She returned to the email on her phone. Creative director for a beautifully on-trend furniture, clothing and lifestyle business up on the north coast. Taking the job would mean having to move the kids away from Brisbane, from Eliza and her free housing and childcare, and from Lara.

More than sixteen years ago, Sunny had made a promise to Eliza in the dim living room, a single lamp switched on, their voices low so as not to wake Lara.

'I'm not going to live forever,' Eliza had said.

'What are you talking about?' Sunny had said, a touch irritated that now she wasn't going to get back to her flat in time for *The X-Files*.

'You saw what happened to your father,' her mother said, wiping her eyes.

'Oh, Mum,' Sunny had said, not wanting to revisit those times.

'*She* could end up like that,' Eliza hissed, pointing down the hall to Lara's bedroom.

Sunny pulled a cushion out from behind her and clutched it across her abdomen. It was true. She knew it. Today, a psychiatrist had put Lara on medication. He'd also sent her home with sleeping tablets so she could finally rest, having been awake for days.

'I know what you're saying,' Sunny said. 'I need to look after her.'

'The three of us have to stick together. Foxleigh musketeers, remember,' Eliza said, a phrase they'd bandied around for years while Leonard was in and out of the house. They'd be okay, she'd told the girls, as long as they stuck together.

'I promise,' Sunny whispered. The awful truth, which had grown like a hard ball inside her, getting bigger with every moment the conversation went on, was that Sunny should have been there for

Lara earlier, back when Sunny was a teenager, even before she'd left home. Instead of taking off when things got rough and leaving Lara in the house while Leonard was wreaking havoc, Sunny should have been there protecting her. At the very least, she should have been a better big sister and taken Lara with her. Given her some respite.

What she would never know for sure was whether she might have stopped Lara's descent, the explosion of the time bomb, had she taken her with her, looked after her, instead of spending her time drinking cask wine down at the creek and smoking with the boys.

Now, if Sunny took this job offer, it meant she would be leaving Lara again.

On the other hand, if the person driving that blue car the other day was who she thought it was, taking the kids away might be the best thing she could possibly do.

22

Lara

Wednesday evening found Lara in a cheerful mood. With buoyed confidence she'd texted Matteo, asking if she could come to see the goats and the cheese factory. She'd told herself that it was all in the interests of education and cultural exploration, and had nothing to do with his lovely hands, eyes and smile. Matteo had replied almost immediately, giving her directions for how to get there.

After she'd made dinner for Samuel and left him watching something on television, she drove to the farm. She'd decided that when she got the chance, she would ask Matteo about Samuel. Was she caring for a murderer? Where did you go in a conversation after someone said something like that?

'Don't worry, it isn't true,' Samuel had said.

She'd nodded and laughed nervously. 'Of course it's not true.' Ha ha. What a joke. That would be crazy.

But crazy was something she knew a bit about.

It was still light as she drove along the country lanes, but the heat of the day was dissipating quickly. The season had begun to turn. She was still nervous on the road, but was improving with each small trip she took into Fiotti for groceries or goat and chicken feed. Samuel's Alfa Romeo was a congenial old thing, starting easily and rumbling up the hills without a great deal of oomph but with a lot of tenacity.

She was rather confused as to which tree-lined dirt road she should be taking, but she eventually spotted a hand-painted wooden sign peeking out from behind a red-flowering bush. Coaxing the car carefully over the dips and ditches of the driveway, she finally arrived in a clearing. There was a *casa* nearby, not unlike Matteo's mother's place—a poor person's house originally, she presumed, given the variety of building materials she could see poking out from the walls. Wooden barrels with rosemary bushes stood either side of the front door—painted the traditional dark green, of course—and many pairs of work boots lay around on the worn patch of dirt at the entrance.

She cut the engine and listened to it ticking down for a moment. But she'd only begun to take in an old tree and a rope swing with a wooden seat when Matteo strode out from behind the house. His khaki shirt hugged his chest nicely, but the best thing about him was his huge smile. He lifted a hand in greeting and Lara unbuckled herself and opened the door, stepping out into the cooling breeze. She ducked back inside the car to pick up her white linen shawl to wrap around her shoulders.

He reached her quickly, appearing at her side just as she was shutting the door.

'*Bella* Lara, welcome,' he said, and swooped down to kiss each cheek.

'Hello,' she replied, air-kissing him too.

'Come, the g-g-g-goats are just settling in for the night.' He took her hand to lead her, and she thought her heart would stop.

They picked their way over the uneven ground, Matteo carefully shepherding her around any deep ditches or slippery places. She was glad she'd worn light sandshoes instead of her gladiator sandals. This was all about embracing the culture, after all, not going on a date.

On the way, they passed a wooden trestle table with two large plates of cut tomatoes under a breathable fly sheet, and then another with plates of sliced zucchini.

'Are you sun-drying them?' she asked, delighted with this small detail of organic farming.

'*Sì*—they will go under oil for the winter.'

She withdrew her hand from his and pulled her phone from the pocket of her pants to take photos of the delicacies with the rolling cornflower-blue hills in the background. She'd text them to her mum, Sunny and Hilary later. One of the things she was enjoying most about Italian culture was how much everyone seemed to *love* food.

Lara put her phone back and continued to follow Matteo. The fencing around the yards was all a little shabby, the grass around the paddocks needed a good mow, and the goat shelters seemed to have been put together with recycled materials; maybe there wasn't a lot of profit in organic farming.

'It's so quiet,' she observed. 'I thought I'd be able to hear them by now.'

'They are too busy eating dinner,' Matteo said. Then he reached out and took her hand *again*.

She allowed Matteo to lead her down the hill to the largest dome shelter. They stopped at the six-foot metal farm gate and she squinted into the barn, but couldn't make out much. The goats were obviously dark in colour, like Meg and Willow.

With a clank and a rattle, the gate opened and they stepped into the yard, a fine layer of straw under their feet. Suddenly, a goat popped out from the barn and into the remaining daylight.

'Oh, she's so small,' Lara breathed.

'These are our baby girls,' Matteo said. 'Four m-m-months old.'

The goat was half the size of Meg and Willow, but with the same deep chocolate colouring and straight horns that leaned backwards from the top of her head. A long stalk of hay stuck out of her mouth as she observed the visitors.

It wasn't long before another goat came. And another.

'What is their breed?' she asked.

'*Camosciata delle Alpi*. Alpine goats.'

'I might need you to write that one down.'

Matteo squatted and held out his hand for a cheeky goat to nibble, a glint in her eyes, ears flicking.

'The babies are very friendly and very interested to know who is here. Come inside.' He rose to his feet and led her into the expanse of the shelter, where dozens of heads looked up from long metal troughs in order to study the visitors. Several came to Lara at once, their soft little noses investigating her hands and her clothes. She knelt down and one put her head into Lara's lap and nosed around to find the buttons on her shirt to chew. More followed.

Lara giggled and gently pushed them away. 'Oh, you are so cute,' she whispered to them, scratching their backs and marvelling at the way their upright tails wiggled to express pleasure.

Matteo joined her, dropping down on his haunches, and a rush of babies mobbed him. His eyes lit up with joy. One climbed into his lap and he laughed, trying to push her off but not before she knocked him backwards to the ground. Taking advantage of his position, others nibbled his hair and clothes.

Lara laughed too. 'Clearly they love you. You've got your own goat groupies there.'

Matteo gently fought them off, with some difficulty, and managed to pull himself up to sit cross-legged, just one persistent goat chewing the back of his shirt collar. Lara couldn't imagine a more delightful explanation for why his shirts always had holes in them.

Around them, many goats stood in the troughs to eat, their back feet on the ground and their front feet inside. Some clambered over their sisters, getting stuck halfway with their long legs dangling at awkward angles. A few even slept in the trough.

'Messy eaters,' she said.

'Very,' Matteo agreed, but his eyes shone and he wore an amused smile as he watched them gambol about, chuckling as one suddenly sprang straight up into the air, launching itself on all four feet.

'Where are their mothers?' she asked.

'They are in their own shelter.' He pointed. 'We take them off their mothers at six weeks and they all come here to live together until they're old enough to have their own babies.'

'When will that be?'

'Now. The men live over there.' He pointed through the wall of the shelter in a different direction. 'There are only two boys. They get fed all year, then spend a month in with the girls when it's time. They have just finished their month of duty. They are very tired now and happy for a rest.'

'Gosh.' She dropped her gaze to the kid that had knelt down next to her, all the better to reach her clothing seams and buttons. 'Are these ones quite young for that?' she asked, rather embarrassed.

'Birthing season is in spring,' Matteo said. 'They should be pregnant now, and they will be about a year old when they have babies.' He pulled himself to his feet.

Lara nodded and also stood up, brushing the dirt and hay and hair from her clothes.

'Do you want to come and see the cheese factory?' Matteo asked.

'I'd love to.'

Lara had imagined a romantic, traditional kitchen setting for the cheesemaking business. But this was all so clinical. White walls and floors that smelled of bleach. Stainless-steel benches that gleamed from energetic scrubbing. Hair snoods, plastic gloves, antibacterial soap, rubber boots. Huge plastic buckets that, while not as enormous as a true factory's would be, still suggested mass production. And of course, it would be. This was a business like any other and it was a business that needed a licence to sell food and would have hygiene standards to adhere to.

Still, it was disappointing.

'Everything is finished for the day,' Matteo said. 'We make cheese straight after milking in the morning.'

'Wow, so it's really fresh when you make it.'

'Straight f-fr-from the goat,' he said, and smiled.

Matteo opened the heavy door of an industrial fridge and the light inside blinked on to reveal dozens of rows of metal racks with hundreds of plastic squares of setting cheeses.

'These we made this morning,' he said. 'They are a fresh cheese and will be ready to sell in four or five days' time. It's easier to make money with fresh cheese, as you turn over the product more quickly. Aged cheese has to be stored for so long. Goat milk is perfect for fresh cheese.'

'Where do you sell the cheese?' Lara asked, peering at the rows of white squares floating in a translucent liquid, lined up like parked cars.

'At markets. The Santo Spirito market in Florence is the biggest. The second Sunday of every month.'

He turned off the lights and locked the production room door.

Outside, a few early stars had appeared in the sky, which was deepening into indigo above them. A light breeze carried the smell of something sweet and floral on the air and washed away Lara's disappointment with the sterility of the cheese room, instantly lifting her heart.

She was in Tuscany. And the man beside her had reached for her hand yet again. Any questions she might have had about whether it had been just a friendly move vanished.

She followed him silently, considering her hand in his. It fitted nicely, their fingers slotting together for a snug, natural embrace, without any kind of *whoops, let's try it this way* awkwardness. And despite what she'd been through in the past, a seed of hope sprang to life.

'Nearly there,' Matteo said.

His hut sat on the other side of a copse of trees. It was perfectly positioned for a view over all three of the goat shelters—the mothers', the kids', and the males'. It was a dark wooden hut—probably some kind of kit home, she guessed—with a tin roof and two steps leading to a tiny porch. A yellow light shone next to the door. Matteo wiped his boots on the mat and levered each one off with the toe of the opposite foot. Lara went to do the same.

'No need,' Matteo said. 'Mine are work boots, yours are . . .' he considered her floral-printed sandshoes, 'too pretty to leave outside.'

The front door slid open on wooden tracks and she followed him into a cosy space, painted white, with a queen-sized bed dominating half the cabin to the right of the entrance, and a kitchenette and dining table on the left. A wall separated off the bathroom at the other end. A skylight over the bed showcased the darkening sky above them.

'This is really lovely,' she said, surprised. She'd imagined him living a bit more rustically on the farm.

'It is part of my wages for my job,' he said. 'I get the best cabin as I am head shepherd.'

'Shepherd?' She wasn't sure he had the right word. Didn't shepherds move flocks of animals around and watch over them at night, wearing long robes and holding staffs in their hands?

He frowned, mumbling some Italian words, trying to find a better translation. 'A *pastore.* A goat manager. I look after their health, choose a diet plan, help with milking and the babies and study what they're eating and how it changes the milk that is turning to cheese.'

Lara nodded, gazing around the space, at the books on his shelf—she couldn't understand the titles, but they looked quite technical. She loved his bright red, orange and gold bedspread, and a chain of carved wooden birds that flew in a line above his bed, attached to the wall on each side.

'*Un caffè*?' Matteo asked, rubbing the back of his neck as though he'd had a long, hard day.

'It might be a bit late for me,' she said, not wanting to be awake and wrestling with her thoughts in the middle of the night.

He went to the kitchen sink to wash his hands and she followed to do the same, washing off the last of the goat love. Matteo passed her a towel to dry her hands.

'Maybe a *vino* then?' he asked, raising an eyebrow.

'I could have one, I suppose, if I wait a bit before driving home again.'

'No rush,' Matteo said, reaching up above the sink to a narrow cupboard and pulling out two extra-large glasses, placing them on the dining table. She suspected they'd hold half a bottle of wine each.

She sat at the table in a simple wooden chair with a tartan cushion, and Matteo began to whistle as he took a bottle of red wine from the shelf. It didn't have a label.

'Do you make your wine?' she asked.

'Of course,' he said, as if this was the most natural thing to do.

'Are there grapevines here too?' She turned around to look out the box window behind her, trying to peer through the velvety darkness.

'Just a dozen rows.'

'How do you make it?' she asked, watching him twist the corkscrew into the cork, watching the muscles in his forearm flex with each turn.

'It is very easy,' he said, shaking his head in a way that suggested he thought it would be crazy to ever buy it. He put down the bottle, the better to gesticulate. 'We make it in one day. We pick the grapes and squash them with a special mallet.' He mimed squashing grapes. 'It must have air to breathe. After you squash it, it begins to boil, because there is yeast in the skin that reacts with the liquid inside. You leave this squashed grape mix in the open barrel for ten days, then transfer it to a big glass barrel with a thin neck.'

She nodded, enjoying following the passage of grapes to wine. It might seem easy to him, but to her it sounded quite miraculous.

'We pour oil over the grapes to seal them from air. Then when you want to get the wine out, you suck out the oil with a siphon.' More charades. 'You don't want any oil in the wine.' Matteo pulled a face. 'And there you have it. *Vino!*' He picked up the bottle he was working on and pulled out the cork with a titillating *thwuck*.

Lara salivated. He poured the wine; just as she'd suspected, half of the bottle went into each glass.

She took a sip. Over the years her tolerance for alcohol had increased but she still treaded carefully. She let it sit in her mouth for a moment, gently swishing it, giving her tastebuds time to wake up. He watched her, his eyes alight, waiting for her response.

'It's good,' she said.

'No, no, it cannot be just *good*,' he admonished. 'Tell me more. What can you taste? How does it feel?'

Lara laughed. 'Okay, I'll try again.' A wine critic she was not.

Matteo watched eagerly, waiting.

'It's, er, kind of . . . well, I want to say *woody*, but that's not right, is it?'

Matteo shrugged encouragingly. '*Sì*, yes, if that's what you taste. What else?' he enthused, rolling his hand in the air to signal to her to keep going.

She took another sip. But before she could offer any more observations, her stomach spoke with a loud and long gurgle. She was ravenous. Matteo seemed unfazed by the late hour but she wasn't used to having to wait hours after darkness to eat dinner.

Matteo lifted one corner of his mouth in a smirk. 'Are you hungry?'

She swallowed quickly and put her hands on her abdomen. 'Yes. Sorry. I normally eat dinner much earlier, sometimes at four-thirty in the afternoon, because the kids have come home from kindy—kindergarten, that is—and are starving. So they want a whole meal. We call that their first hobbit dinner.'

He frowned, confused.

'Did you see the *Lord of the Rings* movies?' she asked.

He nodded, his head tilted, obviously trying to remember what she was getting at.

'At the beginning of the first movie, after the hobbits have left their village and are following Viggo Mortensen's character . . . oh, what was his name?'

'Aragorn.'

'Yes! So they're following Aragorn and one of the hobbits complains he's hungry. When Aragorn counters that he has already had breakfast, the hobbit says something like, "But that was just the first breakfast!" and says that hobbits have several more breakfasts. Or something like that.' She laughed, relaxing more with every moment they were together. 'So anyway, that's what Daisy and Hudson do. They have their first dinner in the afternoon and then they have another, smaller one later, normally *right* after they've cleaned their teeth.'

'The second hobbit dinner,' he said, catching on.

'Exactly.'

He watched her for a moment, smiling, studying her. Something ignited inside her; his gaze was like a physical caress.

He rested his chin in the cup of his hand, elbow on the table, relaxed. 'Your eyes light up when you talk about your niece and nephew. You are close to them.'

Lara shifted in her seat, crossed one leg over the other and shrugged, feeling helpless before her feelings of love for those two kids. 'Our little family is very close. I love them like they are my own.'

'Would you like kids one day too?'

There were so many different directions this conversation could go and she didn't want to go in any of them. Instead, she deflected it back to Matteo.

'You never know what life will hand you,' she said, then quickly followed with, 'Tell me about your family. In fact, what I'd most like to know is why no one other than you is talking to Samuel.'

Matteo huffed and rubbed his nose.

'He told me everyone believes he killed his wife. Is that true?'

Matteo took a breath and nodded slowly. '*Sì*. It is true.'

23

'Wait a minute,' Lara said, staring at Matteo and spreading her fingers wide on the tabletop for support. 'Are you kidding me? Samuel killed his wife?'

'No, no, no,' Matteo said. 'I did not mean that. I mean that everyone *thinks* he killed her.'

'I don't understand. What happened?'

Matteo took a deep breath and let it out slowly, accompanied by a small, anguished groan. He scratched at the back of his neck and then looked down at his shirt as if seeing it for the first time that day. He pinched the fabric and lifted it to his nose to sniff.

Lara giggled.

'It is a long story,' he said, dropping his shirt. 'I think I need to shower first.'

'Yes, of course.'

He stood and waved a hand at the fridge. 'There's cheese and grissini, olives too. Sun-dried tomatoes, zucchini, prosciutto. Help yourself, *per favore*. I don't want you to waste away on me.' He smiled at her then, and held her gaze until she melted into a buzzing, light-filled puddle.

'Okay. Take your time,' she said, holding up her glass of wine.

Matteo disappeared behind the sliding door and she heard the shower water running. Not long after that she heard him singing.

She wandered around his tiny cabin, peeking in his cupboards (well, she had to look for a serving platter, didn't she?) and marvelling at how little he had in material stuff. In years gone by, she would have expected to see stacks of CDs and a music station, a television, a DVD player, a computer station and a telephone at least. But now, she realised, all these could be reduced to a pocket-sized phone and a laptop. Even books could be sucked into the technology, though she was still a staunch fan of the paper book and was glad to see Matteo was too. There wasn't much else on his bookshelves other than a small figurine of the *Pietà*, Michelangelo's famous statue of Mother Mary and her son Jesus, just taken down from the cross. It was an artwork she suspected would break even the hardest of hearts.

Samuel had Catholic artworks in the villa too. And in Rome, she'd seen a statue of the Virgin on almost every building corner, some with tiny gardens adorning her feet. Lara's own family had no religion. Eliza had ditched her Protestant upbringing long ago, though she raised her two girls with at least a cultural appreciation of Christianity. Lara found herself loving how much this country loved Mary, the mother.

Behind her, the water turned off and she heard the shower screen slide open. Matteo was still singing and she realised that she hadn't heard him stutter the whole time he'd been crooning in the shower. In fact, she hadn't heard him stutter at all since they left the goats.

Or maybe he had but she'd simply stopped hearing it.

She drained the rest of her wine, enjoying feeling her limbs go just a little bit numb, her medication and lack of food increasing the effects of the alcohol.

'Did you find the food?' Matteo called from behind the door.

'Oh, yes, thank you,' Lara called back, rushing to the fridge and placing the goodies from inside on the bench. She pulled a large blue platter from under the sink. The bathroom door slid open with a whoosh and Lara turned to see Matteo, hair dripping, wearing nothing but a white towel around his hips, bright in contrast to his olive skin. His chest hair was wet too and a line of it trailed downwards to his belly button.

He grinned at her and it felt like a challenge.

She held her gaze steady. 'I've nearly got everything ready.'

'*Molto bene*,' he said, coming over. He plucked an olive from its jar and popped it in his mouth. The scent of soap rose from his steaming body. He was so close to her that as he reached for a piece of prosciutto a drop of water fell from his bare shoulder and landed on her arm. She looked down at it, watching it run towards the ground.

She looked up at him, her face inches from his.

He winked, the devil, and smirked. 'I just need to get some clothes,' he said, moving past her, his damp towel bumping into her hip.

'Okay,' she said, turning to focus on the food in front of her, pulling a knife from a squeaky drawer and carefully cutting into the pecorino cheese. *Holy shit*, was what she'd really wanted to say. The man was gorgeous and she'd turned to liquid in seconds.

She could hear Matteo pulling clothes from drawers but refused to turn and watch him, instead delicately placing olives and cubes of feta and pecorino slivers and . . . whatever else was in front of her. She could barely pay attention.

He whistled as he walked back to the bathroom and put his clothes on.

Lara's hands trembled as she carried the tray back to the little table and resumed her position on the seat with the window at her back.

She'd had wine on an empty stomach; she needed food. She began shovelling grissini and cheese into her mouth.

Matteo returned dressed in navy linen pants and yet another simple but beautiful linen shirt. He really did scrub up well.

'All better?' she asked.

'Yes, much. Sometimes I forget that I'm not meant to smell like a goat.'

'I can tell you're a great goat handler,' she said. 'They all love you.'

'Not as much as they love the male goats.' He noted her empty glass and turned to pull another bottle from the cupboard.

'Oh, no more for me,' Lara said. 'I still need to drive home.'

'Plenty of time,' Matteo said, popping the cork and setting it aside to breathe.

Lara reached for more cheese instead.

'Have you tried the prosciutto?' he asked, sitting opposite her once more and swirling his wine in the huge glass.

'It's fantastic,' Lara said.

Matteo rolled up three pieces at once and popped them into his mouth, licking his fingers.

'You were telling me about Samuel and why everyone thinks he killed his wife.'

'It is very sad,' Matteo began, reaching for more prosciutto and cheese. There were artichokes on the plate too, Lara noticed. She didn't even remember putting them there during the out-of-body experience of seeing Matteo nearly naked.

'Assunta was such a beautiful woman,' he said. 'She was my great-aunt, and our whole family was very close. Always together. Always feasting. Assunta was a wonderful cook. She loved to make pasta herself. She thought it was an awful thing to buy it. She would make it fresh several times a week and invite everyone over on Sunday evenings. My grandparents, parents, all the extended family. I grew up running around the grounds of the villa with my brothers and cousins, all of us playing football.'

Soccer, Lara reminded herself.

'These feasts, you have no idea. The food, *incredibile*. It would go on for hours. Mostly, as *bambini* we would all fall asleep somewhere in the house while the adults kept talking and laughing and drinking wine and limoncello. Assunta was a great actress. She would recite monologues from plays. And Gilberta—you met her—she would join her and they'd be a two-woman show. Assunta played the piano too. If the weather was bad we would all be inside on the ground floor, the fire going, everyone gathered around the piano while she played. Gilberta's husband, Mario, he would sing opera. Gilberta would dance. My mother recited poetry.'

Lara tried to picture the stern woman she'd met reciting poetry.

'*Incredibile*,' Matteo said again. 'And Assunta would make it all happen. She was, what is the phrase . . . over the top, you know?'

'I think so.'

Matteo reached for the new bottle of wine. It didn't seem the moment for Lara to decline so she let him refill hers too.

'Everyone loved her. She would hug and kiss and hold hands with everyone. Especially with Samuel. They were great together. He was a different person then. He would sing too.' He chuckled at the memory. 'Terrible singer.'

Lara smiled. 'But he did it anyway.'

'Yes, yes. Assunta made everyone bigger than they were.'

'What a gift,' she said, sad for the loss of such a light in the family.

'But since her death, it has all stopped.'

Despite her best intentions, Lara took a sip of the wine in front of her. It seemed the thing to do, to toast Assunta's memory. 'What happened to her?'

'The villa had a leak in the roof, above one of the bedrooms. It had been there for many months. Assunta kept asking Samuel to fix it. It had become a joke. She would tease him about it at the big dinners and everyone would laugh.'

Lara did some mental calculations. 'How old was Samuel then?'

Matteo squinted and looked up at the ceiling, doing the same. 'Must have been late sixties, I guess.'

'Was he able to get up on the roof and fix the leak?' she asked, feeling defensive on Samuel's behalf.

'Yes, yes. He was very fit. When he came to Italy he worked as a labourer for a long time. He had a lot of skills.'

'But he wasn't still working as a labourer then, surely?'

'No, he taught English in private schools. He was still working at one when Assunta died.'

Lara took another sip. 'So what happened?'

Matteo leaned back in his chair with his glass of wine and swallowed a large mouthful before he spoke. 'There was a big storm. Lots and lots of rain. Samuel was late coming home from work. Assunta, sick of waiting for Samuel to fix the roof, decided she would do it herself. She was like that, you know. Fearless. So she went up there and slipped. She fell from the roof. Broke her neck. Samuel found her.'

Lara's hand flew to her chest. 'That's so awful.' She reached again for her glass. 'Poor Samuel.'

Matteo nodded and also sipped more wine.

Lara frowned and tapped her glass with her finger. 'So, why is the family ostracising Samuel exactly?'

'They blame him,' Matteo said. 'Everyone knew Samuel should have fixed the roof. If he had, Assunta would never have gone up there. She'd still be with us, dancing, singing.' He shrugged helplessly.

'That seems a bit harsh. I mean, Assunta didn't have to go up there. It was an accident. An awful, tragic accident, but I don't see why an entire family would stop talking to him.'

'You don't understand Italians.' Matteo laughed emptily. 'Haven't you seen *The Godfather*? Family is everything. And Samuel was an outsider who had captured the heart of the young Assunta and married into the family and inherited her family's villa. To her sisters and nieces and nephews and all the rest, Samuel had stolen her from the family. She'd had to fight her own parents very hard to be with Samuel. They didn't trust the Englishman. Anyone who was foreign wasn't to be trusted. He was despised and then only accepted when it became obvious Assunta loved him and he wasn't going anywhere. And then they had children, so he had to be part of the family—the christenings, the birthdays, the Holy Communions, Sunday masses, Sunday feasts. Christmas. Easter. Holy days. But once he'd broken their trust and allowed their precious Assunta to die, that was it. He was cut off. Blacklisted. *Finito*.'

'Poor Samuel,' Lara said again. 'No wonder he is so . . .' She was going to say 'grumpy', but changed her mind. She had much more sympathy for him now. 'He's so alone.'

Matteo's glass was emptying quickly, she noticed. She glanced at her own, trying to estimate how many standard drinks she'd had. A couple of glasses? She wiggled her leg a bit and noted the heavy weight in it. She pushed the wine away.

'What about his children and grandchildren? Were they still here in Italy at the time Assunta died?'

'Antonio had already gone to America, but the rest, yes.' Matteo continued. 'Then Lily got the scholarship not long after and things were so difficult with the families, and maybe it was too painful to stay here without Assunta. I think they thought it was best to leave. They believed Samuel would follow.'

'But he didn't.'

'He is stubborn.'

'But *you* come to see him,' she said.

'Yes.'

'Why?'

Matteo inhaled, his lovely chest expanding beneath the light linen of his shirt. 'I didn't think it was fair,' he said. 'And I guess I know a little bit what it is like to be an outcast, to have people snigger behind your back, to have them not hear what you say.'

His eyes met hers and she felt a wave of deep, long-held sadness come from him. Instinctively she took his hand in hers. It was warm and sturdy and she had to fight the urge to bring it to her cheek and rest it there.

He looked down at her hand, then wound his fingers through hers. He locked his eyes on hers and suddenly the cabin felt very small. She stood, releasing her hand. 'Water,' she squeaked, and cleared her throat. 'Would you like some water?'

She moved towards the kitchen sink but he snatched back her hand, simultaneously standing and pulling her towards him so that they were standing face to face, her hand in his and her heart galloping within her breast. His free hand cupped the back of her head, his thumb rubbing gently behind her ear.

She looked down at the floor. 'Matteo,' she breathed, not daring to look at him; she'd be drawn into those eyes and lost for good. 'I've had too much to drink and I don't think I can drive home, not yet anyway.'

He leaned forward and rested his forehead on hers. She could smell the wine on his breath. 'Stay here,' he whispered.

Inside her, a triton wrestled wild horses. Here was a lovely, gentle man, who wanted her right now. And she was free here in Italy to do things she normally wouldn't even consider. But she couldn't lose her heart, or her mind.

'I will sleep on the floor,' Matteo said, and lifted his head.

She raised her eyes in surprise. 'What?'

He grinned at her and stepped back, then brought her hand to his lips and pressed them gently to her knuckles. '*Bella* Lara. I will sleep on the floor and you can have the whole bed to yourself.'

'No, you can't. I just need to wait a few hours, I think, until I'm ready to drive. I can rest in the car. You can't sleep on the floor, that's crazy.'

To her great disappointment, he let go of her hand, and her skin cooled too quickly. He went to the bed and tossed off a pillow, tucking it into a slot beside the door. Then he got down on the ground and lay with his hands behind his head on the pillow, grinning at her. 'I'm a goat herder, remember? During kidding season I sleep on the barn floor sometimes. Believe me, this is much more comfortable. The goats? They kick like mules.'

Lara burst out laughing with relief and joy.

'Besides, I am an easy sleeper. No fuss.'

Gosh, how appealing.

'Do you snore?' he asked.

'I don't think so.'

'I will let you know,' he said, folding his hands on his chest and closing his eyes.

After Lara accepted that this was the plan and it was going to happen—she was going to sleep next to Matteo, kind of—he got up off the floor and they talked and ate some more and washed the platter and glasses together and then, finally, they said goodnight and turned off the lights.

Lara lay awake in his bed, listening to him breathing, feeling happier than she had in a long, long time. But there was no way she'd be able to sleep. Every nerve in her body was awake. She waited a few hours, till she felt the effects of the alcohol subside, then tiptoed out of the cabin and drove home to the villa.

24

Lara and Dave

Lara lay in bed, the curtains drawn and her limbs heavy. Dave came to sit on the edge of the mattress, a mug of coffee in his hand.

It wasn't for her.

Impatient to drink it, he blew on it three times, watching her. She hated the way he did this after an episode, studying her as if she was an insect. She sometimes feared he would pin her to a board, splaying her legs and arms wide, leaving her most vulnerable parts exposed. He was biding his time, that was all.

She should call someone. Sunny would come for her. Her sister would kick the door down if she had to. But then Lara would just be the hopeless little sister pulling Sunny away from her fabulously bohemian life.

Her mother, then? No. Then Eliza would know that all her worst fears had come true. Leonard had completely disappeared by now, at last an officially listed missing person, having melted into the underworld population of the homeless. Eliza had been warned he was unlikely to ever return, and so she was stuck, still married to a phantom. So no, the last thing Lara wanted was her mother to see her like this.

Eliza and Sunny thought Lara was safe in the care of her kindly psychologist boyfriend.

'I've sorted out your pills,' he said, sipping his beverage.

'I don't need them.'

'Yes, you do. I'm the doctor here, remember.'

He wasn't actually. Not yet.

He laid his hand on her face the way a mother might check a child's temperature, except it wasn't comforting. It felt heavy; he was slowly pushing down on her. He moved his hand to her neck. She tried to move her head, to get the weight off her, but the pillow held her on the other side. She had to escape. She flung her arm up to push him away but he caught her wrist in his hand, his fingernails sharp in her flesh.

'Stop being so childish.'

She began to sob. Again. She'd gone through two sets of clothes today already, discarding them as they became wet with tears.

'You don't know what you're doing. You need to trust me, Lara. I'm here to help. You're not in your right mind.'

He released her wrist and she rolled away from him, burying her face in the pillow. She felt his weight leave the mattress.

'I'll get your pills.'

'I don't want them!' she screamed. 'Please,' she begged, whimpering now. 'They're making me worse. I know they are.'

You're making me worse.

'Oh, honey,' he said gently. 'How much worse could you get?'

25

Lara

First thing the next morning, Lara sent Matteo a text message, knowing he'd be up at dawn too, to explain that she hadn't been able to sleep and needed to be home for Samuel, thanking him for a wonderful evening and bravely saying she hoped she would see him in the near future.

His reply was instant—*Please come back soon*—and it was all she could do not to squeal and happy dance around her room.

To her surprise, when she went downstairs, Samuel was already up at the barn and feeding the goats. It was just six a.m., exactly when she needed to start work. He looked up at her as she made her way over. Meg was tugging at some hay in his hand and Willow was gobbling something out of a bucket, her tail wagging furiously.

'Good morning,' he said, his voice fatherly, his eyebrows high and questioning, as if he'd been up waiting for her to come home last night.

'*Guten morgen*,' she sang, waving at him. 'Oh, sorry, wrong language.' She dissolved into nervous giggling, her head still way up in the clouds, thinking of Matteo. Her skin flushed under Samuel's twinkling gaze.

Lara went to the gate and scratched Meg behind the ears while the goat chewed at the hay, breathing in her beautiful smell. She was going to try to explain everything—she could only too clearly imagine what he was thinking—but decided to hum mysteriously for a moment.

'Well,' she said, feeling she'd stretched the silence as far as she could. 'I better get the pails to start the milking.' She smiled sweetly at Samuel. His lips twitched, and his hand gripped tightly on his walking stick on the uneven ground.

Lara turned to leave, then stopped. With determination, she covered the few strides between her and Samuel and kissed him on the cheek.

'Thanks for my job,' she said, her hand resting on his bony shoulder. 'I love it here.'

Then she turned and left to get the pails, singing loudly into the cool, gentle dawn light.

If she was totally honest, not everything about type II bipolar disorder was awful. The upside? The absolute power that came with the mania swings. It was as though she was transformed into a sleek, strong superhero figure, like Buffy the Vampire Slayer, or Wonder Woman—nothing could touch her. She could fly through the air and take down a monster with her fingernail alone. True, her medications usually kept the sharp highs and lows at bay, but they each still sneaked in from time to time.

Now, here in Tuscany, a bridled mania on her heels, she could smell the lavender that grew in the rockeries around the villa before she even got out of bed. The red geraniums that sprawled over terracotta pots were so bright they almost hurt her eyes. Food became six-dimensional in her mouth and blew her senses with its taste, smell and texture. She imagined these highs might be akin to taking some kind of illicit drug, though as she'd never experimented with those kinds of drugs she could only assume. She could work or study all day and all night. She composed poetry in her head. The world was full of love and joy. When in the company of others, she made them laugh with her witty banter and enthusiastic conversation.

There was also the liberating feeling of disinhibition, and with Matteo on her mind, she began to fantasise. What might it be like to be with him? It wasn't just his physical attributes that commanded her attention, it was his soft manner with the goats and his gallant care for his great-uncle. She wanted to lose herself with him, lose her old self, shrug off the old dead skin. It was something she hadn't even realised she wanted—*needed*—until now.

No one had touched her in that way since Dave. She didn't want to go through life with those being the last physical memories she had.

So here she was, with her confidence soaring and Matteo so close, someone she intuitively trusted and who seemed to want her too.

She was still thinking of Matteo as she took Henrik a coffee. He was digging holes for fence posts so he could keep the chickens and the goats away from his newly terraced earth.

'Here, look at your pants,' she said, putting his coffee down on the soil a bit too hard, some sloshing over the side. She pointed to his falling-down trousers.

Henrik straightened, sweating and puffing, wiping his forearm across his face, and glanced down. Lara wondered if he was wearing underwear. It seemed like there was nothing under there but acres of tanned skin.

'Would you like some help?' she asked, taking a step forward to pull them up for him.

Henrik's eyes widened in surprise as he stepped backwards. 'No, it's fine.'

Truly, it was nothing more than she would have done for Daisy or Hudson. They were just trousers, for goodness' sake. But she held up her hands in apology and stepped back, picking up his coffee once more, feeling her face warm.

She handed him the cup and glanced at his rippling abs. He was a pleasure to look at. And she felt things, things she really hadn't felt much of in the past six years. Matteo had awakened those feelings and she happily let them burn like a cleansing fire.

'Thank you,' he said, eyeing her cautiously.

Henrik was silent for some time, staring at her over the handle of his spade. A long strand of blond hair hung loose and it was all she could do to stop herself from reaching up and brushing it from his cheek. She'd bet his hair was soft and well-conditioned.

'See you later on for lunch,' she said, and forced herself to leave before she did something she'd regret.

❧ ❧

She decided to clean the villa's walls to rid herself of excess energy. They clearly hadn't been done for some time, with dirt, dust and scuff marks on the paint and small spider webs in between the exposed bricks. She tied a red and white scarf around her head and got to work.

Outside, attached to the bricks next to the huge double wooden doors into what would have been the receiving room, Lara found a diamond-shaped metal plate. *Giardino dei Fiori*—garden of flowers. She rubbed at it carefully, wondering who had named the house and what her intention had been for this land. For surely it had been a woman who'd named it, giving the sign a four-petalled flower, in the shape of a cross, with a circle at the centre.

There were flowers on the property now. Small white bursts from oregano, basil and parsley joined the lavender and geraniums and the wildflowers that grew in the lawn. She turned to survey the vista of greenish-blue hills strung with vineyards or dissected patchwork fields of crops. She tried to imagine a time when flowers might have filled every inch of the view. What a magnificent sight it would have been.

Samuel interrupted her after lunch as she hoisted up a bucket of grimy water to toss out onto the aloe vera plants. 'The walls look good,' he said.

'Thank you.' Lara had been working very hard. She gestured to the name plate on the wall. 'Who named the property?'

Samuel stroked his whiskery chin, something she hadn't seen before; he was usually clean-shaven. 'The villa was built by Assunta's ancestors Sara and Guido Falco in the sixteen hundreds. They were from Venice originally, having made their wealth in investments in glass and jewellery workshops. But Sara was unhappy in Venice so they moved here. I believe she named the property.'

'Lucky her.'

They stood side by side in silence for a moment, considering the metal plate. Samuel looked as though he was about to say more on the subject, but then seemed to change his mind. 'You know, you can take a break from all this work. It's a very big house. It could take days to clean it all.'

'Oh, don't worry about me; I've got plenty of energy,' she said, shifting her bucket of water from one hand to the other. And she did. Her body felt like a well-oiled machine. This was another thing she loved about mania: the lack of pain. No headaches. No exhausted or strained muscles. No sore feet. She'd once fallen down the front steps of Eliza's house while in an upward swing and not realised she'd torn a ligament in her knee until several days later, when the high fell away and the pain unleashed its fury.

'Trust me, it's better I just keep going,' she said, flashing him a reassuring smile. 'Use me while you can.' Samuel nodded, seemingly somewhat relieved that he'd tried to help but it was unnecessary.

It wasn't as though she didn't know she was having a mini manic episode. Quite the opposite. Lara knew it and she loved it. She was well-practised at self-monitoring as best she could, and at channelling her energies into positive pursuits such as exercise or cleaning or cooking. But it still felt great. So much of her life had been spent not feeling good at all—in fact, feeling terrible—that she couldn't help but love these times. It was almost like a reward for getting through the lows. She felt she could conquer the world if someone would only give her half a chance; she'd sort out all those warring nations in a jiffy. She didn't know how long this would last, but she was going to love it while it did. Usually, it was a few days. Sometimes a couple of weeks.

Of course, there was the small voice in the back of her head telling her she'd regret it tomorrow when it all came crashing down. It was a bloody smug voice, that one, like having a boring accountant sitting on her shoulder while she was on a shopping spree. A complete party-pooper.

There were so many voices. So many opinions. Some were her own. Some were other people's. Some . . . well, she didn't know whose they were.

'The medications aren't enough on their own. You still need to work to keep the swinging moods at bay,' Constance had told her. She was a petite, fairy-like psychiatrist with long white hair and wrinkles that showed years of laughter. Her easy good humour gave the impression that she really had mastered her mind in her lifetime. 'People with chronic illnesses that affect their body need to exercise and eat right every day to keep themselves at their best. You need to do the same for your mind. Meditation is your medication,' she was fond of saying.

Mindfulness was the key to everything, according to Constance. Being present, keeping your mind solely on the task in front of you, living in the moment rather than the past or the future, keeping gratitude diaries, meditating morning and evening. And yes, in Lara's case, medication as well. 'They are two halves of the one orange,' she would say.

Now Lara wondered, as she went to the outside tap to fill her bucket with water yet again, if she should contact Constance to check if her medications were still adequate. But it wasn't as if she hadn't been here before. This feeling wasn't new, just unexpected. It was probably brought on by these insanely beautiful surroundings and maybe a blossoming relationship with Matteo. And she was beginning to realise that being away from the family home, away from Sunny and Eliza, was allowing her to find confidence in herself. She was caring for Samuel and getting about by herself. She was doing it, this thing, this *life* thing that others seemed to do so easily. Maybe she wasn't manic at all. Maybe this was what it felt like to be normal.

She lifted her face to the blue sky while the fresh water tumbled into her bucket, enjoying the feel of the sunlight on her closed eyelids, and the warm breeze caressing her arms.

Matteo.

A flood of pure lust washed through her and she dropped her head back, exposing her throat to the sun's touch. There may have been a sensible voice telling her to slow down, but the desire to replace Dave's imprint was much stronger. She needed to move on.

Matteo.

Lara opened her eyes and turned off the tap. She gazed over the hazy valley, then acted before she could change her mind.

She tapped out a message.

Can I come tomorrow? X

His reply came within seconds.

Yes please.

Everything was changing.

26

Lara and Dave

The sky was still black outside, though dawn wasn't far away. The light was changing colour the same way the blackened knuckle of the ring finger on her right hand had been changing for the past couple of days, the result of her own stupidity during an episode—episodes that had been escalating, much to her shame. Lara had just pulled another all-nighter to polish the nineteenth draft of her screenplay, driven by today's deadline for a prestigious state award for an unpublished script. Her fingers tapped across the keyboard of her laptop, ignoring her sprained finger, rewriting a sentence here and there, ensuring her formatting was exactly what the competition guidelines required.

She was elated. This draft was good. Really good. Dave had read it a couple of times, laughing in the right places, offering some solid advice now and then, praising her for her work. 'I can't wait to see it on the big screen. You'll be able to keep me in the lifestyle I so desire,' he'd said, grabbing her around the waist and kissing her long and longingly.

Lara had been working on her screenplay for three years now. It had all the makings of a great movie. An underdog from Italy, determined to make his mark on Australia after surviving the Second World War as part of the resistance against German occupation. A wealthy young woman from England who'd lost her whole family in the Blitz, but escaped with her mother's jewellery collection, seeking a life away from a loveless marriage. And the man who chases her to Melbourne to claim her as his own.

Lara had been smiling for hours now, watching the words scroll by, a delightful shiver of excitement dancing down her spine. She just knew this script was going to win.

Sometimes that happened to her in these long periods of mania. It was as if the veil between reality and the endless sea of possibility thinned, allowing glimpses of past, present and future to play like movies in her mind.

She was going to win.

Her heartbeat could barely keep up with her excitement. A whole new career and life was coming her way, and finally she'd be able to show Dave that she had so much more to give to this world than making lunches, running errands, folding his socks and meeting his physical needs. She wasn't the easiest person to live with. She knew that, because he told her often. Finally, she could make him proud.

The light was turning bluish-grey outside and the birds were chatting up a storm. Lara saved her document, then backed it up to her USB stick, and shut the laptop, leaving the stick on top of the lid. Later today she'd take it to the printers to print and bind copies to post to the judges. But right now, she needed sleep. Finally she could rest, knowing she'd done it.

She yawned, the tidal wave of sleep deprivation washing over her and, just like that, her eyes closed.

ര ൭

She awoke in the afternoon, slumped painfully over her desk. She felt confused and thirsty, as though she'd taken a sleeping tablet, and had a horrible pain in her neck and shoulder, her right arm numb. She began to cry with the pain, stumbling to the kitchen to find water and painkillers, willing her head to stop spinning. On the bench, near Dave's favourite gold-rimmed coffee mug, he'd left a note.

Hey sleepyhead. I tried to wake you but you were snoring like a navvy :) I'll be home late again, sorry. Vicki's helping me with an assignment. Thanks for putting up with me.

Lara smiled, her head-spin slowing, and checked the time. It was already three o'clock. She needed to get to the printers right away if she was going to get this script into the post today.

She staggered upstairs and showered, wetting her hair, washing away the dregs of exhaustion. Back downstairs, she grabbed her handbag and car keys, wincing as her sprained knuckle bent too quickly, and went to her laptop for the USB stick. But it wasn't there. She must have knocked it off while she was sleeping. She searched the desk, moving the laptop, shoving her research books and reams of pixelated drafts of the script to the side, moving the chair and climbing under the desk.

Nothing.

Biting her lip in frustration—she was always losing things; it drove her mad—Lara turned on her laptop and rummaged in her handbag for another USB stick, taking calming breaths against the rising panic and the ticking clock. It was okay; she could just copy it from her hard drive. It wasn't a big deal.

Except it was a big deal, because she was clumsy and inefficient and must be going crazy because she couldn't find the file. She went to the folder labelled *Screenplay*, but it was empty. She used the laptop's search function, but nothing came up. It was ludicrous. It had to be there. It was there just ten hours ago.

Wait. If she'd accidentally deleted it, it would be in the trash.

But that too was empty.

She continued searching for the USB stick long after the deadline had passed, distraught but consoling herself that when she found it she could submit the script the following year.

Over the next few days, Dave helped her look, even emptying out all the rubbish in the bin and searching through it with rubber gloves, assuring her it would turn up.

But it never did. Her screenplay was lost for good. Lara felt truly broken. How crazy and dysfunctional she must be if she couldn't even print out a document and get it in the post. The darkness descended over her, and there it stayed for the longest time.

27

Lara

The white broderie anglaise dress was sleeveless, cinched at the waist and came to just above the knee, and it allowed the light breeze skimming through the open driver's-side window to caress Lara's skin. Her hair was freshly washed, and drying in long ringlets. She smelled of roses—it might be old-fashioned, but she loved it. She pressed her lips together, tasting the vanilla lip gloss she'd applied. Her sandalled foot pressed down on the brake and she acknowledged a slight tremor in her hand as she cut the engine. There was soft light coming from the windows of Matteo's cabin, and when she opened the car door she could hear gentle mandolin music playing inside. She stood, placing her feet firmly on the ground, smoothed down her dress and breathed.

She still had time to back out.

But she didn't want to, even though she'd stared at her scar in the mirror for a long time and known there was no way Matteo wouldn't notice it.

Suddenly, she felt sick. What was *wrong* with her, organising a sex date?

Then again, maybe it wasn't a sex date. Maybe Matteo just wanted to share some food and get to know her better. Share more wine, talk more about their lives.

Who was she kidding? It was a sex date.

Oh, popsidoodles.

The front door opened. The light from inside the cabin backlit Matteo's body like a golden halo.

'Lara, please come in,' he said, striding to the car. He stopped in front of her, smiling broadly, holding out his hands for hers, his gaze running down her body. 'You are beautiful.'

'Thank you.' Her heart beat wildly under the dress. She registered his newly ironed cotton shirt and it touched her, thinking of him going to that trouble.

He kissed her on each cheek before resting his forehead against her own. Her stomach flipped with nerves. She closed her eyes and breathed in the scent of him once more. Toothpaste. Laundry powder on his cotton shirt. And something else. Raw sexiness, maybe.

He lifted his head, his eyes dark and liquid. He traced his fingers lightly down her bare arm, sending waves of goosebumps spinning across her skin. Blood drained from her head, gathering force further down.

She giggled. This situation was overwhelming.

'You are nervous,' he whispered.

'No, not at all.' She wanted that to be true.

Then he kissed her, his lovely lips catching hers and holding them there, his beard rubbing against her skin and igniting new sensations. A small moan escaped her throat and his lips smiled against hers. He lifted his head and admired her as if she was the loveliest thing in the world.

'Come inside,' he said, his voice husky.

She followed him, shimmied out of her sandals at the door and left them near his filthy work boots, and crossed the threshold. Inside the cabin, Matteo had lit a dozen candles, which flickered inside glass jars. A bunch of fresh pink flowers overflowed from a pottery vase on the tiny dining table. His bed was made with fresh white sheets.

He scratched the back of his head, suddenly not as confident as he had seemed a moment ago. 'I forgot to make dinner,' he said, heading to the cupboard doors.

'No, please, I don't want dinner, really.' Lara caught his arm and pulled him towards her.

'Wine?' he suggested, but it came with a raised corner of his mouth, a knowing smile. He was just going through the motions.

'No,' she whispered, pulling him even closer, relieved to feel the sharp edge of manic power coursing through her, turning her into someone confident and stunning. She wanted this. She needed it.

He gathered her to him, crushing her against his chest. One hand cupped the back of her neck as he kissed her again, this time harder, hungrier.

She longed for him to take her out of her mind and into her body and bring her to the edge of madness and maybe even just over it, where she could spin in the light and the ecstasy and fly free of her past.

Very gently, he inched her towards the bed. She went with him, her eyes closed, lost to his touch as his lips traced down the side of her neck and along her collarbone. When they reached the mattress, he broke their embrace, smiling, holding onto one of her hands as he flung back the sheets and sat on the edge with her standing in front of him.

Her fingers wound through his soft curls as he kissed her hip, his hands holding the backs of her thighs, slowly raising the hem of her dress.

Her fingers moved to the buttons on his soft shirt and worked them open, unwrapping his torso. Her palms moved over his hot skin.

His lips nibbled their way around her navel.

And then they found her scar. She froze.

He leaned back, dropping her dress, his hands still on her body, and looked into her eyes. She held her breath, waiting for the questions. But he continued to hold her gaze with his.

Before he could speak, she bent and locked her mouth onto his and climbed into his lap, her legs either side of his muscly thighs. She hadn't come here to dredge up her past. She'd come here to feel even more amazing than she already did. She'd come here to cross the final threshold of moving on.

He welcomed her, his hands running up her spine, sending bursts of pleasure over her skin. He murmured words of appreciation in Italian—words she couldn't understand but which filled her with excitement. He was relishing her body.

She ran her hands down his upper arms and helped him free himself totally of his shirt. Those muscles. So perfect. Just muscly enough. Muscles that could just lie back and relax under the sun or could save you from drowning in a river if the need arose.

All the pain of the past six years fell away and she was here, almost naked—and almost with no secrets—starting life all over again.

But suddenly Matteo froze, his arms wrapped around her. He turned his head to the side, his chest rising and falling.

'What is it?' Lara looked down at him in the candlelight as she returned from the stratosphere, the hard edges of reality gouging into her skin. 'What is it?'

'Shh. Do you hear that?'

Lara looked at the walls, as if she'd be able to see through them into the night. 'No,' she said, feeling a mixture of rejection and confusion.

Matteo gently but firmly lifted her body away from his and moved her to the bed so he could sit up properly, leaning forwards, his ear cocked towards the walls.

'What is it?' she asked again, worried now.

Matteo didn't answer but sprang off the bed, at the same time gathering his discarded shirt and deftly slipping his arms into the sleeves. He managed to get a couple of buttons done up before he reached the door and flung it open. Lara searched for her dress, with no clue what was going on.

She found it, fumbling to pull it the right way over her head. Matteo already had his boots on. And now she could hear what Matteo must have heard.

Terrified bleating.

'What's happening?' she asked, following him, struggling to get her sandals laced.

'*Lupi*.'

'*Lupi?* Do you mean wolves?'

But Matteo was already off the small porch and crunching over the ground towards the main *casa*. Lara followed him into the darkness. She'd had no idea Italy even had wolves. One thing she did know was that they were supremely intelligent and first-class hunters.

They must be after the goats.

It was terrible. Those poor animals.

She kept as close to Matteo as she could, not knowing if a wolf might sneak up behind her.

As they reached the *casa*, outdoor lights sprang on, and there were shouts and people moving.

'Domenica!' Matteo shouted, jogging the last few metres to the house. '*E i lupi?*'

Lara, a step behind, was puffing when she stopped in the blinding floodlight.

Domenica, a short, wiry woman with cherry-red hair, answered him in staccato Italian, ignoring Lara, who briefly wondered if she was simply used to seeing Matteo with strange women. Domenica threw open a wooden trunk, the metal catch rattling as the lid hit the stone wall behind it. She reached inside and pulled out a rifle.

Lara gasped.

Domenica handed the rifle to Matteo. Lara wrapped her arms around herself and stepped backwards, further into the dark.

She was awash with horror, simultaneously terrified for the goats' safety, pushing away images of bloodshed and carnage, and also of this thing in Matteo's hand. This weapon. A thing constructed to inflict injury and death, to give power to the person wielding it.

The only thing worse than seeing Matteo holding a long, dark weapon was that he appeared to know his way around it with ease, holding it deftly, moving parts around that made ghastly metal clanking noises, exactly the type she'd heard in movies or on television. She began to shake.

She could hear more shouting now, down at the goat shelters, and urgent bleating from hundreds of goats. She was scared for them, the sweet young goats that had climbed into her lap. She didn't want them hurt. But still, she didn't want the wolves shot down either. Guns . . . they were . . .

Leonard, home after three weeks on the streets, a gun in his hand. Lara thought it was a toy. Tried to smile and say thanks for the gift, even though it was an odd thing to bring a nine-year-old girl. She reached for it.

'Lara! Stop!'

Her mother lurching from the bedroom, everything in slow motion, Leonard swinging to face her, his smile disappearing, his eyes going hard, Eliza's body between Leonard and Lara, her hand on the gun.

Leonard's other elbow jabbing at Eliza's throat. Her mother falling, gasping. Lara screaming, backing away. Sunny running up the stairs from the yard, noise, noise everywhere. A struggle. Lara hiding behind the couch, her hands over her ears. Don't hurt them, don't hurt them.

Matteo and Domenica were oblivious to her distress. They were already jogging down the hill, their rifles at their sides. She knew they needed to protect the goats, yet she still felt terror in her body at the memory of a weapon smashing open a peaceful afternoon. She stood rooted to the ground, both clenched fists at her mouth. Paralysed.

A gunshot cracked open the air and bounced around her skull. She doubled over, her hands over her ears. Another shot. She screamed and held her hands to her ears even harder.

A cacophony of shouts from down the hill.

Lara pulled herself upright, tears sliding down her face, her feet moving towards the car then back towards the *casa*. She threaded her fingers together in front of her while she waited for the others' return. And it seemed she waited an eternity in the dark, her senses on high alert, not knowing what would come next.

Finally, Matteo appeared, walking gingerly around the *casa* and into the light.

'What happened?' She went to him, casting her eyes down at his filthy pants. It looked as if he'd tripped and slid on his knees. She stopped a few metres from him. The rifle hung at his side, the veins in his arm engorged. He looked stricken at whatever he'd seen or done.

'What happened?' she asked again. And then, more gently, 'Are you okay?'

'F-f-fine,' he said.

She took a breath; he'd stuttered, and she'd noticed. Her stifled sob was still audible. 'Did you . . . find a wolf?' she whispered.

He looked her straight in the eye. '*Sì. Due lupi.*'

Two wolves. Two shots.

'Did you kill them?'

'No.'

'But you would have,' she said.

'If I h-h-had to.' The gun was still in his hand. She couldn't take her eyes off it.

'I think I'm going to be sick,' she said, not long ago feeling nothing but passion and adoration, and now feeling nothing but horror.

'Lara, they had already attacked three g-g-goats. We'll have to put them out of their misery.' His face twisted. He stepped towards her, metal still glinting at his side. She recoiled.

'Get that away from me!'

Matteo halted, as if she was a frightened animal.

'I have to go.'

There was another shot in the distance. Lara yelped and jumped, then spun on her heel.

'Wait,' he called, as she strode up the hill.

Another shot.

'Lara, please wait.'

And another shot. A sob erupted from Lara's chest. But by then, she was climbing into the Alfa Romeo and starting the engine, not allowing herself to look back.

28

Lara and Dave

Lara was twenty-six years old.

Dave suspected first.

He brought home a test kit and presented it to her late one night while she was in bed reading.

'What's this?' she asked, confused and on edge. There was a hardness to his eyes she knew well and her fear spiked.

'Are you pregnant?'

'What?'

'You're late.'

She frowned. 'Maybe a couple of days.'

He reached out and squeezed her left breast.

'Ow! What are you doing?' She shoved his hand away.

'Tender,' he said, as if delivering his foregone conclusion.

He made her take the test while he waited downstairs for her. He was pacing when she arrived. He held out his hand for the test strip to see it for himself.

She handed it to him like a guilty child, and pulled the sleeves of her jumper down over her hands and tucked them under her armpits. She was pregnant and in shock and feeling a whirlpool of emotions, from hope and joy through to dread and shame. She stared at the floor, waiting for him to say something.

At last he stopped pacing and took a deep breath. 'Lara, please come and sit,' he said, and his voice was quiet and soothing. They went to the wooden dining table with the hard, uncomfortable chairs.

She sat as directed. He continued to stand. The overhead light was a little behind him, casting his face in shadow.

'You have to have an abortion.' His tone was flat, calm and authoritative, the same manner in which she imagined he might one day deliver bad news to a patient. No room for discussion. Yet the impact of his words on her was like running at force into a brick wall.

'What?'

'Lara, you've been on medication for a long time and it has a high chance of affecting the foetus.'

'But it might be okay,' she said, shoving her hands underneath her legs, her shoulders hunched. What he didn't know was that she'd stopped taking her mood stabilisers months ago because she couldn't cope with the drowsiness and nausea. She couldn't see straight and had felt herself forgetting what the world looked like without them.

She'd developed a sneaky method of pretending to take them when he handed them to her each morning, tucking them up between her back teeth and cheek until he'd gone, when she would spit out the pills and wash them down the bathroom sink. Maybe one or two of the tiny contraception pills had been accidentally washed away too.

The mood stabilisers were the dangerous ones for pregnancy. She and Constance had talked about it during one of their sessions about possible futures. It was a long time ago now. Dave wasn't a fan of Constance; he said she gave Lara false hope. But back then, Constance had made it clear that having bipolar didn't mean she couldn't one day be a good mother. When the time came, she said, they would have to look carefully at her medications. Lara knew a little bit about which ones were safer for pregnancy. She'd have to check with Constance, of course, but it might still be okay.

'And you have an illness,' the medical voice went on.

'Yes, but . . .'

'You aren't capable of raising a baby.'

His words punched her. She looked up at him, the shadows moving across his face as he walked around the table and came to sit beside her. She didn't even know if *she* wanted a baby. But shouldn't they at least be talking about it?

'Lara, I work and study eighty hours a week. I can't be here to help you the way you would need. And then there's the high probability that you would pass on this very serious, debilitating illness to the child.'

She was defective. Shouldn't be bred from.

'Can we slow this down a little?' she asked, her hands under her legs going numb now, distracting her from the pain Dave's words had just injected into her heart with surgical precision. 'You've always said you wanted children—one day, I know, in the future when your career is settled. But maybe this is it? You're doing well now, nearly finished your med degree . . .'

'I don't want this baby,' he said, sounding disgusted.

The room spun. Her heartrate increased. 'Because . . . ?'

He looked at her pityingly and pulled the hand nearest him from under her thigh and held it, stroking it like a cat. 'Because it's yours.' He sighed regretfully and discarded her hand.

Lara struggled for breath. 'I don't understand.'

'I don't want a baby of yours,' he said again, slowly, as if explaining to a child.

Mocking her.

He was never going to marry her. He'd never intended to. He'd been playing her this whole time.

'I think I'm going to be sick,' she mumbled.

'You need to have an abortion,' he said again, back to his soothing, trustworthy doctor's voice. 'It's the best thing you can do for yourself. You'll never handle the huge hormonal surges that make even the sanest woman struggle.'

Sunny. The sanest woman she knew would be Sunny.

'You'd have to go off all your medications, medications that might have already deformed the baby's heart, spine or brain.'

'Stop saying that.' She clutched at the edge of the table as the world began to sway.

'And even then it might not survive. Then you'll have the trauma of miscarriage and maybe surgery, and you and I both know you couldn't handle that. And even if the foetus is okay and you somehow make it to term without falling into a pregnancy-induced psychosis and having to be hospitalised, you'd still have the postnatal depression and all of that before you got to be a real mother.'

A real mother.

Dave folded his hands neatly on the table, the overhead light now making his cheeks hollow out and the greying hairs over his ears take on a yellow glow.

Lara gave up trying to talk. He'd out-argue her at every turn.

Besides which, he was right. All discussion of medication aside, she wasn't fit to be a mother. Dave was the person who knew her best, and if he was telling her she was delusional to even consider keeping this baby then she was sure he was right.

'And then there is the child to consider,' he went on.

Please stop. Her body had frozen rigid while her insides were slippery with movement.

'*If* the child survived, and *if* by an absolute miracle it wasn't harmed by the medications you've been on, it would have a mother who was completely dysfunctional and unhinged. Devastatingly for all concerned, it would probably grow up to be your carer.'

She vomited then, right into her lap, trying to catch it with her hands. She stared at the mess, her nose pinching and her throat burning.

Dave flinched and moved his chair away. 'And then of course the great tragedy would be that it might be just like you.'

Tears slid down Lara's face.

She'd never realised how truly fucked up she was.

She'd never truly let herself think about what a burden she could be in the future.

Dave got up and went to the kitchen, where he rummaged through cupboards and turned on the tap. He returned with a wet tea towel and handed it to her. She dabbed weakly at herself.

'Thank you,' she managed to squeak between the sobbing.

He sat beside her and rubbed her back. 'Lara, honey, you see? You see what a mess you are? I hate seeing you this way. It hurts me so much that I can't be a better partner for you. It hurts me that I can't heal you.' He dropped his head, his fists balled to his forehead. 'I should be able to fix you.'

'What?' She was shocked into silence.

'I'm a psychologist and almost a medical practitioner but still I can't help you. You are so filled with pain,' he said. 'I don't want to see you like this. It hurts too much.' He beat his chest with his fist.

'Stop,' she said, catching his wrist.

'I need you to have an abortion,' he said, his words grinding out through his teeth. 'I can't stand the thought of watching what it will do to you. If you won't do it to save yourself or the child then please, do it for me.'

'Okay, okay,' she whispered, just needing it all to stop. 'I'll do it for you.'

Dave made her an appointment to request the abortion pill for two days later. But when the time came, she was still curled up crying in bed, where she'd been ever since she found out about the pregnancy. Dave came to sit in the heavy chair near the bed, one he'd put there because he said he spent so much time at her bedside he may as well be comfortable, and placed his leather-bound book on the bedside table.

'I can't do it,' Lara sobbed. 'I know I can't keep it, but I can't do it either.'

He'd been listening to her for two days, and for two days his voice had drilled into her, reminding her why she couldn't keep it, reminding her she couldn't cope, that she was defective and no one would want her for a mother, and this episode she was having, right now, was further proof of that.

'I can't go,' she pleaded, reaching for his hand.

'I know,' he said. 'It's an impossible situation, isn't it?'

'Yes,' she said, relieved he finally understood.

He nodded slowly. 'So because I love you so much and because I want so much for you to be out of this pain, I've come up with another solution.'

Lara gulped. 'You have?' She pulled herself up to sitting, leaning against the headboard.

'My love for you is so great that I would sacrifice my own happiness for yours.' He paused and shoved his hand into the pocket of his taupe pants, then brought out a medicine bottle.

'What are these?' She wiped her nose on her sleeve.

'These are a ticket to freedom, to a place of no more pain for you or the baby.'

She reached for the pills. A whole bottle.

'I want to help you. I can't stand seeing you in this much pain.'

'I'm sorry.' She began to cry again, clutching the bottle to her chest.

'It's okay. It can all be over now for everyone. We will all be better off.' He stood and went to the wardrobe and opened the doors. Up on the shelf above the rack was a large mound of cream coils. He pointed to it. 'Rope. I thought I might take up sailing.'

Rope.

He was giving her options. Not to live, mind you. Just options on how she died. But she could see it, the welcoming abyss. Finally, she'd be free of this pain. She wouldn't have to make the awful choice to terminate this baby. She and the baby could both just drift off together.

'But won't you miss me?' she whispered.

'Yes. But my love for you is greater than any concern for myself. Please, honey, let it all go. Escape this illness that is ruining your life. Let all this suffering end and finally find the peace you've been looking for.'

She did want it. She wanted peace, to be free of this pain and free of the torture of her mind and free of fear.

The rope was too difficult. But the bottle of pills in her hand? All too easy.

Dave stood and kissed her on the forehead and picked up his book. 'Goodbye,' he said firmly, and there was no question in her mind that he wanted her gone. He left the room, leaving her to make her choice.

29

Sunny

'Mum! There's someone at the door.'

Daisy's voice rang out through the living room and into the kitchen where Sunny and Eliza had been discussing Sunny's job offer.

'I can't go,' Sunny said, stretching her arm out to the side. She'd been doing so much sanding of her furniture pieces that she had developed a bit of tendon strain in her shoulder.

'What terrible timing,' Eliza said.

'Is it, though? I wondered if it might actually be a sign, since—you know.'

Eliza grimaced. 'Yes.'

The vision of a blue car lurking outside on the street hovered before them both, Sunny was sure.

'Mu-u-um! A man's at the door,' Daisy repeated, thundering to Sunny's side and tugging at her arm.

Sunny allowed Daisy to take her hand and pull her through the lounge room, towards the front door. What she saw there made her stop in her tracks, with a bolt of adrenaline so strong her hands flew up defensively. She'd thought the door was locked, but there he stood, with nothing between him and her child.

'What the hell are you doing here?' Sunny instinctively pulled Daisy to her, her hand firm on the little girl's shoulder, pressing her slender body into her hip. Daisy must have sensed Sunny's alarm and went quiet, wrapping her arms around her mother's waist.

He said nothing, but his gaze homed in on Daisy. During the ensuing silence, Eliza followed Sunny into the living room.

'Who is it?' Then, just like Sunny, she stopped dead. 'Oh, my God.'

It had been a wet weekend a couple of months ago that started it all. The kids were climbing the walls by half-past nine on Saturday morning, and by Sunday the three women in the Foxleigh household held serious concerns for their own safety, let alone the twins'.

'They're at such a tricky age,' Eliza had offered sagely. 'Too young to concentrate on a single activity and still needing to move their bodies so much.'

'The movies?' Lara suggested, vigorously playing balloon volleyball over a net formed by a string of washing hanging between two dining chairs. Sunny was impressed by just how hot and worked up Lara and the kids were getting over a 'ball' that could only drift through the air.

'Daisy's a chance, but not our other little friend here,' Sunny said, motioning towards Hudson. She'd never managed to get more than twenty minutes out of him in the cinema—roughly the amount of time it took him to finish the popcorn.

Sunny had a terrible headache, ruling out the art gallery and the museum as just too much effort and the indoor playground as way too noisy, so they'd given up and chosen the significantly easier option of taking the kids to the local shopping centre.

'Right, twenty bucks to spend in Big W, sushi rolls, a play in the food court playground, and an ice cream on the way out if you're good,' she'd announced.

Both kids yelled and squealed their excitement, which made Sunny wince in pain.

'Poor Sunny Bear,' Lara said. 'Maybe a good strong coffee from a real barista would help.'

'My coffee machine is perfectly good,' Eliza huffed. 'It's exactly the same as you'd find in a cafe.'

'I'll take my chances in the cafe,' Sunny muttered. She noticed her sister's lips twitch, but dared not make eye contact in case they started laughing and offended Eliza further.

And it was at the sushi counter in the food court, ordering teriyaki chicken nori rolls, that they ran into *him*.

Lara had noticed him first. She dropped her plastic takeaway box on the ground and didn't even try to pick it up.

'What's the matter?' Sunny had asked. Then she followed Lara's eyes all the way to his, about ten metres away. He'd registered them too, his jaw set, his eyes sweeping between Lara and Sunny. A woman in a red cardigan chatted to him about something and ran a hand through her jaw-length black bob. Sunny caught sight of her wedding ring. So he had a wife now. A grocery bag swung from the woman's elbow. She hadn't yet registered Dave's faltering step beside her.

Dave's mother—gosh, she'd aged—was walking alongside them, wide-eyed and smiling as if she was heavily affected by some mood-altering medication, her arms out in front of her like a zombie. Sunny took in Susan's trackpants and ill-fitting jumper with a lightning-fast glance, but her gaze was drawn back to Dave's face. To those almond-shaped eyes and that thick dark hair. Her heart banged just once, like a horse kicking a stable wall. *Boom*.

'Oh, my David!' Susan was saying, now only a few metres away, hovering over the kids. Dave regained his cool and hurried forward to catch her elbow. His wife followed him.

'Mum, I'm here,' he said, playing his role perfectly.

Dutiful son, my arse, Sunny seethed. Behind her, she heard Lara whimper. The wife placed her hand on Susan's back and spoke soothingly to her.

'Hello,' Daisy said to Susan. 'I'm Daisy. I'm five and I've got sushi.' Sunny's innocent, charming daughter held up a sushi roll. Somewhere in the back of her mind, Sunny realised she must be eating one from off the floor, but that was the last thing she could worry about right now.

'David, come here,' Susan crooned, bending low and reaching forward.

As though in a slow-motion horror movie, the other four adults followed Susan's gaze down to where Hudson—with his almond-shaped eyes and that thick dark hair—was pushing his new Minion car along the ground.

'It's been so long since I've seen you,' Susan said, her eyes filling with tears.

Hudson jerked away from her and got to his feet, running off to the playground.

'Wait for me,' Daisy called through a mouthful of sushi, and took off after him, and for once Sunny was pleased at their impulsiveness.

'Oh, come back,' Susan called, her face crumpling, her voice choked. 'Why is he running away? My baby. I haven't seen him in so long.'

Dave's wife's eyes flicked between them all, caught Lara's for a moment, then looked away. Dave, clearly thrown, patted his mother's arm. 'Shh, Mum, it's okay. I'm here. I'm Dave. *I'm* your son.' Despite what a horrible bastard Dave had been, Sunny still found in herself a sliver of pity for him. Imagine your own mother not recognising you.

Then his gaze snapped back to Lara. She flinched and turned away, but he stared openly at her, taking in everything about her, his lips twitching, as if unsure whether to smile or speak.

Sunny stepped closer to her sister. It wouldn't take Dave long to gather his wits and approach her. 'Right, well, we need to go. Goodbye, Susan,' she said, taking Lara by the arm and walking straight past Dave and his wife without a backward glance, though she could feel his razor-sharp glare piercing into her.

'Don't look back,' she ordered Lara. 'Let's get the kids and leave by the side exit and keep going.'

'He mustn't know. He mustn't know. He mustn't know.' Lara was losing her composure by the second.

Standing in the doorway, Dave lifted his eyes from Daisy and let them rest on Sunny. Something changed in his face and he switched to charming mode. 'Hello, Sunny, hello, Eliza. It's nice to see you both again.'

'We can't say the same,' Sunny said. Beside her, Eliza stiffened.

Dave's face twitched, his countenance ruffled.

Sunny's mind raced. Where was Hudson? She'd seen him just a few moments ago, downstairs in the yard on the swing set, Midnight under his arm, her little ears blowing back and forth with the pendulum movement. He loved that dog fiercely.

'What a surprise it was to run into you at the shops the other weekend.' His gaze had fallen back to Daisy, tucked into Sunny's side. He rubbed one palm over the other in a circle—nervous perhaps? No. Calculating, more likely. Sunny took in his trousers with the perfect crease down the centre, his shiny shoes, his shiny belt and collared shirt. He always looked so polished, so goddamn upstanding. Bile rose in her throat. Fear was flickering, but she refused to let it ignite. She straightened her shoulders.

Dave could have crossed the entrance at any time, but he stayed where he was, as if trapped by glass, his welcome to the house revoked a long time ago. Beyond him, out on the road, cyclists and dog walkers passed by, as if this was a totally normal day.

Hudson was the one who looked like a miniature Dave. It was the thought of Hudson that made her chest constrict.

Her children were not really hers.

This man could destroy everything.

'What do you want?' she demanded.

Dave lifted his head so he could look down his nose at Sunny. 'Let's get to the point,' he said, pacing a little on the porch, still rubbing his palms together, like a lawyer getting ready to deliver his speech to a court. Sunny was pleased to see him stumble against the tiny pots of pink and white dianthus flowers that she and the kids had planted a couple of days ago. He recovered himself quickly. 'My mother, as you observed, is suffering from dementia.'

A play for sympathy.

'She was adamant that Hudson was her son, David. That is, *me*.'

Cold water ran down Sunny's spine and made her shiver. Dave had used Hudson's name. But they hadn't said his name in the shopping centre. How did he know?

'I did some maths. Your daughter—' he paused to give Sunny an amused smile, '—told us she was five.'

'What's your point?' Sunny asked, almost unable to bear where this was going. They were *her* children. Hers. Not his. Not even Lara's. *Hers*.

'Alright.' He stopped pacing and stood squarely facing them. 'I believe the two children I met at the shopping centre are mine.'

Sunny laughed, loud, empty and cutting. 'You're crazy. Of course they're not yours.'

Daisy, clinging to her leg, whispered, 'Who is that man?'

'Come with me,' Eliza said, taking Daisy's hand and leading her away.

'Thanks,' Sunny said, eyeballing her mother as they passed, each of them silently panicking.

With Daisy gone, Sunny could think a little more clearly. 'Look, Dave, your mother is obviously in a terrible state. That's a great shame. It must be painful for you when she doesn't even recognise you.' Shamefully, she did actually enjoy saying that.

Dave was standing with his hands on his hips. Her eyes flicked to the gold wedding band on his left hand. *That poor woman.*

'But Susan was wrong. And you're wrong. Daisy and Hudson are my children. I'm very sorry about your mother's dementia, but you're both barking up the wrong tree.'

Dave said nothing, appraising her, then looked behind her into the house, taking in details, assessing, perhaps searching for evidence. She felt his gaze roaming over their home as though his hands were on her body. It was repulsive.

'It's time for you to go now,' she said, moving closer to the front door.

'Where is Lara?'

'No idea.'

He narrowed his eyes.

'I'm sure you'll understand that you're not welcome here, given how things ended between the two of you.' She gave him the steeliest stare she could muster over the pounding of her heart and reached across the threshold for the handle of the screen door.

'Goodbye, Dave.'

He moved back reluctantly and she closed the screen door, but he continued to stand on the porch while she locked it with the key. Then she shut the heavy wooden door from inside and turned the deadlock. She leaned against it for support, her ears thundering with her own blood, listening for him to go.

She heard him knock over one of the children's plant pots; she heard the terracotta smash, and his footsteps as he walked away. Then she watched through the corner of the window as he got into the blue car she'd seen idling outside their house the other day and drove away.

Sunny unlocked the doors and stepped outside to rescue the dianthus plants that he'd kicked down the steps, cradling them to her chest. 'It will be alright,' she whispered. 'It will be alright.'

30

Lara

Lara started the morning in the goat barn, feeding Meg and Willow double the amount of hay they normally got, brushing them tenderly, trying not to let her tears fall into the milk pail as she imagined the terror these two might face if a pack of wolves descended onto the property. They would kick as hard as they could and use their mighty horns. But a wolf was a top-level predator, and a goat—as fierce and determined as she might be—was simply a meal. Not that it was the wolf's fault. It had to eat to live. Everything deserved to live, didn't it? And as for Matteo, he was a goat handler; his loyalty lay with his goats. His *duty*, in fact, was to protect his goats. What choice did he have?

And yet.

Seeing Matteo handling a gun had awoken a memory she hadn't even realised she'd smothered. Over the past six years, she'd had to work through so much after what Dave had done to her that the childhood traumas with Leonard had paled in comparison. But . . . guns.

There was nothing good about them. Nothing gentle or safe. She'd thought Matteo was a gentle man of the land, but he was prepared to kill. If he could kill an animal, then . . .

Lara scratched at her wrist till she bled, finding some release in the pain. She'd been so stupid to think she could force herself into a better place, to force things between her and Matteo. She grieved for herself right now, for the loss of a relationship—whatever it might have been—that never even had a chance. Because how could she ever look at Matteo the same way again? The image of him last night, holding the gun, lifting it, cocking it, carrying it with purpose, made her sick to her stomach.

The weather had changed today, as if knowing that a horrible event had happened and Lara would need extra layers around herself for comfort. She wondered if this was it, then: summer finally gone and autumn here, perhaps a sign that other things were ending too. Her time here, maybe. Samuel was much stronger than when she'd first met him. He still needed help but maybe Matteo and Henrik could fill the need until a new *badante* arrived. Perhaps she should go back to Rome and start again.

31

Samuel

Samuel had lain a long time in bed reading while Lara had been cooking in the kitchen. He'd smelled the frying onion and garlic, heard the chopping of vegetables and the bang of the soup pot lid. He'd taken his time getting up, feeling weary for no reason that he could pinpoint other than age. But at last he'd forced himself into action.

The temperature had dropped today, the bathroom tiles cold under his feet, and he'd pulled out his good slippers. They'd been a lucky find at the piazza markets a couple of years ago, stylish, in a buffed charcoal grey. Assunta would have hated them and teased him for being such an old man. If it were up to her, she'd have had him in something outrageous with bloody bells or tassels. But he liked these ones; they made him feel smart when he had his feet up on the footrest in front of the fireplace. He liked looking down at them, liked the way the skin around his ankles was still smooth, if a little blotchy.

He couldn't remember the last time he'd been to the markets unattended. He'd been sharing his space with *badanti* for such a long time, and had grown to need their help to get out and about more than he'd ever imagined. You could never predict what you'd go through as an old person, what you had to do simply to keep living from day to day. If you were lucky, you had someone who loved you to look after you. Like Rocco had.

Rocco had been old when they'd got him, which made him perfect for the kids. He was unflappable, safe, slow and steady. Exactly what you wanted in a first pony for your children. But as happens to ponies, his children grew up. And then Lily was gone. Samuel and Assunta argued about what to do with Rocco, Assunta insisting he was too old to sell and Samuel saying it was a waste of money to keep a pony no one was using. If they couldn't find him another home, they should call the slaughterman to come and take him away. But Assunta refused, more than once literally putting her foot down in a stomping rejection. She was fiercely protective of Rocco and said he deserved to live out his days with his family. He was a living link to their beloved daughter. By pouring love into Rocco—carrying food and water to him when he couldn't walk easily—Assunta could keep loving Lily.

That was what Samuel wanted, deep down, for himself. Assunta by his side, caring for him till the end. But Assunta was gone. So if not Assunta, then who? His daughter Giovanna? Perhaps, if things had worked out differently.

He walked into the dining room where Lara was seated at the table, her head resting on her forearms. A plate of orange blossom amaretti sat in the centre of the table, golden and fragrant. Lara must have been cooking up a storm while he'd been reading. She looked up as he approached, surprise on her face. The sight of her wet, red eyes snapped him out of his reverie.

'I didn't hear you come in,' she snuffled, wiping at her eyes with the heels of her hands.

'Sorry, I couldn't resist the aromas from the kitchen. Is it soup?'

'It's my version of a Tuscan white bean soup,' she said quietly, then bit her quivering bottom lip.

'Are you alright?' he asked, without a clue what to do.

She nodded, staring at him a bit too hard, her eyes fixed a bit too wide. Suddenly, Samuel was a father again of daughters—Italian daughters at that—who cried and screamed at the drop of a hat, whose emotions were only ever just under the surface at any time. Back then, he'd learned not to try to solve the problem right away. Later, maybe, over a coffee or a *vino*. But while there were tears he'd found the fewer words the better. He always said the wrong thing anyway, especially with Giovanna, and her tears would turn to rage as she declared that he never understood her. If the house hadn't been made of stone, he'd have worried for the walls from all the door-slamming.

Giovanna was probably right; he hadn't understood her and hadn't really tried to. He'd been a stern father, if he was honest, and hadn't paid half as much attention to his children as he now wished he had. His relationships with them had always been strained, and sometimes he wondered if Giovanna and Gaetano had stayed in London simply to avoid him. Back when they were growing up, times were different. Men worked; women took care of the children. But he'd missed out on so much. He knew that now.

Samuel looked to the floor and scratched behind his ear, sighing with the memory.

'Last night, I visited Matteo,' Lara began, sniffing disconcertingly. She paused and searched her pockets, for a tissue, he assumed; when she couldn't find one, she wiped her forearm across her nose. Samuel winced and swapped the walking stick to his left hand, holding it loosely through the mouldable splint, and reached into the pocket of his trackpants for a handkerchief. He always had one. Years ago they would have all been ironed, but now he let a few things slide. He swapped the walking stick back to his right hand so he could rest his weight on it, and stepped towards Lara, extending his clean blue hanky. She hesitated, but then reached over and took it.

'Thanks.' She blew her nose, noisily, then balled up the material in her fist.

Samuel hovered uncertainly for a moment, wondering if he should sit at the table with her. It wasn't easy for him to stand still in one spot; it was easier to keep moving forward. But he didn't want to put pressure on her, either. Finally, as her eyes welled again, he pulled out a chair and sat.

Lara slumped back in the chair, defeated by the tears that just wanted to flow.

'There were wolves,' she said, her voice small and pinched on the last word.

Samuel stiffened. 'Wolves?'

She nodded, blowing her nose again. 'They came for the goats.'

Samuel's stomach plummeted. He turned his head towards the window in the direction of Meg and Willow's barn, even though he couldn't see them. He immediately began thinking of ways to improve the security of their housing. He'd need help. He couldn't wield a hammer anymore. Once upon a time, Carlo would have come and done it with him. Now, he'd need Matteo. Or, if Matteo couldn't help, then Henrik. He could pay Henrik. He had a little money set aside for home maintenance. He was old enough to remember the destruction wolves caused to livestock, back before the widescale trapping.

'They tried to shoot them,' Lara squeaked, dissolving into sobs.

'Of course they did; they had to protect the goats,' he said gruffly.

Lara gave him the look, the same look Giovanna would have given him. He'd misinterpreted her feelings. He rubbed his forehead. She'd shut down now, holding back her tears and folding her arms across her body, looking to the other side of the room, her chin lifted.

He tried again. 'Look, people here in Italy, they are very much at one with the land. People still raise their own animals, tend to them from birth through to death and the dinner table. They work with the seasons and hunt for boar, pheasants and rabbits. Food is their way of life. Men are part of the ecosystem and, like it or not, sometimes other predators get in the way.'

Lara was looking at him as if he was deliberately trying to cause her more pain.

'It's harsh, but that's the reality of farming,' he said, trying to be reasonable. 'They can't let their stock be taken.'

'But Matteo.' She shook her head. 'I thought he was different.'

'He has a job to do, and that's to protect his stock. End of story.'

But reason wasn't what she wanted to hear. Her breath shuddered as she pushed herself to her feet. 'I'm sorry, Samuel, but this isn't the place for me. I'm going back to Rome.' Then she rushed from the room.

32

Sunny

Sunny stared at the text message on her phone, cold dread in the pit of her stomach.

She was at one of the local parks, with Hudson scaling the house-sized spider net that enticed boys to climb higher than their mothers felt comfortable with, while Daisy, never one for climbing had given up at the third level of ropes. Instead, she was throwing sticks for Midnight and the puppy galumphed after them on her short little legs, a cluster of children and adults alike *ooh*ing and *ahh*ing. Technically, Midnight wasn't allowed here, inside the childproof fence that surrounded the brightly coloured climbing equipment and sensitive urban stone-scaping and green foliage. But a little of the old rebellious Sunny remained.

Sundays were always a busy day at this park, with its undercover tables and free barbecues on offer for family gatherings. But as it was late in the day, nearing dinnertime for young children, the crowds were thinning, birthday balloons and bunting being taken down and picnic rugs and tablecloths being shaken and rolled up.

Sunny probably looked no different from many other parents, sitting on a park bench and keeping one eye on her children while she scrolled through social media, occasionally taking a photo of her kids. But what those other parents didn't know was that her world had just been shattered by four words from Dave. A day after she'd told him to go away, here he was, popping up on her phone, paralysing her like in one of those nightmares where she was being pursued by a madman, a monster or a gigantic snake, but no matter how hard she tried to run, her legs just wouldn't move.

Somehow, Lara had kept the secret of Dave's violence throughout their years together. It was only at the end, when the pregnancy had changed everything, that she'd been forced to flee and confess to Eliza and Sunny the true darkness under which she'd been living. Even then, it took years of therapy for it all to come out. None of them wanted to see the kids end up in Dave's hands now.

The day after they'd run into Dave at the shopping centre, the Foxleighs had wanted to clarify their legal position. Sunny would financially qualify for legal aid—having no assets and no regular income—but it would take too long to get the forms in and be granted an appointment. Lara had a bit of money saved from her part-time job, so she'd paid for an appointment with a family lawyer.

Martha Beckett wore a white kaftan dress and her braided hair was pulled back into a ponytail, little beads at the ends clacking together as she moved about. Behind the navy-blue rims of her glasses, her eyes held decades of experience and empathy.

'I'm sorry to hear of your situation,' she said to the trio of women, her voice husky. 'And I'm equally sorry to tell you that the family law court system in Australia is beyond broken and cannot help you.'

Sunny felt sick. To her right, Lara had begun to take deep breaths in an effort to calm down. Eliza had been scribbling notes with her favourite silver pen, but paused as Martha delivered her sombre assessment.

'Look, I'm not going to beat around the bush. You don't have many options. The family law system is, ironically, set up to support parenting arrangements rather than safety from violence. I've seen many a woman's life ruined because she sold her house, lost her job because she had to take time off for court, and spent every last dollar she had trying to defend herself and protect her kids. And even if she did get what she wanted—full custody and protection for her kids—her partner simply waited until she was back on her feet to drag her through the courts all over again, financially ruining her, ruining her health with stress, forcing her into the same room with him to relive the horror again and again, and continuing to terrorise her perfectly legally through this system.' Martha stood up and moved to the corner of the room to boil the kettle, clattering cups onto saucers and pulling teabags from a canister.

'But Dave is violent,' Eliza said, her voice barely audible.

Martha grunted. 'A woman in Australia is more likely to be killed in her own home and at the hands of her partner than anywhere else and by anyone else.' Her tone conveyed that she had sadly repeated this statistic many times.

'He nearly . . . he tried to get Lara to kill herself,' Eliza said.

Martha raised a thick eyebrow. 'The perfect crime—and not uncommon, I'm sorry to say.' That rendered them silent, while Martha continued to fuss at her kitchenette.

Lara began to scratch at her wrist. Sunny reached her hand over and laid it on her sister's, giving her a small, sympathetic smile. Lara tipped her head back, staring at the ceiling.

'We lied on the birth certificates,' Sunny blurted. 'I'm listed as the mother.' Beside her, Eliza stiffened. She'd always been against the idea but they'd done it that way to add another layer of protection between the kids and Dave.

Martha eyed her steadily, then said, 'There are two things you need to know about that. The first is that if Dave initiates paternity testing, the birth certificates won't play any part in determining who the parents are.'

'Really?'

'Really,' Martha affirmed. 'Secondly, if this goes to court, I would have to disclose that I knew that fact. Fortunately, I am not officially representing you here today. Still, I think it's best if we don't talk about that particular situation any further.'

'Okay.' Sunny's whole body turned white hot just imagining how much trouble they'd be in if their fraud came into play. 'What can we do about Dave now?' she asked at last.

'He does have the right to seek paternity tests through the courts, but that will take him some time, which is a good thing—perhaps the only thing you have going for you. He would have to file an initiating application for paternity testing, along with an affidavit and his intentions to spend time with the children. Then he would have to wait for a court date, which could take a few months.'

'Are you saying we shouldn't do anything?' Lara asked, biting a nail.

'At this stage I would simply like to make it clear that if you officially enter into the system, things will get rough. Aside from anything else, you can burn through a hundred thousand dollars just like that.' Martha snapped her fingers. 'The most frustrating thing of all is that, given Lara's medical history, the courts wouldn't look favourably on her as a mother if parenting arrangements were to be contested.'

'But that's ridiculous,' Sunny said, still hoping there was some sort of reason in this madness. 'He took advantage of her sickness and made her worse. Sorry, Lara.'

'It's okay. It's true.'

'And now he's a doctor,' Martha said sadly. 'And probably, on paper, a fine upstanding citizen with a lovely wife. And Sunny, I'm sorry to say you won't have much sway as the acting mother in this either. Staying out of the system as long as you can will actually keep your kids safer.'

'But that's mad. I don't understand,' Eliza said, sitting forward in her chair. Her pen hung loosely in her fingers. 'Lara has seen a psychiatrist for years. There would be reams of documentation about the things Dave did to her.'

Martha grimaced. 'Regrettably, it doesn't always help. His lawyers would argue that since Dave has no history of violence with the children then there would be no cause to keep them from him. If he was to be proved the father then I suspect his application for access would be granted.'

All three of the Foxleighs reacted audibly to that. Eliza reached for Sunny's hand.

'And if visitation rights were granted, you would have to send the kids to him, regardless of whether or not they wanted to go or whether or not you thought they'd be safe in his hands. And if you didn't, if you went against the court orders, you would potentially lose custody.'

'Wait,' Sunny said, aghast. 'The kids would become a test case to see if he hurt them or not? And the courts wouldn't protect them until *after* he'd hurt them? That's ludicrous!'

Sunny could hardly believe it had come to this so quickly. If only they'd gone to the movies yesterday instead of the shopping centre, none of this would be happening. The picture Martha had presented of the lack of support for women who wanted to protect their children was bad enough, but their situation was even worse, really, given that Sunny had no history with Dave to warrant demanding an apprehended violence order and no biological claim for parenting arrangements.

'I am sorry,' Martha said again. 'This part of my job brings me no pleasure, I assure you. I would say, though, that sometimes men like this get most of their thrills from the chase and from the psychological torment they inflict. Right now, Dave believes Lara is the mother, so he'll be coming for her. But for him to proceed through the courts, he will have to have served you with papers outlining his intentions for establishing proof of paternity. If he can't find you, then he can't easily ensnare you in a legal tangle. I would suggest then that if you are not easily found . . .' she paused and looked at them meaningfully, '. . . there is a small chance that he may simply tire of any games he might want to play. While there are no court orders in place, you are free to go wherever you want to.' She looked at Lara. 'Anywhere in the world.'

Sunny looked at Lara, who was so pale she was worried she might faint. 'What about the children? Should they leave the country too?'

'If you can afford it, I would certainly recommend it.'

Beside Sunny, Lara's eyes welled up. They both knew they couldn't afford for all of them to go. And the kids couldn't go without Sunny because Sunny was their mother. But they could make it difficult for Dave, by sending Lara overseas.

'If I were you, I know what I would do.' Martha delivered their cups of tea on a tray with milk and sugar and Iced VoVos. Sunny thought it was exactly what would be handed to someone in shock, then realised with a jolt that that described *her*.

After a few minutes of stunned, silent tea-stirring, Martha spoke again.

'I've come to the conclusion that when you're dealing with these guys, sometimes you're better off tackling the situation on a psychological level rather than a legal one. The problem is, though, you'd have to get close enough to him to have a chance at working that out. So truly, if I were in this situation, I would simply get as far away as I could go, preferably to the other side of the world.'

ꕥ

Hudson called out from the top of the climbing apparatus and Sunny waved and smiled. 'Great job!' she called. She held her smile until he looked away and began his descent.

Then she reread Dave's text.

I have custody rights.

33

Lara

'Hi, Sprout.'

'I'm so glad you finally answered,' Lara said, sorting her clothes into two piles, one to wash and one to pack. 'I'm not in a good state,' she admitted, climbing into her bed and leaning against the bedhead, pulling her knees up.

'What's happened?'

'How are the kids?'

'They're good. They're asleep. I wore them out at the park this afternoon,' Sunny said, her gentle smile floating down the line.

'Oh, of course. I'd forgotten what time it was. I was hoping to speak to them, to Daisy at least, though I'm missing Hudson's bear hugs.' Hudson wasn't a big hugger, but when he did, he did it well.

'What's happened?' Sunny asked again.

Lara told her about Matteo and the wolves, about her upward mood swing and how she'd let it carry her away, thinking she had found someone lovely, and thinking she could just sleep with him and fix something in herself that had been broken so long ago. Sunny clucked sympathetically.

'I think I should leave, maybe go back to Rome,' Lara finished. 'I'm sorting out my washing now. It shouldn't take me long to pack.'

'No,' Sunny said firmly. 'I don't think that's a good idea.'

'Why not?' Lara asked, a tad annoyed. She heard Sunny open the fridge door. It had a small magnetic cow bell on it, put there to alert them if one of the kids was breaking into the fridge unattended. Too many milk and juice spills had driven them to that.

'Um . . .' Sunny paused. 'Hang on, I'm just pouring a wine.'

'It's late for a wine.'

'I've had a big few days,' Sunny said, and Lara could hear the heaviness in her voice.

'Are you still working on that project for the bed and breakfast?'

'Yeah.' Sunny poured the wine; Lara could hear the *glug glug* as it filled the glass.

'How's it going?'

'Good.'

Sunny was quieter than usual, Lara noted, but assumed it was because she was tired. Her sister was probably starting to feel the effects of Lara not being around to help with the kids, she realised with some guilt. That was where she was needed.

'Look, Sprout, I think you should give Matteo another chance. Have you seen any other evidence of cruelty or violence?'

'No. Quite the opposite.'

'Well, there you go. It's not like he was just randomly heading out to kill things. He wasn't tanked on beer and riding in the back of a ute with a spotlight and a gun.'

'No, but . . .'

'He was attempting to humanely remove one animal to save the lives of many others. He was being gallant, really, trying to save his goats. From the goats' point of view, he's a hero.' She paused, then added, 'He's not like Dad.'

'No,' Lara admitted.

'I really think you should stay where you are. You've been doing so well there, haven't you? Until this hiccup with Matteo, you've been feeling good.'

'I guess so.'

'You've been caring for Samuel and milking goats, driving into the village and to the hospital. It's fantastic. Your moods have been steady until the other night. From my end it sounds like the country has been the best therapy you could have asked for.'

Lara had to admit that was all true. She *had* been feeling good. She'd been feeling proud of herself and confident and stronger than she had in . . . well, forever, if she was honest. And she hadn't even really had to try to feel good; it had all happened naturally. She'd just jumped in. Samuel had taken her by surprise on her first day and she'd had no time to dwell; she'd just had to act. And she had.

With her free hand, she folded her scarf over on itself on the bed and laid it next to her open bag.

'Any word from Dave?' she asked quietly, almost not wanting to know the answer.

'Haven't seen him,' Sunny said firmly.

'Well then, there's no reason for me to stay on at all if he's gone away.'

'It's too early to say that for sure. You know what he's like. He's a plotter. And you know what the lawyer said: disappear for as long as possible.'

'I miss the kids,' she said, tears filling her eyes and blurring her vision.

'I know,' Sunny said gently. 'They miss you too. Let's Facetime tomorrow, okay? Maybe Hudson will join in if both Mum and I are there too. We'll all talk to you and you'll feel better just seeing everyone's faces.'

Lara sniffed. 'Okay.'

'Just stay where you are. Everything will be better in the morning. Give Matteo another chance. And, honestly, it sounds like Samuel might need you too.'

~

Lara hid in her room, her washing and packing half completed. Her limbs were heavy with indecision, her chest tight. She'd thought she'd be on a train this evening. But now she didn't know.

Matteo texted.

Can we talk?

She couldn't blame Matteo for frightening her with the gun. But she couldn't yet think of him the way she had before, as a gentleman who cared for his elderly uncle despite his family's disapproval. He had seemed the opposite to Dave. But now he was also someone who handled guns and was prepared to kill. Those things were difficult to reconcile.

A cool breeze skittered through the room and brought goosebumps to her skin. She lifted up the duvet and covered her face, closing her eyes, feeling the weight of the fabric on her forehead and nose, her warm breath quickly turning stuffy.

'Lara?'

She froze, listening.

'Lara? Are you there?' It was Samuel's voice from downstairs, calling up the stairwell. She never closed her bedroom door; there was no need. Samuel wasn't able to ascend the stairs, so she had the whole top floor to herself.

'I'm here,' she said, swinging her legs out of bed and padding to the top stair. 'Are you okay?'

'Could you come down here for a moment, please?' he asked.

Her bare feet made tiny sounds on the tiles as she descended. Samuel was standing at the foot of the stairs, resting on his cane, looking painfully upwards to watch her. She came to the bottom and put her hand on his arm. 'What's wrong?'

'I . . .' His face looked drawn, the skin pinched around his blue eyes.

'Come and sit down,' she said, and helped him to his room. He sat on the edge of his bed, and she sat in the chair nearby. He had the same look on his face he'd had that day in Rome when he'd asked her to help him.

'I'm sorry for upsetting you,' he said. 'Sometimes I forget, you know, what women . . . or young women . . .' He rubbed his hand across his mouth. 'I know the thing with the wolves must have been shocking, and I should have said something different, to make you feel better. I was never good with words with my daughters and it seems I'm not much better now. I'm not like wine.'

'Huh?'

'I didn't improve with age.' His eyes sparkled.

'Ha! Good one.' She smiled. 'It's okay, really. It's not you. It's me.' That made her giggle. 'I know that's a line people use when they're breaking up with someone, but it's really true in this case. I'm easily upset, easily thrown off course.' She tapped her temple. 'I struggle.'

He nodded slowly, as if now understanding better. 'I hope you're not breaking up with me,' he said softly. 'I want you to stay here, if you can. I've come to rely on you and enjoy your company, but if you're leaving because of Matteo, or because of me and the way I blunder on . . .'

Sunny had been right—Samuel needed her. It felt . . . wonderful. Lara held up her hand. 'It's okay. I'm not leaving.'

'You're not?' His face relaxed.

'No, I'm not. I like it here. I think Tuscany has been good for me.'

Samuel nodded knowingly. 'It has that effect on a lot of people.'

'I don't know how long I'll stay, but for now, this is where I should be.'

'Thank you,' he said.

Lara felt herself glow with an unexpected sense of belonging. 'You're welcome.'

34

It had been a week since the disastrous sex date. Lara had not replied to Matteo's text messages. He was confused, understandably, and wanted to see her. But she didn't even know how to start explaining, either to him or herself. She'd spoken several times to Sunny and Eliza, and Sunny had been right: seeing them all on the screen and having a big long chat—even with Hudson!—had done wonders for her spirits. Although their worst fears hadn't been realised and Dave hadn't appeared, they said it would make everyone feel better if she stayed where she was, hidden away in the Tuscan hills.

'Just enjoy yourself,' Sunny had enthused. 'Who knows when you'll get the chance again to be overseas?'

'Yes, you deserve it,' Eliza chimed in, though she sounded a little jittery—but that was probably just the slight delay in audio. 'After everything you've been through, you really need this retreat.'

Lara had to admit that it felt right to be here. She would just take it a day at a time.

Matteo came to the villa to fortify the goat pen, and she made sure she was out of sight, busy cleaning upstairs. But he texted again.

Please, can we talk?

She didn't know where to begin. It was all so big.

Lara had spent years in therapy learning about the profile of abusers like Dave. They were suave, perfect on the outside, and role models in the community. Sometimes they even volunteered in areas where they could find their victims, such as in charities for survivors of domestic violence, or children's charities—or animal shelters. They dressed well and helped old ladies across the road. They would love-bomb you in the beginning, then withdraw affection and make you think you were crazy. They said you were imagining things, that you were being ridiculous, that you always forgot things. This was Dave's trademark too—just as described.

Gaslighting.

The gaslighting was well established before he began physically hurting her. It took years after she'd escaped him for her to piece it together. Dave was a craftsman.

And then there was the sex, the 'games' he'd wanted her to play, making her feel immature and silly if she didn't like it. Childish, he called her. He intimated that he could find his pleasure elsewhere if he wanted. So she gave in, suffering his hand tight on her shoulder, or throat, or across her face, blinding her, or pushing her face down into the pillow as he forced his way inside her. He only climaxed when she cried. It only stopped when she cried.

He explained to her that psychological studies showed over and over that *all* men had these desires. It was totally normal. He was a psychologist! He knew what was healthy and what wasn't. He *loved* her.

Was it true, she asked Constance, that all men had rape fantasies?

Not just a fantasy, Lara. It was rape. Full stop.

It made her sick now, remembering it.

She couldn't explain all that to Matteo. She could barely explain it to herself.

~

Samuel's confession that he wanted Lara to stay had deeply affected her. It must have been difficult for him. She wanted to nurture him, rather than just do the basics, so recipe research became her new favourite pastime, even when she'd technically clocked off from work.

Late into the night she would lie there, the glow of the phone screen keeping her company as she scrolled through mouth-watering pictures on Pinterest. She found recipes for bulbs of fennel, brushed with chicken stock and roasted in a deep baking dish, braised until they were brown, tantalising juices escaping. A hearty rust-coloured lentil soup, with fire-roasted tomatoes floating on top, decorated with sprigs of fresh thyme. Handmade focaccia, browned around the edges, olive oil and rosemary sprigs on top. So many of the recipes she found were based on 'peasant' food, once a staple of working families who relied on dense nutrition in economical packages, and now on-trend, with broths and cheap cuts of meat featuring prominently.

In Fiotti she wandered the provedores' stores and picked fresh ingredients to take home and experiment with. She went through the hundreds of books lining the shelves near the fireplace in the living room downstairs, and found battered, yellowed, musty recipe books in Italian, which she couldn't read but still enjoyed turning the pages. Many of the old books had grainy pictures in black and white. She loved to find pages that were stuck together, splattered with real food made by a real person who'd cooked just over there in the kitchen with the pans hanging from the walls and ceiling, a chopping board in constant use.

The recipes she saw in these books made her hungry. But it wasn't just a hunger for food. It was a hunger for connection, love, family. Putting food on the table was a great act of love. When she'd been with Dave, it was an act of service, one she did to earn her keep.

She sat on the edge of the fireplace in the kitchen, facing the dining table, and imagined preparing the recipes in the books in her hands. The huge boards of antipasto, with the herbed balls of bocconcini, the rolls of shiny prosciutto and salami, the mounds of khaki and black olives, the fire-roasted capsicums and the deep purple figs. She could see the bruschetta with its finely chopped tomatoes and flat-leafed parsley, a drizzle of golden olive oil on top. The main courses might have included a rich mushroom risotto, just like the one in the heavy, musty book she held now, alongside meatballs in burgundy sauce, and *spezzatino con patate e piselli*—a thick beef stew with potatoes and peas—to fill the workers' bellies. For dessert? Tiramisu, of course. Who didn't love coffee-flavoured sweet mascarpone, preferably laced with liqueur?

Food and family went hand in hand. Bonding together over meals. She ran her palm over the matte texture of the pages in front of her. Food connected people all over the world, in every city and village and home. Samuel had lost his feasts and his family. She wanted to get them back for him, somehow. Lara was so supported by her mother and sister, she knew she'd simply shrivel up and die like an untended flower if they left her.

She began to form a menu in her mind for a dinner party. She had no one to invite other than Samuel. And the food budget he'd given her wouldn't cover a banquet. But that part was easy; she could help with that. She'd be happy to pay for all the food if she could organise something special for him. A surprise party, perhaps. A dinner here in this villa that, according to Matteo, used to hold many such feasts, laughter and love spilling out the windows and doors. Samuel had probably not known anything like it since Assunta's death fifteen years ago. Fifteen years. That was a bloody long time to be without connection and celebration.

This was a house built for big families.

She'd known it the first morning she'd woken up in this house. It was not a house for a lonely old man and his *badante.* So as she was sitting there, hard red bricks beneath her, a fireplace with no ashes in it because it hadn't been used in so long, a copper frying pan hanging on the wall next to her, reflecting the light from the chandelier over the dining table, her gloominess disappeared, replaced by this new vision. She knew then why she'd been so drawn to Samuel when she'd seen him in that street in Rome. He'd needed her, but the truth was she'd needed him too.

35

Samuel

Samuel could see plain as day that the incident with the wolves had damaged any early romance between Lara and Matteo. It had been a week, and still she was hiding in her room, another recipe book from the library shelves tucked under her arm as she'd taken the stairs two at a time at the sound of Matteo's truck. Samuel pondered this as Matteo and Henrik spread goat manure around Henrik's rows of vegetables, the black pellets spilling from large hessian bags, raining down on young green leaves of eggplant and capsicum. Henrik wasn't the greatest gardener that Samuel had ever seen, but he'd been true to his word and had been here almost every day since they'd met, slowly building up terraces of reddish-brown earth and transplanting seedlings.

Matteo stood and stretched his back, then left Henrik to finish up, coming to Samuel's side, dragging empty hessian bags beside him. 'The f-f-farm has more manure than it can d-d-deal with,' he said. 'At least it's going to a good home here.'

Samuel eased himself down onto the bench seat that Matteo had kindly brought over for him, resting his broken wrist in his lap. 'I'm surprised they're not a fully permaculture farm,' he said. 'It seems like that would be an easy thing to do with so much free labour around in people like Henrik.'

'I agree,' Matteo said, sitting beside him. 'I g-g-get frustrated with the limitations there and I would like to see it grow and diversify.'

The two men sat in silence a moment, Samuel enjoying the scent of fresh earth and straw coming from the garden terraces, and even the goat manure. Goats, being herbivores, had manure rich in earthy smells, like any good compost really.

'Is Lara here today?' Matteo asked casually, eyes straight ahead on Henrik, who was using his rake to spread the pellets.

Samuel scratched under his chin, thinking quickly. 'She's upstairs. She's been studying recipes from the old books in the library.'

Matteo nodded and kicked out his muddy work boots to stretch his legs, leaning back in the seat. 'I'm having time off this week,' he said. 'It's a s-s-slower time after mating season and before winter.'

'What are you going to do?'

'Trip up north.'

'North?' Samuel felt a twinge of worry. Lara's question the other week about who had named this villa had stirred up uneasy feelings.

'I want to visit some farms and cheesemakers along the way. I am researching, in truth. Thinking about career options.'

Samuel waited. He had the same sense he'd had when his now son-in-law Marco had come to see him, wearing a formal shirt and a slightly crooked tie, requesting a special meeting to ask permission to marry Giovanna. Samuel continued to watch Henrik, one brace of his overalls swinging loose behind his shoulder, now heading to the tap to turn on the water and wet down the fertiliser.

'If I could c-c-convince her to come, would you let Lara accompany me for a couple of days? I know tomorrow is her day off; I could take her with me and she could see some of the country, then

I can p-put her on a bus back to you on Monday. I just thought . . .' Matteo shrugged. 'She's on holiday, you know.'

Samuel stroked the skin of his throat, now so loose. Sometimes when he looked in the mirror those folds of skin reminded him of a Brahman cow.

'That would be fine,' he said.

'Really? Thank you.'

Henrik came back with the hose and began to water the vegetables, a wide mist of fine spray catching the sun and casting rainbows over the seedlings.

'Are you going to visit Carlo, by any chance?' Samuel asked, as inconsequentially as he could. The guilt of unfinished business nagged at him.

Matteo shifted in his seat, signalling they'd entered tricky territory. He was a good Italian boy, Matteo. Of course he would visit his relative while he was up north.

'Yes,' he said. 'It's a long time since I've seen him. He's been up in the mountains years now.'

'Yes,' Samuel agreed.

Carlo. Once a treasured in-law and friend. Samuel missed him and he needed to resolve their outstanding matter before . . . Well, neither of them was getting any younger. The opportunity to make amends could be taken out of their hands at any moment. He wasn't sure he believed in premonitions or visions, but he'd been dogged by a feeling of doom lately. Time was slipping away. Death was coming for him. So be it. He would stare Death in the face and quell its enthusiasm. He wouldn't lie down for Death. Instead, he would take this chance to mend some old broken fences.

He *could* ask Matteo to take him north so he could visit Carlo in person but, to his utter disgust, he truly didn't think he could make the trip without collapsing. And right now, he wanted that wrist to heal so he could get back to milking his own damn goats; he couldn't take the chance that his health would be made worse by a road trip.

His only consolation was that he might be able to help Lara and Matteo, two young lovebirds who had flown off course, to find their way back together.

'Actually,' Samuel said, 'why don't you take Lara with you for the week? Then she could really see some of Italy.'

Matteo turned to look at him, his raised eyebrows and a small smile showing his disbelief. 'She hasn't spoken to me since the whole wolf thing,' he said, shaking his head, his smile vanishing. 'I will be lucky to convince her to come for a couple of days, but a week?'

'Leave it to me,' Samuel said. 'I've got an idea.'

'But even if you c-could conv-v-vince her, you still need her here to look after you.'

Samuel's pride prickled at this even though he knew Matteo was right. His wrist was halfway there, but he wouldn't be able to do enough for himself. And then there was the highly disagreeable thought that he could have another fall and no one would be there to help him. Also, he still couldn't milk the goats.

Henrik began to sing quietly to himself while he hosed the plants. To Samuel, he looked like an overgrown teenager at odds with the world, determined to do his own thing.

'There's always Henrik,' Samuel said quietly, leaning close to Matteo. 'Could the farm spare him for a week? Maybe he would like to spend more time here and really get into his study of bacteria or whatever it is he's trying to do.'

Matteo jiggled his knee from side to side, his thoughtful frown turning into a smile. In a conspiratorial voice he said, 'You know what? He's not very good in the factory. Domenica is worried he will break something expensive. She'd probably be happy to have him away for a while.'

'But can he milk?'

'He's no expert, but he gets the job done.'

'Then it's settled. Leave Lara to me.'

36

Sunny

It was going to be one of those October days when the temperature soars into a dry heat that sears the grass brown. Sunny felt the need to get out of the house and to take the kids to the coast for the day, to play in the sand and splash in the waves, get an ice cream, gaze at endless blue sky and soak up the sun. There were several dog-friendly beaches up there to choose from, so Midnight could join them.

'Do you want to come?' she asked Eliza, shoving sunscreen into the pocket of the beach bag.

Her mother sipped on her Moroccan mint tea, standing near the door to the front deck, morning sunlight falling across her in stripes from the louvre. 'Maybe not. I'm not good with sand.'

'Neither am I, these days. But the kids don't seem to care if they're smothered in it, have it packed in their swimmers and filling up their shoes. Pretty sure I was the same.'

'You were.'

'I wonder when we grow up and become so precious about sand.'

Daisy and Hudson had finished breakfast long ago. They'd been up at the crack of dawn demanding pancakes, their Sunday morning ritual, and they'd scoffed them down and ran down the back stairs to play with Midnight. Daisy was coveting Lara's granny flat, Sunny knew. Her daughter wanted to turn it into a little girl's 'she shed'. She'd be having high tea in there right now, pouring Midnight imaginary cups of tea.

'Are you going to check out the business while you're up there?' Eliza asked.

Sunny kept rolling up beach towels. 'I might drive past and have a look.'

'It's a good job offer,' Eliza said.

'It is,' Sunny admitted, putting the towels down and pulling out a dining chair to sit on. 'I don't know what to do. Part of me thinks I should take it to put some distance between us and Dave.' She had the uneasy feeling, though, that if Dave wanted to find them he would do it no matter where she went. But it might buy them a little time, and according to Martha, time was their best asset. 'If there are legal battles ahead, having a full-time income will obviously help pay the bills.'

'What a bastard,' Eliza muttered. 'How dare he ruin your life and finances just because he can.'

Sunny nodded.

'But then what if your disappearing antagonises him into action?' Eliza said, coming to join Sunny at the table.

'It's possible. He's unpredictable. And with Lara out of his direct reach, I'm the next best thing.'

They were both silent for a moment.

'You should change your phone number,' Eliza said.

'I thought about that. But the absolute last thing we want to do is alarm Lara. We need her to stay away, but if I tell her about Dave she'll either want to come home or she'll be trapped over there without us to support her, and we both know she might have an episode of some sort. She has to believe that everything's okay.'

'Agreed.' Eliza put her elbows on the table, her hands in prayer position under her nose. 'You could tell Lara that you've changed phone plans and you got a great deal but you had to take a new number?'

Sunny nodded. 'That would work. But then if I did change my number and Dave couldn't contact me, how will I know what he's doing? If Martha is right and we need to play the mental game with Dave, shouldn't I have some idea of what he's doing?'

Sunny thought back to that day six years ago. Lara turning up in a taxi at Sunny's house in West End, a pale, disoriented mess, with nothing but the clothes on her back, without even enough money to pay the cab driver.

Sunny's urgent phone call to Eliza, who was in the middle of organising a lengthy and difficult diplomatic tour of Indonesia.

The revelation of the pregnancy, and then the scan that revealed the twins.

The confessions of Dave's abuse.

Lara's terror that he would find her.

The late flight to Sydney, back to one of Sunny's old stomping grounds in Redfern, just the two sisters.

Sunny's life-changing decision to become a mother.

Eliza flying down to visit them in the hospital, and her unexpectedly emotional outburst, which had surprised them all. Eliza, who had spent decades living with an erratic, unreliable husband who'd managed to disappear into the shadows, and whose entire career was founded on her ability to hold it together under pressure, was broken by the sight of two tiny babies swaddled tightly in bunny print sheets and matching yellow caps, sleeping with their faces turned to each other. Their band of musketeers had grown to five.

Those babies would be heading to school next year.

Sunny blinked rapidly. It felt as though it had all happened yesterday. 'You know what?' she said to her mother.

'What?'

'I think I should stay here with you.'

'Why?'

'Because we've all been in this together from the start. We've survived and thrived, and breaking us apart and breaking us down is what Dave wants. It's bad enough that Lara had to go. Besides, I don't want to leave you here alone.' She let her fears hang in the air, the words unspoken but the meaning clear to them both.

'I *am* nervous,' Eliza admitted. She shook her head, dismayed. 'The past six years have been hard on you too. You've been beyond generous, and so strong. Few people could have done what you've done—you've held it all together for all of us.'

Sunny felt embarrassed by her mother's words, yet also proud. She had given up a lot, and she'd navigated tricky territory with Lara, and somehow they'd both grown stronger over the years. But she wasn't too old to glow under her mother's words of praise.

'I wouldn't change anything,' she said. 'I got two gorgeous children that I might not have ever had. Every mother's life changes once her children arrive. I've just done what any mother would do. You didn't get a dream ride of motherhood either.'

Eliza's eyes went bright and her mouth pinched downwards.

'My time will come,' Sunny said. 'I'll talk to Ari. Maybe he'll hold the job for me a bit longer.'

'You shouldn't pass it up. This is your chance.'

'I don't think we only get one chance in life,' Sunny said, with as much conviction as she could muster. 'Right now, we just need to get Dave off our backs. Best case scenario, he gets bored and finds someone else to mess with. Until then, we have to stick together.' Her tone was excessively confident, and she knew it. Dave had just learned he was the father of two children. For an abuser like him, that was pure gold.

37

Samuel

Samuel needed to talk to Lara. He'd waited until she'd come home from Fiotti, weighed down with paper bags that rustled in a way that stirred joy inside him. Decades of paper bags, bringing delicious market foods into his home, had etched the sound into his psyche like the bell for Pavlov's dogs. He waited until she'd settled into the kitchen before choosing his moment to explain what he needed her to do. Now here he was, suddenly feeling as though he should be wearing something more formal for such an important discussion, not his collared t-shirt and pilled trackpants.

There was a wooden shelf above the stove that was crammed with decades-old trinkets he didn't even recognise anymore. Lara had taken it all down and was singing as she wiped down the shelf with a wet cloth.

'I can't believe it's taken me so long to get to this,' she said cheerily, folding over the cloth to cover half an inch of gathered dust and wiping again.

Samuel picked up a small figurine of a Dutch windmill that one of Assunta's wealthy cousins had sent during a trip away. He tossed the windmill across the room in an arc and it landed neatly in the bin.

'Wow! What a shot!' Lara said, and held up her hand for a high five.

Samuel felt his lips curve in a smile and clapped her hand, inordinately proud of himself for making the throw. At his age, any small triumph of a physical nature was rather thrilling.

'You shouldn't be cleaning; it's your day off,' he said, picking out a canister with a rooster on the front containing some type of herbal tea. His granddaughter Aimee must have brought it when she popped in for a surprise visit last year on her way from London to Spain. It had been a delightful few days and he'd been buoyed by her stay. Aimee was into herbal teas, green smoothies and positive thinking. She'd been a breath of fresh air.

'I know.' Lara lifted one shoulder helplessly. 'But I actually like it here. It feels . . . I don't know.'

Like home? he wondered, an unexpected—and totally irrational—sense of hope rising inside him.

He wrestled the lid back on the canister and threw it across the room too. It hit the stone wall and rebounded into the bin.

'You're on fire!' she cheered.

Samuel laughed, soaking up the praise.

Lara stopped a moment to pull out her hairtie and rearrange her locks into a bun high on her head. Her skin was shiny with sweat. The oven was thrumming. 'I didn't mean to start a decluttering party,' she said, indicating the pile of bric-a-brac she'd collected from the shelf. 'I just wanted to clean it up a bit and make space for some things I bought today.'

He looked curiously over to where her market bags were standing on the kitchen table. She followed his gaze and went over to them, opening one bag and pulling out some Fido glass jars with rubber seals and metal hinges.

'I wanted to get some Tuscan herbs.' She placed the jars on the kitchen bench and dived back into the bags for an array of dried botanicals. 'I'm trying to improve my cooking while I'm here, learn to make some authentic regional dishes, and I wanted to do something nice for you for, you know, giving me a job and putting up with me,' she said, self-deprecatingly. 'I know I haven't been all sunshine and cheer this past week.'

Samuel considered Lara, a young woman hiding from *something*.

'Whatever you've got cooking in there smells good,' he said, suddenly hungry.

'Spinach and ricotta cannelloni. I made the ricotta myself! Well, the goats helped,' she said, hands on her hips, proud of herself.

Samuel pulled out a chair from the table and eased himself down onto it. Lara began sorting her dried goods: oregano, sage, rosemary, chilli. He had all of those things growing in the garden, but he didn't say as much.

'Lara, I have a favour to ask,' he said, his voice beginning quietly but gathering strength with each word.

'Sure, what is it?' she asked, pouring garlic flakes into a jar.

'There is a man up north. His name's Carlo. He is Assunta's cousin, though they grew up as close as siblings and he was more like a brother to her, especially since she didn't have any of her own. She was the oldest girl; her two younger sisters are gone now too.' He paused, momentarily shocked at just how fast time went and how anyone could be taken away at any instant with no warning. He gathered himself and ploughed on. 'I want you to go and see him.'

Lara stopped pouring herbs and stared at him. 'What, up to the north of Italy?'

'Yes.'

She gave him a bemused smile and wiped her hands on a tea towel, directing her full attention to him. 'Why?'

Samuel levered himself to the left so he could fish deep into the pocket of his pants to find the wine-coloured velvet box and put it on the table. 'Because I want you to give him this.'

Lara shook her head, confused, and reached out to touch the box. But he covered her hand with his before she could take it. 'And I want you to tell him something.'

Her eyes studied his face, serious now. He saw her swallow.

'It's a long story,' Samuel said. 'You might want to sit down.'

38

Lara

Matteo had rented a small silver van. 'Just in case I f-f-find a goat that needs to come home with us,' he explained, lifting her bag onto the back seat for her.

'You're kidding,' Lara said, unsure whether or not to believe him.

Matteo merely gave her a cheeky smile and shrugged. *You never know.*

He closed the door with a satisfying new-car-sound click and turned to face her. She squirmed under his direct gaze, remembering their night of almost-passion and the upsetting events afterwards, embarrassed that she'd not replied to his messages and now was heading on a road trip with him, something that was always an intimate experience, regardless of whether the other person was your mother, friend, lover or almost-sex-date.

'I'm so sorry about how things ended the other n-night,' Matteo said, thrusting his hands into the pockets of his cotton cargo pants.

'Yes, me too,' she said, genuinely sad.

'Maybe we can be friends again?'

'I would like that,' she said. He looked hopeful and she was pierced with guilt. 'I'm sorry,' Lara added, wiping her damp palms down her hips. 'I shouldn't have ignored your messages. I just . . .' She trailed off, feeling ridiculous, and also deceptive because of what she'd been hiding about her family situation. Also, his presence here in front of her, with the smell of wood smoke in his shirt, was distracting. Without a shadow of a doubt, she was still attracted to him.

They climbed into the van and waved goodbye to Samuel and Henrik as their wheels bumped gently over the uneven surface of the driveway.

'We're going to have a great week,' Matteo said. His huge grin made her smile too, giving her heart a kickstart. She wouldn't forget seeing him with a gun. But Matteo wasn't Leonard. These were entirely different circumstances. Sunny was right. It was just possible that he was the hero in the story after all.

⁂

They'd been driving in comfortable silence for over an hour. Things were a bit too stiff and polite, but easing as the time went on and they were bound together on this journey, with their van wending its way over the magnificent Apennines towards Bologna. Lara was simultaneously soaking up the grandeur of the mountain range—the giant backbone of the country—while also feeling the weight of responsibility of the task Samuel had set her.

'I'll pay you your week's wage as usual, since you are still working for me,' he had said.

'But shouldn't you go and see Carlo yourself and tell him all this?'

Samuel had simply gestured to his wrist and his legs, and Lara had cursed herself for suggesting it.

'What about calling him, then? Surely he needs to hear this from you.'

'He no longer speaks to me,' Samuel said. 'In that regard, he's like all the others.'

'Maybe if you posted this to him,' she said, tapping the box, 'then he'd speak to you.'

'I can't risk something this valuable getting lost in the mail.'

'Courier?'

Samuel shook his head firmly. 'No. It must be delivered in person.'

'Matteo, then?' she pleaded. 'He's a blood relative.'

Samuel had wiped a hand across his mouth. 'He is,' he conceded. 'But he's already defying the rest of his family to be in contact with me. I don't want to burden him with this too.'

Burden. That was a good word for it, Lara thought now, picturing the claret-coloured box tucked inside her bag on the back seat, thinking of the story she had to relay to Carlo.

She pushed that thought away in favour of watching the world drift by outside her window. The road passed through many tunnels and they popped out the other side to be greeted by open yellow farmlands with flocks of sheep huddled under oak trees, or huge round bales of hay curing in the sunshine, or dense groves of olive trees clinging to sheer drops by the roadside. A stone house with curls of smoke serpentining into the sky. Ice blue lakes reflecting dazzling light. A lone cyclist resting on the side of the road, her water bottle in one hand and a map in the other. It was all wonderful, luring Lara into a place of calm and wonder.

Then, Matteo flung his hand towards her.

She'd been so lost in her place of calm that his sudden gesture gave her a spike of adrenaline. She flinched, pulling herself towards the car door and turning her back to him as she buried her face in her hands.

'Lara, what is wrong?'

She uncovered her face, immediately mortified. 'Oh, nothing, sorry!' She looked up and took a breath.

'I just needed water,' Matteo explained, holding up the bottle, glancing at her quickly.

'Yes, I know. Sorry. It was just a reflex. I was off in a daydream and got a fright, that's all.'

Matteo nodded slowly, but she could tell he knew there was more than she was saying.

The thing was, Dave *had* hit her. And not just during his messed-up sex games. Sometimes she lied to herself and pretended it hadn't happened. But it had. She may have been able to block it from her mind, but her body still remembered.

They had been in Bologna for half the day and the beautiful city had worked its magic on Lara, loosening the knots of tension in her body, easing the racing of her mind and heart. 'I think I'm in love,' she told Matteo, her words muffled as she gnawed on a rind of parmesan, determined to get every last sliver of cheese she could. The *formaggio* was smooth and creamy—another class entirely from any she'd ever eaten in Australia.

Matteo leaned back in his chair and grinned across the table at her, his eyes catching the light from the flickering candles. Any residual awkwardness between them had all but disappeared during several hours of wonderful sightseeing on top of a red tourist bus, Matteo offering her the best seat.

They saw the Basilica San Petronio, the light-filled, expansive Piazza Maggiore, Neptune's fountain, and the University of Bologna—the oldest university in the world. They pottered about in the warren of backstreets filled with shops. There were fishmongers with huge white boxes of fish, lobsters, squid and prawns on ice, and fruit and vegetable sellers, and spice merchants. The colourscape in this city was different from the villages in Tuscany. Here the walls were muted orange or lemon, with blue shutters. Her heart was bursting with the beauty of this grand university town with its huge basilicas, its ancient towers, its kilometres of arched stone porticos that wove their way around the city, and its young and energetic vibe.

It was in this city that Matteo had completed his degree, and he was an entertaining guide. She was seeing another side to him—more enthusiastic academic than quiet goat handler. She liked this version of him too. Which was frustrating, really, as she was most certainly trying *not* to like him.

The edges of the white tablecloth lifted and ruffled in the swirling breeze that had picked up as the day went on. Lara shivered. She welcomed the coolness of this city—feeling much further north than it actually was—but pulled her new coat around her just the same. She'd found the coat in a vintage shop tucked away in an alley. It was simple and durable, made from a heavy cotton fabric, stiff like denim, and perfect for a traveller to roll up into a bag.

Today on her wanders, she'd learned that tortellini was the invention of this region. She'd walked past dozens of shops that displayed the pasta not in packets, as she'd only ever seen it in Brisbane, but in their front windows, freshly made and sold by weight. The stores were pokey and delightful, crammed not just with extensive displays of the prized pasta, but also with huge wheels of cheeses, and scores of hams and other cured meats that hung from the ceilings on chains, along with chandeliers that cast romantic light over the produce.

'How am I ever going to eat pasta again when I go home?' she said, sighing deeply.

'It is good, yes? I think you will have to learn to make it properly,' Matteo said, reaching for another slice of mortadella and rolling it up like a cigar before folding it into his mouth and chewing with glee.

'Maybe I could find a class while I'm here. I've been reading the recipe books in Samuel's villa and trying to improve, but nothing beats learning from another person.'

Matteo swallowed the last of the mortadella. 'I am sure Gilberta would love to teach you. You remember her?'

'At your mum's house,' she said, wincing at the memory of that awkward day. 'That was the day you and Alessandra . . .'

'Broke up,' he said decisively.

Lara played with her fork. 'Have you seen her since?' The question was out before she could stop it.

Matteo smiled and dabbed at his mouth with his serviette. 'Not once.'

She couldn't suppress the smile that sprang to her lips. 'And what about your mother? Has she found you another suitable partner yet?'

'It wouldn't matter if she had,' he said steadily. 'Trust me, I learned that lesson long ago. I'm the only one who knows who is right for me.'

Lara bit her lip to stop herself asking more questions. She changed the topic. 'So, you mentioned Gilberta. I liked her very much. We have acting in common, though she had an actual career whereas I was just . . . filling in time, I guess. Waiting.'

A waiter in a starched white shirt and slicked-back hair wove his way through the tables under the restaurant's stone portico, approached their table and refilled their wine glasses.

'*Grazie*,' Matteo said. Then he turned his gaze back to Lara. 'What were you waiting for?'

Lara, aware this conversation was heading into tricky territory, turned her attention back to the cheese board, scraping up a soft white sheep's cheese with a cracker. She chewed thoughtfully. She supposed, since she had decided to be over Matteo, and there was no possible future for them, that it really didn't matter what she told him.

'I lived with a man for several years. I thought . . .' She frowned, not entirely sure what she'd been thinking at the time. 'I guess I thought Dave would marry me one day and we would have kids.'

'But you didn't get married?'

'No.' She quaffed a mouthful of wine, appreciating the acidic fizz in her mouth as *vino* met *formaggio*, delaying her story.

Matteo leaned forward, his arms folded on the table, his linen shirt open enough that she got a good look at his collarbones and fleetingly imagined laying her lips on them. 'What happened to this man?' he asked. And she might have imagined it, but it seemed his eyes dropped down her body to rest on her navel. She felt herself flush and wanted, briefly but urgently, to flee this conversation. Instead, she put her hand where his eyes seemed to be focused. 'He didn't want me,' she said, smiling through the humiliation.

Matteo frowned and shook his head slightly. 'Then he was a fool.'

Lara looked away. Someone riding a bicycle along the flagstone road beside the portico *tinged* their bell and the rubber tyres made a whizzing sound. A family arrived at the entrance to the restaurant, two young children clinging sleepily to their parents' legs, one holding a teddy bear. They were ushered inside with loud enthusiasm.

'I had two babies—twins, a boy and a girl,' she said, forcing herself to be strong, focusing her eyes firmly on her plate. 'But I knew I couldn't keep them.'

'Why?'

It was now or never. She had to tell him the truth. Playing games didn't sit well with her, especially after what she'd been through with Dave.

'I have bipolar affective disorder,' she said, any fantasies she had harboured about a romance with Matteo fluttering to the ground. 'Dave convinced me that I couldn't possibly be a good mother and that the best thing for everyone was for me to end the pregnancy.' She sneaked a peek at Matteo. 'But I couldn't go through with it.'

He was watching her intently, twirling the stem of his wine glass between his fingers. 'And where are they now?'

'My sister is their mother now. My niece and nephew, Daisy and Hudson, are actually my babies.'

Matteo groaned quietly. 'That must have been very difficult. I can't imagine.'

'It was. It still is, some days.'

It had been a slow release, starting with the moment Daisy was pulled from her belly, Sunny holding Lara's hand so tightly, tears in her eyes as her daughter immediately screamed in protest, while the surgeon worked to pull Hudson out next. Both babies had been strong and were quickly swaddled. Lara had lain on the table, tears leaking from her eyes while the doctor stitched her up, knowing that the babies looked perfectly *right* in Sunny's arms.

Lara had been unable to breastfeed, both because she needed to go straight back onto her medication and because she knew she couldn't share that level of intimacy with the babies when she wasn't to be their mother. Sunny had been sensitive and patient, only holding the babies or bottle-feeding them when Lara suggested it, steeling herself for the chance that Lara would change her mind.

They'd taken the babies back to the flat in Redfern, where they'd stayed a couple of weeks, caring for them together. Then Lara flew home to Brisbane first, to be with Eliza, while she and Sunny made the mental adjustment to their new roles, with Sunny as mama and Lara as aunty.

The first few years were the hardest. During the pregnancy, Lara had had to block out so much in order to hold things together. But after the birth, she'd had to get on with the deep and difficult work of recovering herself, spending so much time in therapy, continuing to deprogram herself from Dave, and dealing with the new memories floating to the surface, threatening to drown her with their intensity. Then slowly coming to terms with what she'd hidden, how many lies she'd told herself and her family while she'd been with Dave, seeking their forgiveness for shutting them out. She'd been in no shape to care for the babies. It had been a relief to know they were safe in Sunny's hands, though it had been her own private hell.

Constance had been her rock. Lara asked her if she'd made a mistake, if she should move out and go far away from them rather than living in the granny flat out the back, and what it would be like when the twins finally learned the truth. They talked through it all.

'First of all, there is no one right way to handle this situation,' Constance had said, calmly as always. 'Your family is free to make its own set of rules. Yes, you might choose to go away if you feel it would help you to heal, but that doesn't make it necessary or right. There are many paths to love and healing. You also might feel you would benefit most from the support of your family for yourself.'

Sometimes, Lara would turn her pain inwards, cursing herself for doing such an awful thing. One day, Constance told her that she wasn't alone, that mothers all over the world had to make decisions every day to keep their children safe—from war, violence, famine, poverty, natural disasters and human traffickers—and sometimes that meant splitting up families, giving children to relatives, sending them far away, sometimes putting them on leaky boats to sail across oceans, not knowing if they would survive, let alone find a better life at the other end.

'Knowing this doesn't make it all better,' Constance said. 'But maybe just knowing you aren't the only mother in the world who has had to make an impossible decision might help you to feel more connected to other women, rather than alone in your struggles.'

They talked through every one of Lara's decisions in detail.

Then when the twins turned three years old, something changed. It was as though a window opened and a burst of sunshine and fresh air poured through her. Instead of learning to say goodbye again and again, pulling herself away, she started to relish her role as aunty, feeling confident to play with them and hold them and not fear the pain that followed. She began to store up good memories instead of bad. She began to live again.

'And what about this Dave man? Where is he in the picture?' Matteo asked, pulling her out of her reverie.

Lara cast her gaze out to the night sky and let out a long slow breath. 'I told him I'd had an abortion,' she said, realising that she might as well throw all her cards on the table. Matteo waited out the silence that followed, and she rushed to explain.

'He wasn't a nice man,' she began.

Matteo's nostrils flared and he lifted his chin.

'He was a psychologist, but he used that against me to trick me and confuse me and play games with my mind, like convincing me I was hopeless and wouldn't be able to look after the kids. It's called gaslighting.'

'He preyed on you?' Matteo clarified, clearly disgusted.

'Very much. Like the wolves on your farm, I guess.' She knew now that protecting the goats from the wolf was the only action Matteo could have taken that night. Gentleness could still equal strength.

Lara swallowed hard against her rising emotion. 'He controlled the money, the shopping, my medications. I believe he got rid of my cat and he destroyed the screenplay that I'd been working on for years, and both times convinced me it was my fault. He isolated me from my family and made sure I didn't keep friends. He had affairs, I think, though I could never catch him out. And when he found out I was pregnant, he tried to convince me to kill myself.'

Matteo froze, staring at her in shock.

There. She'd said it all. Lara reached for her glass of water and brought it to her lips, gulping, then choking and coughing. Matteo came and knelt at her side and patted her back until she could breathe properly again.

'This is why you flinched in the car,' he said.

'Yes.'

'Because he was violent.'

'Sometimes, yes,' she said, instantly regretting saying *sometimes*. It was a qualifier Dave didn't deserve. She should have just said *yes*. Yes, he was violent.

Matteo took her hand in his. 'You didn't deserve that.'

Her eyes filled. 'No, I didn't.'

Very slowly, he reached up and laid his hand tenderly against her face. She leaned into it, relieved to have told him her story, regardless of where it went from here. For the first time in a long while, she felt hope for her future. But as for romance with Matteo, she knew that everything she'd just told him wasn't exactly her winning pitch.

❧ ❧

Back at their old, labyrinthine hotel, Matteo walked her to her door and watched while she slid the room key into the lock.

'Thank you for such a wonderful day,' she said, suddenly very tired.

'Thank you for coming with me,' he said.

She was reminded of the awkwardness between the two of them that first night at the villa, standing outside their bedrooms, back so late from the hospital. She wanted him to reach out and touch her once more, but instead he tucked his hands into the pockets of his trousers.

'I am in room 204, just over there.' He pointed. 'If you need anything, just call or knock.'

'Okay, thanks,' she said, a bundle of confused emotions now weaving themselves together. She'd expected that telling him her story would turn him off—if he'd even been 'on' in the first place—but then the moment after she'd finished choking, when he'd put his hand on her face, she'd felt something real. He was probably just feeling pity for her, though. And pity was the last thing she wanted.

Nerves loosened her tongue. 'But you know, if you wanted to come inside, like if you needed to sleep on the floor to help you feel as if you're at home or something like that . . .'

He was frowning at her.

'But of course it's been such a long day,' she went on. God, how she needed to stop talking. 'You'll be tired. So much driving. All those mountains.' Her hand was gesticulating wildly all by itself.

In his pocket, his phone began to play an opera tune, which she recognised as the one identifying his mother's call.

He closed one eye in a wincing gesture. 'Er, I think I will say goodnight,' he said, looking at her gently.

Gently!? Oh, the shame of it.

'I must take this.' He held up the offending phone. 'I will see you downstairs for breakfast in the morning?'

'Yes, yes, breakfast. Will do. No problems. Best of sleep to you.'

Best of sleep?

He backed away a step, as if unsure whether he should take his eyes off her in case she did something crazy, then nodded and turned and answered his phone, talking and walking.

Lara fumbled with her key again, scurried inside, shut the door firmly behind her, staggered to the bed, texted Sunny, then flopped face down. What an idiot she was.

> You're not an idiot, Sprout. You were brave.
> It will be okay in the morning. Remember?
> Everything's better in the morning. Try to
> get some sleep xx

39

Sunny

At the indoor swimming pool, Sunny sipped a takeaway coffee and chatted to Tracey, her almost-friend at swimming lessons. She'd never joined a mothers' group, and she wasn't one for hanging around after music lessons and having tea and cake. But five years on, she'd found that she liked Tracey and had begun to look forward to swimming lessons.

Sunny yawned and blinked heavily. She'd been losing sleep lately, fretting about Dave.

Tracey's son, Damon, was in the same group as the twins—Dugongs. The blue water of the pool was choppy with small bodies churning up and down the lanes with kickboards, the instructors' voices and whistles echoing painfully in the space, the fumes of chlorine enough to singe eyebrows.

'Have you decided which school the kids are going to next year?' Tracey asked, her bangles jangling as she ran her fingers through her long hair. Tracey had brought two coffees with her for afternoon tea. She was nearly finished the first, the second waiting in its cardboard carry tray. She tossed back more of the first—a double-shot soy latte.

'Just the local state school,' Sunny said.

'What's the uniform like?' Tracey asked, her green eyes wide with apprehension, and probably caffeine.

'It's okay. Blues and greens.' The exact same uniform both she and Lara had worn when they were young, in fact, though it had been updated to wash-and-wear synthetic materials rather than cotton.

'Damon's going to St Martin's. The uniform is crap, but the music program is good.' Tracey crushed her empty coffee cup and picked up the full one, slurping loudly.

'Mummy!'

All the mums sitting in the plastic seats either side of Sunny and Tracey looked up. But it was Daisy, goggles on, standing on the side of the pool, arms out straight, ready to dive.

Sunny gave her a huge smile and two thumbs-up. She knew that learning to dive was important, but she always worried that one of the kids would slip on the tiles and split their head open.

Daisy dived, disappearing beneath the surface and emerging a few metres away. Sunny cheered and clapped. Hudson was up next, followed by Damon. Sunny and Tracey paused their conversation to watch. After both boys were safely in the water, Sunny zoned out, yawning again, the fumes and the noise getting to her. She took a sneaky moment to close her eyes, to feel the heaviness of her lids and imagine that she was in a tiny micro sleep.

She didn't know how much time had passed, but she was suddenly wide awake. Her scalp bristled. She straightened and looked around, scanning the other parents, seeing nothing out of the ordinary. But then she caught the movement of a shadow beyond the plastic curtain on the other side of the pool. A man retreated, the details blurred by the thickness of the blinds, but she could see enough of his outline to make her break out in a sweat. She craned forward in her seat, but he was gone.

40

Lara

If Lara had needed convincing that she should learn a second language, the Dolomites would have been the clincher. The iconic, UNESCO-listed mountain ranges of northern Italy left her both breathless and speechless. There simply weren't enough words in the English language to describe them.

Matteo guided the van carefully along the narrow, winding roads, which fell away to sheer drops down into vast valleys, so far below them that she'd long ago lost sight of the villages nestled into the folds of the mountains' skirts. The vista was stunning. Ginormous mountains fading to pale blue on the horizon, white clouds gobbling up the peaks. A panorama of endless blue sky. Steep green hills populated by brown cows and the occasional house or inn.

They were now in Trentino. For the next couple of days, before heading even higher into the mountains to visit Carlo, they would be working their way along *la strada dei formaggi delle Dolomiti*—the Dolomites cheese trail—as Matteo wanted to visit some farms and factories to see what others were doing.

'Aren't you on holiday?' Lara had asked lightly, buttering toast in the Bologna hotel restaurant that morning.

He had smiled at her, cradling his coffee in two hands, taking his time with it. 'I am very lucky that I love what I do. I don't ever really feel that I work. So this will be a holiday for me. I am excited to see what others are doing and what I might be able to take back to the farm.' Then he shrugged self-consciously. 'Or maybe a farm of my own one day.'

'Would you have a goat dairy, like the one you're on now?'

'Maybe. I love all food, so I think I would be happy on most farms.' He paused. 'But I do love the goats. They amuse me.'

Lara smiled, thinking of Meg and Willow grumbling at her and kicking up their heels. Some mornings when Lara went out, she would find one of them with her front feet in a bucket for no discernible reason other than fun.

'I envy you,' she'd said, thinking of her real estate job back in Brisbane. 'There must be a deep bliss in having found your dream career. I wouldn't even know where to start looking.'

Now, as they pulled into the gravel driveway of a Trentino restaurant on a hillside, she took in the scenery and considered that if she had a job here in the mountains, she might even start to love her job too. 'Look at this,' she said in awe, motioning to the restaurant and the surrounds.

The straight cypress pines of Tuscany had long since given way to the wide Christmas-tree pines; the rows of grapevines and flat yellow wheatfields that sat between mountains had opened up to green fields of cows, sheep and goats; and the slower rivers and canals had opened up into fast-running rivers of melted snow busting down from the peaks above them.

But it was the buildings that astonished her. She felt wholly ignorant and naive, but she'd just had no idea how *Austrian* northern Italy was, and felt even more stupid when she'd mentioned it to Matteo and he'd informed her that that was because this land *had* been part of Austria.

'Italy annexed it in 1919,' he'd said.

'That's not that long ago. Do people still speak, um . . .'

'Austrian German,' he supplied. 'Maybe some elderly people, those whose parents were born in what was Austria and spoke their language to their children. But mostly everyone speaks Italian.'

In front of their van now was a classic example of this Austrian past. It was a huge stone building, whitewashed and with dark wooden beams around doorways and windows, a sharply pitched wooden roof to allow the snow to slide off, and bursts of bright pink, yellow and purple flowers overflowing from balconies. Moving through the doorway, carrying trays laden with food and drink, were women with their hair in braids, wearing white blouses underneath green pinafores.

Matteo removed the key from the ignition. 'Let's eat.'

'Why is the cheese here so good?' Lara said half an hour later, feeling bloated and sleepy from the warmth inside the building and the rather large house beer she'd been working her way through. Matteo cleaned up the last of the semi-hard, dark-rind Nostrale d'Alpe cheese, originating from this area, and washed it down with his own beer. She envied his ability to eat so much. She could live on cheese, oh yes, she could.

'Fifty or sixty years ago, everyone in these mountains had their own house cow. They milked their own cow to make cheese, yoghurt, butter. Not everyone can afford to live in these mountains now—they need jobs—but the traditions are strong. Each village has its own cheese and is fiercely proud of it. Some families will still have someone in the mountains who continues to make their traditional cheese.'

'Like Carlo,' she said, the thought of the box back in the van like a stone weight on her.

Matteo nodded. 'Carlo's whole family lived up here for centuries. He lived down in Tuscany for a long time, but moved back here when his father died. He is the last one still living the old way.'

A wiry, white-haired man walked in the door wearing lederhosen and a brown felt hat with a small feather sticking out of it. Lara expected someone to start yodelling at any moment, and rather wished they would.

She shifted the conversation away from Carlo—she'd have to think more about Samuel's message for him later—and brought her attention back to the cheese board in front of them, small white flags on toothpicks bearing the name of each cheese. 'I really don't understand what all these names mean,' she said. 'Back at home, you'd be lucky to find ten different types of cheese in the supermarket. Here, there are thirty different types on the menu in this restaurant alone.'

'It's very complicated; you're not alone. I am a cheesemaker and I could not tell you everything.'

'Well, that makes me feel better.' Lara suddenly realised how much she loved the fact that Matteo never talked down to her, never made her feel inferior or dumb.

'Essentially, that thing you call parmesan or brie isn't really a parmesan or brie.'

'Huh?'

'It is cheese made in the *style* of brie. There are only two real Brie cheeses in the world. They have been registered as being authentic to the region of Brie in France. Everything else, any cheese called a "brie" anywhere in the world, isn't really a brie. Does that make sense?'

'Sort of,' she said, watching the white-haired man ordering from a braided waitress, and tried to ignore the large deer head nailed to the wall above the fireplace behind him.

'Cheeses are classified on firmness: hard, firm, semi-soft and soft,' Matteo continued.

'Ah. So parmesan would be hard and ricotta would be soft.'

'Yes.'

'And the harder the cheese the more flavour it has?'

'Often, but not always. Have you tried Stilton?' He smiled.

'Oh, yes! The smell! It got so far up my nose I couldn't get rid of it for hours!'

'That's it,' he said, laughing. 'You can change flavour with the cultures you add or the type of milk you use—Guernsey milk has a high fat content, and fat gives flavour, but Jersey milk has higher protein. And of course how long you mature the cheese is a big factor.'

'Now I can see why you have a degree in this stuff,' she said, loving how animated Matteo became when talking about his favourite subject.

'You can change a cheese's flavour by cutting it months earlier than you intended. Most of the time, soft cheeses mature quickly, in weeks, but with less flavour than hard cheeses that mature for years.'

'So what you're saying is that there's no one formula for how long to mature a cheese? The cheesemaker needs to decide that.'

'Not if the cheese comes from a mass production factory. There everything needs to taste the same, always, or the customer gets cranky. But in the hands of a craftsman, making cheese like we do back in Fiotti, from our own goats, yes. What I make this year should taste different to next year because my goats will be different, the grasses and weather will be different, I might feed the goats different foods, I might be having a bad day—or a really good day—when I make the cheese. All of that will change the taste.'

'That's amazing.'

'Just think of it like wine. Each wine that a winemaker makes is different, which is why a certain year will sell really well and everyone wants it and pays a high price for it. Cheese is a living thing—or it should be, when you use raw milk. In a tiny isolated village, like in these mountains, a family may have been making their cheese, using the grandfather's culture that he created, which they re-culture each year. That family would have a totally unique cheese, not found anywhere else in the world.'

'That's so beautiful.' Lara had really only dipped her toes into the Italian approach to food, their reverence for food, but she loved it. They celebrated difference. They *wanted* difference.

She was different.

Perhaps she too could be loved, not in spite of her difference, but because of it. She stared at Matteo for a moment, speechless, then pushed the thought aside to ponder another time.

'So what do the names of all these cheeses mean, then?' she asked.

Matteo smiled, plucking a toothpick from a dark yellow, holey cheese. 'Nothing.'

'Nothing?'

'It's like naming a child. Mostly, cheeses are named for the region they come from, or the cheesemaker who made them. The name won't tell you what it tastes like if you've never tried it before or have nothing to compare it with.'

'So what you're telling me is that I must just keep eating cheese to learn all about them.'

'Yes! See what I'm doing here?' He popped more cheese into his mouth. 'This is work, yes?'

'You have the best job in the world.' Lara picked up a wedge of delicately creamy, truffle-laced goodness—because, surely, there was room in her belly for one more piece.

41

Lara lazed under the duvet and stretched her arms out wide in the deep and comfortable bed. Here in the Austrian-like Italian inn, the walls adorned with shields bearing coats of arms, cowbells hanging from hooks and a dreamy green landscape outside her window, the world felt peaceful. *She* felt peaceful. Here in Italy, she was sinking into herself, really feeling like Lara for the first time in as long as she could remember. Yes, she missed her family and the kids, but she'd found something unexpected here: a place where she wasn't defined by her past. Instead, she could see new possibilities.

Matteo had told her last night that he'd be up early, talking with the innkeeper to find out more about cheese production in the area, so she took the time to check in with her people back home.

First, she messaged Samuel to make sure he was okay and Henrik was looking after him, and told him to give Meg and Willow a kiss for her.

Then she messaged photos of the Dolomites (*the photos just don't do it justice!*) to Hilary, Sunny and her mother. And she sent another text message to Hilary to wish her a happy forty-second birthday.

Hilary replied with a photo of herself dressed in fairy wings and a crown. *This from my kids*, she said. Then a photo of a whistling key chain for her car keys. *This from my hubby. WTF? Doesn't anyone understand I just want a massage?*

Poor Hilly Billy. Maybe next time you should tell them what you want? x

Next time I'm hopping on a plane to Italy. On. My. Own. Speaking of which, have you shagged that gorgeous goat farmer yet??? I need details! Not photos, mind. But long details of romance and wooing.

The resultant thoughts of Matteo made Lara's head spin. She pushed them away and instead tapped out an email to the kids for Sunny to read to them, telling them all about the little children she'd seen in Bologna, staying up way past their bedtime and eating pasta in restaurants with the grown-ups, and the tiny buskers playing their violins in Piazza Maggiore, their instruments at least half their size.

She also told them about the trio of dark-haired beauties, about the same age as Daisy and Hudson, wrapped up tightly in little coats and long pants, blowing bubbles outside a shop selling wooden Pinocchio toys and books, each bubble a perfect whirling circle of rainbows, scattering in the busy wind.

She'd always loved blowing bubbles with the kids, particularly very late on summer afternoons, when the sizzling, stinging heat had finally left for the day, sitting on the still-hot concrete of the driveway, blowing gorgeous bubbles to fill the air, the kids chasing them till they popped, then coming back for more.

Often, Hudson would pick flowers and put them behind his and Daisy's and Lara's ears. It was one of his sweetest traits, she thought, and it gave her hope that he wouldn't turn out like Dave. This was something she never wanted to think about, but sometimes the dread sneaked in. Sunny said it was rubbish, and that any son of hers would know from the start how to be kind and loving. Maybe that was what had prompted her to get a puppy.

A tsunami of love for the children washed over Lara, temporarily rendering her unable to breathe. She closed her eyes, waiting for its intensity to pass.

The first trimester had been a sea of terror, despair and instability. She had run from Dave, run away to Sydney to get as far from him as possible, but she couldn't escape the awful realisation that Dave was right and there was no way she was fit to look after a baby—let alone two, as the scan revealed.

But then there'd been Sunny, her beacon of light.

The second and third trimesters had been much calmer. A heavy stillness fell around her, like huge, rich velvet theatre curtains that kept everything backstage a secret. Lara felt long moments of calm such as she'd never felt before in her life, even though on some level she knew it would all end, the babies would be born and she would give them away. But it was as though she knew if she could just get this one thing right, if she could just hold onto her mental stability long enough to deliver two healthy babies for their chance of freedom and happiness, she'd have done what she'd been put here on earth to do.

People misunderstood the supernatural love of a mother. Lara had it; it was what brought those children into the world, and of that she was proud. But then it had transformed into a different sort of love, one that meant she could willingly and consciously choose the woman who could *be* the real mother, in action, every day. Sunny had it too, this supernatural force of selfless love. Sunny would die for those kids, no question.

42

Lara and Matteo arrived at their next stop on the cheese trail and were shown to their cabin by an ancient, unspeaking man who shuffled across the clearing to open the door for them, then shuffled away again, leaving Matteo and Lara in the deep silence of their surrounds.

Their cabin shared the clearing with an enormous store of firewood, the same height and width as the cabin, both buildings with sloped roofs. They were nestled at the base of a steep rise in the mountain: a platform above many other cleared platforms all the way up and down this range. No key was necessary for the door. They dropped their bags, admired the rustic beams, flagstone flooring and open fireplace, then both glanced at each other.

'There is only one bed,' Matteo said. 'I am so sorry. I didn't realise. I will sleep on the floor, of course.'

'No, don't be silly. I'll sleep on the floor. I'll sleep over by the fireplace.' Lara tried to sound cheerful and as though she really meant it, though the idea was terribly unappealing.

'No.' Matteo held up his hand. 'Absolutely not; I will sleep on the floor.'

Lara bent down to look for a rollaway mattress beneath the sagging queen-sized bedstead in front of her, but only discovered dust. She opened the doors of a wobbly wardrobe, but there were just clothes hangers and extra blankets.

'Maybe we could see if there is another room inside the house,' she said feebly.

'It is no big deal,' Matteo said gently. 'Goat handler here, remember? The barn floor is my friend.'

Lara placed her hands on either side of her face. There was no need to panic, she told herself. They were travellers, on an adventure. This sort of thing happened when you were travelling. She was no stranger to a night with no sleep; she should just count on staying up, maybe snoozing a little on the couch, being useful by tending the fire.

Matteo walked across to her, his strong farmer's frame bulked up by his coat, his deep brown eyes terribly seductive. He put a hand on her shoulder and a spark of energy bolted to her chest so that she almost jumped under his touch.

'Lara, trust me. It is no big deal.'

'Okay,' she said quietly. She was grateful, of course, but she was also starting to feel fractious with Matteo, and couldn't put her finger on why. She smiled it away. 'Let's go for a walk.'

They put on their sturdy shoes and slipped out into the crystal-cool air, heading for the slope behind the cabin, wanting to find a view from up high, like eagles. They hiked in silence, taking their time, nowhere else to be, and Lara's irritated mood evaporated.

They climbed through soft brown leaf litter high up in the hills behind the farmhouse and their accommodation hut, dappled sunlight fell through the pines, and ferns cast magical rainbows at every turn. The only sounds were those of birds taking flight from the grasses around them, the breeze shifting through the treetops high above, and the rhythmic fall of an axe far below them in the valley as it chopped through even more wood to add to the huge winter store. The steepness of the track tested Lara's heart rate.

She stopped, put her hands on her hips and puffed. Matteo, his legs far more used to this kind of exertion than hers, turned and smiled. 'Should we rest here?' he asked.

'I . . . think . . . I'll . . . have . . . to,' she puffed. 'Woo! This hill is steep.' Her calves pinched with burgeoning cramps.

A new sound entered the air then, the loud, tinny clangs of cowbells from the hidden animals meandering through the trees.

Matteo sauntered back down the hill and she was pleased to see that even if he wasn't as breathless as she was, his face was at least beaded with sweat. As if reading her mind, he wiped his forearm across his brow. They stood side by side gazing out at the view.

'Spectacular,' she said, struggling to believe that something so stunning could be real and that she was actually here.

'It is *bellissimo*,' he agreed.

They stood together in peaceful silence, drinking in the view. This was something Lara wanted to be able to see in her mind again and again after she . . .

Went home.

The thought fell hard, just like the axe.

Something odd had happened. Right now, she could say with certainty that she didn't want to go home. Where had that come from? It wasn't as if she was never going home to Australia. Of course she would; her family was there.

It was just that the further she travelled with Matteo into the Italian countryside, the more she felt strong and . . . and . . .

Joyful. *Truly* joyful—the kind that came with assured peace.

She peeked at Matteo's profile and his thoughtful gaze on the magnificent view spread out around them like a living map. Her eyes fell to the fullness of his lips. As if sensing her attention, he turned to face her.

She had no idea what he thought of her, and realised that was where her earlier irritation had come from. She wanted him to touch her. She wanted him to hold her in his arms and run his fingers through her hair. She wanted to feel those lips on hers, feel his heart beating against hers, feel his fingertips on her skin.

But she feared that in telling him the truth about her past she'd ruined any chance of him feeling the same way. How must she now appear to him?

The panicky swirl had started again, a whirlpool of fears and insecurities. She had to do something to stop it.

Instinctively, she reached out and took Matteo's hand in hers, linking her fingers with his, the touch of his roughened skin halting her spiral and landing her right back here in this moment on the mountain, where nothing else mattered.

He pulled gently on her hand, drawing her to him.

Her feet inched their way forwards. Then she made them halt, digging them deeper into the soft leaf litter. Her chest felt as though it might explode, but she had to ask, before he kissed her. She had to know.

'Why don't you blow on your coffee to cool it down?' she asked.

Matteo's shoulders rose, startled. '*Perdono?*'

'Your coffee.' She could hear her voice shaking. 'You hold it to your face to check the temperature.'

'*Sì*.' A corner of his mouth drew upwards and he shook his head ever so slightly, confused.

'Why don't you just blow on it?'

He studied her a minute, thrown by her questions. 'The coffee is sensitive, yes?'

'Um, I don't know—I guess so, sort of.'

'Most people blow . . . *fff ffff*,' he mimicked, '. . . to force it to cool down, but I respect the coffee. It will be ready when it's ready.' He shrugged. 'I am happy to wait; it will be all the sweeter.'

Lara stared at him, blinking fast against a wave of delicious tears.

'Oh my God, I love you,' she murmured.

Matteo leaned towards her. 'What did you say?'

'Nothing. Kiss me,' she said. 'Please,' she added.

His lips met hers and she felt the solidness of him pressed against her, the full length of his body against hers.

If she'd been carrying wings on her back up that mountain, they would have opened right at that moment, stretching, ready to soar.

43

Samuel

Samuel limped as fast as his stick would let him into the kitchen. The tremendous crash had roused him from the sitting room, where he'd been cleaning his old pipe collection. Henrik was standing stock still, his jaw fallen open, staring at the pile of shattered plates and glasses on the terracotta tiles, the bottom drawer of the dishwasher on top of them, cutlery scattered all the way to the fridge.

'What the hell happened?' Samuel asked sharply, already cranky because his favourite blue dinner plate—the one he'd picked up in Milan about fifteen years ago—was in three pieces.

Henrik began to splutter and gesture to the dishwasher, its door dropped open like a drawbridge.

'In English!' Samuel snapped.

'It's not *my* fault,' Henrik said, a finger thrust accusingly at the debris.

Samuel waited, his heart rate still recovering from the ear-splitting crash.

'I just opened the door to finish loading it, to be helpful.'

The old man barely contained an eye roll. *Helpful* was not an adjective he would use to describe his current *badante*. He went for narrowing his eyes at the impossibly blond and pale Swede.

'I pulled out the tray, then turned around to get just one more fork—' Henrik picked up the utensil off the edge of the sink to show his employer, '—but the tray didn't stop. *Whoosh!*' He demonstrated. 'It kept going, so full of dishes and with so much weight behind it.'

'You must have yanked it out,' Samuel said, poking the broken edge of a red baking dish with his stick.

'I did not,' Henrik said with a defensive tilt of his chin. 'It came out all by itself. Whose dishwasher *does* that?' he demanded, incredulous.

Oh, so he wanted to pick a fight, did he? Put the blame on Samuel's dishwasher?

Samuel took a breath, ready to remind Henrik that he'd only been here a short time and the list of 'accidents' would make a coroner suspicious. Already he'd snapped off the slide bolt to the goat yard (and had no practical idea how to fix it), tried to move the terracotta pot with the bougainvillea in it and dropped it, cracking one side, and rested his foot on the edge of the short stone wall outside the kitchen door, tumbling a stone to the ground, leaving the wall like a row of teeth with a tooth missing.

In fairness, his blunders weren't restricted to Samuel's property alone. Henrik had tripped over uneven dirt in his experimental vegetable patch, flattening a sizeable section of young chilli plants and ripping his trousers; fallen *up* the stairs twice; and whacked himself fair and square in the nose while attempting to pull a cork from a bottle of wine. That one had really smarted, if the tears pouring from the boy's eyes were anything to go by.

The lad might have some science smarts about him, but he simply wasn't blessed with any of the physical dexterity that one required to live on the land.

And his pasta bake was terrible. That one had kept Samuel awake into the night as it repeated on him, not once tasting any better than it had the first time.

Samuel released the breath he'd been holding. It wasn't as if he could fire the boy, unfortunately. And there wasn't that long to go, really. Maybe he should just remove anything precious from the Swede's reach. Toddler-proof the house, perhaps. The thought almost made him chuckle.

'Just clean it up,' he said, and noticed the visible relief on Henrik's face, like a little boy who'd escaped a bollocking. Then Samuel turned on his slippered feet and went back to his pipes, wishing for some nice leaf from the village *tabaccaio*. Maybe he could send Henrik for some tomorrow. Surely he could handle that.

44

Lara

Matteo led Lara down the hillside. Her fingers were tingling in his, and she could feel a stupid smile on her face that she just couldn't suppress. At the cabin, he nudged open the door with his shoulder and smiled at her, equally excited, she thought. Her skin hummed beneath her clothes.

Matteo held the door open for her to cross the threshold. She was careful to show restraint this time, not wanting to be that heady, mania-filled person who'd tried to seduce him once before. Still, she noted how on fire her senses were. She could smell him as she passed—moist earth and pine needles and maybe even the fresh mountain air embedded in his clothes—and she wondered if this might be a touch of elation that was just outside the range of normal.

He closed the door and leaned against it, his eyes taking in every part of her, from her windswept curls to her numb-with-cold finger-tips, and down her legs. She didn't know where to look, acutely conscious of that bed a few metres away—a bed with a brown paisley quilt and an ugly navy-blue throw cushion, which nevertheless begged to be messed up.

Matteo moved to her, each step assured of its destination.

She was his destination.

He paused an arm's length from her and she took the chance to gather her wits, determined not to rush this, determined to enjoy every tiny moment, to be truly and fully present.

But then he blinked, and the invisible cord she'd felt holding them together fell away.

'Er . . .' He stepped back and rubbed his beard.

She thought her heart would seize. He didn't want her? How could she have got that so wrong?

Matteo stepped swiftly away towards the kitchen and began whipping open cupboard doors, looking for something.

'What are you doing?' Lara asked, trying to sound amused rather than ashamed.

'Um, we haven't eaten, and it's a long time until *cena*, and I know you get hungry.' He pulled open the bar fridge, found it empty and muttered in disapproval.

'I'm not really thinking about dinner right now,' she said slowly. The fire of rejection burned hot.

Matteo straightened, looking in the cupboards above the sink. 'Ah!' He pulled down a kettle, its cord banging against the door in his rush to get it connected to the power point. 'Coffee?' he asked, already searching for cups.

'Coffee? No.' She stared at his back, his shoulders, his neck, trying to piece together what she must have done wrong, thinking back to the moment on the mountain. She'd been straightforward about wanting to kiss him. She'd been unambiguous. She'd told him she loved him! Though she was sure he hadn't heard her. And he'd kissed her back. *Hadn't he?* Surely she hadn't imagined it. Maybe she'd been too blunt, too forceful. Men liked to chase and feel in control, didn't they?

Dave did.

But Matteo wasn't Dave; Matteo was the anti-Dave.

'I am making one anyway.' He turned to face her and smiled. Then frowned. 'But there is no milk in the fridge, and I know you like milk.'

'Matteo, I don't need milk, really.'

I just need you.

'Hm.' He bit his lip and rested against the sink.

'What?' She struggled to find words. The kettle was rumbling gently beside him. *What the hell is happening*? was what she wanted to say. Maybe he really needed a coffee. He did have a high caffeine requirement; she'd lost count of how many coffees he had a day. Or maybe he *really* needed a coffee to, well, *perform* or something.

'Right, okay, then. I'll have a coffee with you,' she said, trying to keep her hope alive. Had she truly misread this situation so badly?

'Great!' He smiled again, too broadly.

'Great.' Lara stood where she was, wringing her hands for a moment until her nails found the sweet spot on her left wrist and began to scratch, digging for calm.

'But the milk.' He slapped his hand to his forehead.

'Please don't worry about the milk. I will drink it black.'

I will take it purple and laced with bleach if you'll just calm down and make love to me.

Matteo drummed his fingers over his lips, then snapped his fingers. 'I will milk a cow.' He launched himself off the kitchen bench, heading for the door.

She grabbed his arm as he neared, pulling him to her. 'Stop. I don't need milk, Matteo.'

He frowned at her and took a deep breath.

'What is going on?'

Matteo's head rocked backwards, and he gazed up at the ceiling where dried wildflowers adorned the rafters.

'Don't you . . . want me?' she asked, about two beats away from a heart attack.

He took her by the shoulders. 'It is not that.'

Lara let out an anxious breath.

'I just don't . . .' He released her shoulders and took her hands instead. 'What you've been through, what you've told me . . .'

'Oh, God.' She'd said it out loud, accidentally, but decided she might as well blunder on. 'I've scared you. It was too much. Now you don't see me as sexy anymore. I'm that helpless woman, the *victim* . . .' She closed her eyes, hating that word. It would define her forever; that was the lens through which she would always be judged in the context of what had happened to her. She couldn't possibly be attractive to anyone.

'No.' He said it firmly, firmly enough that she felt it could be true.

'Then what?'

'I just want to do it right.'

Her hands were sweaty in his and she wondered if he'd noticed.

'I should be taking you to dinner, serving you wine, serenading you under a full moon,' he said. 'Not just hiking through a cow paddock and falling into a saggy bed. It should be perfect.'

She reached up a hand and stroked soft curls from his forehead. 'It already is,' she whispered.

Lust exploded inside her, an aching need.

He must have felt it too, because the next thing he was shucking off his jacket and kicking off his boots. She did the same, both of them stumbling in their haste, grinning like love-struck fools. And then he kissed her, his muscly thigh between her legs, his hands cupping her shoulder blades, gently but firmly guiding her backwards to that musty, saggy bed.

She pulled at his shirt, loosening it from his trousers, the skin on his back almost too hot to touch. He moaned as her fingertips traced his spine and she felt his hardness against her, and was ridiculously pleased that she had made him feel that way. She smiled against his hungry mouth, so excited to be here with him in this moment, both of them starting something new.

They tumbled into the sagging bed. He pushed her shirt over her head, his hot kisses on her neck and chest and, oh, her breasts, her nipples, her abdomen. She arched her back, staring up at the open beams, breathing hard now, helping him to pull off her trousers, and knew that she was totally safe in Matteo's hands.

45

Sunny

Sunny pulled into the driveway and cut the engine. Down the back of the house, her current project lay waiting. It was an old television cabinet that she was turning into a dog bedroom for Midnight. She had taken off the cupboard doors to open it up and was just about to start sanding it all back. She planned to paint it bright red and wallpaper the backboard and fit a gingham-covered mattress inside, with a little pillow for Midnight's head. It was a dream project, one Sunny hoped she might be able to replicate for customers. The creative prospects were endless—tiny pictures framed and hung on the 'wall' of the canine bedroom, doonas, tin roofs to waterproof them, windows and wall-mounted potted plants on the outside.

Sunny walked down the drive towards the gate, feeling so lucky that Midnight had joined their family; as well as giving the kids so much pleasure, the pup had brought a whole new inspiration to her work. She was just about to reach for the child-safe lock when she realised that the gate was already open.

'Midnight?' She hurried into the yard. 'Midnight?' She whistled and looked under the steps, then headed down to the vegetable garden in the corner. The pup had recently enjoyed digging up all the kale and lettuce, and loved to flop onto the earth and smile as though she was the cleverest dog in the world. Sunny's throat tightened and her eyes stung, her mind going to the worst possible places.

She began to run. She ran up the back steps, let herself in and checked all the rooms, just in case Eliza had somehow accidentally left Midnight inside when she went out. 'Midnight!' Sunny called again and again. 'Here, girl, come here.'

Sunny jogged along the street, hoping Midnight had somehow got out and chased a cat into a yard and then forgotten how to get home. She asked everyone she met along the way if they'd seen her puppy. But no one had.

Five blocks away, she gave up, crying loudly as she made her way home, not caring at all who heard her, and sat down by the phone, her head in her hands.

She called the local vets and left her details, called the council and the pound and left information there too. She called her mother, who was out again at mahjong.

'I don't understand,' said Eliza. 'Midnight was there when I left, I'm sure. She was chewing a bone, last time I saw her.'

'What time was that?' Sunny pressed.

'I don't know. Maybe eight-thirty, just after you left for kindy. But I'm not sure. I'll come home now and help you look.'

Their elderly neighbour on the high side said she hadn't seen Midnight at all. The work-from-home dad on the low side said he hadn't seen the pup either, but he had seen a blue sedan out on the street not long before Sunny had come home from the kindy run. He'd noticed it because he'd been making a coffee about then and had been looking out the window while waiting for the kettle to boil.

'A blue sedan?' Sunny could barely get the words out.

'Definitely blue. My brother has one quite similar.'

Sunny swiped at the tears on her face and staggered back home.

A blue sedan.

She went back downstairs and searched the yard again, hoping that maybe Midnight was sick or injured and lying somewhere in the garden, needing help. Hoping, because it was a preferable alternative to what she now feared.

She looked at the cabinet that was supposed to become Midnight's kennel. 'Please be okay,' she whispered, then started her search all over again.

46

Lara

The next day, Lara practically skipped outside, every cell of her body singing its own happy little song. Matteo had stayed longer than he should have inside the cabin with her, their naked bodies nestled together, their rumbling bellies ignored, sleeping just enough to refresh themselves enough to celebrate their pleasures again.

But finally he'd pulled himself away, shrugging into his clothes and battered jacket to brace himself against the stiff breeze outside. He headed off to visit the cheese factory, another whitewashed, dark-roofed, flower-adorned Austrian-style building on this dairy farm. Lara—knowing she had no self-control when it came to cheese—had chosen to stay outside in the fields, talking to the cows.

Accompanying her now was Isabella, a tall woman in her early twenties, Lara guessed, who strode across the hills in her boots and pinafore dress as though she'd been doing it since babyhood. Which she had, actually, having been born in the very hut where Lara and Matteo were now staying.

Lara scanned the scene before her, taking in the dozens of pale brown and white cows lying down together and chewing their cud, drinking in the sheer brilliance of the day.

Then she stepped in a huge cow pat.

'Oh, shit,' she mumbled, gingerly extricating her horribly stained sandshoe from the suction of the poo.

'Ha, exactly!' Isabella hooted, clapping her hands. 'You are blessed, yes?'

'Blessed with shit,' Lara muttered.

'Ah, it is hard to look down at where you are going when you have all this to enjoy,' said Isabella, motioning to the endless rows of stony Dolomite mountains in the distance, some capped with white snow and some disappearing altogether into slow, moody clouds.

'When I was young, on cold morning with the fire had gone out, I would put my feet inside a big cow poopie to warm them up,' Isabella said, without a hint of embarrassment.

'That's . . . really gross,' Lara said, laughing, and wiping her ruined sandshoe sideways on the grass in a futile attempt to clean it.

'It gets very cold up here,' her guide said. 'Very soon, in few days, we will herd the cows down the mountains, through the village, into lower pastures. Too cold up here for them. The grass stop growing. It is a festival we do each year to celebrate the old ways. Hundreds of years of history for shepherds to bringing their animals up here in the summer to eat the grasses, herb and flower, and make cheese all summer long. Then back to the lower fields, and the shepherds they do other works while the mammas are pregnant with baby cow. So we celebrate this and decorate the cow in headdress of flowers and everyone come to see them walking through the streets.'

'I'd love to see that,' Lara said.

'You should come.' Isabella took the moment to stretch up tall. Sunlight bounced off the long plaits that wound neatly around her head.

'I will ask Matteo if we can come to the festival before we go home.'

Home. That was a strange thing to say. Home to Samuel? Lara didn't allow herself to ponder that for too long, though, and instead pulled her shoe back on and straightened up to resume their walk. They were nearing the cows; a gentle tinkling of bells rang in rhythm with the slight swaying of their heads as they chewed.

'It's like they're in meditation,' Lara observed. 'It's so sweet the way they all lie down together, as if someone said they should stop work now and have a break and they all agree. Like council road workers having smoko.'

'Smoko?'

'It's what we call it in Australia when all the men working on the roads put down their tools and stop for tea and cigarettes.'

'Ah.' Isabella nodded. 'Like *riposo*?'

'I guess so. But not as long.'

They stopped a few metres from the herd, as huge bovine heads turned in the direction of the intruders, considering their options but in no hurry to move. Their ears—easily as long as Lara's forearm—flicked lazily against flies.

'Cows are *gentile*,' Isabella agreed. 'They lick each other and all be together like this. I call this cow council,' she said, grinning.

'That's perfect,' Lara said. 'I wonder what they're discussing.'

'World peace, I think.'

'I like that.'

'Come, you can pat,' Isabella said, leading the way to an enormous animal with lethal-looking horns, wearing a thick collar and a metal bell the size of a dinner plate.

'Are you sure?' Lara said, tiptoeing over.

'Of course. This is Serafina.' Isabella squatted down at Serafina's shoulder and began to stroke her neck. The cow turned her head to Isabella and licked her arm. 'See, she is very docile.'

Lara approached too, also squatting beside the cow's shoulder, but just a little behind Isabella. 'Hello, Serafina. What a beautiful name you have.' She offered her hand for the cow to sniff, which she did, her rubbery wet nose—the size of Lara's fist—snuffling at her skin before extending her blue tongue and licking her arm too. Lara squealed. The cow's tongue was rough, like a big piece of sandpaper affectionately nuzzling her.

Isabella laughed and lowered herself to sit on the ground, a few yellow wildflowers bending under her weight. 'The tongue is so rough so they can to grab the long grass and pull into their mouth. They do not want to lose out on the food.'

'That's how I feel about chocolate,' Lara said. 'A big long tongue would help me too; I could just snatch it from the shelves on my way past and keep going.'

'That is it exactly!' Isabella said, delighted.

Lara sat down too and admired the sheer bulk of Serafina. Her two-toed hooves were big, yet very small, really, when she considered how much weight they needed to carry. They sat in blissful silence for a few minutes, simply stroking Serafina's warm body.

'Do all your cows have names?' Lara asked, looking around at the rest of the group, some obviously much younger, some with smaller horns, some pale with spots. And many of them were now also licking and grooming nearby friends. It was as if Isabella and Lara had started a circle of massage.

'Yes, of course. We love our cows. This is Rosina, Marcella, Sofia, Luisa . . .' Isabella rattled off a dozen names before stopping. 'And that one over there is Freya. She is little, only one horn, but she gives good milk. She thinks she should live in our house. Arrives to the door and tries to come inside.'

As though she knew she was being spoken of, Freya lay down on her side and stretched out all four legs like a cat before closing her eyes in the sun.

'I don't want to leave these hills,' Lara said, suddenly overcome by all this peace around her. Isabella looked at her, but said nothing. Lara put her hand over her mouth, shocked by her own admission. For the first time, she had begun to imagine the possibility of a life away from her mother, sister and kids, and it was both glorious and devastating at the same time.

47

'I'm sure my tastebuds have nothing left to give,' Lara said the next day, licking her fingers. She was eating unladylike amounts of cheese, some of which had been blended with dried wild lavender flowers, and she was decidedly high on deliciousness.

'Come on, be brave.' Matteo sat facing her across a picnic-style wooden table in the shade of the main farmhouse. Lara was in the enviable position of being able to gaze at Matteo's thick lashes and locks as well as the green hills and grazing cows. The air was full of repetitive clanging from their bells.

Isabella appeared, in knee-high white socks today, proffering a tray of olives and fizzy orange drinks. 'More aperitifs?' she asked, placing the tray between them. 'Time for some Aperol, yes?'

Lara exhaled, torn.

'Go on,' Matteo said, reaching for one and giving her a wink. 'It will help you digest.'

Defeated, Lara nodded her thanks to Isabella. The drink tasted of tangy orange and it went straight to her head.

'I've had such a great time here,' she said, reaching out a hand to entwine her fingers with Matteo's.

'Me too,' he said, giving her a cocky smile.

'Not just because of that! Though that was excellent.'

'Of course,' he agreed.

'Hey, I've been thinking,' she said, sipping on her drink.

'Less thinking, more eating,' Matteo said, reaching for yet another slice of marbled salami and blue cheese. Lara envied his ability to eat and eat and apparently not gain weight.

'Well, it's funny you say that, because I've been loving this great food tour of Italy I'm having—and I've read a lot of cookbooks in Samuel's bookcase, and I really want to do something for him.'

Matteo nodded his interest, still chewing.

'I would love to see him enjoy a big family feast again, you know, like the ones you were describing from when you were young, from when Assunta was still alive.'

Now Matteo frowned and tapped the table thoughtfully. 'But the family is not . . .' he searched for a word, 'the same.'

'That's what's so sad. He's an old man and needs . . .' She trailed off. 'Anyway, you would come, wouldn't you?'

'Of course.'

'And there's me, and Henrik—and do you think maybe Gilberta and Mario would come?' she asked, remembering how kind they were to her the day she met them at Matteo's mother's house.

From down the hill came the sound of car doors closing. New visitors to the farm were arriving this evening.

'They might,' Matteo finally said. 'There has been a lot of history there. Gilberta is Mamma's friend, so it might be tricky. But Gilberta is very generous. She loved spending time with Samuel and Assunta. I'm sure she has missed him.'

Lara grinned. 'That's what I thought.'

'If Gilberta went, Mario would go too.'

'Okay!' she said, excited. 'So we've got, what?' She counted on her fingers. 'Five of us and Samuel. Six is a nice number for a feast, isn't it?'

Matteo nodded, open to this conversation, she was pleased to see. 'I could bring cheese and wine, the antipasti.'

'And I might ask Gilberta to teach me how to make pasta, just as you suggested. But we'd need a distraction to get Samuel out of the house for the day so it can be a surprise.'

'Henrik could do it.'

'And do you think . . . I know it's a long shot, but could we get your mother to come? Maybe your brothers? Anyone else? I want it to be a feast to remember.'

Matteo shook his head. 'My mother would never come.'

Lara wasn't surprised, but it was still disappointing.

'My brothers, *sì*, maybe,' he said. 'It's been a while since we have all been together anyway, much to Mamma's great sadness.'

'Why so long between visits?'

He raised one shoulder. 'I don't mind so much.'

'Go on,' she encouraged.

He inhaled and blew out his cheeks, holding the air for a moment, then letting it go in a rush. 'My brothers are a lot . . . *tougher* than I am, you know?'

'I think so.'

'I am not a black sheep, but maybe the odd sheep.'

Lara gave him a sympathetic smile. She was an odd sheep too.

'Besides, they are all busy with family and businesses. I think it's convenient for them to have me still around the family home. I am Mamma's only baby left nearby. That is why she calls me all the time. Family is everything, you know. We are expected to do our duty. She is ageing and getting nervous.'

'But that's the key, isn't it? Your mother sounds desperate to see everyone. If you could get them all to the feast, then she'd come, wouldn't she?'

Matteo grimaced, and wriggled in his seat as if wanting to escape from a net. He raised his eyes to the sky and sighed heavily. '*Mamma mia*.'

Lara grinned.

'Alright,' he said. 'Let's do it. We'll work out the details as we go.'

A gust of wind suddenly raced up Lara's jeans, freezing her ankles and making her shiver. Matteo looked up into the clear sky—a sky almost too clear, as if it was the eye of a storm. 'Winter is coming fast,' he said. 'It will snow here.'

'Isabella was telling me about the festival this Saturday when they walk the cows down through the village. Do you think we can make it back to see it?'

'I think so. We'll only be with Carlo for tomorrow night, so we can drive through there on the way back.'

Lara wondered, not for the first time, if she should tell Matteo in advance the story she needed to tell Carlo, to prepare him. Her allegiance was torn between Samuel and her *boyfriend*. At least, that's what she thought Matteo was. She felt herself frown, wondering if he thought the same. Should she ask him? It felt ridiculous to have to ask, as if they were teenagers, but she also knew she had to protect her heart.

Then again, if she asked him now and he didn't say what she wanted him to say, the rest of this trip would be a nightmare.

'What are you thinking?' Matteo said, circling a finger around his face to indicate that hers had clouded over.

'Oh, nothing that matters.'

48

Sunny

A noise pulled Sunny from her uneasy slumber. Since Midnight's disappearance she'd barely slept, just snatching scraps of disturbed dreams between cold sweats and nausea.

The kids had cried themselves to exhaustion for the second night in a row. Sunny felt both the crushing weight of helplessness and searing fury at that vile man for torturing her children in this way. But she knew she shouldn't be surprised; this was what Dave did best, messing with heads, making his victims either feel crazy or actually turn crazy.

There was that sound again. It was a scraping, banging noise.

Her heart accelerated and she flicked off the blanket, her bare feet hitting the cold floorboards. Then she heard Eliza's doorhandle open too. They met in the hallway.

'Did you hear that?' Sunny whispered.

'I thought it was the kids at first, but . . .' Eliza pressed her hand to her throat, the streetlights outside catching the whites of her eyes.

They stood frozen, listening, trying to hear over Hudson's snoring from the kids' room.

There it was again: a scraping noise. Eliza reached for Sunny's arm.

'Come on,' Sunny said, far more bravely than she felt. She moved slowly towards the front door, Eliza following, still clutching her arm. They were in the lounge room now, just metres from the front door. Sunny strained to listen, but could barely hear a thing over the pounding in her ears.

They paused near the door. Silence.

'Who's there?' Sunny called, her legs shaking now.

The reply was instant: crashing and scratching and yipping and a flurry of puppy barks.

Eliza gasped. Sunny wrenched open the deadlock and hit the switch for the outside light. There on the front porch was a fruit box, its lid fastened down tightly with gaffer tape, and small slits in the side from which Midnight's tiny soft nose and tongue and paws were crazily poking as she fought to free herself.

'Oh, Midnight, thank God,' Eliza cried, bending to help Sunny pick up the box and bring it inside. Sunny shut the door hard behind her and locked the deadlock again.

'Hurry, get her out,' Eliza said.

Sunny pulled at the tape and they both dug their nails under the edges trying to lift it off, but it was stuck hard. Midnight was barking nonstop, throwing her body against the sides of the box, making their job impossible.

'Get a knife,' Sunny ordered, continuing to wrestle with the box. She crooned to Midnight, 'Shush, baby girl, shush. We're nearly there.'

Eliza returned with a small knife and Sunny held the box still while her mother carefully cut through the tape. Finally, enough of it was broken so that Midnight could buck and jump her way out of the box to land in Sunny's arms, a writhing hot body, her tongue all over Sunny's neck and face, whimpering and shaking as though she'd been through hell.

Eliza started to cry. 'Oh, dear girl, where have you been?' Then she stopped. 'Sunny, look.' She reached into the box, drew out a note and read it aloud.

Next time.

'Next time what?' Sunny hissed. The stress and loss of sleep in the weeks since seeing Dave had frayed her nerves. 'Next time *what*?!'

Eliza held her hand to her mouth and spoke through her fingers. 'I don't know.'

Then they both saw it: the string of coloured beads attached to Midnight's collar. One of Daisy's bracelets.

49

Lara

Carlo's home was in the Domodossola mountains, in the tiny town of Oira. The houses here were medieval, with rough stone walls, sloping shingle roofs, narrow windows, no balconies or awnings. There was one building that looked like a castle, with a tower and turrets. Narrow cobblestoned roads wove crazily between the houses. The effect was eerie, as though they had slipped through a keyhole and into the past by accident. Lara wouldn't have been surprised in the slightest had a horse and cart and washerwoman passed by, perhaps a prince in full armour atop his horse, or an unfortunate man in the pillory, rotten fruit being flung at his head. The mountains rose high above them. The air was even colder here, and Lara had to pull out a woollen scarf and gloves she'd bought along the way.

She was pleased to see smoke coming from Carlo's chimney when they pulled up outside his tiny stone home. The wind was blowing hard, the grasses and flowers bent almost to the ground. Three cows grazed on the steep slope that leaned into the back of the house, their bells all ringing. Heavy, dark clouds filled the sky, threatening a downpour.

Carlo met them in front of the house, flinging his meaty arms around Matteo and rocking him from side to side with many effusive words and pats on the back. He kissed him on both cheeks, and then held him out with his huge hands as if to study him. Carlo was as solid as Samuel was frail, Lara noted, although he was even older. His thick head of white hair didn't give away his true age at all. At last, having squashed the young man to his breast so many times that Matteo began to protest, Carlo turned his gaze on Lara.

'And who is this who has come to see me?' he asked, launching straight into English as though Lara had *foreigner* written all over her.

Matteo came to her side and put his arm around her shoulder, and beamed widely as he said, 'This is Lara. She is *Australiana*.'

'*Australiana?*' Carlo whooped. 'You must be cold.'

Lara laughed. 'I am, actually!'

'Come! Come inside,' he said, moving to her other side, and both men frogmarched her indoors.

The welcoming area was more spacious than it looked from outside, though it was sparsely furnished with little more than a couple of shabby couches, a full bookcase, and a large woven rug on the floor.

The kitchen was even more sparse, set up more like a commercial kitchen than a home. In the centre was a huge, blackened fireplace with an enormous copper cauldron sitting to the side. This was attached to a swinging, extendable arm—for moving the full cauldron over the fire and back out again. Stone benches ran along one side of the room. Putting the pieces together, Lara recalled that Matteo had said the building had been in the family for generations, used solely during the summer when making cheese was the prime focus.

On the other side of the ground floor, a simple wooden staircase turned on itself and led to the upper floor.

'Please sit,' Carlo said, gesturing to the couches. Lara and Matteo sat down together. Lara removed her woollens and Matteo reached for her hand, and her whole body warmed instantly, not just from the fire's heat. She felt totally comfortable and welcome here, and in that moment wasn't even worried about having to tell Carlo Samuel's story.

Carlo tugged on the red and yellow braces holding up his trousers. 'It's so good to see you,' he said, his eyes shining with emotion as he took in the younger man's face. Lara couldn't remember the exact relationship betwen them.

'It's good to be here, *zio*,' Matteo said, using the word for *uncle*. 'It's been too long.'

Carlo clapped his hands together. 'Time for grappa!'

ꕥ

The day progressed so smoothly, with Carlo and Matteo sharing many stories of what had been happening in their lives, and Lara felt so at ease, that she almost forgot the real reason she was here. Carlo assumed that she and Matteo were a couple and showed them to the spare room upstairs—bare timber floors, dark wooden wardrobe and nightstand, and an old double bed with another paisley bedspread.

Then he said it was time to make cheese. 'The milk is waiting!' He grimaced, checking his watch. 'It is a little late, what with the joy of guests coming to visit.' He put a paw on each of their shoulders. 'But still time. Come, you help.'

The milk was sitting in large metal pails outside the kitchen, but with the icy breeze that blew through the back door, Lara had no concern that it might have gone off. She inched closer to the fireplace as the men dragged the pails inside.

'You like cheese?' Carlo asked Lara.

'Oh, yes,' she said. 'I've been loving getting behind the scenes and learning how everyone makes their cheese. Matteo taught me how to make ricotta,' she said, beaming at her man.

Carlo frowned. 'You make from milk?'

'Yes,' Lara answered, a little confused. What else would anyone make ricotta from?

Carlo wagged a finger at Matteo and *tsk*ed. 'You should know better.'

Matteo shrugged and smiled, already pulling the huge copper cauldron away from the wall on its industrial arm. It was big enough that Lara could have easily climbed into it. 'Sometimes you have to improvise,' he said, then squatted to pick up one of the pails of milk, hoisted it to the lip of the cauldron and poured. A torrent of milk gushed into the pot. Once that pail was emptied, the men hefted the next two pails.

'How many litres is that?' she asked.

'My cows, they are good milkers, so in here—' Carlo gestured to the cauldron and waggled his head, '—about fifty litres.' He stoked the fire to break apart the coals and generate more flame, then pushed the cauldron over the fire pit, where it stayed, suspended in the air.

Noting Lara's keen interest and clearly proud to be able to share the cheesemaking process, Carlo seated himself on a wooden chair and began to lecture.

'First we will be making *Bonomo formaggio di montagna*, which is my family name—Bonomo—and *mountain cheese*.'

Lara smiled at Matteo, remembering him explaining to her that you could call cheese anything. This was Carlo's family's special recipe.

Matteo had taken a seat too, leaning forward and paying close attention. She didn't think it was for show either. She'd seen that Matteo was an eternal student, voraciously soaking up new information. It was one of the things she loved about him.

Carlo got up again. Lara couldn't help but admire his fitness. The old man picked up a metal shovel and began to stir the milk over the flame. Then he put his hand in it to check the temperature. Satisfied, he pulled the cauldron off the flames, picked up a packet and sprinkled white powder into the milk.

'This will start the ferment,' he explained to Lara.

Matteo jumped up, picked up a long-handled slotted spoon and began to stir, his muscles flexing against the weight of the milk.

She whipped out her phone to take photos. This was what she'd hoped to see the day she visited Matteo's farm, not the sterilised, white-tiled kitchen with tall silver fridges. This, with its open fire and a cauldron (a *cauldron*, for goodness' sake), and two generations of a family making cheese together.

Now Carlo poured in a small amount of tea-coloured liquid from a test tube. 'Rennet,' he explained. Matteo stirred a little longer, then returned to his seat.

'Now we wait about twenty minutes,' Carlo said, also resuming his place near the huge pot of fermenting and coagulating milk. In English, he chatted with Matteo about the goat farm and his brothers, his mother and cousins. The time passed quickly and then the men were up, testing the milk, which was now thick curd, like custard, stiff enough that a hand shovel could stand up straight in it. Carlo declared that this was the point at which the cauldron should go back over the flame. But first they had to break up the curds. Each man picked up a tool like a shovel, dipped it into the curds and pulled it through, raising a sweat with the effort, the custard-like curds breaking into smaller and smaller pieces.

The cauldron swayed its way back to the fire and Carlo seated himself again. Both men were puffed and Matteo stretched his arm and shoulder after the effort, Carlo chuckling at him. 'You come, you build muscles, yes?'

'Gladly,' Matteo said.

'Will the lumps that are left in the milk break down now they're back over the flame?' Lara asked.

'Good question,' Carlo said. He gave Matteo a look that said, *Hey, your girlfriend is smart*. 'The size of the curd determines how long it can age. The smaller the curds, the longer the ageing. We are not going to age for long with this cheese—a few months over winter, maybe—so the curds can be bigger.'

They let the curds cook until they reached forty degrees, stirring constantly, Carlo occasionally picking up a handful to check the texture and temperature. He didn't use gloves; apparently, the traditional way of making cheese involved a stray arm hair or two.

'You must keep stirring,' Carlo said. 'The texture must be even or there will be mistakes in the ageing.' He indicated that Matteo should have a turn dipping his arm into the mixture, which he did. 'Spin the milk around, then hold your arm still. You will be able to feel the curds as they move against your skin.'

Matteo nodded, his eyes alight.

'I love watching this,' Lara said. 'This is a really beautiful thing. Thank you for showing me.'

Carlo's face became solemn; instead of making him happy, her words seemed to have had quite the opposite effect.

'My family has done this for hundreds of years,' he said finally. 'Thousands of years, perhaps. This cheese is the same cheese they all ate, made the same way, passed on from one to another every summer. This cheese, it has come through my ancestors' hands, all the way to mine.'

Lara took a moment to really feel the depth of that tradition, sensing the spirits of Carlo's family still living here in this home, in that fireplace, in that cauldron and, ultimately, in that cheese.

'And now I might be the last one,' Carlo said, his eyes filling. He wiped at them with the back of his hand. 'My children and grandchildren, they all live away in cities. They work, you know, in offices, in front of screens.' His distaste for that notion was palpable. 'When I go . . .' He let his words hang there, and allowed his eyes to drift to Matteo's. His loss and loneliness and fear hung in the air.

'It's . . .' Carlo was lost for words again for a moment. 'This is the way cheese should be made, not in big steel factories, milk coming from many farms all over. No identity. No care. This is art,' he said, flinging an arm out towards the fireplace. 'Living art. And it will be lost forever.' A log on the fire popped and crumbled. 'Sometimes I feel helpless. All this will be lost.'

'Teach me,' Matteo said automatically, still stirring the curds. 'I'll come back again soon and stay with you. Teach me the old ways. I will carry them for you till it is my turn to pass them on.' He dropped his shovel in the cauldron and went to Carlo and put his arms around him. Carlo buried his face in Matteo's shoulder and patted him firmly on the back. They whispered in Italian. Then Matteo stood back, his hands still on the older man's shoulders. 'So teach me, yes?'

Carlo gave Matteo one final pat, then pulled himself together, sitting up straighter as Matteo returned to the pot.

Watching them, Lara's heart had squeezed up into her throat; tears trickled down her cheeks. She wanted to fling herself on both of them, hug Carlo and take away his worries—and maybe adopt him as her own uncle, since she didn't have any of her own—and to kiss Matteo all over his face and tell him what a great man he was and how much she loved him.

She sniffed quietly and the silence stretched on, but not uncomfortably, filled only with the fire's crackling, hissing and popping.

At last Carlo felt the milk and declared it ready to be made into cheese. Matteo swung the cauldron back out into the room, the curds lapping the sides.

Carlo bent over the cauldron and buried his arms in the cheese, his nose practically touching the surface of the liquid. He began to move his submerged hands, his face reddening with exertion. One arm swept in from the left, then the other did the same from the right, working mysteriously beneath the surface of the now watery whey bath, over and over until, with a grunt and a heave, he lifted an enormous ball of hand-pressed white cheese, which broke through the surface like a baby birthed in a bathtub. He held it there for a moment, this huge and obviously heavy creation, floating in the sea of whey, while he got his breath back.

'Oh, wow,' Lara breathed.

Matteo stood by the cauldron, nodding. 'Magnificent.'

Carlo took a wire with a handle at each end and used it to cut the ball of cheese into two, each about the size of a fat cat. He heaved both out onto the stone bench nearby. Whey ran from the balls, draining down a gutter and into a bucket on the floor.

Matteo reached to the shelf above for wooden rings with clips, about the size of bamboo steamers. They were moulds, lined with cheesecloth, and the men stuffed each cheese ball into a ring, tightening it with rope, more whey gushing out and running down the drain into the bucket. They tied the cloth around each ball and placed heavy wooden weights on top, squashing the cheese further.

'Now we drain them,' Carlo said, removing the full bucket that had been catching the whey and replacing it with an empty one. He heaved the first bucket to the cauldron and Matteo assisted him to empty it in.

'*Now* we make ricotta,' Carlo said, his words dripping with superiority.

'With the whey?' Lara asked.

Carlo was already pushing the cauldron back to the flames.

'Ricotta means *recooked*,' Matteo said.

'Recycling at its best,' she marvelled.

'Nothing is wasted,' Carlo confirmed, taking a seat again while he waited for the whey to heat once more over the open flames, this time reaching a much higher temperature. He was sweating, and reached into his pocket for a handkerchief to wipe his brow. 'The whole reason we have cheese is to preserve the goodness in milk,' he said. 'The cows, they give milk in summer, lots of milk. We want to save it for the harder, colder months. This is how we save it.'

Lara nodded, seeing clearly the way cheese had been invented. It had always been about preserving the nutrients to keep people healthy during the hard months. It was genius.

Matteo rested by her side, one ankle on the opposite knee. 'That's why cheese comes in round balls,' he said, grinning. 'So they could roll them down the hills at the end of summer and collect them at the bottom. That way they didn't have to carry them on their horses or donkeys.'

'Seriously?' Lara asked, unsure if he was joking or not.

'*Sì, sì!*' Carlo said. 'Everything for a reason.'

Before long, Carlo declared the whey was ready, and the process of making ricotta began. Lara jumped in to help fill the cheesecloths with the white clumps of cheese, straining off the last round of whey, which Carlo said he would use to water his vegetables.

Near the end of their ricotta-making, Carlo suddenly asked, 'Where did you two meet?' and Lara's bubble of joy popped. The time had come. Once Samuel's name was mentioned, she would have to explain why she was here.

Minutes later, with everyone seated in the living room once more, she began the story.

50

Samuel, 2003

It had been raining for two weeks.

When Samuel got home it was already dark, his Alfa Romeo's headlights casting erratic beams across the grass and the short rows of young olive and pine trees that he and Assunta had recently planted around their outdoor table where they held their feasts. It would give them more shade during summer, and become a boundary to show the kids where the footballs had to stop. Not that there were many kids left. Giovanna's children, Lily and Antonio, were nineteen and twenty-two, and Gaetano's daughter, Aimee, was fifteen. They were past the footballs now. But then again, at the rate Assunta made new friends and collected people along the way, there was always someone's child or grandchild coming. And some of the young men of the family, like Matteo and his brothers, still wanted to play football. Anyway, all this soaking rain would at least be giving the trees a good head start. When they were bigger, he and Assunta would hang kerosene lanterns on the branches to create atmosphere.

Samuel cut the engine, bracing himself to get drenched, regretting that he hadn't yet built a carport. He was late getting home, the students' English-speaking exams having run over time; he couldn't leave them half done. Assunta would be unhappy with his late return, as she had been for many weeks now in the lead-up to the exams and with Samuel's extra tutoring responsibilities, but they would benefit from the extra money. She'd be happy when he told her it meant they'd saved up enough for their trip to Holland. Assunta had seen the little windmill figurines her cousin had brought back from there, and fallen in love with the idea.

He slammed the car door and held his document wallet above his head as he jogged lightly to the back door, water dripping down his shirt collar, reminding him that the roof in the spare bedroom would be leaking too. Again. Shutting the door to the kitchen behind him, dripping water all over the floor, he resolved that as soon as this rain stopped he would get up there and fix that leak once and for all. He'd get Carlo to help him if necessary. He hated asking anyone for help, truth be told, because he felt he was forever having to prove to the Palladino family that he was worthy of their Assunta.

To provide for her and their family was his job. And he prided himself on it as much now as he did back when he first met her, her contagious laugh ringing through the geranium-filled street.

'Assunta!' he called, stripping off his soaked white shirt and tossing it on the back of a dining chair, heading for the stairs. She must be upstairs. He took them two at a time, excited now, imagining her face when he told her about the money for Holland.

'Assunta!' he called again, popping his head into their bedroom. It was empty, just as it had been when he left this morning, the white duvet pulled up tight and the pillows tucked in neatly. Mother Mary on the wall above the bedhead. Lace doilies and fresh flowers from the garden a bright contrast against the mass of dark wood in the room. But the double doors that opened to the balcony were ajar, the curtains flapping wildly in the wind, rain blowing in. He crossed the room and slammed the doors shut, nearly slipping in the puddle on the floor, but righting himself just in time.

'Assunta!' he called, annoyed now. Where was she?

Then he heard a scrape and shuffle up on the roof.

Surely not. His darling wife had been threatening to get up there and fix the leak herself, but he'd laughed off the suggestion along with her teasing. Well, mostly it had been teasing. Sometimes she set her jaw and lifted her chin, hands on hips, challenging him. He called it her bull stance—the moment the bull stands square and stares the matador in the eye, metaphorical steam shooting out of its nose, daring the challenger to wave his red cape. Samuel never waved the cape; instead he merely took her in his arms and nuzzled her neck until she softened and slapped him away, laughing.

But she couldn't have gone up there in this downpour.

He swept the wet curtains aside to peer out onto the balcony. Sure enough, there in the corner was the old wooden ladder, paint-spattered from when they'd freshened up the bathroom.

Christ!

Rain stung his eyes as he lunged out into the weather, almost toppling the ladder as it protested under the violence of his ascent. One foot after the other, his fingers digging into the wood as he pushed himself higher and higher, his heart galloping.

The truth was, Samuel was afraid of heights.

That was why he hadn't been up to the roof. He'd been ignoring it, somehow convincing himself that it would fix itself in time. Assunta didn't truly understand the depth of his fear, thinking he was being melodramatic, and he was too embarrassed to admit his shortcomings to her family. Instead he buried his anxiety under jokes and teasing. Long dry spells allowed him to forget there was a problem with the roof. Or with himself.

Now Assunta had done what he wasn't man enough to do. He cursed himself viciously as he neared the roof, his head starting to spin, his vision blurring and failing in the low light. His hands were shaking so much he was sure he wasn't going to be able to climb up onto the roof. He couldn't get a grip.

A sob caught in his chest.

'Assunta,' he called. But it came out as a whisper. He paused and leaned his forehead on the gutter, working hard to control his terror, closing his eyes so he couldn't see what was around him. A huge gust of wind rocked the ladder and he squealed. He *squealed*.

He was paralysed. He couldn't go up and he couldn't go down.

And then, like an angel, Assunta was above him, squatting on the edge of the roof, water running in rivulets down the terracotta tiles around her. She reached out a hand and placed it on his cheek and he cried, with relief, with shame, with love.

But she didn't say a word.

That was when it hit him.

If he'd been terrified before, now he'd stepped into another dimension of hell. Suddenly, everything stopped around him. The rain, the wind, his fear of heights. It all fell away, because when he looked up into her face and her eyes, he saw she'd gone to the dark place.

Her long hair hung around her face in wet strands. Her eyes were black. The skin on her face was lined with age. Yet all he saw was his beautiful young love. A love he didn't want to lose. Not now. Not yet. They were supposed to die at an ancient age in each other's arms.

Her hand rested on his cheek.

All too soon, the moment ended. The rain was still pelting down on him. His weak and useless legs were shaking on the ladder. And the space where his Assunta's hand had been was ice cold.

She stood up.

'No!' Samuel was moving now, his arms pulling him up and his legs finding strength born from pure desperation. 'No! No! No!'

He kept screaming it, hoping it would help. Hoping it would break the spell she'd fallen under, reach her somewhere, wherever she was, in that place she fell into at times like this, times that had started after Lily died. Who wouldn't feel their world had ended when their child was dead? But the episodes had never gone away.

He was scrabbling now, awkward, ungainly, doing whatever he had to to get on the roof. But Assunta was on her feet and walking, already strides ahead.

Later, he would look back on that moment a million times, and each time he would marvel at how calm she appeared. She was walking, just as if she was off for a stroll on a hilly slope, heading home.

There! He'd made it! He was up, on his feet, staggering but not falling, negotiating the steepness of the roof. He was doing it! He was gaining on her.

He had to get to her.

To touch her. To hold her.

He had to stay on his feet.

'Goddamn it!' he yelled, slipping dangerously on the roof. 'Come on, God, I need you now. Send your angels. Send yourself. Please!'

But it was too late. She walked to the edge of the roof and simply kept walking. Without a backwards glance, she took flight.

51

Lara

Lara felt shaky and empty. The burden of relaying Samuel's story may have been lifted from her, but it had been replaced by the heaviness of seeing the pain on Carlo's face and the shock on Matteo's. She felt guilty for passing on such grief.

She took a deep breath and let it out unhappily. 'So that's why I'm here. Samuel sent me. He needed you to know but he was . . . afraid,' she finished lamely. 'It was too much to send in a letter or something . . . and . . .' She was lost for words. She'd said so much already.

From the lounge room, she could still hear the fire crackling gently in the kitchen, and the constant drip of the whey making its way down the stone channel and into the bucket.

'I don't know what to say,' Matteo said, inching forward on the couch next to her.

'And nor do I!' Carlo boomed, making Lara jump and Matteo visibly flinch. 'What you say is false. It is not true!' His face had turned beetroot in seconds. His meaty fists conducted an orchestra with every word. 'Assunta fell! It was an accident, one caused by Samuel's laziness and failure to protect his wife.'

'*Zio*,' Matteo interjected. 'I don't think Lara would come here to lie.'

'Then it is Samuel who lies,' Carlo said, heaving himself to his feet. 'Assunta did not . . .' His face twisted. 'She could not have.' A spray of Italian followed, his eyes on Matteo but his hand flying to point at Lara every so often, making her wince. She shrank into the cushions. Matteo got to his feet as well, standing protectively in front of her, forcibly quietening his own voice, hands in front of him in a *let's all calm down* manner.

This seemed to infuriate Carlo further, his hands ascending in response. Matteo let out a frustrated sigh and scratched his head. Carlo made some sort of final declaration before glaring at Lara and stalking from the room, slamming the heavy wooden door behind him.

There was a moment's silence while they each breathed.

Lara bit her lip and shook her head slowly at Matteo, who stood with his hands on his hips. His eyes held hers and she was certain she could see disappointment there. She'd ruined his beautiful reunion with Carlo.

'Are you okay?' he asked her.

She nodded.

'He's not . . . I know he is loud, but he isn't . . . he would never—'

'It's okay, don't worry about it.' She brushed off his concerns, though in truth Carlo's anger had unnerved her. 'I'm sorry I didn't tell you this story before, but I . . . I don't know, I felt loyalty to Samuel, I suppose.'

Matteo rubbed at his forehead, whether to ease some sort of pain or to help him think she wasn't sure. 'I should have known he had something up his sleeve,' he muttered.

'What do you mean?' Lara hoisted herself from the sofa so she could look him in the eye.

Matteo paced in a circle. 'I asked Samuel if it would be okay if you came away with me for a couple of days.'

'You did?'

'I felt so bad after the wolves. You were so sad and wouldn't talk to me. I didn't want you to think of me that way, you know. If you never saw me again . . . or if you left Italy and that was the last memory you had . . . I just wanted to give you good memories.'

Lara melted. 'You are so beautiful.' She took his hands. 'I'm still sorry I didn't tell you. I didn't want to do it at all, but he pleaded with me. I tried to talk him out of it; I tried to get him to ring up, or write, or ask you to do it.'

Matteo grimaced at that.

'You are his family, not me,' she went on. 'I thought it would be better coming from Carlo's own family, but Samuel thought it was too much of a burden. And you and I weren't exactly talking at that point. I thought I was coming on this trip to help Samuel, not to . . . you know,' she said softly.

Matteo's set mouth relaxed.

'What are we going to do about Carlo?' she asked, partly anxious about how to get through the night here in the house with him and partly sad for this *zio* she'd grown so fond of in just one afternoon. She'd like to give him the benefit of the doubt that his reaction to her story had been a wild exception to his normal behaviour.

'He's gone out to feed the cows,' Matteo said, his thumbs gently rubbing the backs of her hands. 'I think we should leave him be for the moment.'

She nodded. 'Is there anything I can do?'

Matteo raised his eyes to the ceiling and drew a deep breath.

Lara laid her palm over his heart. 'Should I leave? You could drop me somewhere in the village for the night, get me out of the way. Maybe then you and he could talk this through.'

He thought about this for a moment, chewing on his bottom lip. 'It doesn't seem right to leave you on your own in a strange village. I should come too.'

'No. Don't be silly. Your uncle needs you. I'll be fine, really. Stay here and talk. You might not get another chance for a long time.'

Matteo kissed her and even under the strained circumstances it was the loveliest kiss she'd ever had.

༄

'Ready to head down the mountain?' Matteo asked later that evening.

They were standing at the top of the stairs in Carlo's home, Lara's suitcase at their feet. She pulled the box that Samuel had given her from her bag.

'Here,' she whispered, handing it to Matteo. 'Samuel wanted Carlo to have this. I was going to give it to him after I told him the story but then things got a bit out of hand.'

'What is it?' he asked, his voice equally low, turning over the wine-coloured antique box in his hand. They didn't actually need to be whispering. Carlo had gone underground to the cheese maturation cave below the house to wash maturing cheese rinds with salty water to prevent spoilage. Lara was disappointed to miss it. Matteo had described the cave as something to behold, with a constant supply of water straight from the mountain running into a small basin attached to the wall, providing a consistent temperature and humidity all year round, something modern-day cheesemakers fretted over even with the latest refrigeration technology.

'I don't know,' she said. 'I couldn't bring myself to open it; it didn't seem right.'

Matteo hesitated. 'Do you think I should?'

Lara shrugged.

Matteo clasped the box in his left hand and prised it open gently with his right, the hinges rusty and unwilling. Inside was a pendant on a tarnished silver chain. He frowned. 'What is it?'

'I've seen that before,' Lara said. 'It's the same symbol as on the name plate on the villa—Giardino dei Fiori.'

Matteo carefully lifted the pendant to study the four-petalled flower inside the silver diamond more closely. 'It looks very old.'

'It does,' Lara agreed, horrified that she'd been carrying something so precious around with her in her suitcase. 'How old is the villa? Sixteen hundreds?'

Matteo nodded, still squinting at the pendant, turning it this way and that.

'It couldn't be that old, surely,' Lara said, feeling sick.

'I have no idea. Jewellery is not my specialty. Goats, good. Jewellery, no.' He dangled it to its full length—about thirty centimetres.

A loud thump from under the house signalled that Carlo had slammed the door to the maturation cave. Matteo quickly replaced the necklace in the box and snapped down the lid. 'Let's hope Carlo will know what it means.'

Residence Briona was a rather stunning fifteenth-century hotel, with multiple storeys of stone archways and porticos, and medieval tunnels. While she wasn't pleased with the circumstances that had led her to be here, Lara was still happy to see the building firsthand.

Late room-service *couscous con pesce* had displaced the knots inside her that had been there since she'd told Carlo her story. Now she sat in her tastefully decorated blue and white room and phoned Samuel.

'How are things with Henrik?' she asked.

'He broke his toe this morning.'

'You're kidding.'

'I wish I was.'

'That's terrible. What was he doing?'

'Collecting the eggs.'

'But that's . . .' Lara tried to picture how such a gentle activity could lead to a broken bone.

'Trust me, I know.'

'Did any eggs survive?' she ventured, trying to lighten the moment.

'A few.' Samuel sounded tired.

'So, who's looking after you now?' she said, anxiety rising—had her charge been left alone to fend for himself?

'I think we're looking after each other,' Samuel said and, to Lara's immense delight and relief, she heard him chuckle. 'I have feet; he has hands. Now we must go everywhere together, like conjoined twins with our walking aides.'

She grinned at the mental image. 'I'm sorry I'm not there to help, or at least to watch you both getting around together.' Lara paused. 'Matteo and I have been to see Carlo.'

Samuel's intake of breath was audible, and she ached with sympathy for him.

'How did he take it?' Samuel asked, and she was sad to hear that the previous lightness in his voice had gone, each word now sagging with weight.

'Not especially well,' she said.

Samuel held his silence.

'And I delivered the necklace too.'

'Good,' he said, relieved.

'Can I ask where it came from? It seemed very old.'

'More than a hundred years.'

'It was Assunta's, I assume?' She knew she was being nosey now, but she couldn't help herself. Besides, after being burdened with that story and bearing the brunt of Carlo's fury, she felt entitled to some answers.

'It was her grandmother's, forged in the late eighteen hundreds. They still had many jewellery-makers in the family then. It was a wedding gift, I think.'

'And it's the same as the plate on the house—Giardino dei Fiori.'

'Yes.'

'Is it very valuable? I only ask because I was kind of horrified that I'd been carrying around this priceless heirloom.'

'No, I don't think so,' Samuel said. 'Not in the way you're thinking. But in terms of its sentimental value to her family, yes.'

'So what does it mean? Why give it to Carlo? Why wouldn't you give it to Giovanna or Lily?'

'Carlo and I fell out after Assunta died. He blamed me for her death. I blamed myself, but not in the way he thought. He believed I was ashamed that I hadn't fixed the roof—and of course there was truth in that. But I blamed myself for . . .'

'Because you couldn't save her.'

Samuel took another moment to gather his strength to go on. 'Carlo came to the villa one night, late, about a week after Assunta's death, a couple of days after her funeral. Her funeral notice was still plastered over the church walls in the village. He'd been drinking. He stumbled out of the car and fell onto the lawn. He was crying. She'd been like a sister to him—his little sister.'

'But you'd been close too, hadn't you?'

'Like brothers. But only as adults. Assunta had been with him from childhood.'

Lara thought of Sunny and the world of intimate knowledge and history they shared. It was true that no one could ever come close to replacing that. And now with the precious cargo they shared between them, they would share a deep bond for life.

'He needed someone to blame, and I was there.'

'What happened?'

'We fought. Wrestled like stupid boys, punching each other.'

'Weren't you, like, sixty-something?'

Samuel laughed, but the sound was empty. 'I was sixty-four. He was sixty-seven.'

'What happened?'

'He kept yelling at me that it was my fault, and it was all I could do not to scream at him and tell him the truth. So because I couldn't scream it, I channelled all that rage into my fists and I broke one of his ribs.'

Lara gasped, too shocked to speak.

'Well, to keep a long story short, it hardened everyone's hearts against me even more than before. Carlo left. He couldn't stay in Tuscany anymore. He said everywhere he looked he saw Assunta. But before he left, he demanded the necklace from me, saying I had no right to it because it belonged to the Palladino bloodline.'

'But your children are Palladinos too,' Lara argued, horrified. (Matteo was right: she should have watched *The Godfather*.)

Samuel sniffed. 'The remaining family asked them to choose between me and their Italian family. They went to London, and it's been too difficult for them to come back.'

Lara's mouth hung open.

'Carlo went up north to be with his ailing uncle and take over the house. If there was anyone left here who felt anything for me, they gave up all pretence once Carlo departed. As far as they were concerned, I caused his leaving too.'

'Goodnight, Samuel!' Lara heard Henrik call in the background.

'*Buona notte*,' Samuel called back.

Lara waited a beat to ensure they'd finished. Then she asked gently, 'So why now? Why dredge all this up again and tell Carlo about the . . .' She couldn't bring herself to say the word *suicide* either, just as Carlo had faltered. 'And why give him the necklace?' She was more than half expecting Samuel to clam up on her, to say he was tired and needed to go to bed, or to tell her outright to mind her own business. He was certainly within his rights. But apparently he recognised that the moment he'd asked her to do this task for him was the moment they'd crossed a line.

Samuel made some noises, sounding almost as though he was chewing his cud like one of his beloved goats. Lara waited, her ears straining to catch his every word. When they came his voice was quiet. 'I held onto the necklace for Assunta's sake when I should have given it to Giovanna long ago. Now it's one thing I can do to set my children free from any further bitterness hanging over their heads from the rest of the family. I don't want the family's anger and resentment to stop Giovanna and Gaetano from coming back to Italy . . . if they want to. It won't fix everything, but it's a start.'

Lara pulled a tissue from the box next to her.

'And as for why I would tell the truth of the story, there are so many reasons,' he said, his voice weakening. 'I did it for myself, selfishly. I'm tired of carrying this knowledge alone. By bearing the shame, protecting Assunta's memory, I have paid the price of not being part of my children's and grandchildren's lives. I know Assunta wouldn't have wanted that. But also I want to be able to say it out loud and tell them all that what Assunta did—taking her own life—it *isn't* the great shame and sin they might have once believed it to be. It was silence around depression that killed her in the first place.'

Lara blew her nose noisily. 'When will you tell Giovanna and Gaetano? They have to know this was not your fault, no matter what they've been told by the family.'

'Soon. I will do it soon.' Each word was heavy with his regret at having waited so long.

She almost let it go there, but it seemed the floodgates had opened, so she might as well ask. 'Why did you throw your wedding ring into the Trevi Fountain?'

He didn't speak for some time.

'The Trevi Fountain has the god Oceanus in the centre.'

'Yes.' She remembered the towering marble statue.

'He is the personification of the ocean. And despite the whole of this country loving Jesus, Mary and the pope, the old mythologies still run deep.'

'Okay.'

'The things the Catholic Church used to say about those who did what Assunta did . . . They said anyone who commits suicide would endure eternal damnation. It would have brought huge shame onto Assunta and the family. I wanted to protect her, our children and the rest of the family.'

'What about now?'

'Officially, some things have changed. Culturally, not really. There is still an ignorant belief that people who commit suicide lose their soul and can never go to heaven. I called out to God to save my Assunta as I was running across that roof to catch her, and He didn't help me.' Samuel's voice was tight with anger. 'My time is coming to an end. Water took my Assunta from me. I wanted to make an offering back to the water god—a sacrifice that would be taken seriously. I want to be sure that when my time comes, wherever Assunta is, I'm swept straight into her arms.'

52

Sunny

Hudson had pulled out his magnifying glass and was finding ants to study, while Daisy lined up dominoes to stand in a row only to have them fall again and again. Sunlight beamed through the open window next to them, lighting up their hair with shimmers of gold. Midnight squirmed in Sunny's lap—she was now firmly an inside dog, under lock and key.

What Dave had done . . .

Sunny had never been someone who found life frightening. Quite the opposite. Yet in a very short amount of time, Dave had brought her to her knees. The stakes were simply too high. She was a nervous wreck. She had no faith in the law; it was up to her to protect them.

As she watched her children play, her mind reeled back to that day in Sydney when her life changed forever.

Lara, having had a seven-week scan, knew that there was not just one baby, but two. She'd been crying for days in the dingy one-bedroom flat they'd rented, engines revving almost constantly outside the windows, the men in the street frequently shirtless, the women pushing strollers and smoking. The deep scratches on her wrist looked red and inflamed. Sunny had been trying to convince Lara to at least put antiseptic cream on them, but Lara wasn't interested in taking care of herself. She hadn't showered for three days, and had barely touched the food Sunny cooked for her.

Lara was folded over on the couch with her head on her knees, her hands in her greasy hair, scratching at her scalp as though trying to dig through to the terrible thoughts in there and pull them out.

'I thought I could do it,' she whispered.

Sunny rubbed her back, feeling her own sanity tested to the limits. How long could this go on?

'But I can't.'

Sunny nodded silently, though she knew Lara couldn't see her. She had no idea if Lara was referring to the abortion or to having the babies. On the issue of having the babies, she had to agree. Right now, given what Lara had been through with Dave, her sister wasn't in a fit state to raise one baby, let alone two.

A termination made all practical sense.

And yet.

Watching the ultrasound, Sunny had felt something deep for those twins—little blobs, with blobby heads and blobby bellies, blobbing along together in their watery home. Just blobs.

But they were her blobs too.

Those babies shared her genes. They were as close to being her own babies as they could possibly be.

Lara bolted upright then, her pupils huge, her hands shaking. 'Help me. Please help me,' she begged, and grabbed Sunny's shirt, tearing it at the collar. 'I can't kill them.' She shook her head wildly, till Sunny restrained her so she didn't hurt herself. Lara stilled under her hands. And then she broke down. A wild, primal, animal wail erupted. 'But I can't be their mother either.' She collapsed into Sunny's lap, rigid.

Sunny took a deep breath and looked at the 1970s-brown curtains covering the barred window. They'd hit bottom. For a second, she was seduced by the darkness that was engulfing Lara, tempted to fall apart and drown in it too.

But the thing with the darkness, she learned that day, was that it only made the light shine brighter. Suddenly, it was all very clear.

'I'll do it,' she said. She nodded strongly to herself, to the darkness that was waiting to ruin them both, and to Lara. 'I'll be their mother.'

Lara sat up, her eyes bloodshot, red-rimmed, puffy. She wiped her arm across her nose. 'What?'

'I'd hardly be the first to do it. It's been done all through history, aunts raising babies as their own. Half the royal family's probably got dubious bloodlines. And none of it makes a bit of difference.'

Meaning. Her life suddenly had meaning. All the drifting she'd done, all the rubbish relationships, all the waiting for . . . something. That *something* was here. Sunny was thirty-two years old, and this was where life had led her.

'You'll do it?' Lara squeaked.

'Yes!' Sunny said, suddenly smiling. She put her hand on Lara's abdomen. 'If you want me to, of course. It *is* your choice, Sprout,' she affirmed, though she was hoping beyond hope that Lara wouldn't choose to abort them. 'Only you can decide your future,' she said gently.

Lara looked down at Sunny's hand, then covered it with her own. 'Oh, Sunny.' And then she crumpled over and slept for sixteen hours, a deep peaceful slumber, as though knowing that everything would be okay.

While Lara had slept, Sunny sat nearby, guarding her, and talking to those little blobs. Those two little blobs that had grown up into these laughing, cheeky, inquisitive children in front of her now.

Dave could destroy them all.

Martha's opinion was that Lara's medical records would stand for little in court as a way to keep Dave from the kids. And she had a mental illness. Dave was a respected physician and any day now he would know that Lara and Sunny had committed fraud by naming Sunny as the mother on the birth certificates.

It had been stupidly easy. No one asked Lara to prove her identity when she went to the doctor or to the hospital. They only asked for a Medicare card. That was it. Sunny handed over hers and Lara became Sunny for a while. The babies were born to Sunny Foxleigh and they stayed that way. When the sisters registered the birth, the paperwork simply asked for copies of identification documents—mother's passport, birth certificate and so on—and the signature from the midwife that the babies were born to Sunny Foxleigh, which, as far as the nurse knew, was true. Sunny presented all her documents and that was that.

The intention had been to hide the children from Dave. Formal adoptions left paper trails and laws seemed to change all the time about freedom of information around sperm donations, open adoptions, surrogacy and the like. Hiding down in Sydney, keeping the pregnancy away from Dave's eyes, it seemed the simplest, cleanest thing they could do to stop him from finding them. But now Dave could take them to court to prove paternity and then ask for amended birth certificates naming him as the father. And then their fraud would come to light and Sunny and Lara would be in even more trouble.

Dave must not get his hands on her children. Sunny had failed in protecting Lara from him. He had tortured her. The revelations had taken years to all come out, and whenever they did, they gave Eliza and Sunny nightmares for weeks. And they knew the man would never change.

There was no way in hell he was *ever* going to touch her children. She would do whatever it took to protect them, or die trying.

Given the options available to her, the answer was simple. She had to take them and hide. She could take them on a road trip, and Dave wouldn't be able to find her, delaying court proceedings again. She'd be gone long enough that he'd hopefully get bored and, regrettably, find another victim to torment. Because that was what men like Dave did. They destroyed one life and moved on to another.

But even if he kept trying to get the kids, the one thing she could hope for was that the older the kids got, the less likely it was that a court would take them away from their mother. From her. She had to buy as much time as possible. Years, if necessary.

She'd long ago bought an ageing but reliable Ford Falcon, a model with not many comforts but a lot of grunt, and it had a tow bar for towing the furniture pieces she picked up for her work. It was capable of towing a caravan.

Sunny spent a total of thirty minutes considering the difficulties—money, homeschooling, sharing the caravan with an energetic puppy, not having Eliza with them—wondering if she should be trying to talk herself out of the plan. But she was a good problem-solver, a capable child carer and talented handywoman and she poured a mean beer: that should be enough to get her started with some odd jobs. She was a gypsy at heart. She got out her laptop, typed in *long-term caravan hire* and watched as the screen filled with websites.

53

Lara

They caught sight of Isabella among her herd of cows, just one of dozens of young shepherdesses walking alongside their four-legged charges. She was dressed in hiking boots, jeans and a billowing long-sleeved white blouse under a black vest, and she carried a hiking stick. Her beautiful bovine ladies were adorned in towering, ornate floral headdresses that bobbed backwards and forwards with the movement of their huge square heads. More flowers encircled their necks, attached to the thick collars, with clanging bells the size of kettles.

The crowd was half a dozen deep the whole way along the narrow cobblestoned streets that were shut down to traffic in all directions, locals and tourists alike staying put—as though time itself stood still for the spectacle of hoof after cloven hoof treading the medieval paths home.

Lara jumped up to wave at Isabella above the heads of onlookers. Isabella walked steadily, following the flicking cow tails, hurrying one along every now and then if it was distracted by the paparazzi. But she looked up just as Lara's head shot up into the cold air, her gloved hand waving wildly.

The young woman returned Lara's enthusiastic greeting. She tried to call something, her hand to her mouth as a mini megaphone, but Lara couldn't possibly hear it. In fact, she was fairly certain she'd never hear again. The cacophony of discordant sounds ringing out from the cows' bells was enough to send her home doing a splendid Quasimodo impersonation. *The bells, the bells!*

Cameras flashed in the dim light, the day heavily overcast. Summer was well and truly over, the weather having turned so quickly since she'd arrived in Italy just a month ago. The oppressive, low-hanging clouds held the stench of cattle manure thickly in the air. Lara hurried to take some photos of Isabella and her brown and white cows, but they were soon swept along in the great current of bovine and human flesh, replaced by the mocha-coloured, leaner cows of the next group, with huge kohl-lined eyes and seductively thick lashes.

Lara leaned back into Matteo and he wrapped his arms around her from behind so they could watch the parade together. This was truly a moment she would never forget.

❧ ❧

After the last of the cows had passed, Lara and Matteo inched their way back to the van through a village that was probably usually sleepy. In the van, Lara turned up the heat to defrost her fingertips, which were chilled despite her gloves. Silly, cheap polyester. If she was going to be here for winter proper, she'd have to invest in some super wool-lined leather gloves.

They were on their way back to Tuscany now, not stopping to see Matteo's brothers as they'd originally considered doing, instead forging on so Matteo could visit another farm he wanted to see—one that ran buffalo and made soft white and blue-veined cheeses.

'I am very interested in seeing what they do,' Matteo had said. 'I am looking forward to sharing ideas about less wastage.'

'What do you mean?'

'I have been reading journals that say buffalo produce less milk per day but with higher solids, so it takes less milk to get the same kilo of cheese. And buffalo are more efficient with their feed.'

'So you have to spend less on feed to get the cheese?'

'Correct.'

While Lara was thrilled to see yet more animals, she was a touch disappointed not to meet Matteo's three big brothers.

'Tell me their names again,' she said, yawning. She'd stayed up late last night talking to Samuel and then lay awake thinking, and missing Matteo's body next to hers.

'Enzo is the oldest; he is forty now, and is an electrician. Sergio is thirty-six, so just a year older than me, and owns a chain of gymnasiums. And Salvatore is thirty-eight and is a textile trader.'

'And they all have families of their own,' she clarified.

'Yes. I have seven nephews and nieces, all between the ages of twelve and fifteen.'

'Wow. I bet that gets expensive at Christmas,' she said, grinning.

Matteo murmured agreement. 'It does. And, you know, I am a simple shepherd man,' he said. 'What can I bring them? Cheese?'

'So you're the only one without kids.' Lara studied him sideways while he steered the van through the countryside, wriggling her toes, willing them to defrost as well. He had such a lovely profile.

He glanced at her quickly, then darted his eyes back to the road and lifted the black leather-clad shoulder nearest to her before dropping it again. 'I was a late starter,' he said.

'Why? You're a hot man!' she said, running her hand up the denim over his thigh.

'This is true.'

'And so modest.'

'That too,' he joked. 'But not so good with the words, huh,' he said, suddenly more serious.

Oh, yes. The stutter. That thing she hadn't noticed once the whole time they'd been away. Was it possible he stuttered less around her? It was an incredibly flattering thought, but a rather far-fetched thing to believe, she admitted. Or was she simply completely blinded by love? Or deafened, as it were.

'I imagine that was difficult for you growing up.'

He shook his head lightly and she wondered if he was going to go on. 'It was. Especially with three older brothers who were all great football players and very popular with the girls. Who all had the right clothes and the smooth skin. I had to go to speech therapy instead of football practice, and nothing fixed my words. I was an embarrassment to them.'

She was about to say, *Surely that's not true*, but stopped herself. Children could be unimaginably cruel. She'd certainly felt the alienation at school, her oddness apparent from a young age.

'I had to choose to be different from them because I already was,' he said. 'I focused on science. At first it was because of my speech. I wanted to know why this had happened to me. But I found my peace with animals. They don't care what I can or can't say.' He smiled, sadly at first, but then with real warmth. 'They have lots of time to listen. No rush. Rushing is no good for me.'

'Do you get on with your brothers now?'

Matteo waggled his head, considering. 'Some days. It depends on their mood and that depends a lot on who is doing well in the World Cup.'

'Would you . . .' Lara stopped, not wanting to ask her question out loud, but knowing she would have to do it sooner or later and that it might as well be sooner. She needed to know what he thought so she could get her head and heart straight. 'Do you think you will want children one day too?'

Matteo was silent a moment, tapping the steering wheel. Then, 'Perhaps, if the time is right and it happens, then yes.'

Okay, that wasn't too bad. Lara released the breath she'd been holding. Silence stretched between them then, with Matteo concentrating on the winding roads and Lara gazing at the deepening blue, purple and grey sky, the approaching inclement weather like a big bruise seeping through the air.

'What about you?' he asked quietly.

'Until recently I hadn't given it too much thought because I have this great relationship with Daisy and Hudson, and while I know that Sunny is their mother, they're still part of me and they're still mine too, in a tribal sense, I guess. We all belong to each other.'

'That is very special.'

'But coming over here, having this time away from them, I see for the first time that maybe I won't always be living with them. Maybe they have a life to lead without me in their face every day, and maybe I have a life to lead too, with all sorts of new adventures. At some point I'll need to learn to fly on my own.' She pressed her lips together to hold back emotion, but when she spoke her voice was shaky. 'I'm at peace with my choice and I know it is *possible* for me to have another child, but I also know it would be a difficult process in terms of medications and managing my condition, and it would put a lot of strain on both me and my partner.'

She fixed her eyes out the window, determined not to look at Matteo. She needed to get it all out, and if she looked at him she'd want to stop. 'I'm not saying it would never happen, but right now I think there's too much risk for me to do it again.'

Sunny and Lara had agreed that one day when the kids were older they would tell them the truth, the story of their birth. Lara knew she had a family for life. That was a lot more than many people got. Sometimes you had to count your blessings and not tempt fate.

The warmth of Matteo's hand cupped around hers. 'That's okay with me,' he said. 'I have a big family already. Sometimes too big. Right now, I just want to keep seeing you.'

Lara blinked rapidly. 'I want that too.'

The first plops of rain splattered on the windscreen and Lara leaned over and rested her head on Matteo's shoulder, her arm across his chest, feeling warm and snug and deeply in love.

54

Sunny

It was after eight o'clock and the kids and the pup had finally fallen asleep. Sunny could hear their noisy sleeping breaths over the bump of the wheels along country roads, though it did little to quiet her mind's chatter about the car that had been following her for the past half hour.

The interminable blackness threatened to swallow the weak beams of her car's headlights. She couldn't shake the two white orbs that had been following her for the past half an hour.

She'd tried slowing down, encouraging the driver to overtake her. When that didn't work, she tried speeding up. But he simply followed whatever she did. Now she was doing the speed limit, yet the other car still sat up against the back of the caravan as though she were crawling.

Every now and then a wallaby sprang out from the dark roadsides and she swerved sharply, almost squeezing her eyes, expecting the too-close car behind her to come through the back end. So far, they'd been lucky.

The next caravan site was still over an hour away. The navigation system's calm voice had been silent for a long time.

Her phone lit up like a torch and vibrated from where it sat beneath the handbrake, nearly causing her to plough off the road.

Still the car followed.

Sunny grappled for the phone, dangerous in the dark, but desperate to connect with someone.

Mum.

'Hi.' Her voice was tight, even to her own ears.

'Are you talking on your phone while driving?' Eliza asked, her motherly voice condemning.

'Yes. I don't have much choice.'

'You could pull over.'

And have the person behind me slash all our throats in the dark on the side of a country road?

She ached for her mother's voice to talk her down from the ledge of fear she'd climbed to. But Eliza was already reeling with worry, for her children and grandchildren but also for her own safety, at home alone.

'I can't,' Sunny said, trying to speak calmly. 'I need to get this lot to the caravan park so I can put them into bed.'

'Put me on speaker, then.'

'No, just talk to me. I don't want to wake them up.' Sunny flicked her gaze to the side mirror again, knowing that the eye of the car behind her would still be there, staring back at her. The brightness hurt. She forced herself to look back to the inky nightscape ahead.

'Where are you now?' her mother asked, casually, as though it was an easy question.

'You know I can't tell you. It's too risky. For all I know, Dave has tapped our phones.'

Eliza paused. 'I don't think that's possible,' she said carefully. 'He's not a spy.'

Sunny could imagine all too well what Eliza was thinking—that her elder daughter had cracked, that she was displaying signs of bipolar too. 'It was a joke, Mum. A bad one. I haven't lost the plot, I promise. But we need to stick with the plan. No one can know where we are, including you.'

'I don't agree with this,' Eliza said firmly. 'This whole thing has gone too far. We need to tell the police about Dave, about what he did to Midnight, and you need to tell Lara what's going on. She has a right to know.'

Sunny couldn't speak for the wave of fury that rose up her chest. *Lara's rights?* Sure, she had rights. But what about *Sunny's* rights? She was the twins' mother.

Instead, with supreme control she kept her voice as even as she could. 'The police can't help us. We have no evidence. They'll start asking questions. It will all go downhill. Remember what Martha told us?'

'Yes,' Eliza agreed reluctantly.

'We have to stay out of the legal system. And as for Lara, do you really think telling her about Dave will achieve anything? She can't do anything from over there, and the last thing we want is for her to . . .' Her words caught in her chest as she realised that she, Sunny, was on the edge of collapse herself.

'Break down,' Eliza finished helpfully.

'Yes.'

Eliza sighed audibly. 'Okay.'

The car behind her dropped off suddenly and Sunny's hopes rose. She watched as it pulled over to the side of the road.

'Mum, I've got to go. I shouldn't be talking and driving. I'll let you know when I've got the kids settled.'

She tossed the phone onto the passenger seat beside her and floored the accelerator, praying like mad that no stray cows would be wandering the road. She didn't know who was driving that car or what they were doing now—maybe it was Dave, maybe it was a random lunatic, or maybe it was all in her imagination. But she wasn't going to waste a second trying to find out. The engine roared and the wheels gobbled up the road, every kilometre inland taking them just that bit further away from Dave's reach.

55

Lara

Downstairs in the kitchen of Giardino dei Fiori, the men were already awake, Samuel sitting with a mug of black coffee on one side of the wooden table and Henrik on the other, his foot up on a chair.

'Well, good morning to you both!' Lara squeezed Samuel's shoulder gently and was more than touched when he raised his hand and placed it over hers, patting it briefly.

'Good morning,' Henrik said, looking the most cheery she'd seen him, the remains of crinkles around his eyes as though he'd been smiling and laughing with Samuel just before she came in the door. He was still wearing dark blue pinstriped pyjama bottoms.

'I better just head out to milk the goats, then I'll be right back,' she said, tying up her hair to keep it out of her face.

'We have already done it,' Samuel said happily.

'Oh! I was looking forward to seeing the girls again,' she said. It had been dark last night when she and Matteo got home and Henrik had already milked Meg and Willow, able to perch on a stool to do it while Samuel assisted as necessary. Lara had heard the goats saying hello to her—*meh, eh, eh, eh*—from inside the barn while she'd leaned against the car with Matteo, kissing him slowly, sad that their special week had come to an end, wondering where they would go from here.

'Well, I'll do the milking this afternoon,' she said, laying claim to the job. She inspected the lump of bandaging under the thick sock poking out of Henrik's open-toed shoe. 'Oo! Is that your second toe?'

'Yes.' His cheeks flared. 'So stupid.'

'Don't be so hard on yourself,' Lara said. 'Accidents happen. Now, would you like some scrambled eggs? Toast?' She went to the fridge. 'Let's see. What about some fried mushrooms and tomatoes, some sort of cheese, some leftover . . . what is that? Lentils? And what is this—' she opened a plastic container, '—bacon?'

'Pancetta,' they both answered at once, like an old married couple.

Lara suppressed a smile, wondering when Henrik would be leaving or if he'd somehow got himself an invitation to stay. It was amazing how quickly friendships could flourish, even between the most unlikely people. 'Pancetta,' she corrected herself. 'How about I do a big fry-up?'

Samuel raised his bushy white eyebrows and Henrik craned his neck to look at her over his shoulder.

'What?' Lara asked, bewildered.

'Are we expecting company?' Samuel asked, nodding towards the bounty in her arms.

'Oh! I woke up hungry, imagining a big Aussie breakfast with scrambled eggs, smashed avocado on toast and salmon. So get ready, lads. It's time I shared a bit of my culture with you, don't you think?'

Samuel looked amused but wary.

Lara closed the fridge door with her hip and carried the food to the kitchen bench. 'You both look as though you could use a good feed.' She clapped her hands and grinned at them. 'I hope you're hungry!'

With both men in the house physically hampered, Lara spent a lot of the morning cleaning, which she really didn't mind because she'd had difficulty doing up a pair of pants this morning, all that lovely cheese nutrition in storage for the harsh winter ahead.

She was changing the bedding in Samuel's room when she got a message from Gilberta.

We make pasta tomorrow, *sì*? xx

Lara sank onto the edge of the bed, thinking. She really wanted to keep this feast a surprise for Samuel, so she'd need him out of the house while the tutorial was going on. But what could she do? Matteo was back at work today and Henrik—who she'd originally thought might be the one to get Samuel out of the house—was off his feet.

Gilberta couldn't come here; it wouldn't work. Mind you, she probably wouldn't simply turn up after all these years anyway.

That would be great. Is it okay if I come to your house? I want to keep it a secret from Samuel.

My lips they are solved! xx

Lara wedged her phone back into her pocket, smiling.

For morning tea, she continued to break food routines in the house and instead of serving pastries she made real English scones, taking her time to rub in the cold butter with her fingers until she had a really fine crumb, stirring in the fresh goat milk and egg and pulling it together, patting it out and using a glass to cut out the rounds. She brushed them with extra beaten egg and milk and set them out on the tray to slide into the warm oven.

This morning's goat milk had been settling in the fridge for a while and the pale yellow cream had risen beautifully to the top. Lara took exquisite pleasure in scooping it off into a delicate glass bowl to serve with the scones. Then she rummaged in the larder and found a jar of apricot jam, though she was momentarily disappointed it wasn't homemade—she'd been spoilt on her little tour of artisan food producers.

Samuel and Henrik had been reading in the large living area, silently, companionably, but both started to make some noises once the aroma of the scones drifted out to them.

'What are you making?' Samuel called.

'It's a surprise,' Lara called back.

'It smells wonderful,' Henrik added.

'It's my mother's recipe,' she said, squatting to peek through the oven door and watch the scones turning golden.

Her family didn't have anywhere near the rich food traditions she'd unearthed in every corner here in Italy, but she did have her mother's scone recipe, which was probably just an everyday workman's recipe, but still it was known by heart by all three of the Foxleigh women. Lara had even employed it as an activity to get the twins learning some kitchen skills, more to manage their boisterousness than impart family tradition. But the effect was the same, she supposed.

She set the dining table with plates and knives and the little bowls of cream and jam, then told the men to come to the table.

'Coffee?' she asked. She'd have preferred a big pot of tea but she hadn't seen either a supply of usable tea leaves or a teapot in the house. Henrik and Samuel came in with their walking sticks and eased themselves into the chairs at the round table, their eyes taking in the beautiful cream and deep orange jam.

'The moka pot is on the stove,' she said, placing coffee mugs in front of them. 'And I'm just getting the scones out now.'

Their eyes followed her hungrily to the kitchen, where she pulled out the tray and slid the scones into a tea-towel-lined basket, trussing them up to keep them warm and soft. This step should never be omitted, according to her mother. Eliza said she could always tell when someone had failed to do this, as the scones were tough.

Lara delivered them to the table like Red Riding Hood and then finished making the coffee. 'Henrik, how long will it take for your toe to heal?' she asked from the other side of the fireplace that sat between the two rooms.

'The doctor said I should keep it strapped up for at least three weeks. It might take longer, but it is more pain management than actual bone management. Not like Samuel's wrist,' he said. 'That is a real broken bone. Mine is just . . . embarrassing.'

'You're not the first person to break a toe,' Samuel said generously.

'And you won't be the last,' Lara added, bringing over the moka pot and a jug of milk. 'How much longer do you have here in Italy?' she asked.

Henrik looked crestfallen. 'I can't work at the goat farm now,' he said. 'I'm not sure if Domenica will hold a place for me, as the dairy will be heading into some quieter times over winter.'

Lara remembered Matteo saying that Henrik wasn't too helpful on the farm. 'Maybe you could find a job in the village.' She unwrapped the scones and passed the basket to Samuel.

'I would like to stay longer,' Henrik agreed, 'even if I am not studying on farms. I like it here.'

'I do too,' Lara said.

There was a moment of thoughtful silence while cream and jam were passed around.

'Do you eat scones in Sweden?' Lara asked, spreading a half centimetre of apricot jam on her scone.

Henrik nodded, his mouth already full, then swallowed and licked his fingers. 'Ours are heavier and thicker, more like a brick on your plate. These—' his eyes widened, '—are light as a feather.'

'Thank you.' Lara beamed. 'It's so simple, really. Lots of people put all sorts of things in their scones, like sugar or lemon juice or raisins, but I think the scone is just the canvas for the cream and jam.'

'They're wonderful,' Samuel said. 'I honestly can't remember the last time I ate scones, let alone ones straight from the oven.'

'Would it have been in England?'

'Quite likely.'

'Did your mother make scones?' she asked, sensing there were some memories there.

'She did. But growing up we had food rationing, so it was difficult without butter.' He smiled wryly. 'My mother used to encourage us to dunk them in tea to soften them. You could break all sorts of social rules while rationing was on.'

Lara enjoyed the morning tea with Samuel and Henrik, feeling very much at home. It was a new but undeniably pleasant feeling, and again it made her wonder what the future held.

56

Gilberta's kitchen was peaceful. Rough-cut stones formed an arch above the fireplace, hundreds of years old. Garlic bulbs and herbs, trussed with string, hung from hooks in what was obviously both a practical necessity to dry them and a casual way to store them. Mother Mary loomed in a painting at least a metre tall above the kitchen sink. Mario was out, helping a neighbour to build something, Lara had garnered, Gilberta's English breaking down a little in translation. So they were alone, other than Gilberta's small collie Greta, a miniature version of the one in the painting of Samuel's Lily. Greta fussed about Lara's feet for a while, suspiciously sniffing her boots and bell-bottom linen pants.

'She must be able to smell the goats,' Lara said, squatting to take the dog's head in her hands and massaging her neck in greeting.

'She is hoping you have treats,' Gilberta said, slipping an apron over her bright red hair and tying the strings behind her. 'I'm very naughty, feeding all the time,' she said guiltily.

Lara washed her hands at the sink, then Gilberta passed her an apron of her own, in a shade that was a near perfect match to the older woman's hair.

'First we make the sauce,' Gilberta said, moving to the stovetop and hefting a cast-iron pot onto the flames. 'Is very simple. We use meat and wine.'

'That's it?' Lara asked, astonished. 'At home, I would use onion, garlic, basil, oregano, parsley, and I'd put in vegetables for the kids, so peas, maybe some carrot . . .'

'No, no, no!' Gilberta said, her hands in the air. 'We no do that. Oregano, yes. Maybe add whole onion, then take it out. But that's all. Meat and wine—*if* you can have leftover wine from the feast the night before.' Her eyes shone. 'Mario, he cannot handle seeing a little bit of *vino* in the bottom of the bottle!' She threw up her hands again, this time in defeat. 'He must get to the bottom. He is in love with the bottom!' She laughed heartily, her hand on Lara's arm. 'So we open another, *sì*?'

'Sounds good to me.'

Gilberta pulled out a bottle, the cork popped satisfyingly and they each breathed in the bouquet.

'To good health,' Gilberta said, raising her glass in a toast.

'To new friends.'

They made the sauce quickly, tossing in the meat to brown and covering it with red wine, then moved on to the pasta.

Gilberta produced an enormous rectangular plank of wood with a lip on one side. It clunked down onto the bench, the lip holding it in place on the edge. 'This board has been in family for many years. Here, you see the wood has worn away where all the women make their dough,' Gilberta said proudly. She patted the board and Lara bent down to eye level to see the groove.

'That's fantastic,' she said, goosebumps erupting unexpectedly over her just at the thought of all those women, their hands, their energy, their dreams and their love transforming the board.

Then Gilberta pulled out a large plastic bowl. Okay, that wasn't quite as authentic. 'We use plastic as it won't make the pasta go cold. If not the bowl, you do it straight onto the board.'

Gilberta pulled out a packet of flour and a carton of eggs. She hummed as she poured the flour into the bowl.

'How much flour are you using?'

'One kilogram of flour. The whole bag. It makes it easy—no measure.' Gilberta scrunched up the empty packet, shook the flour in the bowl, made a well in the centre, then reached for the eggs. 'And ten eggs.'

They broke eggs in silence till Gilberta said, 'It is always better to aim for abundance. Overshoot the ingredients.' Then she waggled her head and muttered, 'Maybe not so if adding water—there's only so much you can fix if goes wrong.' She wiped her hands on her apron. 'Like going to bad hairdresser!' she said, and burst out laughing. Then she settled again in front of the bowl and began to pull the flour into the middle to cover the eggs, then expertly worked the eggs through, pulling it all together. It was mesmerising to watch.

'The colour of the pasta comes from the eggs,' she said. 'If it's yellow, it's the eggs. And we use *grano duro* wheat, type double zero.'

'What does that mean?'

'Is hard wheat. Pasta made from the tender grain is not so good. It breaks apart easier. Hard to get *al dente*.'

When a smooth, pale ball of dough had formed, Gilberta picked it up and laid it on the board. Rhythmically, she pushed it with the heel of her hand, then pulled it back into shape.

'After the war, when people had no money, they made pasta with no egg. It is eaten with *fagioli*—white beans or chickpeas. Poor man's food. Here,' she said, shifting to one side and motioning for Lara to come to the dough. 'You work it now.'

Lara placed her hands on the dough. It was slightly cooler than skin temperature. She pushed the heel of her hand into it and it moved like a wave, silky smooth yet with a bit of grit. She adjusted her stance and got both hands into the dough; it was stretchy but sprang back again. It was resistant, but flexible.

If she was a poetic type of person she might see a metaphor for people in this dough, certainly for herself and her own healing. She could push that dough around and stretch it to its limits, yet it always came back into itself—a whole, gathered ball of potential, which could be turned into any number of things.

She smiled softly to herself, working the dough more vigorously, building heat in her body and in the dough itself. 'How do you know when it is ready?' she asked.

'When it feels the same as your earlobe,' Gilberta said, and laughed once more.

Together they kneaded the dough and tested their earlobes to come to an agreement on when they should stop.

'Now, we let it rest,' Gilberta said.

'For how long?'

'Ten minutes. In between, we drink wine.'

Gilberta's Italian ten minutes ballooned out to an hour while she told Lara all about the 1966 flood in Florence when the river Arno rose four metres.

A knock at the front door interrupted her story. They heard the door open and a voice shout out to them.

'Matteo!' Gilberta called, rising from the small stool. Lara did the same. Gilberta got to him first, wrapping him in a bear hug and muttering all sorts of Italian endearments, by the sound of it.

Matteo—in working clothes and with a big goofy grin—winked at Lara over Gilberta's head, then kissed the woman on each cheek. When Gilberta released him, she wiped at her eyes. 'I advise you, I am easy tears, huh. We hope none go into the pasta.'

Lara's grin was so wide it hurt her cheeks. They'd been apart two nights and she'd missed him terribly. She was even more thrilled when he reached for her, kissing her full on the mouth and each cheek, embracing her as though he hadn't seen her for weeks, rather than just a couple of days.

'Oh, lovebirds!' Gilberta clapped, then squeezed her strong dough-pounding arms around them both and wept some more.

'What are you doing here?' Lara asked Matteo when finally all the crying and cheek-pinching and hugging had subsided.

'It's *riposo* time,' Matteo said, moving easily in Gilberta's kitchen. He helped himself to some wine and leaned over the dough, nodding in approval. 'Everyone on the farm is resting. But I choose to come see my favourite girls.'

'You are perfect time,' Gilberta said, draining the last of her wine and rinsing her hands. 'We are about to roll out the pasta.' Lara admired the way the woman moved, as though she was about to break into dance at any moment.

Matteo came to Lara's side and put his arm around her, pulling her close. She leaned into him.

Gilberta brought over the squat little pasta machine and clamped it onto the edge of the bench. 'Now, we need many space to roll out the pasta and have it to dry. They can't be all like sardines top of each other or will stick.'

She beckoned Lara to the bench and handed her a knife. 'Cut off a slice of the dough, squeeze in fingers to the right depth.' *Thickness*, Lara mentally corrected, and pressed the dough flat. 'It needs two people,' Gilberta said, pulling Matteo to the bench. 'Now, Lara feeds the little machine and Matteo catches the ribbons at the other end. Like catch baby,' she teased.

Lara fed the warm dough into the machine and cranked the handle. The pasta came out the other side in perfectly flat, if not perfectly straight, golden lengths, much like the shape of bandages as they unrolled.

First aid food.

Matteo held out his hands and the pasta fell gently across them.

'There!' Gilberta whispered, watching the pasta come to life.

They kept rolling, the volume of the final product far exceeding what Lara would have expected. They floured the sheets between the layers so they didn't stick. When the dough got tacky between the rollers, Gilberta sprinkled more flour. Broken pieces were simply put back together and rolled again. Mostly, they worked together in silence, the methodical turn of the wheel and the slow emergence of the ribbons creating a meditative space. Finally, they had used all the dough. Lara's arms burned from all that turning of the wheel.

'Now we let them dry,' Gilberta said. 'Later, we tear into pieces. This is *maltagliati*. No fancy pasta!'

'It means something like rustic, homemade or badly made,' Matteo explained. 'It's as authentic as you get.'

Lara checked the time and realised it had run away on her, the whole pasta-making experience taking much longer than she had thought.

'You need to get going?' Matteo asked, coming to her side.

'I have to get to the village shops.'

He nodded but frowned, then took her hand and led her out the door and into the yard, where a biting wind raced up Lara's clothes and made her wrap her arms around her body.

Matteo pulled her against the stone wall of the villa, positioning her out of the wind. 'I wanted to talk to you, but we got caught up in the pasta and now you have to go and so I am rushed,' he said, scratching behind his ear.

'What is it?'

He leaned his shoulder into the wall. She did the same.

'Will you stay on here in Italy, with me?' he blurted, his dark eyes even darker under his serious brow. 'I don't know when you thought you might move on, but I want more time with you.' His voice was strong but his eyes betrayed his nerves. 'In my head there was more of a lead-up than that.'

Lara reached out her hand and laid it on his cheek, taking in the scattering of tiny freckles under his eyes, feeling the roughness of his beard in her palm. He covered her hand with his.

'I want to see where we can go, here together. I don't want you to leave. You have a lot waiting for you back in Australia, I know that, but I think I have something to offer you here, too.' He took a quick, sharp breath. 'Our time away together . . .' He lost his words then, clearly unable to express everything he wanted.

But he'd said enough, more than he'd ever risked all at once while they'd been away together. He'd learned to hold his words back, but now they'd just tumbled out for her.

The stiff cold she'd been feeling vanished.

It would have been so easy to feel overwhelmed at this moment. Because while she may have felt that it was so right that he had asked her to stay, and it may have felt so right to agree that she would, they both knew it simply wasn't that easy.

But when had it ever been simple?

What she did have now, for the first time, was confidence in herself. It allowed her to envision something new, something she hadn't even known she wanted. Above all else, she had resounding faith in her sister and their shared ability to channel their love for the kids into something great. With no more word from Dave, she felt more confident every day that the future was bright for them all. She didn't know how she and Matteo could make it work; she just knew that it was entirely possible.

'Yes!' she said, grinning like a fool. 'I want to stay here with you too.'

'Lara, *mio amore*, I love you.'

'I love you too,' she said, loudly this time, so there was no way he could miss it.

He picked her up and twirled her around and she squealed with joy.

From the doorway, Gilberta clapped and cheered. 'Bravo, bravo!' Lara felt her cheeks flame.

Matteo took her hand and led her back to the doorway and inside. Gilberta grabbed them both and hugged them tightly, kissing first Matteo's cheeks and then Lara's.

'We are in love!' Matteo announced to the room, sweeping his arm wide. Lara thought her chest might actually crack open with the emotion swirling inside.

'We must celebrate,' Gilberta said, looking around for something fitting, then stopping at the kitchen table. 'But look at all this pasta!' she said, her arms wide. 'We cannot eat it alone!'

'We'll take it to Samuel,' Matteo said, turning to Lara. 'Your feast that you wanted, it's here. We can take it over and I'll pick up cheeses and Gilberta will come, and Henrik is already there.'

'We will find Mario too,' Gilberta said, catching on. But then the woman's face fell.

'What is it?' Matteo asked, placing his hand on her shoulder.

A shudder went through Gilberta's chest and her breath caught. 'Samuel,' she whispered. Matteo nodded and pulled her into his arms for a moment while she sniffed. 'I listened to your mamma,' Gilberta said. 'But . . .'

'I know,' Matteo said 'My mother is a difficult woman.'

Gilberta widened her eyes in implicit agreement.

'I too have been guilty of listening to her when she thought she knew best and I thought that maybe she was right.' Matteo shot Lara an apologetic look. 'But it's in the past. What's done is done. Let us bring Samuel a feast today.'

57

Just outside Samuel's villa, on the lawn, there was a rectangle of mature trees—olives, a leopard tree, a pine tree, and something that looked like it belonged in the Australian bush. There was a long table beneath their shady branches, for lengthy dinners outdoors during the hot summer.

This evening it was cold but still Lara had brushed down the metal table and chairs, rusted paintwork flicking off under the bristles. Then she laid a dark green tablecloth over the table. Lit lanterns hung from the branches. Sometime during the heyday of feasts, rows of blue, red and yellow bulbs had been strung through the leaves, and these too glowed happily.

The trees stood like thin clusters of curtains, defining the space but still allowing sweeping views over the valley and mountains surrounding them, the colours of the landscape changing as the light fell, muting into swathes of delicious Monet-style blues and greens, layer over layer, punctuated here and there by rusty red rooftops and white-walled villas. It was breathtaking.

Mario arrived, carrying hurricane lamps. He placed them down the centre of the table, while quietly singing something operatic. Gilberta was in the kitchen, boiling a pot of water for the *maltagliati*. Matteo would be here soon, bearing platters of antipasti—cheeses, cured meats, olives, sun-dried tomatoes and zucchini from the farm, white-bean dip and flatbreads, as well as ingredients for Gilberta to make sage-wrapped deep-fried anchovies, and baked preserved lemon ricotta bites. Or so his text had said. Lara had replied with effusive gratitude and added that maybe he could invite his mother too. *Not good chance, but I will try*, he'd replied. *Just for you.*

The pasta they'd made with Gilberta today would be the *principale*. The homemade wines would be plentiful. And for *dolci*—given they didn't have much time to get it organised—they were serving bunches of frozen grapes on boards with hunks of chocolate and shot glasses of grappa on the side.

Of course, the food was the easy bit. It was Samuel who posed the biggest challenge.

Lara went to check on her employer. He'd been hiding in his room since she'd come home from Gilberta's and announced the surprise. Okay, this feast wasn't going to be the really big occasion she'd first hoped—with Matteo's brothers and their families, or even, as she'd once naively believed possible, with Carlo and a big reconciliation. And maybe that was a good thing, given Samuel's response.

'Cancel it. Now.' His words had been sharp.

'I can't,' she'd said, holding her ground. 'Everyone is on their way.'

'You have no right,' he'd said, standing as straight as his hunched back would let him, eyeing her with outrage.

'That's probably true,' she responded, carefully. 'But try to be open to this. People are on their way to celebrate . . .' Here she paused. It was Matteo and Lara's love that had sparked the idea for this feast tonight. But Lara's original intent had been to celebrate Samuel, and Gilberta had quickly realised that and jumped on the idea.

'. . . life,' she finished. 'They're coming to celebrate life, just like you used to in the old days when Assunta was here.'

At the name, Samuel blanched.

'You can do this,' Lara said firmly, motherly. 'Don't waste golden opportunities when they fall into your lap.'

He'd left the living room then and shuffled to his bedroom, closing the door with excruciating quietness—far worse than if he'd slammed it.

Now here she was, standing outside Samuel's door.

She knocked twice, hard. He didn't answer, but she went in anyway.

Samuel was sitting on the edge of his bed, his back to her, the bedsheets pulled up as neatly as they were every morning. Even with his broken arm he'd managed to wrangle them into smoothness each day. It had never been her job to straighten his room; he wanted it to himself.

The hunch in his back looked more pronounced in the shadowy light. She hesitated then, almost losing her nerve.

'What is it?' he asked.

'Can I come in?'

'No.'

'Okay, well, I already have, so . . .' She was walking across the room. She needed to face him. But then Samuel started to speak, catching her off guard.

'When you said you'd organised a feast, I panicked,' he said, his voice raspy. His right hand fluttered to the walking stick leaning against the bed and touched it briefly, as if to check it was still there. 'I don't really speak to people anymore. Gilberta and Mario—they were part of the old crowd.'

Lara stood in front of him now and reached behind her for the edge of a wooden chair and eased down onto it. 'It brings back memories,' she said.

He nodded, his eyes catching the light of an outdoor lamp whose muted rays glowed through the curtains. 'Assunta.' He whispered the name, then looked at Lara sharply. 'Does everyone know now? About what you told Carlo? About . . .'

'I'm not sure. Matteo does, obviously.'

Samuel sniffed, bitter. 'He will have told them.'

Lara opened her mouth to defend Matteo, then closed it. She was sure he was too sensitive than to run off and spread the story like salacious gossip. His loyalty to his family was strong, but even if he had told his mother, Lara knew he would have done so with great tact. And more to the point, there was no shame in the story. Assunta had had a medical condition. She'd never got the help that she needed. Her death was tragic, but it shouldn't have been covered up.

'For what it's worth, I think people would be more receptive to the truth now than they might have been at the time she passed,' she said.

'You have no idea of the things people say about those who take their own life. Weak. Selfish. Insane. Evil. Lost to God. Gone to hell. Stuck in purgatory. Doomed on Judgement Day. That they don't deserve to be mourned. That they shouldn't be buried in a Catholic church.'

Anger flared within Lara on Assunta's behalf. How close she herself had come to doing the same. Some of those pills had even made it to her mouth before she spat them out.

She was angry for Samuel too. The world had come a long way in understanding mental illnesses and differences, but maybe not as far as she'd like to believe.

'The way Carlo reacted was just the beginning,' Samuel said.

'Are you wishing you hadn't told him?'

Samuel straightened himself a little, stretching his back. 'Maybe.'

Lara nodded. 'I understand.' They sat in silence a moment, listening to Matteo's truck pulling up slowly over the gravel drive, a sweep of headlights crossing the bedroom window, momentarily casting Samuel's face into deep shadows.

'I know the power of second chances,' she said quietly. 'I was once a heartbeat away from where Assunta was when she was on that rooftop. I can't tell you why I'm here and she's not. But it wasn't an easy road back from that place to where I am now.'

The silence between them filled with understanding.

'This is why I think you should go out there and hold your head high tonight, because your second chance—no matter how hard it is to face it—is right here waiting for you. Don't let it go.'

He almost looked convinced, then raised his face in defiance. 'But it's hardly anyone, just Gilberta and Mario—'

'Precisely the reason you should go,' she countered. 'You've nothing to fear.'

'—none of the people who really matter.'

She tilted her head. 'I'd like to think that the people who really matter are here for you right now, hungry, thirsty and waiting for you to come out and declare that this feast has started.'

'Alright, alright,' he grumped.

Lara smothered a smile of victory and stood up, helping him to his feet, her hand wrapped around his twiggy bicep.

'You know, the day I first met you, you were at the Trevi Fountain—the fountainhead for an ancient aqueduct, the water travelling more than twenty kilometres to its terminus.'

'I know the history.'

They were out of his shadowy room now, squinting in the bright lights of the hall.

'I've thought a lot about the fountain since that day, particularly since reading about its history. I like to imagine where the little trickles of water come from—a spring, or down from the melted mountain snows. Just drops, joining with more drops, forming tiny rivulets, which join to form a stream, gathering force until it bursts out of the fountain, a mighty, unstoppable, never-ceasing flow of life.'

'Your point?'

They were at the front door now, about to step out into the courtyard. They could hear joyful chatter out on the grass, the pop of a wine cork, a cheer, the scrape of metal on metal as chairs were moved about.

'Maybe not everyone who is really important is here right now. But this is a start. The first trickle. Momentum is gathering. And who knows where it might lead? The Trevi Fountain led me to you, and for that I will be forever grateful. Maybe tonight is the start of something wonderful too, the first of many feasts that will grow into the one you really want, with everyone here—Carlo, your children, your grandchildren—all of them breaking bread and dancing into the night.'

Samuel's eyes were bright pools of blue. Then he looked down at his trackpants and ran his hand nervously along the bottom of his t-shirt. 'I should change.'

Lara kissed him on the cheek. 'No you shouldn't; you're perfect as you are.' But she did lift his heavy woollen cardigan down from the coat hook by the door and wrap it tightly around him, covering his chest well. Then she stuck out her elbow like a wing for him to hold. 'Let's go.'

Lara walked Samuel across the steps and stones between the house and the feast table, feeling a little like she was walking him down the aisle. Gilberta sprang up to hug him warmly, tears pouring down her cheeks as she rocked him from side to side and murmured a joyful welcome, like a mother who'd found her lost child. For his part, Samuel seemed unable to speak, his jaw working with emotion.

'I'm sorry, I'm sorry,' Gilberta said, kissing him on both cheeks. 'We should never have abandoned you.' She turned to Matteo, still holding Samuel's hand.

Matteo smiled at Lara, and winked. *Well done*, it said. He held out his arms and she nestled into them, relishing the feeling of their strength around her.

Mario cheered then and began to clap approval for the newest couple in the clan. Henrik, too, raised his glass of wine from where he was sitting with his leg raised on a spare chair, grinning at them, his enviable hair tucked neatly behind his elfin ears.

Lara felt herself flush, and sneaked a sideways glance at Samuel, who raised one eyebrow at her and smiled just a little smugly. She probably did have him to thank. If he hadn't asked her to go to Carlo with that terrible burden, she might not have found her way to Matteo. It was a small price to pay for finding such happiness.

Mario was at Samuel's side now, hugging him—nearly lifting him off his feet!—kissing him, singing to him.

Samuel cracked. He burst out laughing. It was a stuttering laugh at first, unused for so long, then gathering force until it became a glorious belly laugh, which led to a trickle of tears. He looked stricken, that stiff-upper-lip British boy still there despite living for so long in a country so much freer with emotions. But Gilberta ushered him into a seat at the head of the table and Mario pushed a glass of wine into his hand. They sat on either side of him, flanking him protectively, talking over one another, catching up.

Lara slipped her arms under Matteo's jacket and wrapped them around his warm body. 'Did you get a chance to speak to your mother?' she whispered.

'Yes.'

'And?'

He shook his head.

'But did you tell her about Assunta? Did you tell her it wasn't Samuel's fault?'

'Yes.' He sounded sombre. 'She was angry, shocked. It will take time. The whole family will need to come to terms with it.'

Lara nodded, sad despite knowing it would have taken a miracle for Lucia to come tonight. She looked at Samuel, more relaxed now, sipping his wine, chuckling at something Gilberta said as she dropped her flame-haired head back and squealed with laughter.

When Lara had first met Samuel, he was on his own. Now there were six of them here, ready to feast on homemade *maltagliati*, so simple with just a sprinkling of sharp parmesan cheese, followed by bitter dark chocolate and sweet juicy grapes, all washed down with fiery grappa.

Trickles. It was all trickles.

ൟ ൟ

It was late. Henrik had been on coffee-making duty for a while now, limping carefully while holding cups. Samuel and Lara had shared a couple of covert looks, each expecting him to trip or drop coffee into someone's lap. But he surprised them and each cup got to the recipient in one piece.

Lara would never forget the kindness and warmth from Gilberta and Mario, their open hearts and instant joy at embracing Samuel once more, and the smile they had brought to Samuel's face. She could swear he was able to sit straighter in his chair, to meet their eyes and hold their hands.

She and Matteo managed to slip away, the chatter and laughter fading behind them as they sneaked down the hill towards the old lemon trees—tall, age-spotted limbs, twisted joints and thorns as long as her thumb, but with a good bounty of green fruit waiting to ripen in winter. It was cold down here, the air heavy with damp. A thick white fog would fill this hollow in the morning.

But for now they kissed, hands under shirts, beating hearts sending quivers through limbs as they leaned against the stone toolshed, the place where they had first met. Matteo tasted of coffee and wine and grappa. An owl hooted rhythmically from somewhere nearby.

Matteo broke away, breathing deeply to steady his pulse. 'Are you happy?'

Lara nodded definitively. 'Samuel looks so joyful. He has the start of a family again.'

'We will keep working on my mother,' he said, brow puckering. 'And Carlo too.'

Her fingers fluttered to his waistband. 'Let's go inside,' she whispered. 'Come upstairs with me and stay. I've missed your body.'

She didn't have to ask twice. He turned and led the way, holding her hand, slipping through the back door, down the hall, past Samuel's room and silently up the staircase. They stepped into the darkness of her room, lights from the feast outdoors throwing golden shadows into corners. They undressed, already knowing exactly how to touch each other. As his skin pressed against hers, she felt the simple truth: if she stayed here with Matteo, everything would be okay.

But it was only a short time later, as they lay entwined sleepily in each other's arms, the chatter and laughter from the garden having moved inside the house, downstairs where it was warm, as Lara was blissfully tracing her fingertips up and down Matteo's chest and abdomen, and he was doing the same down her arm, that her phone rang.

The noise was painful. Her heart kicked and she pulled herself over the bed to retrieve the offending item. The caller's name was illuminated on the screen.

'Hi, Mum, is everything okay?'

'Hi, love. No, I don't think it is.'

'What's happened?'

'It's a letter,' Eliza said. Lara could hear paper rustling. 'It came for Sunny and it looked important, so I opened it,' Eliza said apologetically. 'I don't know where she is, she's not answering her phone, and what with everything Dave's been doing . . .'

'Dave?' Lara sat up straight on the edge of the bed. Behind her, she felt Matteo lift himself to sitting. 'And what do you mean, you don't know where Sunny is?'

'We didn't want to upset you,' Eliza said, her voice small.

'About what?'

Her mother told her about Dave, each word like a steely finger closing around Lara's throat. Lara listened and paced. She was dimly aware that Matteo had brought her a blanket to wrap around herself against the chill. Out of the corner of her eye, she noticed him pull on his jeans and shirt, watching her closely, on guard.

'And then he took Midnight!' Eliza said, her words trembling. That was when the shakes set in.

But it only got worse. Because not only was Dave stalking Sunny and the kids, but he had already armed himself with legal weaponry. Her mother read her the letter.

> Dear Ms Foxleigh
>
> I am writing to inform you that I act on behalf of Mr David Hyne who has approached me to assist him with issues relating to the paternity and custody of Daisy Foxleigh (5) and Hudson Foxleigh (5) who reside in the care of yourself, allegedly the biological aunt on their maternal side.
>
> This letter informs you that we have initiated an application to request the Federal Circuit Court to authorise paternity tests to prove that Mr Hyne is the biological father of the children. We assume the result of this test will positively confirm this, at which time we will move to formalise Mr Hyne's parenting arrangements with the children.
>
> Mr Hyne alleges that your sister, Lara Foxleigh, is the birth mother. We will be contacting her in due course. If your sister cannot be contacted, we will apply for substituted service of papers to yourself as you are identified as a person concerned with the welfare of the children and who Mr Hyne reasonably believes has knowledge of Lara Foxleigh's whereabouts.

Included with this letter you will find an information booklet about these processes and your rights and responsibilities under Australian law. I encourage you to read it and also to secure legal representation for yourself.

Sincerely
Rudolf Dunkirk
Principal Lawyer
Dunkirk & Wayne

Lara made her mother read it again, but it was only more terrifying the second time around. How stupid Lara had been to believe for a moment that she might be alright, that there might be a bright future ahead for her, one with joy and love and family and safety. How completely in denial she'd been to trust that *he* would let her go. He would never let her go. Now he was coming for her, then Sunny, and worst of all, the children.

58

Lara arrived back in Brisbane on a stinking hot October day. The jacaranda trees that stood camouflaged all year long were in full bloom, turning the streetscapes purple and emitting a mauve haze across the skyline. She had the worst sleep-debt hangover she'd ever known, even when she'd been coming down from days of mania. It felt as if she'd gone through the spin cycle of the washing machine. She almost wished for an episode of mania right now, just to lift herself up.

She'd wanted to come home as quickly as possible and Matteo had helped her book a flight the very next morning, driving her to Rome later that day.

She said goodbye to Samuel on the driveway of the villa, amid whirling, frigid winds. She embraced him, his curved spine beneath her hands. He'd held her, not speaking, emotion close to the surface. She'd been brave; she refused to cry.

Henrik hugged her and Samuel gave her arm a final squeeze. 'Come back soon,' he said, sternly. Then he instructed Matteo, leaning against the truck, to make sure she did.

'I will,' Matteo said, opening the truck door for Lara to get in. She smiled gratefully at him, but the sadness in his eyes almost broke her resolve to hold it together.

Both Samuel and Henrik had stayed outside, waving to her for as long as they could see the truck.

She cried hopelessly in Matteo's arms at the departure gate, for too many reasons to even begin to express. His face was pinched, awash with misery. He stroked her hair and loaded her up with magazines and chocolate and kissed her all over her face, and waited with his hands in his pockets until she was out of sight. As the plane ascended, she had no idea if she would ever see Matteo again, and she had no idea what would be waiting for her when she got home.

Now, she was here.

The taxi pulled into the familiar driveway and Lara paid the driver. Eliza came to meet her at the passenger door.

'Oh, I've missed you,' she said, holding Lara close before helping her up the stairs with her bags.

Lara wheeled her suitcase into the dining room and parked it parallel to the large potted peace lily, which was bathing in the strong mid-morning sunlight that sliced through the tree branches in the yard. No muted tones of the Tuscan valley here in Brisbane.

'Any news from Sunny?'

Her mother glanced at her, then set two mugs on the benchtop. 'Nothing.'

Lara's chest tightened at the thought that Sunny and the kids were out there somewhere, and that no one—at least no one they knew—had any clue as to where. She just hung on to the knowledge that Sunny was the capable one, and said as much to her mother.

Eliza shook her head, switching the kettle on. 'I've felt sick since we spoke.' She stood still a moment, her hands over her face, then went to the fridge, which was still covered with photos of Daisy and Hudson as well as their messy artworks, a sight that almost undid

Lara's threads of self-control. Eliza pulled out a baker's bag of jam and cream doughnuts and held them high. 'Fancy one? I've been emotional-eating around the clock.'

'You don't need to ask me twice.'

The doughnuts were plated up, the kettle boiled and teabags infused. Eliza cut into her doughnut and bright red jam oozed across the plate.

'I need to speak to Dave,' Lara said, blowing gently on her tea, then thought of Matteo holding his cup to his face and did the same.

'You're not serious.'

'I am.' She held her mother's gaze. 'It's me he wants to hurt because he thinks he still can. He thinks he can get to me through Sunny.'

'Because he *can*! And he can hurt those children.' Eliza took off her glasses and polished them with the hem of her t-shirt, something she never normally did, rather using proper spray and cleaning cloths.

'I know. And there's no point in contacting the police, because we know they won't do anything until he actually *does* hurt one of us.'

'This bloody system!' Eliza pushed herself back from the table and stood, folding her arms. 'It let your father down, it let me down, it let you down, and now it will let Sunny and the kids down too.' She let out a primal roar of frustration that stunned Lara. 'How can one man get away with so much?' She burst into tears.

'Oh, Mum.' Lara got up and wrapped her arms around her mother while Eliza struggled to control herself.

'You can't meet Dave, you just can't,' Eliza pleaded.

'I'll meet him in a public space.'

'And what will you say that could possibly do any good?'

'Something I should have said long ago. I'm going to tell him to leave us alone, that I'm a different person now from who I was when he knew me, and that I won't tolerate this behaviour. I will tell him that I'm applying for an apprehended violence order.'

'Are you?' Eliza looked up, surprised.

'No. But he won't like that because it would make him look bad, and we know that appearances matter to him. He's a doctor and something like that could damage his reputation.'

Or it might do nothing at all, of course. The man was like Teflon.

'What about Sunny and the kids?' her mother sniffed. 'What if they never come back?'

'They will,' Lara said, determinedly, because what else could she say?

Eliza patted her younger daughter's arm then, revealing a touch of embarrassment over her outburst. 'What should we do now?'

Lara stepped away to give her mother some space. She studied Eliza's blotchy, teary face and pondered this question. 'Well,' she said at last, 'I guess I'm going to have to phone Dave.'

59

Sunny

Sunny turned off the engine and considered her choices.

She'd already endured over an hour of crazy-making behaviour from Hudson in the doctor's surgery in order to get a script for antibiotics for an ear infection that was keeping him awake at night. And in their tiny caravan, that meant all three of them, and the puppy, were awake. Everyone was overtired and irritable, which didn't help anything.

It certainly hadn't helped her patience while he'd practically torn the doctor's room apart, pretending to take everyone's blood pressure, pulling the anatomy charts off the walls—and then fighting with Daisy, who screeched at him because she'd been busy studying the spinal nerve pathways with the doctor's magnifying glass—turning the surgical light on and off, on and off, on and off, climbing up on the bed with his dirty sneakers and jumping up and down.

Sunny and the doctor—a young and probably childless woman who gawked at Hudson as though she'd never seen such behaviour before—could barely hear each other over the noise. The doctor had hardly been able to get the light into his ear with all his squirming and yelping. She'd even glanced at the clock in the room while they were there, probably wishing this consultation would end as rapidly as possible. Sunny suspected she hadn't been able to see anything in Hudson's ear at all but had decided a course of antibiotics probably wouldn't hurt and it would get them out of her room.

Now it was past dinnertime. Daisy was complaining that she was hungry, and Sunny had run out of handbag snacks to thrust at her. There was nothing prepared back at the caravan. From memory, their little travelling fridge contained some milk, stale buns no one wanted to eat, a splash of wilting lettuce, and some butter, soiled by toast crumbs from knives that were never clean. Sunny had just wrangled them both back into the car, anxious to get home to Midnight, who was stuck inside the van and probably peeing all over their beds, but she really needed to rush into this town's small general store. She could see a sign advertising hot chooks just beyond the rainbow waterfall of flimsy plastic streamers that hung in the doorway. She hesitated. The thought of bringing Hudson, let alone both the kids, with her was unbearable. Dave had broken her. She should have asked the doctor for sedatives while she was there.

'Kids, I need to go into the shop for a moment, okay?'

Hudson kicked the seat in front of him. 'I want an ice block!'

Sunny started to refuse, but the wailing and anger overwhelmed her. Then Daisy joined in. 'I'm *starving*,' she whimpered.

'Okay, okay. I'll get you a lemonade ice block. Here's my phone.' She loaded up *Paw Patrol* on YouTube and passed it to Hudson, the only thing guaranteed to calm him when he got worked up like this. 'Let Daisy watch too. I'll be back in a minute.'

She wasn't sure if he'd heard her. He didn't answer, totally absorbed in the most exciting thing in his world: flashing lights on a screen.

'Daisy? Did you hear me?'

Her daughter's head lolled back in her booster seat. 'Yes.'

Sunny wound the windows down a few centimetres, got out and locked the doors, guiltily eyeing a couple of other cars parked nearby, their owners no doubt doing the same thing as her: trying to find something to fill empty stomachs with their children in tow. *Should* she take them? Yes, technically it was against the law to lock her kids in the car. But she would only be a couple of minutes. It was late afternoon and rather overcast. It wasn't as though it was a hot summer's day. And she honestly just couldn't face it. Her nerves were shattered. She began to walk.

Dogs die in hot cars. That was the mantra the animal refuges promoted, trying to stop beloved pets collapsing from heat exhaustion, abandoned in cars while their owners shopped or swam or dined out. But her kids weren't dogs. And she would only be two minutes.

She sidestepped milling parents and school kids still in uniform who were standing and chatting. Everyone knew everyone in this small town. There were only two hot chooks left, and she nabbed one along with a tub of coleslaw and headed to the checkout. She was stuck for a couple of minutes behind an ancient, bent man shakily counting out coins for his white bread and baked beans. She jiggled her knee and pushed aside the repetitive thought of *dogs die in hot cars*. When it was her turn, she paid as quickly as possible, forgoing a bag or receipt.

But back at the car, a woman and man stood at the window where Hudson sat strapped into his seat. Sunny eyed them nervously and clicked the key tag to unlock the doors. They whipped their heads around to stare at her accusingly.

'Your son is screaming in there,' the fox-like woman said.

'We were just about to call the police,' added the unshaven man.

Sunny opened the driver's door and shoved her head inside. 'What's wrong? What's happened?'

Hudson was hysterical, his legs thrashing against his car seat restraints, his face purple, tears leaking from his eyes, strangled sobs and hiccups forewarning that he was on the verge of vomiting from distress. Daisy stared forlornly out the window, distancing herself from her brother's meltdown.

'What's wrong?' Sunny repeated, frightened now, while also piercingly aware of the woman and man still standing there.

'It went off!' Hudson screamed, and thrust the phone at her. She looked at it: set on the home screen. He'd obviously pressed something he shouldn't, and *Paw Patrol* had disappeared. Not exactly a national emergency, but to him the world had ended.

She popped her head out of the car to reassure the bystanders. 'His movie stopped,' she said, with a slight eye roll to convey the ridiculousness, desperate to get away.

The foxy woman waw not appeased. 'Couldn't you leave him some air?' she growled. The man lost interest and padded away.

Sunny fought the urge to defend herself and point out that the windows *were* open a fraction, and instead fiddled with the phone to get *Paw Patrol* back on to end Hudson's crisis.

There! She handed the phone back to him, *Paw Patrol* once more in action. He sniffed, but settled instantly, his eyes fixed on the screen.

'It's illegal to leave children in a car,' the woman added helpfully, showing no signs of moving on.

'Yes, thank you,' Sunny said, not meeting her eyes but getting back into the driver's seat as quickly as possible and turning the key in the ignition. 'Troll,' she added, under her breath.

A quick look over her shoulder as she reversed showed her the woman was still there, murmuring in disgust about Sunny's appalling mothering.

Sunny drove out onto the road, feeling the knives in her back, and turned towards the caravan park, already making plans to hitch up the van and drive on into the night to get away from here.

But no sooner had she taken a deep breath to lower her blood pressure when Hudson released an ear-splitting scream from the back seat. Sunny slammed on the brakes and turned around. 'What? What *now*?' she demanded.

He thrust the phone at her. 'It's stopped again!' he whined.

'For God's sake!' She grabbed the phone, a car behind her beeping at her to get moving again. But she couldn't move. She had to get the video working to end this screeching meltdown before she lost her mind.

'Troll,' came a small voice from the back seat—Daisy, repeating her mother's indiscretion.

Sunny thrust the phone back at Hudson. 'There!' she snapped, unable to find any sort of maternal serenity.

She turned around again to drive on, but there was a man at her window. She jumped, her hand to her heart, adrenaline coursing through her blood like electricity.

Tap, tap, tap on the glass.

The man bent down to eyeball Sunny through the window. He was wearing blue.

60

Lara

Lara had asked Dave to meet her at the local library. Her heart banged the moment she saw him appear through the automatically opening doors and pause, looking around for the meeting room. She had the advantage in being able to see him first, having got there fifteen minutes early, enough time to try out every seat around the rectangular table and break into a decent sweat.

She watched him walk—that self-assured, arrogant stride. Time concertinaed in on itself and she felt the blood drain from her face. She had to forcibly stop herself from running.

He queried the librarian at the counter, who pointed towards the meeting room and he followed the outstretched arm. His gaze collided with hers.

He may as well have hit her.

The shiny new belt around his trousers made her face twitch with unwanted memories.

He came straight to the meeting room, standing tall on the other side of the table. Lara suddenly wished she was standing, preferably nearest to the open door, and berated herself for not keeping open that escape route. He ran a hand down his neatly pressed collared shirt.

'Lara, it's lovely to see you.' He cast an eye over her. 'You're looking well.'

'I *am* well.' She stopped herself from adding *thank you*. We have a lot to discuss. Please, take a seat.'

His smile suggested he knew how nervous she was. 'I might just get a coffee from the cafe. Would you like one?'

'No.'

He tipped his head and left her to stew in her frustration at his games while she waited for him to return. Finally he sauntered back in, carrying a takeaway cup. He seated himself, leaning back in the chair, hands clasped behind his head. 'Well, you've been a busy little girl in the past six years.'

'So have you,' she said, nodding to his wedding ring.

'Oh, yes, Vicki. You remember her, don't you? We married a month after you left me.'

The poor woman.

'She helped me heal from your abandonment,' he said seriously.

She had to stop herself from scoffing. She would not let him bait her into arguments.

'Little did I know I was a father.' He folded his arms at his chest.

She was tempted to deny that was true, but knew it was futile. 'Well, I had good reason to hide them from you, didn't I?' she countered.

His forehead furrowed in mock confusion. 'What are you talking about?'

'You tried to get me to kill myself.'

'What?' He shook his head. 'That's crazy. I've always wanted to be a father—you knew that. You're imagining things, Lara. You have always been shockingly unreliable, due to your illness, I'm sure, but this whole situation is a tragedy.'

'It was certainly a tragedy for me. It's taken me years to recover from the damage you did to me.'

'Lara! All I ever did was look after you,' he said, aggrieved. 'I supported you financially, and supported your dreams to write your screenplay. I looked after you when you were sick. Not many others would have done what I did.'

His speech was intended to make her feel ashamed, to remind her she was unworthy. But she knew the truth now. 'You're right about that. Not many men do behave the way you do.' She faltered. 'At least, I'd like to believe that's true.'

He narrowed his eyes at her and leaned forward, almost as if to sniff her. His eyes lingered on her neck, the spot where his thumb used to fit, pressing on her voice box, silencing her cries. 'You've been with another man,' he whispered.

She was unable to stop the shudder that shot up her spine. He noticed, and smirked with pleasure.

'Dave, you will never get Daisy or Hudson. Ever. You will never know them or touch them in any way.' She injected as much steel into each word as she could muster over the skittering of her heart.

'I have rights, Lara. And remember, I'm not the certified crazy one here; you are.'

It was near impossible to keep herself from falling apart at that moment. On paper, what he said was true. Add to that the falsified birth certificates, which would be uncovered in due course, and her stocks would fall fast. Her heart threatened to burst through her chest at the idea that what she'd done—giving false information on birth certificates to hide her children from a violent man—might actually be the thing that convinced a court to allow him access to them.

'I'm a respected psychologist and GP. I'm married to another doctor. We are flawless.'

'On the outside, that might appear to be true. But I know what a monster you are behind closed doors.'

He tapped the table in calculated contemplation. 'I don't know what you're talking about. I'm concerned by these delusions. Have you checked in with your doctor lately? You might need to change your medications, because you are clearly very muddled.' He picked up his coffee and blew on it sharply three times.

She grimaced. 'Look, I needed to see you today for one reason only, and that is to tell you that you have no power here anymore. I am strong now. I've just come back from Italy where I've been caring for a frail old man, his villa and animals and doing it all rather well. I've travelled the country. And I never once *lost* anything,' she said, hoping he caught her emphasis. He lifted his chin and his lips pulled down to suppress a jeer. 'I didn't have a breakdown. No one had to rescue me. I didn't get confused, forget anything, or injure myself. I barely even scratched my wrist,' she said, looking down now and realising her skin was without a single mark. 'I did it all. You have no power over me and no power over my children or any other member of the Foxleigh family. Got it?'

He snickered, though there was an infinitesimal moment when she wondered if she'd made him nervous. But then he flung his hand through the air and slammed it down on the table.

Lara jumped and twisted herself away from him to stare at the ground. She knew not to make eye contact.

'You don't get to tell me what to do,' he said quietly. 'No one tells me what to do.'

She continued to focus on the tiny flecks of green and brown in the carpet at her feet, frozen, silently pleading with him to leave her alone.

'Tell Sunny to return my lawyer's calls or it's going to make me very angry.' He leaned across the table, closer to her ear. 'And I'll see *you* again soon.'

Back in the car, she drove numbly, having to wrangle her mind to stay focused on the road. Dave's violent outburst was all the more shocking because he'd lost his composure in a public place. That was a change, a progression, and she didn't know what it meant.

Her phone rang, startling her; she pulled over beneath the jacaranda tree at the beginning of her street.

Sunny.

With shaking hands, Lara answered it. 'I'm so glad to hear from you,' she said. 'Are you alright? Where are you?'

'I'm fine. I'm sorry to call so late . . .'

'Late?'

'It's the middle of the night, isn't it?'

'Huh? Oh, no, I'm back home. In our street, actually.'

'What? Why aren't you in Italy?'

'Because Dave is after the kids and we didn't know where you were!' Lara burst into tears, all the anxiety of Sunny's disappearance and of her meeting with Dave erupting at once.

'How do you know about Dave?' Sunny sounded gutted.

Lara explained that Eliza had read the lawyer's letter to her and she'd felt she had no other choice but to come home and face her pursuer.

'Are you crazy?' Sunny demanded, then paused. No one was allowed to say that. 'Sorry, I didn't mean . . . you know.'

'I know. But yes, I might be crazy.'

'Did you see him? What did he say?'

'The usual. That I was imagining things, that I'd been a naughty girl to hide the kids from him, that he was an upstanding citizen and we'd never make anything stick. And then he slapped the table and made me cry.' Tears leaked down her face.

'I want to kill him. I truly do,' Sunny hissed. 'Mind you, I'm relieved to know he isn't out here, stalking us through Queensland.'

'Where are you?' Lara asked.

'That's what I need to talk to you about. I've just stepped out of the police station in Winton.'

'As in the middle of Queensland?'

'Yes.'

'What happened?' At the mention of the police, the world outside Lara's car had begun to dip and bend. 'Where are the kids?'

'Playing with Midnight and the police dog out in the yard behind the station. I'm walking up the street so they don't hear me.'

'What happened?' Lara repeated, more gently this time. A sudden breeze sent a shower of delicate mauve flowers falling from the branches above her car, pattering softly on the roof and sliding down the windscreen.

Sunny took a deep breath. 'I'm so stupid.'

She told Lara about the incident yesterday, leaving the kids in the car and Hudson's meltdown, the policeman witnesssing the scene and following her, then running a search on Sunny's licence number and finding she was a long way from Brisbane and asking questions. He seemed to have a hunch that something was up, and had clearly come up with an unflattering picture of this woman travelling on her own with two children, a puppy, no employment and no real plan of where she was going. Still, given it was late in the day and she did have these two young and exceedingly hungry children, the police officer had followed her back to the caravan site to let her settle the kids, asking her to come to the station in the morning. Apparently, he could either charge her or issue a warning for leaving the children unattended in the car—even though the windows were down and she was only gone a few minutes!—an offence which carried a maximum sentence in Queensland of three years' imprisonment.

'Sunny!' Lara slapped her free hand to her forehead.

'It was a few minutes. I was just so tired. But I wish I could take it back.' She paused while Lara digested this. Then in a quiet, non-Sunny voice, she asked, 'Did Mum tell you about all the things Dave's been doing?'

'Yes.' Lara swallowed hard. 'I'm so sorry.'

'It's not your fault,' Sunny said, sounding more like herself again.

'I can't help feeling that everything is my fault.'

'Stop it. None of this is your fault. It's Dave's fault, end of story.'

Lara considered the sweet spot on her wrist, but forced herself to look at the sky outside instead. 'When will the policeman decide what he's going to do with you?'

'I don't know. Sergeant Crook has just been to the bakery with the kids to get them vanilla slices for morning tea. I left them to it to clear my head. It's a little weird, but I feel safe here with the kids in the care of a policeman. He's a little bit cute, actually.'

Lara opened her mouth, barely knowing where to start. 'Are you for real? His surname is Crook?'

That set Sunny off on a bout of barely suppressed giggling, and Lara couldn't help but join in. It was a truly awful thing to have happened—who knew how it would affect their legal proceedings with Dave? But because it was far too awful to contemplate, they could do nothing but cry tears of laughter over the phone.

At last, wiping her face, Lara pulled herself together. 'Oh, this is really quite dreadful,' she said.

Her sister was instantly sober. 'I know. I don't know what to do.'

Lara experienced a flicker of pride that, for the first time ever, Sunny had called *her* for help. If only the circumstances were different, she might have enjoyed that realisation just a little more. 'Tell me what I can do.'

Sunny thought for a moment. Lara heard a cockatoo screech in the background and could imagine its white wings bright against the same blue sky that stretched above them both. 'Lara, could you come here, to Winton? I'm so rattled and tired and it's hard driving on my own with the kids. I don't think it's safe to go back home, not after everything Dave's done, and especially because he'll only be angrier now he knows you're back in town.'

'I agree. I think Martha was right: the more distance and time we can put between us and him the better. What if he snatched one of the kids?' A stone fell through her chest.

'We won't let it happen,' Sunny said.

It was unthinkable. 'I'll fly up and meet you there,' Lara said, considering a new life on the run, wondering if she would ever see Matteo again, or when they would see Eliza. 'But will Sergeant Crook let you go?'

Her sister took in a sharp breath. 'God, I hope so.'

'He has to,' Lara said firmly. 'Everyone leaves their kids in the car to duck in to pay for petrol or buy milk.' She'd done it herself more than once when she'd been caring for the kids, Eliza too. 'It's not like you left them at the casino or anything. I'll go back to Mum's now and look up flights and be on the first plane I can get out that way. If I can't get a direct flight, I'll get as close as I can and hire a car.'

'Thank you. I'm so sorry.'

'Hey, it's not like you haven't saved me a thousand times over.'

Sunny sniffed. 'That's true.'

'We're strongest together.'

'All for one.'

'We might be running away, but at least we'll be running together and doing it on our own terms. Besides, it might look better to the courts if the kids at least seem as though they're in my custody.' She knew that would hurt Sunny, but it was true. Lara *was* the birth mother. 'Call me back as soon as Sergeant Crook has made up his mind about what he's going to do. I'll call Martha. We need advice.'

'Oh, hold on, I've got another call coming through. I better get it in case it's Sergeant Crook wanting me to come back to the station.' Sunny hung up.

61

Sunny

'Hello?'

'Sunny Foxleigh?' A woman's voice.

'Yes,' Sunny said, guarded.

'I'm so glad . . . Are you alright?'

'Who is this?'

'Oh, sorry, I don't have much time. My husband will be home soon and he can't know that I've called you.'

'Who is this?' Sunny repeated, stopping in the middle of the concrete footpath on her way back to the station. She squinted, raising her hand to shield her eyes from the bright sun. Someone's brown chicken had escaped from its yard and was waddling slowly up the green verge towards her, cocking its head to the side and staring at her with a yellow-rimmed eye.

'My name is Vicki. I'm married to Dave Hyne.'

Sunny went rigid.

Vicki continued, her words tumbling over each other in her urgency, talking about Dave, about danger.

'Wait,' Sunny said. 'What did you say about a journal?'

'He's been writing everything down. I knew he'd been calling you; I went through his phone. I was jealous and nervous and—anyway, your name was there over and over: Sunny, Sunny, Sunny, Sunny. I thought, who is this woman? I'd never heard him mention you before. Normally with the others—'

'Others?'

'—he doesn't bother to hide it. He doesn't care that I know. But I thought this was strange, so I . . .' She paused to take a few deep breaths. 'I went and found his journal. He writes in it every day, but I'm not allowed to look in it. He told me they're confidential patients' notes but . . . well . . .'

Sunny closed her mouth, which had fallen open, and gently pushed away the chicken who'd begun to tug at her laces with its beak. 'The journal,' she reminded Vicki. A cold shadow had passed over her, despite the bright sunshine.

'Yes, so I found it, just today while he was out. God, I really don't know when he'll be back, and he can't find me talking to you . . .'

'Don't lose your nerve now,' Sunny commanded. 'You called me to tell me something. What is it?'

'It's all there. His plan. Everything.' Vicki started to cry. 'I wish I'd known sooner; it's so terrible I can barely say it.' Her voice rose as if trying to strangle itself.

'Say it!'

'He's planning on getting the children. And he's planning on making sure you and Lara will never get them back. Look, I can't talk, Dave's on his way back, but I had to warn you.'

'We know. Lara saw him today . . .'

'She did?'

'Vicki, listen to me, you are in danger. I know what Dave's like. I know what he's done to Lara and what he's been doing to our family lately. He's not going to change. You have to get away. I know you feel you can't leave, but you have to. You have to save yourself. Right now. Just walk out the door and don't look back.'

'No, I can't, he'd find me . . . I didn't phone to . . . There's not a lot of time.'

'Okay, if you won't listen to me you have to listen to Lara. She's been where you are, she can help you.'

'No, I can't, please . . .'

'I'm going to hang up the phone now and get Lara to call you back. Please, just hold on. You *have* to speak to her.'

62

Lara and Dave

Lara stood in front of the bathroom mirror, pills in her shaking hand. She stared at the reflection, barely recognising herself. Her swollen eyes, her tangled hair, her hollowed cheeks. Days of crying—rivulets of despair changing the landscape of her face.

There were other marks too. Three fingers of bruises on each of her upper arms from his tight grip when he'd tried to shake sense into her. A patch of hair missing from above the left temple where it had been ripped out by his exasperated clenched fist.

She hiccupped a sob. She felt like crying again but no tears came. There were simply no more tears left. She was empty.

Who *was* this person in the mirror?

She lifted the handful of pills to her mouth and forced them in, some spilling into the sink with tiny rattling noises. The others clung to her lips and tongue. She raised the glass to flush the pills down.

But she couldn't swallow.

She gagged. Dropped the glass into the sink where it cracked in two. Tried to spit out the tablets. But they were sticking. Panicking, she cupped her hands and splashed in water, washing the last of them out into the sink.

Her legs shaking now, she gripped the sides of the sink and stared at herself again, gazing right into her own eyes.

You can do this.

A voice. Her own?

You can do this, Sprout.

Sunny!

Lara almost smiled as her big sister's voice rose up from somewhere in her memories, floating through time to right now, right when she needed to hear it. It was exactly what she needed.

She didn't want to die.

But she knew one thing for sure: Dave wanted her to die and to take the child with her, the child that so disgusted him. If she didn't take care of it herself, then he would find a way to make it happen.

She had to escape, right now.

63

Lara

Lara phoned Vicki three times before she answered.

'Hello?' It was a voice as brittle as cracked toffee.

'Vicki, it's Lara.'

They were silent for a moment, a universe of shared experience swirling around them. Lara spoke again. 'Thank you for answering. I need to speak to you.'

'I'm so sorry. I should have known,' Vicki said, her voice shaking.

'It doesn't matter, really. I understand where you are because I was there too. Dave has broken you down and you believe you can't survive on your own, but you can. You are stronger than you think, people will help you, *I'll* help you, and you will get through this.' Lara paced the lounge room, Eliza watching on, her hand over her mouth.

'No, it's not that, you have to listen to me.'

'Please, Vicki, I know that Dave will be home soon. I've just seen him and he's in a mood. You and I both know what will happen. Please, just get out. *Please.*'

'You don't understand!' Vicki's voice was suddenly strong, desperate. 'I have to tell you something.'

'What is it?' Lara asked. All she really wanted was to hear Vicki walk out that door *now*, because the way Dave had slammed the table and left the library . . . it made her sick, knowing what he'd want to do when he got home.

'He's going to kill them,' Vicki said. 'The kids. He's going to kill them. I read his journal. It's all there. He has maps and . . .'

Lara lurched to the couch and crumpled onto it, loud buzzing filling her ears.

'It's punishment, for you taking them away and lying, making him look like a fool and . . . it will look like an accident . . .'

'*Who are you talking to?*' It was Dave's voice in the background.

Vicki fell silent.

Lara whimpered. *Oh, God, oh, God.* There was a clatter, as though the phone had fallen to the ground.

She could hear it—the scraping of feet, a sound like furniture being dragged across the floor. Muffled cries. The grunts and puffs of brute force. She felt the blows as if they were landing on herself.

Eliza stood. 'What is it? What's happening?'

'Call the police,' Lara said. 'Dave's got Vicki.'

64

Vicki

I can see myself down in the hospital bed, surrounded by machines, driplines and a variety of tubes and wires, blue curtains drawn around the few people by my side. My mother is holding my hand. She looks as pale as the white sheets that cover me.

There is a tube down my throat, taped at my mouth, the other end attached to the ventilator. That machine is keeping me alive.

My eyes are closed, the flesh around them swollen, red and purple, my neck too. I do remember his hands around my neck, dragging me backwards. I remember the dining room chair smashing against my spine as I struggled for air. But I don't remember anything after that.

It looks like my arm is broken too. My writing hand, which is a shame. It is heavily bandaged and splinted, though not in a cast. That's not their priority right now.

The doctor speaks quietly to Mum and lays her hand on Mum's shoulder. I could never have been this sort of doctor, one who bears witness to such exquisite suffering, right on the precipice between life and death.

Though, of course, suffering is still something I know about.

When I met Dave I'd been an overworked doctor for so long, and had moved around the country so often, that relationships had been on the backburner. By then I was late thirties and I knew only too well that my reproductive years were almost done. I knew he was with Lara, but he kept promising me it was nearly over. He kept telling me that he had to find the right time because she was so ill and he was really her carer, not her lover. He couldn't wait to be with me and start a family. So I kept holding on, despite the belittling words he slid into my mind, like creepy crawlies that nested in there and multiplied. I knew things weren't right. But I'd invested so much time already. And there was just No More Time!

It was so stupid. I am a doctor! This sort of thing just doesn't happen to people like me—educated, leaders of the community, intelligent, advocates for women and women's health and, yes, even their safety. We are trained to look for signs. I can rattle off statistics: *In Queensland, almost half of all homicides are the result of domestic violence.*

If I'd been my own patient, I would have handed over the literature and given myself the phone numbers to call for help. I could have left at any time. I didn't need him to support me. But I kept thinking there'd been some sort of mistake. Truly, this couldn't be my life.

And yet it was.

I knew that it was a sick relationship, of course I did. But I couldn't stop it. Like eating peppermint chocolate ice creams. I know they're bad for me too, but still I kept bingeing. Dave kept telling me I was fat and needed to stop eating them and that when we tried for a baby I wouldn't be able to get pregnant. But the more he said it, the more I ate them. I'd begun to realise that we were never going to have a baby; it was one of his cruel games—maybe the cruellest one of all.

Anyway, I digress.

Another man has entered the room. He reaches out to shake Mum's hand and she reluctantly, tearfully, unclasps my wrist to take his palm in hers. He has a small book tucked under his arm. A Bible.

God. Is it really this bad? Don't they know that I'm still right here? I'm just resting, I guess. My body is probably too banged up for me to fit in there comfortably.

I want to shout at Mum, *I'm coming back soon!* Oh, poor Mum. Her husband gone and her only child here so critical. I haven't seen enough of her over the past six years. She never liked Dave and couldn't keep that hidden, though she tried hard. It just became too difficult to be in the same room with them both.

She was right about him, though.

She'll be so happy when I wake up and tell her that I'm leaving him. Yes, it's taken too long, but I'll do it as soon as the swelling comes down in my brain and I wake from this coma. I will start a new life, a free life, a life filled with joy. I'm sure Mum will let me live with her while I get back on my feet again.

I'm in a bad way. I get that. I regret that it had to come to this to make me see sense.

But I'm not sorry I phoned Sunny. I'm not sorry I warned Lara. Knowing I could protect those two innocent young lives was worth as much of a beating as Dave could deal out, which, by the looks of it, was quite a lot.

I'm glad now that I never had children with Dave. Look at what could have happened to them. My time for children has passed but there is still so much life out there for me to live. Maybe I will travel the world, join Médecins Sans Frontières, learn to scuba dive, or get a dog. Maybe one day I will even find a man who is kind and who loves me, and we will walk on the beach at sunset, and argue over whether we should holiday in Bali or South Africa, and drink wine at food festivals. And laugh. So much laughter.

I'm still young, really. There's still so much good I can do in the world. There is still time for me to find happiness. I just need to get out of here and I'll be on my way.

Hold on, Mum. I'm coming.

65

Lara

Lara, Sunny and Eliza sat on dining chairs in the backyard under the glorious electric-blue sky of a warm Brisbane spring day. Daisy and Hudson were playing with green magic sand at the outdoor table, building a small city of pyramids with leaves as flags on top and plastic jungle animals prowling at the base. Midnight, now at an awkward gangly stage, legs too long for her body, tripped over her feet as she chased a speedy grasshopper through the grass.

Lara clutched a pentagonal white cardboard box in her lap. She hadn't said much all morning, which was a change from the past two and a half weeks, during which it seemed all she'd done was talk.

That was how long it had been since Dave had attacked Vicki. Lara had stayed on the line, calling out, trying desperately to get Dave's attention, to get him to stop. Afterwards, she'd relived it in statements for the police.

Eliza had been able to get the police to send a car around to Dave's house immediately, but it was too late. Vicki was still breathing when they'd arrived, then had stayed on life support for two more days, after which her mother had made the unbearable decision to let her go.

Apparently, Dave claimed it was an accident.

They'd all spent so much time with the police, giving statements, especially Lara, who'd not only had to describe the phone call but also testify about her own time with Dave. His journal had included alternative plans for ways to harm Lara. She'd had counselling. They'd all had counselling.

She was in shock, of course; that was what Constance had told her. 'Knowing the very real threat Dave posed to your own life, and to your children's lives, will affect your body as if he'd actually tried to do it. Your primal brain knows no difference. Whether it "almost" happened or did happen, the trauma is as deep and needs as much time to be healed.'

Lara knew they'd all had a narrow escape.

Vicki's funeral was taking place today. The Foxleigh women had decided not to intrude. They had spoken to Vicki's family in the past couple of weeks, and didn't want their attendance to cause any more distress. Still, they needed to do something, together, to recognise this moment.

Sunny wiped under her eye and sniffed. 'Can I say something?' she said, watching her children. Daisy was tiring of the sand building and gazed up into the trees, daydreaming.

Sunny had brought down one of the white roses from the bouquet that had arrived this morning, along with a note from Sergeant Mitch. He'd been so wonderful, organising to have Sunny's car trucked back to Brisbane and the caravan returned to the rental company. He'd been her rock up in Winton for a couple of days, helping to look after the kids, bringing his dog around to wear out Midnight, then helping to organise a crate for Midnight to take her first plane ride home with them all. And, of course, he'd let Sunny off with a warning.

As far as Lara knew, he and Sunny had spoken at least once a day since they'd met, long after they'd finished dealing with official business.

Now, Sunny cleared her throat, twirling the rose stem between her fingers. 'I just wanted to say that wherever Vicki is now, I hope she's—no, I *know* she's—at peace.' Her voice faltered, and Eliza took her hand and squeezed it. In silence, they all watched Daisy as she skipped around the yard, gathering a fistful of yellow dandelions that had sprung up with some recent rain.

'And I hope they never let Dave out of jail,' Sunny finished.

After a small pause, Eliza began. 'Well, I would like to say again how grateful I am to Vicki that she gave her life to save my grand-babies.' Her voice hitched and she pressed a fist to her mouth. 'She was a hero,' she whispered.

'She *is* a hero,' Lara agreed, finding her voice at last, shifting the box on her lap.

A flash of blue caught her eye and she looked over to see Hudson rushing after Daisy, who was skipping around the bushes like a nature sprite, collecting blooms. Her heart squeezed as she willed him not to hurt Daisy's feelings or ruin her fun.

Instead, he ducked down to the ground behind her and picked up a couple of flowers that had fallen out of his sister's fist. 'You dropped some,' he called to her. Daisy turned and went back to him. Hudson took a dandelion and tucked it behind her left ear. 'There,' he said. 'You look beautiful.' Daisy's face broke into a toothy grin and she spun around, her skirt twirling, and continued on her way.

The three Foxleigh women smiled tenderly at the kids and then at each other.

He's going to be okay.

'Lara, how are you feeling?' Eliza asked.

Lara closed her eyes. What could she say? She shrugged, lost for any words.

Instead, she opened the lid of the box on her lap. Inside, six large orange and brown monarch butterflies sat waiting. The sun's heat and light had been doing their work, waking them up from hibernation. They slowly began to stretch their wings up and down, and move their antennae, searching their surroundings. Lara dipped her hand in, knowing it was safe to touch them, and nudged one gently. It stepped up onto her fingers and continued to open its wings. She passed the box to her mother and sister and they did the same. The butterflies sat on their hands, and took little flights into the air, coming back to rest on a woman's shoulder or head. One even paused for a moment on the soft petals of the white rose Sunny held.

Lara realised she was smiling. They were all smiling. The simple purity and hope in each of these butterflies seemed to shimmer around them.

One by one, the butterflies alighted into the air, gently, in no rush to go anywhere. They dropped onto nearby bushes, then flew a little further and landed on the swing set, on a tree, hovering in the air, beating their wings so effortlessly and gracefully. One landed on Daisy's arm and she squealed in delight. Hudson, with extreme gentleness, cupped another in his hand and grinned at it, then let it go on its way.

'Fly free,' Lara said, and at last felt a tiny shift towards peace in her heart.

66

Samuel

Samuel watched Matteo close the kitchen door behind him, his face reddened from the cold outside; it was barely four degrees out there. Beside him, Gilberta hummed, her hips swaying, as she nursed along a bubbling pot of *passata*. Matteo balanced the logs in his arms and headed to the fireplace at the back of the kitchen. Henrik was there, stirring white bean soup over the open flame. Matteo dropped the wood into the box near Henrik's feet, then straightened and caught Samuel's eye.

They were both nervous.

Samuel walked slowly to the dining room, reading a text message from Giovanna, who assured him they were on their way, just a little later than they'd hoped. He tugged at his collar, unable to tell if the tightness in his chest was from nerves or excitement.

In the library, Mario sang while aligning tables. The long space had been cleared of the green wingback chairs, and Henrik and Matteo had brought in long tables from the dairy, along with bench seats.

More than thirty people were coming to their early Christmas feast. All those people! The thought made Samuel have to sit down for a moment on the sofa near the piano.

'She's a clever woman, my Gilberta,' Mario said to the room at large, though Samuel was the only one nearby.

'Yes, she is,' he agreed. Gilberta and Matteo had organised all this, and Samuel couldn't fathom how they'd managed to get all the family to commit. The pair of them would make good politicians.

Gilberta had dressed the tables with red cloths. Squares of honeycomb sat atop round slices of pine logs, along with nuts and dried fruits. Terracotta pots held tall slices of crostini. She wanted people to start grazing the second they got here. Other pots held living thyme and oregano plants. Candles flickered, their bases wrapped in olive leaves.

So much effort, and it was all for him. Samuel had agreed to Matteo and Gilberta's plan and deep down he really did want this. But as the evening drew closer, more and more he found himself longing for a grappa to steady his hands.

Matteo carried in his last load of wood, dropping it beside the big fireplace in the library just in time for a gust of cold air from the front door and a babble of voices announcing the arrival of one of Matteo's brothers and his family. Matteo shot Samuel a quick look. The boy looked like he needed a grappa too. Samuel nodded at him almost imperceptibly, encouraging. *We can do this.*

Matteo met his oldest brother, Enzo, in a suit as always, and his wife Carlotta in sparkly jewels alongside their daughters.

My word, how the girls had grown! Samuel could barely recognise them with their shiny hair and their grown-up clothes. They'd only been toddlers when he'd seen them last. He pulled himself to his feet to greet them all, as the head of the household should do.

'*Zio!*' Enzo called, his arms held wide, and Samuel was pierced with gratitude, realising that a part of him had feared they might all come only to unleash fury on him. But Enzo kissed his cheeks and Carlotta did the same, her natural warmth smoothing over any stiffness. He'd missed her. The girls followed suit, shyly but affectionately.

More family arrived then, the villa echoing with cries of greeting and laughter. Matteo's other brothers, Sergio and Salvatore, came with their families. Then Gilberta and Mario's friend Costantino, and his granddaughter Teresa, came bearing wine and silver-wrapped gifts, which Teresa raced to place at the foot of the Christmas tree. Next was Gaetano and Sarah, and Samuel's granddaughter Aimee, all the way from London.

'Thank you for coming,' Samuel said into Gaetano's shoulder as they hugged.

'I'm only sorry it's been so long,' his son murmured. 'I'm deeply ashamed to have left my father alone here all these years. Please, forgive me.'

Samuel couldn't speak. He merely clapped Gaetano on the back and nodded, his throat tight. Aimee introduced herself to Henrik and they shook hands.

Each time the door opened to admit a new arrival, Matteo craned his neck to see who it was. So did Samuel.

Giovanna arrived, along with Marco and Lily. Giovanna burst into tears when she saw her father, wrapping his thin frame in her voluptuous one. 'You must come to London!' she wailed. 'Look how small you are! I need to feed you!'

Samuel raised his eyes to Matteo across the room with an *I told you so* face, but relaxed into his daughter's arms.

Lily, long beads around her neck, her long hair falling to her waist, called, 'Nonno!' and rushed to kiss him. A lump rose to his throat.

'Will you play for us?' he asked, nodding in the direction of the piano.

'Of course,' she said, and led Samuel by the hand to the lounge room. She sat him on the three-seater and then positioned herself at the black Steinway.

Samuel kept his eyes glued on her as she played Scarlatti, but felt his mind drift away, back to a time when Assunta was there in that seat, or maybe even his own Lily. He pulled his handkerchief from his pocket and wiped at his eyes.

Then he looked around his house, marvelling at all the people in it.

The young ones had gathered on the bench seats at the long tables in the library, their backs to the fireplace, sharing photos and games on their phones and catching up with their cousins.

Mario opened wine and filled glasses while Gilberta heated chocolate on the stove. Her handmade pasta—magnificent yellow knots of tagliatelle—waited in a pyramid on the kitchen bench near bunches of fragrant basil.

Henrik and Aimee stood in a tight twosome in the doorway to the dining room, each with a glass of wine, their cheeks rosy as they laughed at whatever the other said; Henrik popped back to the kitchen occasionally to check on the bean soup.

And then Lucia arrived, in a black trench coat, her eyelids heavy with smoky colour, the white streak in her hair dramatic. She paused in the doorway and pulled her scarf through her hands, a gesture that may have betrayed her nervousness. Her head was high, searching for Matteo, Samuel assumed, but her eyes met Samuel's first. She flinched at the sight of him.

Samuel, automatically assuming the role of the host, pulled himself to the edge of the lounge in order to rise and greet her.

But she held out her hand and frowned. 'No, please, don't get up.' It wasn't unkind, more concerned for his physical dexterity, and he could see she was shocked by his body's decline since they'd last met. In her mind, he had remained the capable man who should have fixed the roof, and seeing him here was forcing her to reassess.

They held each other's gaze, awkwardly, suspended in time and space, until Matteo entered, breaking the moment.

'Mamma,' he said, kissing her and taking her bag. He gave Samuel a supportive smile, then led Lucia towards the kitchen where she could relax in Gilberta's presence.

Lucia would take time to warm to him again, but at least she was here.

Samuel eased himself back on the sofa once more. They were all still waiting for Carlo to arrive.

And there was another guest he and Matteo were particularly eager to see.

67

Lara

The hire car rumbled slowly up the villa's long gravel driveway. A golden glow emanated from cracks around curtains and blinds. Outdoor lights reflected off the bonnets of several cars stationed up near the house, towards the goat shed. Lara parked alongside them and pulled on the handbrake.

'We're here,' she said.

'Oh, Lara, it's beautiful,' Eliza said.

A deep midnight blue sky surrounded the stone home.

'Are you nervous?' Sunny asked from the back seat. Daisy had fallen asleep against her shoulder, still jet-lagged and confused by the shortness of the days, even after three days in Rome, where they had taken a little time to get their bearings and do some sightseeing. Hudson gazed silently out the window.

'Horribly,' Lara confessed. It had been two months since she'd seen Matteo and she felt as though she'd lived a lifetime during her time apart from him. They'd spoken frequently, but there had been long stretches after everything that had happened when she just couldn't muster enthusiasm, or even many words. Even talking to her mother or sister had been difficult.

Funnily enough, the one person she'd felt able to talk to had been Samuel. They'd spent long hours talking on the phone, about her time with Dave, and what it had been like to have the twins, and the shocking events with Vicki. And he talked to her too, about Assunta, the old days with Carlo, how much he regretted not seeing his mother in London before she died, and about how he missed his extended Italian family now and hoped one day they'd all be together again. And his stories of his adventures with his latest *badante*—Henrik—were nothing if not amusing. He'd made her laugh, a precious gift in those weeks.

But as for Matteo, she'd been frightened to let him into that dark period of struggle. She knew he understood, but she also knew theirs was a new relationship and feared that level of intensity would be difficult for anyone to deal with.

But now her feelings had changed. Knowing that Dave would be behind bars for a long time gave her a sense of freedom she hadn't had before. For now she felt safe, though the survivor guilt (as Constance called it) was taking its time to abate. But she'd get there. They didn't call it *survivor* guilt for nothing. She *was* a survivor. She *was* strong. Deep in her bones, she knew it to be true.

One night after dinner, a week or so after Vicki's funeral, she'd opened her mouth and words came tumbling out without any preamble.

'I don't want to be here anymore. There are too many bad memories in this place. I need to start again.'

What she really wanted was to go back to Italy, back to Samuel and Matteo and the peace she'd felt with them. The blue hills and the green pines, the olive trees, the gentleness of the air. The wine. The goats.

'You should go back to Italy,' Sunny had said, as though she'd read her mind, completely sure of herself, licking gravy off her finger. 'It was great for you.'

But what about Sunny, Eliza and the kids? Lara now knew it was inevitable that one day she would leave their shared home to lead her own independent life. But not yet. It was too soon. Not after what they'd all just been through.

'I want to go to Italy too,' Eliza had said dreamily.

'Why not?' Sunny encouraged. 'You and Lara could go together.'

'What?' Eliza said in disbelief.

'That's what retirement is all about, isn't it? It's a great idea,' Sunny said, beginning to clear plates.

Eliza and Lara had looked at each other. Eliza's hand drifted to her chest. 'It would be nice,' she said.

Sunny put her hands on her hips, determined now. 'In fact, why don't we all go? We all need a break—an extended one at that.'

'What?' Eliza and Lara said in unison.

'It will be great for the kids.' Sunny scraped leftovers into the bin. 'We'll teach them Italian. They'll be citizens of the world. We can all share a house together. Besides, the last time Lara went to Italy and left me behind, I got arrested and nearly ended up in jail.'

Lara and Eliza grimaced at each other.

'And Mum's been lonely and lost since retiring.'

Eliza opened her mouth as if to protest, but settled for widening her eyes in disapproval and letting it go.

'What about school?' Lara said.

Sunny shrugged, smiling, wiping her hands on a tea towel. 'They'll go to school there, for however long we stay.' It seemed there was still a bit of the gypsy left in her after all.

'What about Mitch?' Lara asked.

Sunny paused. She'd been having a phone relationship with the policeman for weeks now. 'Well, we're fifteen hours' drive away from each other now and we're doing okay. It probably won't be any different if I'm a twenty-two-hour flight away.' She shrugged. 'Besides, if he really wants to see me, he can come to Italy.'

Lara and Eliza smiled at each other, glad to see a bit of the old Sunny back.

Over the next week, it was all they could talk about—the pros, the cons, the money, practicalities, bank accounts, and the clothes. None of them had a European winter wardrobe and they were in the middle of an Australian summer. They didn't have a lot of money to play with but Lara had taken a chance to go the first time and it had all worked out. Surely, luck was due to come their way. Finally, it had been settled.

'Poor Hilary,' Lara said. 'She'll be trying to stow away in my suitcase.'

Hilary had indeed been crazy with jealousy. 'Oh, if only I hadn't had that whole career and husband and kid thing . . . I could come too.' She sipped on her cocktail. Then she suggested that Eliza rent out her house for short-term lets while they were gone. Hilary could manage it for her and it would give them a bit of play money so they could travel around if they wanted to. Hilary had also become Midnight's foster mother and had begun taking the dog to the office with her. She swore that sales had increased due to Midnight putting everyone in a good mood.

When Lara had nervously told Matteo about the idea of the entire Foxleigh family coming to Italy, he'd been unequivocally supportive.

'Yes! They are your family. You must bring everyone,' he said, as though it would be strange to do anything else. 'I can't wait to meet them.' He paused. 'As long as I can have you to myself sometimes too?'

She assured him that would be no problem.

Then when she told Samuel they would be looking for a place to rent in Fiotti he insisted they all stay with him.

'No, we can't,' she protested. 'Daisy and Hudson will drive you mad with the noise. There are five of us!'

'Don't be daft,' he said sternly. 'There's plenty of room here. Your sister and the kids can join you upstairs. I think maybe my room with Assunta has been closed up for too long.'

'Oh, Samuel, no.'

'No arguing. It's time for new life in there. And there is still the former caretaker's flat under the house for your mother to have her privacy.'

'But it's too much.'

'Rubbish. I won't hear another word about it. This was a house built for big families,' he said, and Lara's skin erupted into goosebumps. She'd known it from the start.

'Okay,' she'd said, hardly believing it was happening. 'Thank you.'

'You're welcome. I am old enough to guarantee you that there are better times ahead, for all of us.'

And now the Foxleigh family was here.

Sunny woke up Daisy, who blinked into the shining lights. 'Are we there yet?'

'Yes. Now we need to put your coats on,' Sunny said, retrieving them from the floor of the car.

Lara stepped out, and the very first thing she heard was the goats remonstrating at her from the shed. She grinned. 'I'll be right back,' she told her family, and dashed up the hill to the barn, shivering without a coat.

Meg and Willow came to the door to greet her. They looked like they'd pulled themselves out of bed, she thought, given they both had wood shavings on their coats.

'Hello, my darlings,' she said, reaching both hands over the wooden gate so she could rub each of them at the same time, loving the feel of their soft noses in her palms, the warm smoothness of their long ears. Meg continued to grumble while Willow made little creaking noises. 'I've missed you too,' she said. 'I really have.'

'And I have missed you.'

Lara looked up to see Matteo standing nearby, smiling. She retrieved her arms from the goats and before she could even straighten up, he'd moved swiftly to her, pulling her to him. She squeezed him back, hardly able to believe the feel of him beneath her hands. 'Oh, I've missed you so much,' she whispered, her voice carrying on the crisp air.

He released her, but only enough so that he could swoop down and kiss her. The feel of the back of his neck was enough to make her hum with glee. She was certain they were going to be okay.

'Goats!' Daisy's voice called, interrupting their kiss. She came running into the barn, her wool-lined boots pounding the earth with each step.

Matteo released Lara, but did not flinch or shy away. Instead he stood solidly, one arm tightly around her.

'Hello,' he said to Daisy as she halted at the gate. 'And hello to you,' he said to Hudson, who'd followed her in.

'Hi,' said Hudson, his eyes on the goats, but giving Matteo a wave.

Lara shivered then, realising how cold she was now that Matteo's body wasn't pressed so tightly to hers.

Eliza and Sunny arrived, puffing and rubbing their hands. Lara introduced them to Matteo and he kissed them each on both cheeks.

'It is so good to meet you,' he said. 'Welcome to the villa. Samuel is inside, and almost everyone else is there too. It is much warmer. You should come down and sit by the fire.'

He shepherded them all safely down the hill, taking Eliza's arm, and they filed into the warm kitchen. Gilberta was 'easy tears' as she met everyone and kissed them all and hugged Lara so hard Lara worried for one of her ribs.

'But you are all so bountiful,' she said, squeezing the children's cheeks. They both giggled.

Matteo put his arm around Lara and turned to Lucia. 'Mamma, you remember Lara,' he said.

Lucia lifted her chin slightly but managed to smile at Lara, seemingly having let go of her preferred choice of woman for her son. She held out her hand, but Lara stepped forward and embraced the woman, kissing her on both cheeks. '*Buonasera*, Lucia.'

The older woman was a little stiff in Lara's arms, but Lara hoped she was pleased with her efforts. She returned to Matteo's side and squeezed his hand. 'Samuel's in the lounge,' he told her.

'Oh, yes,' Gilberta said. 'He will be so happy to see you.'

'I'm hungry,' Hudson said.

'Me too,' chimed in Daisy.

'*Sì*, we must feed you,' Gilberta said, pointing to the platters of food out in the dining area.

Lara excused herself and headed past the boiling pots and pyramid of pasta in the kitchen, waved to Henrik, who was in the corner of the dining room with a young woman, and entered the living room.

Samuel was on the three-seater. His snowy hair was brushed back. He was dressed in a charcoal suit, with shiny shoes and a crisp white shirt, and he looked amazing. Years younger. Several people sat around him, all watching another young woman playing the piano. Lily, it must be—the pianist. Lara couldn't help but smile. Samuel appeared so transfixed by his granddaughter's performance that Lara almost didn't want to break the spell he was under.

He must have sensed her presence, though, because he suddenly snapped out of his trance and turned towards where she stood, just inside the doorway, Matteo behind her. She grinned and raised a hand to wave, and Samuel straightened up and beckoned her over. She tiptoed through the crowd of music lovers and bent to hug him. He patted her back as a father might, and she crouched down on her haunches to gaze at him.

'Welcome home,' he said.

'It's so good to be here. And look at *this*,' she said, gesturing to all the people around the room.

Samuel chuckled. 'Unbelievable, isn't it?' He scratched at his head in disbelief. She rubbed his other arm, pleased to see the cast off and him all better.

'Are you happy?' she asked, looking around. People seemed to fill every corner, their faces illuminated by firelight and candles and strings of fairy lights, drinking, eating, laughing, pulling books from the shelves and flipping pages, the young ones texting and talking.

He nodded, seemingly lost for words to express just how happy he truly was.

'What about Carlo?'

'He's supposed to be coming,' Samuel said, his face falling. She wished she hadn't asked.

'Who's supposed to be coming?' came a booming voice from behind them.

And there was Carlo, looking almost exactly as Lara had last seen him, except for a thick grey cable-knit jumper snug around his girth. He stared straight at Samuel.

Everyone stopped talking. Lily's fingers faltered on the keys and then stopped. A child sitting at the long table squealed and was shushed by an older cousin.

'Carlo,' Samuel said, his voice barely audible.

Lara got to her feet and held out her hand to Samuel. He took it and, with some difficulty, pulled himself up from the lounge. Lara handed him his stick, and he straightened his shoulders and walked over to Carlo, who towered over him.

Samuel stopped in front of him and held out his hand. 'Thank you for coming.'

Carlo looked at Samuel's outstretched hand, then back at Samuel's face. He shook his head and Samuel dropped his hand.

Lara gasped quietly, her gaze flicking to Matteo, who was still standing near the doorway. He chewed his bottom lip.

Then Carlo stepped close to Samuel and took his shoulders, kissed him on both cheeks and said, 'Little brother. It has been too long.'

68

The table was near to overflowing with food. Wooden boards piled with prosciutto-wrapped melon, pastrami and pancetta bumped up against platters of olives with slivers of preserved lemon and capers, anchovies and tomatoes. Hudson returned for crostini and white bean dip again and again. Daisy had eaten her own weight in bruschetta and chunky pesto dripping in olive oil. Teresa had taken a shine to Daisy immediately, and sat next to her on the bench seat, teaching her Italian words for *plate* and *knife* and *glass*.

'They seem to be taking to this Italian thing,' Sunny said, sitting to the right of Lara, a glass of red wine in her hand. 'You know, I think it's going to be okay.'

Lara smiled. Actually, she simply grinned wider, her face aching from the endless smiling and laughing. Beside her, Matteo had barely taken his hand off hers since they'd sat down. He was talking in Italian across the table to his brothers and sisters-in-law, but often stopped to talk to Eliza, who was to his left. Lara signalled to her mother by leaning behind Matteo's back while he was busy with his brothers, raising her eyebrows. *Well? What do you think?* Eliza beamed and nodded her approval.

Gilberta carried in plates filled with her handmade tagliatelle and rich red sauce, grated pecorino sprinkled on top, its aroma making Lara's mouth water. Mario followed with more plates, carrying six at a time.

'Gilberta, you must sit down and eat,' Lara said, then murmured in delight at the charred zucchini strips adorning the plate in front of her. 'You're working too hard.'

'This is the fun part,' Gilberta said. 'I can to feed you all!'

Mario placed his dishes down in front of the children, singing to them and doing a little sidestep shuffle, making them all laugh.

Henrik was at the head of the table, still in conversation with Aimee, two scientists together discussing the glory of the microbial world.

Samuel was diagonally opposite her, flanked by Giovanna and Gaetano, the three of them deep in conversation. Samuel was too far away, with too much noise from the raucous crowd around them, for Lara to talk with him. But she was enjoying taking in the sight of him, observing his face light up as he looked at his much-missed children, watching him sit a little straighter and pat down his formal shirt whenever it puckered. She would have time to talk to him. Lots of Italian time. She would be here for him, as long as he needed or wanted her.

Lucia was next to Gaetano, in surprisingly close proximity to Samuel, and Lara had seen her pass him a smile and a cheese board a couple of times. There would be a long way to go for them, she suspected. But it was the first little trickle of hope.

When all the pasta was gone, Matteo's brother Salvatore sent the nieces and nephews to clear the plates, giving Gilberta and Mario a break, and Carlo cleared his throat, loudly, as he was able to do with his stentorian voice. A few heads turned his way, sentences tailed off.

He was seated at the other end of the table, and had a single chair to sit in rather than the bench seat. He pushed it back and stood. All voices hushed and all eyes turned to him.

'It is not my place to make a speech here to welcome you all to this villa,' he said, speaking in English for the benefit of the Australians, Lara supposed. There was some translation for the younger guests, in whispers, mums and dads leaning towards eager ears. 'But I do come here to confess.'

Lara peeked at Samuel, whose face was apprehensive, a slight wobble in his chin. Giovanna and Gaetano appeared guarded too, the exiles returning to the family home.

'I was wrong.' Carlo put his hand on his heart, gazing at Samuel. 'We were all very wrong,' he said gravely, looking at Lucia first and then at others around the table. 'Assunta was our much-loved sister, aunt and mother. Her passing was terrible.' He paused. Giovanna had started to weep quietly, pulling tissues from between her breasts.

'We blamed Samuel.'

Samuel lifted his chin and swallowed.

'But we were wrong.'

The room was silent, bar the crackling of the fire.

'We have mourned Assunta too long. We still have so much life to live. Let us not waste it.' Carlo picked up his wine glass and raised it high. 'To Assunta's memory,' he said.

'To Assunta,' came the collective reply, more glasses held aloft.

'And to Samuel,' Carlo said, bowing his head in Samuel's direction.

'To Samuel,' came the response, with many smiles and a few cheers.

Samuel stared at his plate and Lara could see the tremor in his hands.

'And I want to give you back this,' Carlo said, pulling the wine-coloured jewellery box from his pocket. He left his spot and walked around the back of the bench seat and stopped behind Samuel, who'd lifted his head. Carlo put a large hand on Samuel's shoulder and placed the box on the table between Samuel and Giovanna. 'It belongs in your family.'

Giovanna opened the box and took out the necklace. She exclaimed in Italian and stood up to hug Carlo, who patted her back and murmured in her ear.

Samuel looked up at his old friend. 'Thank you.'

Carlo, seemingly lost for words now, simply patted Samuel's shoulder and returned to his seat, where he picked up his wine glass and drained it.

Matteo put his arm around Lara and kissed her on the temple. 'Look what you did,' he whispered.

'Nice job, Sprout,' Sunny said beside her.

Eliza reached behind Matteo's back and squeezed her hand, staring at her proudly.

Then Samuel caught her eye and lifted his glass to her.

She returned the gesture. 'Thank *you*.'

Late in the evening, when the twins were falling over with fatigue and Sunny had bade her farewells, leading them up the stairs to their new bedroom, and Eliza was nursing a coffee and chatting with Lucia, Lara pulled Matteo into the receiving room. Yet another fire burned brightly in there, warming it so much she had to take off a layer. She collapsed happily onto the chaise longue, Matteo joining her, wrapping his arms around her, his lips meeting hers.

'I'd invite you upstairs to my room but now there are children up there,' she said, smiling against his mouth.

'There is always my cabin back at the farm,' he suggested, his hand on her thigh. 'Except we have had too much wine,' he added sadly.

'Tomorrow,' she whispered.

Matteo gazed at her as if he couldn't believe she was really here. He ran the back of his hand gently down her cheek, her neck, her shoulder. 'You know, you are all part of the family now—once you meet us and feast with us, it's a done deal. The Italian way.'

'That's lucky,' she said, lacing her fingers through his, 'because Gilberta has already adopted the kids as grandchildren.'

He stilled and his eyes widened. 'Did you see your mother and my mother?'

'Yes!' she said. 'They looked like old friends.'

Matteo shook his head in disbelief, but smiled at the idea. He rested his elbow on the back of the chaise longue and studied her. 'Thank you for coming back to me.'

'Tell me when I wake up tomorrow that this won't have all been a dream.'

'It's not a dream.'

'I'm really here?'

'You really are.'

'I made it,' she said, almost not believing it. That one sentence meant so much.

I made it.

Out in the living room, Lily had begun playing the piano again and Mario was just warming up for an operatic piece. There were cheers and whistles.

'What shall we do tomorrow?' Matteo asked.

'Honestly, I'd be happy to hang out with you in the goat shed and feed berries to Meg and Willow. Actually, I think I'd be happy to do that every day for the rest of my life.'

'Then I think that's what we should do.'

Lara thought back to those three gold coins she threw into the Trevi Fountain—one to return to Rome, one to find love, and one for marriage. The first two had happened. Would the third? She didn't know. What she did know for sure was that life didn't always turn out the way you might have thought it would, but that she could survive anything, and even the darkest of days would one day turn bright again.

ACKNOWLEDGEMENTS

I love writing acknowledgements. Creating a book is a long and potentially treacherous journey into creative oceans, but I am always buoyed by so many beautiful souls along the way.

This book wouldn't even be here had I not attended Vanessa Carnevale's writing retreat in Tuscany in 2016, where I made the bold decision to throw away fifty thousand words of a different novel, to instead embrace the story that wanted to be told here, born in the garden of the villa in the Tuscan hillsides. Thanks to the writing sisters on that retreat, Vanessa, Amanda, Tracey and Pascale, for giving me the push I so needed in order to let go. And to Fabio, Gilberta, Mario and Jen for the feast of a lifetime. Gilberta Sangiorgi Nuccitelli, again, for your pasta-making tutorial and your permission to use your recipe, as well as a fictional character named after you (I hope you like her!), and to Mario for the same.

And very importantly, to my husband, Alwyn Blayse, who encouraged me to take the trip in the first place and who is always my number one fan (and even threatens to be the founding member of 'The Moonies' fan club, bless him).

Christian Nobel from Fromart here on the Sunshine Coast for inviting me to come and visit your lush green hills to ask a hundred questions on what it is like to be a cheesemaker.

Alison Brien and her YouTube videos on Channel Cheese TV for so many mouth-watering episodes, particularly those in Northern Italy.

My sister, Amanda, for being my travel assistant, making sure I turn up to the airport on the right day (!), and making me laugh till I cry, all in the name of research and cheese-eating extravaganzas. (But I will never be able to eat Stilton. Ever. Though I will accept the cider that goes with it.)

My publisher, Annette Barlow, for being flawless in your confidence in me to write a book at all, let alone one you'll love; your faith is both gracious and nerve racking. All at Allen & Unwin who work so very hard to bring out the best in my book and promote its socks off to find new readers. My agents, Fiona Inglis at Curtis Brown (Australia and UK) and Haylee Nash for doing what you do best.

To my early readers (I'm sorry you had to endure such a poor quality draft, but I promise your feedback really did help it grow up into a real book): Vanessa Carnevale for checking all my Italian words (and of course any errors are totally mine); Dr Tracey Hay (aka 'Big Sis') for medical matters (again, any errors are mine); Haylee Nash for great structural advice and much-welcomed enthusiasm; Clara Finlay, my favourite ninja of the editing world, who endured not just one but two *completely* different (and much poorer) versions of this novel (including the abandoned fifty thousand words) . . . I hope for both our sakes that next time I crack the story on the first draft; Marie-Louise Willis for picking me up when I was lost out at sea, and your helpful feedback on characters and plot; and the multi-talented Kate Smibert, who always sees to the heart of my stories.

Hilary Reynolds for your keen eye for detail and helping make my words shine. This is a much better book for your efforts. Thanks also to Genevieve Buzo for overseeing the book's progress through to publication.

Sharyn Wagner, from Briese Lawyers, for advice on family law matters. (Again, all errors are totally mine.)

Rosie Batty for your courageous testimonial at the parliamentary inquiry into family law and family violence. I don't have enough words to express my gratitude for the work you do for the women and children of this country.

My goats, Meg and Wilbur, for lending me your personalities for these fictional goats.

I read through countless recipe books while writing this novel, too many to name here, but I do want to mention Jamie Oliver's *Jamie's Italy*, a book that is as brutal as it is beautiful and made me think deeply about our relationship to food.

To Jill, Nicky, Sam, Misty and team at the Goodness Gracious cafe in Yandina, for taking care of my caffeine and cake needs and for the love notes of encouragement that came with the coffees. I am superstitiously glued to 'my seat' now, so please don't ever renovate!

And my final but largest thanks go to Flynn, just for being you, the most precious gift of all.

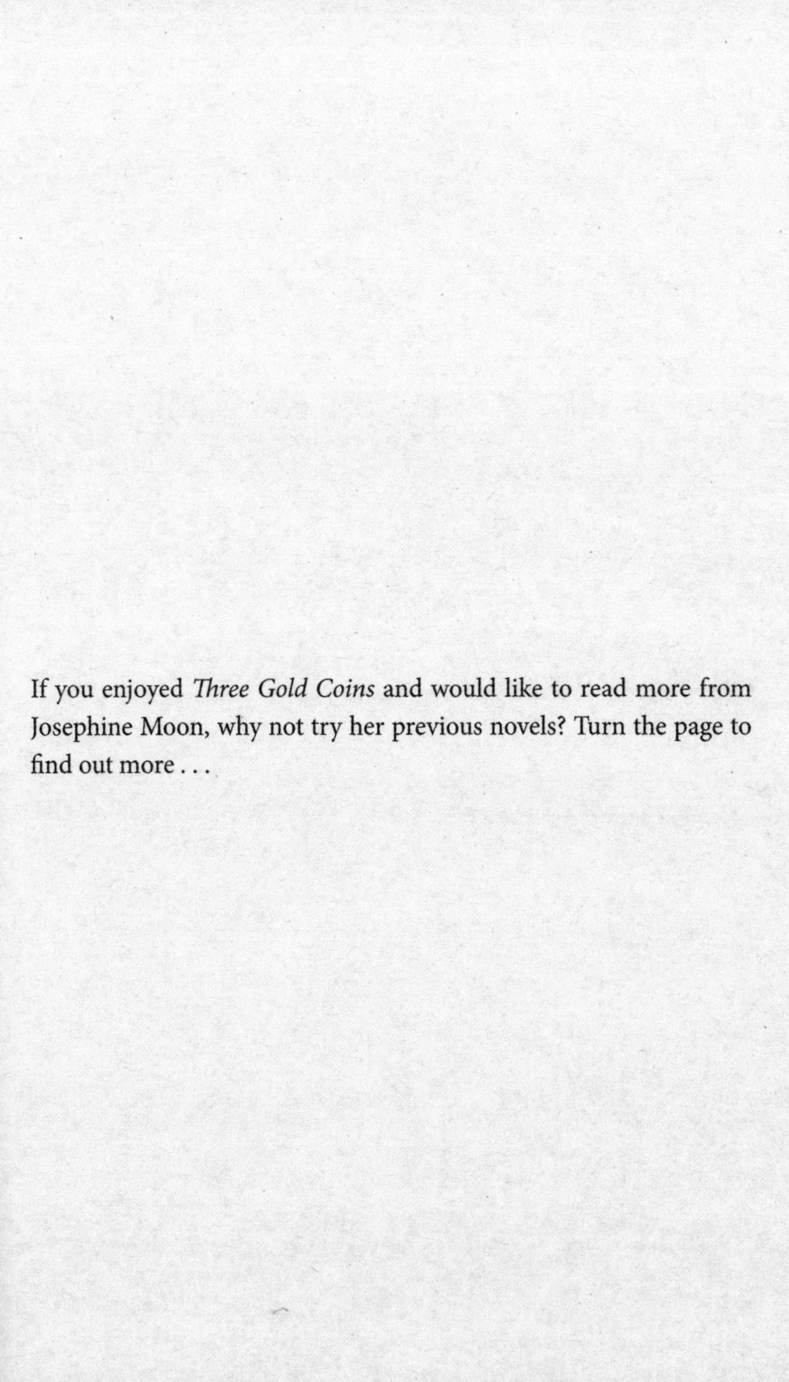

If you enjoyed *Three Gold Coins* and would like to read more from Josephine Moon, why not try her previous novels? Turn the page to find out more . . .

The Tea Chest

Kate Fullerton, talented tea designer and now co-owner of The Tea Chest, could never have imagined that she'd be flying from Brisbane to London, risking her young family's future, to save the business she loves from the woman who wants to shut it down.

Meanwhile, Leila Morton has just lost her job; and if Elizabeth Clancy had known today was the day she would appear on the nightly news, she might at least have put on some clothes. Both need to start again.

When the three women's paths cross, they throw themselves into realising Kate's magical vision of the newest and most delectable tea shop in London, The Tea Chest. But every time success is within their grasp, increasing tensions damage their trust in each other.

With the very real possibility that The Tea Chest will fail, Kate, Leila and Elizabeth must decide what's important to each of them. Are they willing to walk away or can they learn to believe in themselves?

'I loved it – a perfect blend of sweet and spice' Jenny Colgan

The Beekeeper's Secret

Maria has secrets to hide. She spends her solitary days tending her bees and creating delicious honey products to fund orphaned children. A former nun, her life at Honeybee Haven has long been shaped by her self-imposed penance for terrible past events. But the arrival of two letters heralds the shattering of Maria's peaceful existence as her past begins to track her down. Pushing aside the misgivings of her family and friends, on the eve of her marriage Tansy made a serious deal with her adored husband, Dougal. A deal she'd intended to honour. But, seven years on, and facing a life-changing decision, Tansy is finding her current feelings difficult to ignore. . .

With captivating characters and an intriguingly tangled mystery, *The Beekeeper's Secret* celebrates families in all their joys and complications.

The Chocolate Apothecary

Christmas Livingstone has formulated 10 top rules for happiness by which she tries very hard to live. Nurturing the senses every day, doing what you love, sharing joy with others are some of the rules but the most important for her is no. 10 – absolutely no romantic relationships!

Her life is good now. Creating her enchantingly seductive shop, The Chocolate Apothecary, and exploring the potential medicinal uses of chocolate makes her happy; her friends surround her; and her role as a fairy godmother to her community allows her to share her joy. She doesn't need a handsome botany ace who knows everything about cacao to walk into her life. One who has the nicest grandmother – Book Club Captain at Green Hills Aged Care Facility and intent on interfering – a gorgeous rescue dog, and who wants her help to write a book. She really doesn't need any of that at all. Or does she?

With an enticing tangle of freshly picked herbs, flowers and delicious chocolate scenting the background, *The Chocolate Apothecary* is a glorious novel of a strong, creative woman discovering that you can't always play your life by the rules.

About the Author

Josephine Moon lives with her husband and son, and their extraordinarily large and diverse animal family, on the Sunshine Coast in Queensland. She has a passion for horses, imported fine chocolate and gourmet teas.